A FLOWER OF ASIA

Bibliographical note:

this facsimile has been made from a copy in the
British Museum
(04410.F33)

A FLOWER OF ASIA.

A Flower of Asia.

An Indian Story.

CYRIL.

LONDON: BURNS & OATES, LIMITED.
NEW YORK, CINCINNATI, CHICAGO: BENZIGER BROTHERS.

—

1901.

PREFACE.

The religions of the East, adherents of which appear in these pages, should be taken for what they are worth—as no better than pagan forms of belief and ethics. The highest estimate that can be made of them scarcely brings them to the level of the best of the old philosophies. The gems that sparkle in them clearly are not their own, and the great traditions they reflect have come from a common source to which no one of them can lay a special claim.

The zeal with which their members act according to their lights, and the efforts they make to capture heaven, as they understand it, must awaken in us thoughts of sympathy; but the Oneness of Faith is not affected by their struggles, nor is the obligation to enter the sheepfold by the door less pressing because a few in their invincible ignorance and longing for God have scaled the fence, and been allowed to mingle with the sheep.

What a revelation it is, if we look over the wide earth, to see man everywhere hastening on to a bourne where he thinks he will find happiness, and straining his human vision to the utmost to see that favoured region in which he hopes to rest for ever! The revulsion of some among the decadent Christians in Europe is a small item compared to the forward movement of the human race as a whole; and its diversity from the general tendency of religious thought declares its origin evil.

CONTENTS.

A FLOWER OF ASIA.

CHAPTER I.

A DRUG STORE IN CALCUTTA.

A COUNTRY never seen and far away may become for a resident in England a place of thrilling interest apart from its beauty and value. If loved ones have abode in it for long, and written home describing its mode of life and its scenes of joy and sorrow, in which they have taken part, a picture may have been painted on the memory which only time can efface. If beneath the soil of that distant land has been laid to rest a father, a husband, a son or brother, it is for the bereaved one a shrine before which the stricken heart bows down, a Calvary to which a pilgrimage must be made in spirit as long as life remains.

Few there are in Great Britain whom some thread does not connect with our greatest dependency beyond the seas ; few for whom a figure does not emerge from the recesses of years gone by, at the mention of the name, India ; few for whom an eye long-closed does not beam again with its old loving light, and a voice hushed into silence for years does not speak again in the well-remembered accents of its last farewell

B

Our tale is laid in India—this "land flowing with milk and honey," like the ancient patrimony of the Jews. What land has such a flora? The varied woods of Solomon's temple are as wayside shrubs in this teeming region. The banana, the vine, the tea-plant, the cotton-trees, the mulberry to feed the producer of silk, and a hundred others— all spring from this soil, while beneath it the buried forests of the young world are stored. Here is everything that can minister to the wants, the tastes, the luxuries of man; everything that even his whim demands is to be found here as in its native home.

Its ancient unique form of civilisation, its history touching on the second dawn of life on our sphere, its fervent and picturesque religious worship, its diverse races, fierce and gentle, with a stamp of primitive beauty impressed upon them, combine to make Hindustan the fairy region of our globe.

No wonder that Sesostris travelled a wide continent to pilfer the gold washed down by its rivers, that Darius Hytaspes seized upon it to squeeze out its treasures for his hungry Persian hordes, that Alexander of Macedon regarded it as the fine flower of his conquests, that the ever-advancing Moslems came to rest on its bounteous plain, that Britain, the greatest of them all, holds it in her grasp with a tenacity, that will never relax until her last soldier shall have fallen, her last ship have been sunk.

Like all great countries India has a capital city; and this Indian capital is large, handsome, and populous. Calcutta is handsome—with a reservation, which means that while its principal section, that is, the quarter occupied by the Whites, is well laid-out, commodious and of striking architecture, its Native quarter is not so ; yet even this, by its very squalor and quaintness, cannot fail to rouse the interest of the traveller from the far West.

Between the White and Black divisions of this city runs a neutral zone ; and in this zone, at its southern extremity, there stood in the year 186— a flimsy detached house. Its walls were full of rents and crevices, its doors and windows were bulged and patchy, and its roof had in places fallen in, partly from age, and partly under the tropical rains that beat upon it. Within this tenement was a small store or shop, giving on the street, divided by a long counter, and so crowded with shelves and drawers that one could not say whether it was round, square, or triangular.

If the house and store were quaint and strange, no less so was the man that owned them. He sat on a low chair, with his legs on the counter, rocking and rolling incessantly. Though short, no doubt, he was not, like the house, light or flimsy. His head was large ; his body was stout and round ; his feet were wide and heavy. He failed only in the matter of his legs, which were diminutive, thin and spindle-like. A sign-board outside bore his name in raised letters, and after that name his title, M.P.S.I., which the wags on the street, who understood English, interpreted " member of parliament," or " sub-inspector," or both, according to their mood. He was not, however, to be put in either category ; he was, in fact, an apothecary posing as a qualified physician and surgeon, and ready at a nod to use the lancet, saw, forceps, or any other instrument known to the surgeon, oculist, or dentist.

As he rocked up and down, he mused and muttered. There was evidently some trouble on his mind; and in his muttering, some words escaped from his lips. They were words of one syllable, and as they were not connected, they conveyed no meaning whatsoever.

He mused and muttered, and as he muttered he shook his head and clenched his fist; he even showed a tendency to grind his teeth. By an effort, he kept back his wrath and smiled; in a moment the smile widened into a broad grin, and from the grin broke out a laugh as, starting to his feet, he said in a pleasant voice: "That birth in France was a great mistake: it played the deuce with my figure. If I had been born at home, I would have grown into a man—little land-tortoise that I am—all body, no legs to speak of! Ahem!"

As this man is to hold a prominent position in our story, we may not pass him over lightly.

His name was O'Dowd, and he was called Septimus at Baptism, in anticipation of a family—of seven—all boys. His father, Mulligan O'Dowd, was steward to an English nobleman, and was, with his wife, on the continent, when he had to leave the latter in charge of a nurse and a doctor, in a village of the Ardennes. But Septimus O'Dowd, though French by the accident of his birth, was not French in manner—grimace, gesture, or movement, in speech or outward guise. His stomach was French, for he was a lover of savoury dishes, and the wines of the Gironde ; but as these luxuries were not within reach of a small and uncertain income, it became cosmopolitan, and learned to take in with equal relish a sherry cobbler, a pint of pilsener, a curry, a tinned rabbit, or an Irish stew.

Septimus O'Dowd was naturally of cheerful disposition ; but he was now in Hindustan, far from friends, and his struggle to live was too acute for even his elastic temperament.

He regretted that he had not gone to some country which was occasionally visited by the plague, or even by yellow-fever or small-pox ; or among a people who understood the value of sweet scents. But to have come to India, where a dip in the Ganges is believed to be a remedy for all the ills of soul and body, and where an outbreak of cholera may not occur twice in a dozen years !—it was depressing.

He strove to raise his drooping spirits by often exclaiming, " Autrefois," thereby deceiving himself into the conviction that his earlier life had been spent in sunshine ; but it was not so ; his present position in India was every way in keeping with his previous career, which had been chequered, shifting and uncomfortable.

His occupation, before he left his home in Ireland, was that of a dispensing doctor. His professional district ran along the mountain slopes of the county Kerry. The peasantry, among whom lay his sick-calls, were perched around on the hills in positions difficult to approach. His salary did not exceed one hundred pounds a year, and his extra fees were next to nothing. He was married, and had a family of five boys, who made such demands on his little purse for food and raiment that he found it impossible to pay his bills as they fell due; which he felt keenly, for he was, in theory, an honest man.

How he loved those boys! He was proud of them, too. They were, perhaps, in shape rather bulky for their respective years, and short as well. Their faces were full and their legs were bandy, but they were lively little dears, and, in their way, witty. He revelled in their society at home, and in his walks abroad, whether for business or pleasure, he was seldom seen without them.

He had an old-fashioned gig in which he drove to visit the sick, and into this little car he thrust his five boys, heads or heels uppermost; and they went through the country, a very lively and noisy party, singing, crowing, cheering, and saluting the neighbours as they passed with epithets of a perfectly original and very lively character.

The doctor was amused by these ebullitions of the O'Dowd family humour; and among a people mirthful themselves and tolerant of fun in others, they were not regarded with disfavour. His boys, however, had other tastes that were more harmful, and the indulgence of these became a source of trouble not only to themselves but to their honoured parent, and led in the end to a serious catastrophe.

They got possession of a blunderbuss which

their father kept for the purpose of bringing down rain and settling the weather. It was a ponderous engine of destruction, with a recoil that would have staggered a bullock. It could not be fired with safety unless the stock were kept well outside the shoulder, and as a consequence, instead of casting its pellets among the convoy of birds at which it was aimed, it was apt to scatter them through flocks or herds in a neighbouring field, or among farm hands working at a distance. Showers of lead came down in places where they were least expected ; domestic fowls were shot away like vermin ; windows were broken ; such, in fact, was the destruction wrought by these adventurous sportsmen that a great outcry was raised, and combinations were formed for the protection of life and property in that parochial district. Complaints were made to O'Dowd of the lawless conduct of his boys. They were met with a smile from the over-indulgent parent.

Complaints of the father and sons were made to the dispensary committee, and the Doctor received from that responsible body a solemn warning—of which he took no notice whatsoever.

Complaints were made to the Local Government Board, which addressed to O'Dowd a forcible letter containing a threat of dismissal from his post unless the outrages ceased, to which he replied in a vein of ill-timed jocularity.

Then the patience of all the aggrieved ran out, for the raids of the sharp-shooters became more frequent and reckless than ever. The Doctor was cashiered—rooted out stock and branches—and

advised to look for a district where there was a rifle
range in which his boys could indulge their taste
for big guns and reckless shooting without imperil-
ling the public weal.

It was fortunate for O'Dowd that he had a
brother-in-law, which brother-in-law was well-to-do
and generous. To him he turned in the hour of
his distress. He told him of his sorrows and
poverty ; he drew a moving picture of the steadiness and docility of his sons ; in a word, he put
such a case before the kind man that he consented
to come to his aid by buying for him a practice in
a certain sea-side town, which was then growing
rapidly in wealth and population.

Here at the opening of his career the Doctor
gained a wide reputation as the possessor of an
elixir of life which he always carried on his person
in a mysterious black bottle buttoned carefully in
a breast pocket. It was probably composed of
ingredients that could neither kill nor cure ; but
such was its reputation that diseases of the imagination and nervous system went down before it as
a demon is said to fly from an obsessed body when
brought under the power of the exorcist. The
effect of it was different on the really sick. It
dosed them and did them no good ; it dosed them
and did them positive harm ; it dosed an indus-
trious widow unto death. The friends of this
woman assembled in troops to make inquiry regarding the treatment she had received in her
short illness, when it came to light that she had
been given three draughts in succession from
O'Dowd's mysterious bottle. Then they recalled

to mind the fact that they had all imbibed from that spring of life; that some of them had indeed recovered, while others had become sick almost unto death. So, putting their heads together, out of a great conflict of tongues they arrived at the conclusion that O'Dowd had only one cure for all diseases, and that he was a quack, if not a fraud. A storm of public indignation broke upon him with such violence that he was forced once more to break up his household and to retire from that district. This was followed by a fresh appeal to his wife's brother for an advance of money to enable him to thrust his sickle into some new and heretofore untouched corn-field.

About this time a change crept over the tastes and tendencies of his bright boys.

Quintus O'Dowd was reading Virgil, and became enamoured of the pastoral life, as described by that poet; and by an adroit handling of that subject brought all his brothers to share his view of the delight of lolling idly on the grass, and playing on a reed in the shade of a wide-spreading beech.

Now they were one and all tenders of flocks and herds, or they were nothing. What was to be done?

"Ahem!" said the Doctor; "there is little common-land in this country except mountain-tops, where the grass is damp from mists, and the sun is seldom seen. But in the colonies, above all in that of Victoria, there are sun-lit plains, with leafy trees, and sheep to tend in countless flocks, and such solitude and silence all around as give an opening to the player of rustic music."

A family council was held ; books and maps were procured ; information was obtained from a returned colonist ; the slender money-chest was unlocked ; the youths were fitted out ; the mother wept, the Doctor blubbered, and the boys took ship for Adelaide, and O'Dowd and his wife found themselves as much alone as in the early days of their married life.

The brother-in-law, though murmuring, consented to give a sum of money for the purpose of retrieving the fortune of the fallen man, but on a certain condition laid down by himself. It was not to be expended in the purchase of a business, but in the purchase of bottles, aqua pura, cheap tinctures, soaps, fundamental drugs in the raw state, sponges, salines, gingers, brushes, and all the other furniture that adorns and enriches the windows and counters of the apothecary.

The venture seemed a success. The business throve, if the clearing out of stock be a sign of prosperity. Shaving sticks, soaps, syrups, fruit salt, pilules of all kinds vied with each other in a general stampede ; it seemed as if the inhabitants of that town, which was little better than a hamlet, had a perennial washing and shaving day, and sustained themselves, for the most part, by an outward application of plasters and an inward drenching of syrups and black draughts.

It was the wonder of everyone, especially the brother-in-law. The shop filled—the shop emptied ! Yet no money in the till, and the Doctor complaining of poverty and calling for a renewal of his stock !

The brother-in-law got tired of the farce, and told the Doctor that he ought to try his fortune abroad. Whereupon O'Dowd declared his willingness to go to the most distant part of the globe— he would have gone among the pigmies into the forest of Central Africa if it had been then explored—on condition that his relative would pay the expenses of the journey and give him a substantial sum of money wherewith to set himself up in business on his arrival at his new abode.

His wife fell ill at this time, owing, no doubt, to the constant care and worry of her life, and the flight of all her children ; and was heard plaintively to prophesy that she would never see the Golden East to which her husband thought of hieing. She besought him to set out without her, and promised that she would follow him if her illness did not take a fatal turn. He left her behind without misgiving, for he was buoyed up with the hope of seeing her soon again ; but he had not been a full month in his new home when the black-edged letter came to announce that she was no more. He shed tears ; he said many loving words of her, as he recalled the struggles in which she had taken part, and the straits in which she had been his chief support ; and then the image of this cherished one began to fade from his memory, and finally he forgot her, and with her his children and all the chequered scenes of his early life.

He had not been many months residing in Calcutta at the time our story opens. He had found it difficult to procure a small house in the city, and was driven at the end of a long search, to hire the kind of hybrid tenement in which we have found him.

He had put in a few articles of furniture, and had stocked a little shop with miscellaneous professional wares, just as he had done in Ireland. In the local journals he had advertised himself as "Septimus O'Dowd, doctor, chemist and druggist," who had come to reside in Calcutta for the purpose of promoting health culture principally among the dark races, and to supply them with a class of medicines adapted to the eaters of rice and similar light diet. The advertisement had taken very well. Crowds of dusky Hindus had streamed into his surgery; the outcome of which was, that they had consumed all his patent medicines, and taken his professional advice, while paying him next to nothing. Very few whites had come to his store, but the few who did paid him but little more than the people of colour. Between them he had sunk into poverty.

On this afternoon he sat in his low chair with his legs on the counter, and now he ceased to rock. He was looking with doleful regards at the empty bottles and crocks and dismal boxes that lay around him.

"Poor creatures!" said he, "there is not one copper pennyworth of stuff in any of them, The niggers have consumed the medicines, and I have consumed the tooth-picks, syringes, shaving sticks, and sponges: and I am this blessed evening on my last case of scented soap."

Starting to his feet he endeavoured to dispel the gloom by a performance of which an account will be given in the next chapter.

He was thus engaged when he saw a Hindu boy enter, who asked for a piece of scented soap for his mistress who had given him two rupees to pay for it.

CHAPTER II.

MISS ADA PHLICK, who came so opportunely to
the aid of Doctor Septimus O'Dowd by the purchase of a small quantity of the only ware he had
in his shop, was a lady who had been residing for
some years in India; to which dependency of the
British crown she had come on a speculation of her
own.

It was not, as can easily be guessed, for the
purpose of trade that a spinster of thirty summers
left her home, bade good-bye to her friends, and
took ship for what she regarded as the most distant
part of the world; nor was it to visit a relative or
take up a legacy, or busy herself with the conversion of the Hindu.

No; Miss Ada Phlick came to British India
three years before the date at which this story
opens, with the unselfish purpose of conferring herself and her charms on some man in the Civil
Service, or wearing the uniform of a British officer
in a home or native regiment.

The Indian matrimonial market happened to be
full at the time of her arrival; and not only was it
well-stocked, but the goods were superior and
attractive. Amidst blooming maidens of eighteen,
just arrived, and well-preserved damsels of twenty-
three, Miss Ada, who had passed her thirtieth

year, and laboured under a serious facial defect,
was nowhere; and she gradually fell out of the
view of the only classes that she cared for, or
thought worthy of her, and disappeared from
fashionable society.

A crisis had come in the affairs of this lady, but
she met it like a woman of spirit. The civil
functionaries, who had turned from her, she
characterized as a set of purse-proud nobodies;
and as for the strutting officers—well, she could
not help admiring them; her heart, if it must be
told, went out towards them still. But she told
herself, and came to believe in it in the end, that
they were wits and wags, and fops, and hair-brained
swells, who amused themselves with butterfly
hunting, and were fitted for little else.

Miss Phlick had a small annual income, that was
just enough to keep her; so when she had satisfied
herself that she had no chance of bagging the
higher game of the capital, she hired a small house
at the end of what was called the White quarter
of the city, resolving to take her ease and look out
for squalls; for she thought that even a slight
disturbance in any part of the peninsula, such as
the revolt of a tribe or a little war of annexation,
would bring new life, and, above all, strange men,
into the hum-drum city of Calcutta.

She was not aware, when taking possession of
her new home, that she had a neighbour who, like
herself, had come across the ocean on speculation;
but she was not displeased when her eyes fell for
the first time on the surgery of O'Dowd over the
way. She saw the house, but not its inmate; and

she sat in her window for some hours straining her
eyes across the street, and hoping to behold a
Briton of stalwart frame and symmetrical build
issuing from the place or showing himself in a
window.

Patience, if we are to believe in an old adage,
brings, in due time, a compensating reward ; but
we should not feel ourselves justified in admitting that the patient spying of Ada Phlick on the
house of her compatriot brought her these pleasur-
able emotions which she might regard as a
reasonable price for her composed and long-con-
tinued sitting.

A head appeared at O'Dowd's door ; it was a
fat and flabby head, and a pair of large flat
feet were set firmly on the ground directly under
it. But the trunk that connected them not appearing, a guess might be hazarded that those members
belonged to a body of great length, which was
bent, in the form of a curve, inside.

How we hug our delusions to our heart when
they support a theory in the truth of which we are
interested !

Ada Phlick would have made a solemn declaration, and signed it, that, to the best of her belief,
the owner of the head and feet was a man of
colossal stature. It could not be otherwise, she
thought ; what business could a little man have
with such large extremities? and how could such
a ball of flesh and bone as she saw over the way
sit upon the trunk of even a middle-sized descendant
of Adam?

Having feasted her eyes with a prolonged and

minute stare at the fragments of humanity presented at O'Dowd's door, and having failed to
discover the connecting link between them, and
having satisfied herself that said link, whether
through design or frolic, was concealing its large
proportions, she turned in upon herself and reflected. Then she left the window, and took a
seat on a bamboo easy-chair that stood in the
centre of the room, and uttered the word " Perhaps "
in a perfectly audible tone of voice.

She was like one sitting for a portrait. Let us
take advantage of the pose in which we find her to
make a pen and ink picture of the lady.

She was of middle-height, and well-formed.
Her hair was golden auburn ; her eyes seemed to
have borrowed a tint from her hair, for they were
not grey, nor blue, or hazel, and of course they
were neither brown nor black, but there was a
sympathy in them which made up for their nondescript hue. Her hands and feet were small ;
her mouth was in good proportion. But it was
her nose that gave character to and lit up her face,
and that gave a tone to the figure of this romantic
young lady. Yes, her nose was everything to
her ; without it, she would have been an ordinary
spinster. Not that it added to her beauty, for it
was neither Grecian nor Roman ; but in some in
describable way it marked her out as a woman apart
And yet it was not a flat nose, for it had an
ordinary bridge, which was not depressed ; nor did
it lack the usual side appendages, nor did it turn
out of the common line, up or down, or sideways.

C

And yet, without that nose, Ada Phlick would have been nobody. It seemed to start out of her face with the best intention, and then to forget itself, not by becoming absolutely bulbous, nor running to a point, as this feature sometimes will, but by growing on until it was out of proportion to her other features and assumed a marked authority over them all. And even the growing process, which must have continued longer in her care than in that of most children, could not account for the bold terminal line of this remarkable feature.

If Miss Phlick laughed or cried, her nose was in perfect sympathy with her emotions, and had a way of showing it. If she was in even mind, her nose seemed perfectly happy.

This indicator (if she would pardon us for so naming this very respectable, and we will add capable, organ of smell), was not quite itself to day ; it was inclined to be restless. It had been put out by something that had occurred—perhaps by the apparition over the street. Miss Phlick knew that it was chafing ; and whether through a wish to give it comfort, or to bring it more perfectly into subjection, she rubbed it hard ; whereupon it became very hot—so hot, indeed, that when she got up from her seat, and went over to a mirror to have a look at herself, she was made perfectly uncomfortable by its appearance.

" I did not mean to hurt you, poor little thing," she said ; " come and let us have another sitting at the window, when perhaps we may receive a reward for our long and patient waiting by getting a full view of this grand man, who is our neighbour, and may be later on our friend."

She went to the window and sat down—she and the nose together ; and if she had on her previous waiting closely examined the house opposite, peering into door and windows, she now turned her eyes upon it with the sweep and brilliancy of a search-light, as if she would penetrate to the interior, and see through the rents and chinks of the flimsy building the figure and movements of the man she knew to be within.

She looked up and down, around and across, but to no effect. Not satisfied with the view of the place which her sitting position commanded, she stood on tip-toe like a dancing girl, hoping to open a new vista through which she might make a discovery of what was going on inside. But the place was sealed against her—designedly, she thought for no idle man, as the Doctor was proved to be by the fact that no one seemed to enter his store, could live and move in so small a house without betraying his presence there—unless he were asleep in bed, which was improbable at that hour, or were purposely hiding in a closet or room behind.

Miss Phlick was a woman of character: though balked, she was not beaten. She continued to work the search-light, throwing it not only on the house, but up and down the street, thinking that perhaps the imprisoned one might try to go out by a postern door, for she suspected that he might be in some way conscious that he was being closely watched.

The curiosity of an ordinary woman would sink

into insignificance beside that of Ada Phlick, who
had come to India to look for a husband and had
been disappointed, and who was now leading a
forlorn hope against a stronghold garrisoned by
one whom she believed to be a very gallant and
desirable member of the sex she had come to
fascinate !

Her curiosity, however, was putting her patience
to too great a test, and she was beginning to feel
weary. An inclination to retire from the window
for good was creeping over her, when sounds of a
mixed and very unusual character came in waves
across the street, telling her, in no uncertain tones,
that her *vis-à-vis* was still at home, and not only
at home but hilarious.

She listened. He was whistling—a practice she
detested—absolutely whistling the air of a vulgar
street ballad, and at the same time he was dancing,
for she heard distinctly the shuffling of feet on his
floor. He was singing too at intervals, and in
French ! What could it mean ? Whistling, singing, dancing by turns ! Then—dancing, singing,
whistling all together ! She listened more atten-
tively : " Au clair de lune ! " she caught ; " un babu
brun ! " Then a railway shriek, or the soft sibila-
tion of an amorous ditty ; then a jump into the air,
followed by the thud of a heavy body coming
down on the floor ; then a gliding along as if he
were waltzing, followed by a quick step, as if he
were doing a sailor's hornpipe ; then a full stop.

The nose was becoming restive, and she gave it
a friendly tap, whispering, " Listen."

He resumed after a few minutes, but in quite a

different style : all that he had been doing up to this time was but a prelude.

From a whizzing and gulping that she heard, she thought he was swallowing a cough mixture, or using some glycerine lozenges to clear his throat. And then he sang out the following :—

> Gin my love were yonder rose
>   That blooms upon the castle wall,
> And I a little drap o' dew
>   Within its bonny leaves to fall.
>   How I would mourn
>   When it was torn
>   By Autumn wild
>   Or Winter rude ;
>   And I would sing
>   On joyous wing
>   When youthful Spring
>   Its bloom renewed.
>   Oh ! my love's bonnie, etc.

Miss Phlick was moved almost to tears by the concluding words of the song. When the performance began, and during the preliminary part of it, Miss Ada had very serious misgivings. She wondered, indeed, whether the singer was a lunatic, and she was even telling up mentally the asylums she knew of in England, with a view to making a guess as to that from which he had escaped. India was not, she was thinking, a bad place for a flying madman : it was out of range ; no keepers would follow him thither, or even suspect that he had chosen it for his home. But that song ! That tender, quaint, loving Scotch song ! So well timed ! So much to the point ! He must have seen her stealing glances at his house and windows, else why the allusion to "yon castle wall"? He must have even had a view of her face and person—"yonder rose." Ah, the dear man!

Ada called Jumri in a voice slightly shaken by a new-born agitation; and when the Hindu boy whose patronymic this was appeared, she said to him with some agitation: "Here are two rupees: take them to the chemist's over the street, and bring back to me the amount of scented soap for which they may pay. And, Jumri, look well at the chemist, and be able, when you come back, to give me a correct description of his face and form. But be cautious; don't let him suspect that you are spying."

The bright boy, in white turban and gown and red sash, said nothing in reply, but bowed low and disappeared.

He went across the street—Ada took a snap-shot impression of his movement—and entered the shop of the apothecary, who was seated behind the counter taking rest and recovering his breath after his exertions.

"Missis want soap of scent," said the lad, laying down the money."

"She shall have it with thanks," said the Doctor. "Pray, who is the lady, boy?"

Jumri pointed across the street and said: "She be there."

"What is her name, my lad?" inquired O'Dowd.

"Miss Phlick only," answered the boy.

"Only—I see: she hopes to add another name to it later on."

This was too obscure for the boy, and he said nothing.

"Phlick O'Dowd!" murmured the Doctor. "It would not sound badly." Then, raising his voice: "Scented soap," he said, "is very dear at present; not a bit of it to be had for love or money. I don't believe there is another house in Calcutta that could supply it. I fear—and for the sake of the lady I regret it—that I shall have to charge you all the money you have brought for one small piece of this invaluable toilet requisite."

The boy shook his head, saying: "I don't know." By which he intended to convey that he did not understand the Doctor's reasoning. Then he took the soap and departed.

Ada was waiting for him patiently, and was disappointed at his coming so soon.

"Why, boy," she said, "you have not given yourself time to do your message in full. You have brought the soap, but, I fear, scarcely looked at the vendor of it."

"O, yes!" said Jumri; "I see him very much. He a very fine man—he's not black."

"You booby!" said Miss Phlick.

"Nor colour of copper," said the boy, thinking that Ada's appellation was complimentary.

"Nor blue, I suppose?" said Miss Phlick, annoyed; "nor red, like an American Indian. Is he tall?"

"Yes, he be tall this way," said the boy, opening his arms horizontally.

"This way and that way," said the lady testily; "what a description you give of him. I don't believe you looked at him at all."

"Oh, yes!" I look very much," said Jumri—"I look in his face."

"Well! and what sort of face has he?" said she.

Jumri grinned. "He's not as ugly as a monkey," he said, "nor as nice as a coolie."

"You may go, boy," said Ada; "you are as stupid as—as—as nature made you," for the want of a term of comparison. Her watching was at an end for the present.

CHAPTER III.

THE FOURTH DUFFS.

MISS ADA PHLICK, in her best days, when she arrived in Calcutta, aspiring and hopeful, with a few introductions in her card-case, was not a success in military circles, though she received and accepted a few invitations to balls at Fort William.

In that sombre citadel still went on the round of parades, reviews, assemblies and mess dinners in perfect oblivion of this lady; though there were among the soldiers who formed its garrison some who, if they had met her in their idle hours, would not have scrupled to amuse themselves at her expense.

Other belles shed their charms on the military dances. Straight-backed broad-shouldered daughters of Britain strolled the Maiden Gardens with military friends, in the early morning or as the sun went down. After dinner chat in the ante-room of the mess often turned on some new arrival who, by her wit or beauty, drew a circle of admirers around her ; but never was the name of a native lady introduced, for the caste restrictions in force among the Hindus kept the daughters of zemindars and rajahs secluded from the society of Europeans.

It was therefore a revelation, when, at a dinner of the Fourth Duffs, who were then in garrison at

Fort William, an officer made reference to a mysterious coloured lady whom, in very clear terms, he declared to be the handsomest woman in Calcutta, or for aught he knew, in the entire peninsula of India.

It came about in this way.

Colonel Baily, a serious yet affable chief, was in the chair, and not far down, on the right and left, were two officers of his regiment, an Englishman named Halbot and an Irishman named Stokes, who were leading spirits in the garrison ; while at the end of the table, in the vice-chair, sat Mayor Staples, a dry man, who spoke little but, in an unconventional way, to the purpose.

The guests were not many, but there were two amongst them of whom a few words may be said. One was a lawyer of dark skin, named Akbar Yassov, as fierce and noisy a follower of the Prophet, as could be met in the bazaars of Stamboul ; the other an Anglican clergyman, the Reverend Nethcoff Bingham, a man who happily combined with the seriousness of his character as a clerk an unaffected gaiety that rendered him very attractive.

The conversation of this mixed party rose and fell, and sometimes ran along and around the table, like the pleasant roll of a drum. The scorching heat, the arrivals by the last packet, the latest mails, the stirrings on the frontier, the general health of India, were the topics they discussed ; and there was no room for friction among the speakers, until the subject of the General's last ball was introduced.

" It was a perfect gathering of rank and beauty,"
began a young lieutenant named Scott, "and as
for the supper, it was exceptional in material and
splendidly served."

' I envy you, Mr. Scott. My impaired digestion
revolts against doubtful dishes and over-crowded
tables," said Captain Stokes.

A smile passed over the company.

" Now, Captain Stokes," said Major Staples,
"you have come down too heavily. I am
of Mr. Scott's view as to the material of the
General's supper, but I predict that you will see
quite as exquisite a menu when our president
entertains."

" Which will be," said Colonel Baily, "when the
Juggernaut car is again set in motion. Where
could I find beauty like that which gave a quite
uncommon charm to the General's gathering ?
Such colours ! Such faces ! Such figures ! Such
dresses ! I fully believe there is not a handsome
woman in the peninsula who was not in that ball-
room."

" Pardon me," said Captain Halbot, "there is
one lady in Calcutta, not much known and seldom
seen abroad, who is far more beautiful than any
of those who accepted the General's invitation."

These words surprised the company. "You are
not serious, Halbot," from a dozen voices. "Is
this lady a new arrival from Europe? Who is
she ?"

" Only a Hindu !" said Halbot smiling.

" How do you judge of beauty, Captain Halbot?"
said Colonel Baily. "What is your standard ?"

" Face, form, height, bearing and proportion,"
replied the man questioned.

" Does colour form an element ? "

" Certainly."

" Marvellous ! " said the Colonel, as he lapsed
musingly into silence.

It was marvellous, they all thought, that a man
of Halbot's critical taste should give utterance to
such an opinion. The subject, however, was
allowed to drop out of the general conversation, to
be taken up perhaps later and discussed at length
when the company retired.

.   .   .   .

We left O'Dowd in fairly good spirits, which had
been raised to a higher level by the arrival of the
Hindu boy and the purchase he made for his
mistress, Miss Ada Phlick.

It was an angel that sent him, thought the
Doctor, and she must have been inspired, for I
would have been disgraced for ever if he had asked
for a tooth-brush or a bottle of saline, or a square
inch of court plaster. May her fair hands grow
whiter under the influence of the detergent !

He tossed the coin into the air, saying : " It is
only a trifle, but it will give me a roll, a dish of
curry and a bottle of beer."

He then fell into a silent study of his position,
and thought that he had made a fatal mistake in
leaving a country where there is much sympathy for
the poor and struggling, and coming among a set of
black pagans whose minds were scanty as their
clothes. And he went out devising plans and
schemes by which to stem the current of ill-luck

which was all but carrying him away. He thought that if he turned auctioneer he might do a good business, for he had quaintness to amuse and a silvery tongue to persuade; but what, after all, was there to sell in this country, unless the clothes of the poor creatures (which didn't half cover them), or their little sticks of furniture which were hardly fit to put upon a decent bonfire? And this, thought he, is the Golden East! But, if there be gold mines in the British portion of Hindustan, what is to prevent me from becoming a miner, and descending with pick and lantern into the depths of the earth and coming up laden with nuggets? Or if the yellow sparkling deposits are out in the country of the tribes that live under their native rulers, might I not go out among them, and barter black draughts for the privilege to dig? The Doctor, though born in France, had inherited a very lively but erratic imagination, and it was probably this defect of the faculty, arising from its exuberance, that produced another idea that now floated across his fancy, and on which he seized with much zest. There is a business, he thought, suited to this land which might be made to pay; and yet it is, as far as I know, totally overlooked. It is a novel business; it might be a dangerous business; an enterprising man only should embark in it. I flatter myself that I am such. Merchants of cotton are numerous here; and there seems no opening for me in that trade. There are many silk merchants around, and many exporters of Indian rugs and carpets; but where is the tiger-merchant? Where is the tiger-merchant?

he repeated.   Is there in all India even one man
that deals in the royal beast?   And if this particular line of goods is lying fallow and neglected,
why may not I rush in and seize upon it, and
ship it in hundreds to the open markets of Europe
and America?   There is the catching of the tiger
to be sure, he impartially added.   That is a
difficulty in the case of the full-grown brute.   But
then the cub!—the toothless, clawless, playful cub!
He might be taken in the absence of his parent
foraging, and I have no doubt but plenty of those
black wooden-legged trotters that one meets everywhere in this city would risk, for a trifle, the chance
of being surprised and eaten in the attempt to
rob the roost.

"There is a mine in this country," he said aloud,
"that has not been tapped heretofore.   If I had
capital, I'd make a fortune of its reptiles and wild
beasts.

"Why, the rattle-snakes alone (I am not quite
sure that they are indigenous) and cobras would
put anyone on the way to wealth, not to speak
of the centipedes, toads, beetles, butterflies, and
parrots.   I believe money could be made of the
alligators that swim in our rivers, and I am quite
sure that if fire-flies were bottled and shipped,
let us say to the Dark Continent, they would bring
back a large return of the circulating medium of
that region, whatever it may be.   If I had capital
I would become a great export merchant of all
the crawling, creeping, roaring, hissing, bounding
swimming and flying things that are found in this
country, but—"   He was stopped by the entry of

a young Hindu maid, who came timidly to the counter and made a sign, with a finger on her mouth, that she wished to speak to him in confidence. He went to her and bent his head to hear what she had to say.

" She want gumra," said the girl ; " she gave me money to buy it."

" A very proper and thoughtful act on her part," said the Doctor, " for neither gumra, whatever it may be, nor any drug or condiment can be had without coin."

" She be very rich, and don't want nothing for nothing," said the girl.

" Which is much to her credit," said the Doctor " I wish all the world was like her."

" Has the Sahib gumra ? " said the girl gaining confidence.

" He has sold it all," said the Doctor, adding under his breath : " be hanged to it."

" She be sick," said the girl pointing to her heart.

" I see—heart symptoms. Gumra is very good in its way, but will never set the heart at ease. Who advised her to take gumra ? "

" Black doctor, Sahib."

" I might have guessed as much ; the name should have told me. Some confounded extract of toads and turnip-tops. These dark medicine-men are killing off the people like a plague. If I could see your mistress I could prescribe something for her that would set her right, and, my word to you, it would be no gimgrackery like gumra."

" No gumra, I go," said the girl.

" No, my love!" said the Doctor. "I may find
something for you better than gumra."

" I no love," said the girl ; " I ugly little thing.
If the Sahib saw Kèsur."

" Pray, who is Kèsur, child ? " said O'Dowd.

" Kèsur sent me," said the girl. "Oh! she be
like the sun rising."

" A poetical comparison, my darling, but not
clear.   Do you mean to convey that Kèsur is
comely ? "

" Kèsur is lovely.   No one like Kèsur," said the
girl.

" Strong words ! " said O'Dowd.

" Oh! True—true!" continued the girl.   " No
one like Kèsur, not even the English Memsahibs. "

" Is Kèsur black ? " said the Doctor incautiously

" Kèsur be not black," said the girl pouting.

" She is a white woman then ? " said O'Dowd.

" Nor white," said the Ayah.

" Perhaps your colour ? " said the Doctor.

" Nor my colour," she answered, " but a beautiful colour of her own : nicer than white, nicer than
brown : and her eyes, and her face, and her form.
Oh! she be a mahwanee."

" If she be of that colour, gumra is not the dose
for her complaint.   It is too nasty.   It is only fit
to be used by pariahs or niggers.

" No gumra," said the girl again, turning to go.

" Not an ounce of it in the shop or store-house
at present."

" I go and tell her," said the girl.

" What a hurry you are in," said the Doctor.
" We may find something else among the drugs

than will suit her, especially as you have brought the money."

" What ? " said the girl.

" Has she any nice scented soap for her ablutions ? " said O'Dowd.

" Kèsur want no soap.   She gets purified in the holy river."

" A dip in the Ganges may be a good thing in its way, but it won't keep the hands clean always. Does she never wash her hands before meals ? "

" I don't know."

" Oh, child ! A woman of such beauty must have a vanity.   She could never sit to the table with soiled hands."

" Be soap good for the heart ? " said the girl.

" Scented soap of this class," said he solemnly, putting a piece of it on the counter, " is good for the whole body.   Smell it."

" It is sweet ? " said the girl.   " May she eat it ? "

" I don't think it would injure her if she did, but it is to be applied externally."

" ' Ternally ? " said the girl, " that's for ever."

" If it were applied for ever, it would be the better for us all.   No, girl, it is not to be eaten : it's to be rubbed on.   She will know what to do with it herself.   It's dear and scarcely to be had now ; it's part of an old stock.   They make no such soap in India.   I must charge you two rupees for a cake of it—wholesale price."

The girl was bewildered, for she could not follow the Doctor in his eulogy of the soap, and yet she understood enough to feel certain that this was a very rare and valuable article.   She laid down all the money that she had to pay for it, which was five rupees.

"I take soap," said she, "you take money."

"How much money?" said O'Dowd. "Five rupees! It is too much for the soap. I could not, as an honest man, take more than two rupees for it. But I will meet you in another way. I will take the remaining three rupees on loan. Do you know what a loan is?"

"No," said the girl innocently.

"Tell your mistress that Doctor O'Dowd, not having at present any gumra in stock, has taken the liberty of sending her some nice scented soap instead, for which he has put aside two rupees out of the money brought; and that being just now very low in funds, he has taken the additional liberty of retaining the balance on loan, to be re-paid on demand, or, if she will be so good, at the end of one calendar month."

"Thank you, Sahib," said the girl bowing low as she left the shop.

"Heigho!" said he when left alone again. "I am in luck to-day—on a small scale, to be sure; but, all the same, I *am* in luck, thanks to the ladies—the darlings! Yet I may not be in luck to-morrow; in truth I cannot, for the scented soap is nearly all off. "'Twasn't a bad idea—selling soap for gumra, which I take to be a perfectly brutal medicine for internal use, which in all probability would have killed the lady. Now, with this soap in her hands she cannot be worse at the heart than she was before, while she will be more sweet and sanitary."

He dropped again into a study of means and ends, and putting aside all his previous speculations which he felt could not be carried into action for want of capital, he thought of an old adage, that he persuaded himself he had heard in France when a child, " Parceque la montagne ne voudrait venir à Mahomet—Mahomet s'approchait à la montagne." Exactly what he would do.

The paying people of Calcutta were not coming to him for advice or medicine. He had been already six months in their midst, and he had not received of their money, but had spent his own —it wasn't much—amongst them. Because they would not come to him, he would go to them. He would pass through the streets of the Black and White quarters of their city and advertise himself by his gravity and his learned appearance. His silent figure moving along would appeal to their selfish feelings, and (ahem) he would await the result.

CHAPTER IV.

A MESS-ROOM STORY.

THE tables are bared, the lights extinguished, the guests departed, and the mess-room of the 4th Duffs is normal ; but the officers of the regiment are in another apartment smoking, lounging, and sipping effervescents mixed with stronger liquids.

They do not resume the subject of the General's ball, which they let drop so suddenly during dinner, nor revert to the discussion to which it gave rise ; and so they leave Captain Halbot's Hindoo Lady on the pinnacle to which he had raised her, to the surprise of everyone at table.

There is not much talk, and such as there is, comes dreamily and at intervals. A gloom had set in, keeping pace with the advancing shadows, when Captain Stokes, always an enemy to depression, started up.

" For the want of something to enliven us," he said, " I will tell you a story, if you will allow me, which cannot amuse you much, I fear, but may help to pass the time."

" Thank you, Stokes," from all sides.

" Don't be prosy or maudlin," from the Major.

" No, I promise to be as brief as the subject may allow, and I shall leave the company to draw the moral from my tale."

" And I, with the consent of the assembly, as

senior officer, shall draw it," said Staples. "Proceed."

"Some time ago," began Stokes—"I shall not, for certain reasons, give the date—a friend of mine was coming to India by the Cape, and during the voyage, he made the acquaintance of the first mate of the ship, and often conversed with him, as they trod the deck of an evening."

"I can already feel," said Mr. Scott, "that we are in for something creepy. Pass the potash, Halbot!"

"Now, Scott," said Captain Stokes, "no forebodings! I am not, as you know, a dealer in horrors. I am simply to tell a story, to raise your spirits, which, when you shall have heard it you may deem creditable to the principal actor, who, in a moment of thoughtlessness, put his hand in another man's pocket, and would take it out again if he could."

"A mild type of the species thief!" said Halbot.

"You will say so with knowledge, when you have heard all," said Stokes. "I resume my narration. The mate and my friend often walked together on deck, smoking and talking freely on many subjects. It was during one of these strolls, that the officer told a somewhat sensational story.

"'We were on a home voyage from the Cape of Good Hope to Southampton, not many months ago,' said he, 'when I observed among the passengers a wild fellow, with a troubled expression on his face, who seemed to me to be striving to drown in beer and boisterous laughter some canker that was gnawing at his heart. His bearing excited my curiosity, so I determined to throw myself in his way, get into his confidence if I could, and come at his history, which should be sad or sensational.

"'I had no difficulty in introducing myself to him, but I was simply amazed at the ease and freedom with which he made me sharer of the great secret of his life.

"'"Skipper," said he, "you have an honest face, I have a weight on my mind. I wish to make it known to you. You will, I know, keep it dark. I am a miner, as you may guess. I have been at the gold-fields, where I have had some luck, and I am returning to Old England with a well-filled purse ; but I have been a dishonest man, and I am very unhappy."

"'"Gone in on another's claim ?" said I, "Or broken a bank in the absence of a cashier ? "

"'"No, sir," said he, "I did not lay a finger on any man's gold or take a spoke out of any one's wheel during the six months that I was working in South Africa. It was before I arrived there, and on the voyage out—it might be in this very ship—that I was guilty of an act of theft, which has ever since made me a desponding and un-happy man. I'll tell you all about it.

"'"Among the passengers in the ship in which I came on from England, was a soft-headed fellow, with whom I became very intimate. He was an unsuspicious creature, always talking of his private affairs ; and it struck me as probable that he would become a victim to some knave before he arrived at his destination, which was India. He tempted myself to be that knave by shaking in my face a large bag of sovereigns.

" ' " I was staggered by the music and glitter of the coin, but did not fall yet. I told him that he was too out-spoken and rash, and that it was my firm belief that he and his money would not be long together. He said : ' So little am I afraid of losing it, that I leave it always where it is now, in my coat pocket, even when in my berth asleep, on the principle that the valuables in a jeweller's shop are all the safer for being seen in a strong light by passers and prowlers, and even thieves of the night.'

" ' " After this avowal, the temptation grew upon me and became irresistible. His money was for the first comer, and I, in a moment of weakness, resolved to take it.

" ' " I continued to keep him company as before, walked with him on the deck as often as I could, keeping him always in view, to the evening of the day before the ship arrived in the harbour of Cape-town. Meanwhile, I was bringing my nefarious plan to maturity.

" ' " For a small gift in money the steward of the ship removed myself and my belongings into the cabin used by my dupe, where I occupied a berth directly under his. I then managed to get some chloral from the doctor—you will guess for what purpose." ' "

" The d—— fool ! " from the Major. " Pardon ! I forgot—old style ! "

" The crisis is coming," from the young Lieutenant. " Pass the nervine." Stokes continued :

"'"I asked him on the evening of that day to have a drink with me, and we sat for a long time over our often-filled glasses. He kept the table closely, and I was beginning to fear that I might not get an opportunity of slipping the chloral into his liquor, when an unusual noise was heard on deck, and he rose and left the cabin for a short time, going up the companion ladder.

"'"In his absence I poured the chloral into his tumbler which was nearly full; and when he came back he swallowed the contents at a draught, grinning a little afterwards, and saying that it was sickening stuff, and that he would go into his berth and sleep off the effects of it. Even then he had no suspicion of me.

"'"He took off his coat, and I watched him hanging it from a hook; and then I went away to walk the deck and think of the imbecile who allowed himself to be so easily victimised. I returned after half an hour to find him, as I expected, in a deep sleep, snoring as if he was in a fit; when I took off my coat, as if preparing for bed, and hung it on a hook by the side of his. I then sat down, burying my face in my hands. I was acting, for there were others in cabin. After some minutes, as if I had changed my mind and would not retire yet, I rose and took down his coat, put it on, and went to the forecastle, which was quite deserted. There I drew out his money-bag, counted two hundred sovereigns, which I put into a belt which I carried round my waist, and then went back to the cabin, where I took off the coat, put it into the position on

the wall which he had given it, and then went
into my berth in my clothes, not even removing
my boots.

"'"The next morning, before he was awake, I
was off with my booty to the gold fields. Poor
soft-headed jester! I am certain that he did
not miss that money until he arrived in India,
and that even then he did not suspect anyone
of having stolen it, and least of all me, to whom
he had opened his heart so freely. But, sir,"
said the miner, as he drew his rough arm across
his eyes, "I am sorry from my heart for that
mean act, and I am ready to give him back the
money if he can be found; but I need not, I
suppose, betray myself, for I should die of shame
if he knew it was I that stole it."'"

"Is there a moral to this story, Stokes?" said
the Major rising to a sitting posture, "or is
it an advanced lesson on the mode and science
of thieving?"

"You can take it as a sermon on repentance,"
said Stokes.

"Maudlin! Pray what do you propose to do
with the swag? Give it to any man who will say
he lost it. I suggest that it be thrown open to
all claimants by a general advertisment in the
city journals."

"You would have hundreds coming forward."

"Great fun! Thousands, I say. It would raise
quite a school of thieves through British India.'

"I think," said Halbot seriously, "that Captain
Stokes has given us this story in confidence, and
does not wish in consequence of the interests

involved, and the danger of one of its actors being arrested and prosecuted for theft, and the other brought up as an accomplice after the fact— to have it go beyond the present circle."

"I thank you, Halbot," said Stokes ; "such was my intention."

"And I promise," said the Major, " to keep it to myself, for I was slumbering peacefully during the greater part of it. But come, Stokes," he continued, "you require change of air and scene after your toil of mind and voice in telling this gruesome tale. Let us have a sort of pro-miscuous stroll through the streets and suburbs. Meanwhile, if you wish, you may tell me another story, provided that it does not inculcate vice or give instruction in any other mode of villainy."

"Smoking not allowed ? " said Stokes.

"Like a blazing furnace," said Major Staples.

They started : it was now quite dark, and the heat was intense. They crossed very slowly over the plain that separates Fort William from Calcutta, and entered the city by a narrow street. The night scenes which met them were like those of the day, presenting few features of interest to those who had so often seen the dresses, or absence of dress, the half faces and the whole faces, the brown and black and white people that jostle along side by side in the beautiful capital of the East.

They passed from the side street through which they entered, into a leading thoroughfare which was well lighted, and then capriciously turned into a dim lane and continued in a straight line until they reached the suburbs. Then they followed the fringe that divides the town from the surrounding country, until they almost touched the native quarter, where they stood and looked around. There was little to see and nothing to awaken curiosity at that late hour, and they were turning to retrace their steps when their eyes fell upon a sign-board on which were written the words—"Septimus O'Dowd, Surgeon, M. . . ."

"What is that?" said Staples, looking at the uneven letters.

"Merely a puff," replied Stokes, "an apothecary posing as a surgeon and doctor of medicine."

"How do you read it?"

"'Septimus O'Dowd, surgeon, M.D.' last letter broken."

The Major throwing a glass into his left (good) eye:

"By Jove! 'Septimus O'Dowd, surgeon, M'— M—M—it's not D, Stokes! Its F. I read it— 'Septimus O'Dowd, surgeon, M.F.' Surely these letters cannot stand for a medical degree."

"They may," said Stokes; "the titles that some of these men add to their names are now quite fanciful."

The major still peering at the board, crossed the street for a closer inspection.

"By Jove! I have made it all out. The second letter is ' F ' evolved out of ' D ' which has come to grief. There is a third letter—small ' h '— which has been pencilled on by an amateur. The whole inscription reads 'M.F.H.' which has only

one meaning on British soil—master of fox
hounds. I feel inclined for a saline. Let us
enter and interview. I foresee that there is more
than medicine to be had here."

On going in they were confronted by a large
pair of feet upon the counter, the soles turned
out ; but the owner of the feet was sunk into a
low chair behind. He started on hearing footsteps : the feet disappeared, and the beaming face
of O'Dowd took their place.

"At your service, gentlemen !" cried the Doctor.

"Which is, I regret to say, merely nominal,"
said Stokes. "We read your name outside and
thought that you might have come from the other
side of the Red Sea."

"And if you added the Suez Canal and the
Mediterranean, you would be nearer the mark,"
said O'Dowd.

"Perhaps the English Channel too ?" said the
Major.

O'Dowd nodded, not quite approvingly.

"And if the gentleman won't deem me inquisi-
tive," said Stokes, " the Irish Sea ? "

"Let it be so," said O'Dowd. " Put me down as
a Hiberno-Frenchman."

They smoked their man at once, and felt inclined to linger and draw him.

" I hope, Sir," said the Major, "that your sojourn
in this land of gold has been agreeable."

" I believe," said the Doctor seriously, "that I
can carry as big a trouble as most men, and even
smile under the burthen of it ; and I suspect that
I could not be quite happy if I had no snake to

cross my path. I have been at war with fortune since I took out my degree, but since I came to this land of glitter, I have had to keep up my spirits by artificial means."

"Stimulants, eh?" said the Major. "You won't, I hope, deem me impertinent?"

"No," said O'Dowd, "I am not a spirit drinker : I have kept myself together by looking out for better times, and I may add figuratively, by playing the lute and lyre."

The concluding words of O'Dowd brought a light laugh with a "By Jove!" from the Major, while Captain Stokes struggled hard to keep his features set.

"I should have thought," he interposed, "that your presence here would be a great boon if not to the white, certainly to the coloured people, near whom you have pitched your tent."

"Not a bit of it," replied O'Dowd. "The creatures are in the hands of a set of black practitioners, and they are pleased and grateful to them for their poisonings and butcheries."

"Innocent, ignorant, but interesting Hindus!" murmured Stokes : "they are fatalists as well, and bound up in their vague traditions."

"Ah!" put in the Major, who seemed to think that he had been too long silent : "you have an infernal lot of drugs."

"Of bottles, Sir," said the Doctor, " and hampers and boxes. But drugs!" He shook his head and was silent.

"Possibly out of saline mixtures?" said the Major. "I thought of having a draught."

"Faith, Sir," said O'Dowd, "it is not saline I'd offer you at this hour of the evening, but something more refreshing, if I had got in the rents of my Irish property ; but the clients are not paying here or there."

"Your hospitable intentions do you honour, Sir," said Stokes ; "and they are worthy of the old land from which both of us hail. We must meet again. You see by our dress what we are. Our place is Fort William, where we shall be glad to see you some day at mess. Meanwhile will you accept this accidental call as a visit and put aside formality ? "

"Certainly, gentleman," said O'Dowd ; "I feel honoured by your presence ; all the more as I seldom get a chance now of meeting persons of my own colour. There is, it is true, a white lady over the way, who is a customer of mine for soap," he added frankly, "but she is like the Veiled Prophet—she is seen only through a blind."

"I hope, Sir," said the Major, "that this accidental call may be the opening of a new vista in which you will see a little of that civilized life to which you have been used when at home. We now bid you adieu, and wish you numerous patients and a replenished exchequer."

The officers left the shop, and went towards home, laughing occasionally at the find they had made, and calculating the use they might make of it.

CHAPTER V.

A PARIAH'S END.—THE DOCTOR IN THE GANGES.

It would be rash to infer, from the Doctor's allusions to Miss Phlick, that he was watching to catch a glimpse of that lady through her window, or that, up to this time, he took any interest in her, save as a buyer of scented soap. And yet he would address himself to Jumri, if he chanced to see him as he opened his door at sunrise, and entrust that youth with a greeting to his neighbour; which, for one cause or another, was never delivered.

Ada Phlick was not so placid. She had cast her net, and it had come back to her empty. She had sent Jumri into a drug store as a spy, to take a secret impression of its inmate, and he had returned with a description of his face and form which was ludicrous, if not malicious. Nothing daunted, she still sat at her window: though it must be admitted that the weariness of her watch was giving rise to irritability.

"What a mole he is," said she, "burying himself in some dark corner of that gloomy shed, without air or light! If I had the patience of a saint— Jumri, come here. Have you seen that man opposite go out or in for the last week?"

"Oh, yes!" said the boy. "I see him early, very early, before lady be out of bed."

"Impertinent boy ! How do you know the hour at which your mistress rises ? "

" I hear no noise nor walking until ten o'clock. I hear kettle singing."

"Whatever does this sharp lad mean by *kettle singing?* He'll drive me to dismiss him. He is insinuating that I warble in my sleep."

" I hear kettle singing loud," continued the boy, " snort—snort—like railway."

" Stop that foolish talk," said Miss Ada, "and tell me if you have met our neighbour in the street."

" Yes, I spoke to him : he spoke to me. ' Jumri,' he says."

"What then ? " demanded Ada Phlick.

" ' How is the Maharana ? ' he says, very nice and kind."

"Did he say that ? " said Ada.

"He did. ' And,' says he, ' give her my combliments.'"

"Compliments ! It's all the same : the dear man ! "

"And he says to me," Jumri continued, becoming quite confidential, " 'is your mistress young or old ?' says he. ' She's old,' says I. "

"You bad boy ! " said Ada.

"' Most as old as yourself,' says I."

" You untruthful, deceptive and unfaithful lad ! How old, do you think, is this gentleman over the way ? "

" I think him as old as Buddha, nearly," said Jumri brightening.

"Go away from me," said Miss Phlick : " I

will never again put a question to you on this
subject. You have placed me in a dilemma: I
must do justice to myself. I shall have to conquer
my timidity, and call on this man in person, that
he may judge for himself of my age and appearance. Miss Phlick indeed as old as Doctor
O'Dowd! And Doctor O'Dowd as old as Buddha!"

She passed into her dressing-room, and stood for
a short time before the glass, contemplating her
really good figure, and searching incredulously for
a silver thread in her hair, or a wrinkle on her brow.
Not finding a blemish to disturb her self-esteem,
she went with confidence to her toilet-making. We
pass by that complex series of moves and pushes
and pulls and washings and crimpings and tintings
and powderings, with silent awe; for it is not
within the power of our pen to do it justice ; and
wait long and patiently in her snug parlour outside,
until she comes forth satisfied, parasol in hand, and
passes, like a bright vision, before us on her way to
visit the Doctor.

She crosses the street with light and juvenile
steps, enters the surgery of the Invisible, with the
air of one who has run her game to earth, looks
straight before her, and then to right and left, but
fails to see anyone or anything beside the gloomy
boxes and bottles. She taps the counter gently
with her fair hand, but there is no response. She
plays upon it with the handle of her umbrella ;
the echo is the only answer.

We leave her, for the present, perplexed and
annoyed, and go in search of the man who has
been unwittingly the cause of her embarrassment.

E

An hour before Miss Ada Phlick left her house
in all the brightness of summer costume, to call
upon her neighbour, O'Dowd had been waited
upon by a wretched pariah, in rags, who asked
him to come and visit his father, who was dying
under a shed, beyond the Black quarter of the
city.

"He be cold and naked," said the boy. "Do
come, good Sahib!"

"Yes, my lad," said O'Dowd, "I will come,
but I shall want a little time to dress."

"May I wait here until the Sahib is ready,"
said the boy, "or go and squat in the gutter
outside? I be only a pariah, that has no caste,
but under the feet of everyone."

"You are a man!" said O'Dowd, "and have as
much right to stand here as the greatest Nabob
in Calcutta."

The slender waif was amazed at the tone in
which the Doctor pronounced the words, and the
tears came down his cheeks, as he took his stand
humbly by the door, waiting until the kind man
should re-appear.

After a short interval O'Dowd came forth, with
his coat buttoned to the neck, carrying in his hand
a small paper parcel, which contained neither dose
nor plaister, but still was redolent of some sweet
confection. Beckoning the boy to go before him,
he followed him out of the shop and along the
street. They entered the dark town after a short
time, and keeping a little to the right, went on
nearly in a straight line, until they arrived at the
outskirts of the city.

" I go on," said the boy, " and be first with him. When he see me, he won't cry. We be always keeping each other up in our misery."

Something rose in O'Dowd's throat, and he coughed. It rose again, and he turned away from the boy, and seemed to gaze with emotion on a half-starved dog that came limping out of a tumble-down cottage not far away.

He entered the shed a few minutes later, and saw before him an old man, lying on a pallet of straw and covered with a robe of white cotton, which was not in keeping with his scant surroundings. His frame was emaciated to the last degree. His eyes were sunk deep in their sockets. His colour was ashy—livid. He mumbled, in a hollow voice, words which the Doctor did not understand. O'Dowd went on his knees to examine his throat and lungs, and remained in that position until he had satisfied himself that his life was ebbing rapidly away.

Then he rose, and after looking with compassion on the face of the dying pagan, turned to his son and said :

" Was this man a worshipper of Brahma ? "

" He knew not Brahma," replied the boy, " nor Vishnu, nor Siva, nor the others. He was only a pariah, that is given over to the Spirit of Evil. For him there were no rules laid down, but to live and die like the beast."

" Did no pious fakir come out of his cell to instruct him ? " inquired the Doctor.

" They be not pious fakirs," replied the youth, " but men of blood and lewdness. But if he had hidden in his wretched rags even a few rupees, they would be soon enough at his bed-side to demand them with threats and violence."

"If you summoned a priest to console him, would he, think you, come to close his eyes in peace?"

"The Sahib is not long in India, else he would know that they have no feeling for anyone or anything but learning and pride."

"Then he must leave us," said the Doctor feelingly, "like a lamp going out, as if he had no soul, and there was no home beyond the grave?"

"No!" replied the boy, brightening, "not so, good Sahib. He knew of a Great Spirit, and he loved Him,—that deals out justice to the poor."

"Where did he find that belief?" asked O'Dowd, who was amazed at the boy's ready reply.

"Ah!" sighed the waif, "if the Sahib saw the beautiful Spirit that hovers about this poor shed! She it was that taught him to believe and to love. She be a zemindar's daughter, of the highest caste, but she drop a tear over the lost pariah."

The Doctor was well-nigh dazed. He looked at the white robe that covered the dying man, and surmised that this was a gift from this tender woman. He was still examining it closely when he perceived a shivering motion in the bed, and a sigh, as a spirit took its flight to the unseen; and the wide eyes of the wan frame it had left seemed to gaze upwards to a place of rest far away.

The Doctor rose to go. He was not the

O'Dowd of old as he sauntered away, but a grave
man, with an air of thoughtfulness and even sorrow
on his usually cheerful face.

The pariah was preyed upon by vermin, and all
his surroundings, including the straw on which he
lay, the floor and the coverlet, were invaded by
myriads of nauseous creeping mites. The Doctor
did not observe this : but when he went out of the
shed ———

We pause. The subject is gruesome, but
the stern facts of history, however distasteful,
may not be overlooked ; and the narrative of
French O'Dowd's adventures in India would be
incomplete, if we did not touch on the mishap
which befel him during his attendance on the
abandoned Hindu.

Let it be said then, but *sotto voce,* that he was
invaded by armies of nameless crawlers and
biters. Some of these were in battle array ;
others were encamped on his shoulders and
knees ; a few of them had got inside his coat,
and were playing terrible havoc with his unpro-
tected skin. Bolder and bolder they became
every moment, because they were neither met
nor punished : and now they were moving on
in force to his face. An adventurous one would
now and again march over the bridge of his
nose, and flanking parties of these vile things
were thrown out on the fringe of his hair to cover
the advance on his forehead.

Again we must apologize for giving these
horrible details, but without a knowledge of
them it would be difficult to understand the

cause or urgency for a strategic move which the
Doctor made on his way home.

The enemy must be met, he must be attacked,
he must be driven off, he must be expelled from
his lurking places and strongholds : but how is
it to be done ? These were O'Dowd's reflections.
Fire, or water, or the sword ? If he could burn
the clothes he wore, it would extinguish the
hostile army, but where was the substitute for
them, unless he went into the scanty costume
of a coolie ? The sword, even in a diminished
sense, could not be used to expel an enemy that
was so mobile and tiny. But water ! Water was
at hand in abundance ; the mighty Ganges was
near. To the Ganges he would go, and dip
himself and the living freight he carried in its
cleansing waters ; and dip, and dip again, and not
cease to dip until every living insect that crept
upon him, within or outside his garments, had
given up the ghost.

To the Ganges, therefore, the Doctor turned ;
and when he arrived on its bank, he walked
slowly down an inclined platform, and from it
into the water, where he began to splash and
plunge like one possessed by a religious or
other mania. His mind contained but one idea,
and this was, to bring relief to his tortured body :
he did not see, or, if he saw, he was indifferent to
the fact that there were many in the Ganges
beside   himself—popping   and   dipping   and
plunging : men and women, all to an extent
dressed, and boys and girls performing an afternoon
religious ablution.

We leave O'Dowd in the river, now disappearing altogether under its surface, now rising above it and shaking himself in the manner of a retriever after a bath, and we go back to Miss Phlick, whom we left standing in dismay at the counter of the Doctor's surgery.

She soon got tired of waiting and listening to echoes, which were the only reply that came to her tapping on the counter with her parasol. She left the store, and coming across a coolie, as she went out, who stood at the side of the door, as if he were in charge of the place, asked him if the owner was long away, and what direction he had taken. In reply he told her that he had been absent half an hour, and that he had gone down the street in front and turned to the left into the quarter occupied by the Hindus.

Now Miss Ada Phlick had no leaning towards the Black city, and no taste for the odours that float in its atmosphere. At the same time, she had a strong desire and a firm resolve to see the Doctor before she returned to her house. She went down the street pointed out by the coolie, but did not turn into the Black town: she came up the street, re-tracing her steps to O'Dowd's door. She went down the street again ; and facing about when she had gone some distance, came back its whole length, passing the drug store and going on to the other end. She went up a lane and returned to the main thoroughfare. She was doing sentry-go on the Queen's highway : and no one, with the face and dress of a home-born Briton, was allowed to pass her by without undergoing a close and searching scrutiny.

Up came a tall man, with a face rather like that she had seen at O'Dowd's door; she was moved to stop him, but refrained herself. He was swinging along with a light and jaunty step. Something made her think that he was whistling internally. She turned to follow him. He stopped —she stopped. He went on—she moved. He looked at her; she bent her glance on a lean dog that was shambling onwards. Rapture! he entered the drug store. It was enough: she had seen him. He was the O'Dowd of her fancy, tall and straight, not going out sideways, as foolish Jumri had said, but running up to a towering height, like a church spire, or a cedar of Lebanon—ah, the dear man!

She went across the street in a state of unusual exhilaration. Well it was for the Hindu boy that he was not before her as she entered her house.

But she must suppress her emotions, or, at least, hide them under a composed exterior. She would allow herself the pleasure of looking across the street, but henceforth it should be through a window curtain. She had nothing to be curious about now. She had seen him! He corresponded to her ideal! He was there, whether she looked at him or not—caged!

Would she meet him? Not just yet. But as time went on, she would, she must, meet him. She could not avoid meeting him: he was her neighbour, and they were the only white people in that corner of the city.

She sat down to her simple tiffin, which consisted of a pillau, a well-cooled bottle of claret, and a dessert of fruit ; and when Jumri appeared to attend upon her, she told him that he might go outside and wait until he was called, which would probably not be for that evening, as she would take a rest after her long walk.

CHAPTER VI.

BRAHMANS AND BUDDHISTS.

Nothing the worse for his dip in the Ganges, O'Dowd sat in his surgery the next day in his usual graceful posture. The enemy that had assailed him was gone—drowned—dead ; not a trace of him on the surface of O'Dowd's dress, which looked all the better for the immersion.

He had never been lower in funds, and with two rupees in his pocket, no wares in his shop, he was dreamily thinking of the future, when a native of grave and learned aspect crossed his threshold, and coming over to where he sat said, without prelude or introduction :

" I have called to wish you joy. I am a priest of Brahma."

" I thank you, Sir," said O'Dowd, " but I am not conscious of having done any act worthy of your greeting."

" Your visit," said the other, "though failing a little in gravity, was a source of pleasure to all who saw it."

" No one saw it," said the Doctor, " but the dying pariah and his son ; and more is the shame for you caste-people ! who fly with horror from the presence of these poor wretches, who are your own kith and kin."

" Allow me to correct you," said the grave man ;

" we, the disciples of Brahma, give respect to each other, in various castes, though we may not mix in business, pleasure, or wedlock ; and if we fly from the pariahs, it is because they are a Brahma-forsaken horde."

" It was a pariah I visited yesterday ?" said O'Dowd. " Is it for that visit you congratulate me ? "

" No, no, " said the priest. " The pariahs are, as it were, soulless, for they can never rise from their abject state."

" Pardon me, Sir," said O'Dowd, " I cannot follow you. Can I understand you to say that all the Hindu followers of Brahma may rise to a higher state except the pariahs ? "

" You have taken my meaning exactly."

" I am in ignorance of the tenets of your religion, and cannot attach a meaning to the rising of which you speak."

" Consider the fall of man from the Infinite ! If you know of his fall and its consequences, you will realize the necessity of his rising."

" I suppose I ought to feel thankful for your wish to enlighten me : I shall give attention to what you may say on the subject."

" Man," said the priest, " came from the Trimurti and wandered from it, and lost his inheritance. He is now so far away, and must go back to them by slow stages. Hence, even when he fasts and hides himself in a desert from the face of his fellow man, he is not worthy, when he dies, to return at once to the Divine, but his soul must pass into another body for purification, and yet another, and perhaps a fourth or a fifth, or it may be through countless bodies ; and many hundred years may elapse before it will be fit to mount again to the pinnacle from which it has fallen."

" Phew ! " whistled the Doctor ; " this is the old story of the transmigration of souls, which I thought was a burst bubble."

" It is," said the priest solemnly, " our method of justification."

" My firm belief," said the Doctor, " is, that it is neither yours nor mine. I don't see, Sir, how travelling about from body to body could make a soul purer than it was. I put aside bantams, and badgers, and boa-constrictors, and animals of all kinds, and ask you where are the laws that regulate the migration of a soul from man to man. Is mine a migrated soul ? Has it been in another body before it entered that of Septimus O'Dowd ? When it leaves its present tenement, may it not as well go into a burglar's carcase as into that of a saint ? "

" That depends on your own good or evil deeds : the rise or fall of the soul is in your own hands."

" Your system does not attract me," said O'Dowd, " and you will excuse me when I say that it cannot work. A soul, you say, by good works passes on to another and purer body at death. I say, that all soulless bodies are equally pure or impure ; and if, for argument's sake, I grant you that the body to which migration takes place is cleaner than the body left behind, it is still liable to sin ; and the soul that has entered it may find, after a while, that it has made a very fatal exchange. In the name of common sense, Sir! how can a poor soul, as I may say, on the run, ever hope to get back to God if it has to pass through a number of bodies, when even one body hinders it so much?"

"We have got into quite an irrelevant discussion," said the priest, who was not prepared for the Doctor's logic: "I did not come here to raise a storm, but to bless a calm—not to discuss with you the grounds of the Brahmanical creed, but to wish you joy on having embraced it."

"Me?" said the Doctor, knitting his brow.

"You," replied the other. "I cannot be mistaken. You performed, on yesterday, an act of Brahmanical worship, though, I must say, with a slight absence of decorum."

O'Dowd looked closely into the man's face, and said quietly: "You are quite sure that you have not come from an asylum for idiots or lunatics?—for your words are as the words of the witless."

The priest opened his eyes, but did not reply.

"I have performed no act of Brahmanical worship," continued O'Dowd, "yesterday or any other day, unless you call by that name an act of humanity to a creature of God on his bed of misery and death."

"My informant was the priest who presided at the religious service. He saw you, he told me, bowing low like the other worshippers, and following them in all their movements, though like a novice, performing them for the first time."

"Well!" replied O'Dowd, "he deceived you— I won't say maliciously, but all the same he deceived you—when he told you that Doctor Septimus O'Dowd attended as a worshipper, or took part in a prayer meeting of yours, or a religious function of any kind."

" As I know my friend to be truthful, and that he is incapable of deceit, I am forced to the conclusion that he mistook you for another," said the priest.

" If there be another like me in Calcutta," said the Doctor, " which I very much doubt."

The Brahman having used all the arguments that he could then think of to convince the Doctor that he was a follower of Brahma, bade him good-afternoon, and left the surgery a more serious man than he was when he entered it.

O'Dowd threw himself back into his old attitude and indulged in a quiet laugh.

But it was to be a day of trouble for the Doctor.

The priest of Brahma had not been gone half an hour, when another man, spectacled, pig-tailed, and looking like a Chinese, came in timidly, and asked if he might have a few words of private conversation with " the curer of bodies."

" He might have any length of time he wished for, to unburthen himself, as the business of the house was more or less suspended owing to the non-arrival of supplies."

" I fear," said the new comer, " that you may look upon my visit as obtrusive, for I can have but a very slender claim upon the attention of a neophyte of Brahma ———"

" There it is again," murmured O'Dowd.

——— " But, before you take what I will name the irrevocable plunge into that system of belief and ethics, I would ask your permission to speak a few words of warning."

"My dear Sir," said O'Dowd, " I have had this day a strong and nauseous dose of religious twaddle from a Brahman, who stuck to me for an hour like a leech, and extracted every globule of patience from my system. If I am to hear you for another hour speaking on similar lines, I fear—and I give you notice of the fact—that I may explode."

" I am a priest of Buddha," said the man.

" Well, Sir ! " said O'Dowd, " what then ? "

" As a disciple of Brahma ———" said the Buddhist.

" Look here, Sir," said O'Dowd, " fix your eyes upon me : examine me from the crown of my head to the soles of my feet : turn me around, and see my back and sides : here is my tongue," putting it forth; "here are my eyes," opening them wide ; " am I set up like a Buddhist? Bless my soul, Sir," he continued, " it is an outrage on all the proprieties, that a man who has been turned out of a Christian lathe should be told that he has the shape of a Buddhist."

The Buddhist, even if he could have followed the Doctor in his rhetorical flight, was too grave a man to be moved by language like this. He made no reply, but nevertheless he stuck to O'Dowd like a barnacle.

" I think," continued O'Dowd, " that, after this profession of faith, you should find it your duty to retire."

" Ah, please," pleaded the staid one, " hear me only a little, while I prove to you that in Buddhism a fallen soul may recover itself by a surer and easier way than by following the Brahmanical method."

" Fire away," said O'Dowd.

"We have all come from the Intangible, Self-existent Being."

" Yes ! " said O'Dowd, " we have all come from God."

"And we have all wandered away from the Intangible."

" Our progenitors and ourselves have fallen into sin," said O'Dowd.

" And our need is," said the priest, " to regain the inheritance with the Self-Existent that we have lost."

"Very desirable ! " said the Doctor.

" How is it to be effected ? " said the Buddhist.

" How do you think ? " said the Doctor.

" By annihilation of self," said the priest.

" My dear Sir," said O'Dowd, "annihilation of self is annihilation of self only—there it stops— and when a man is annihilated, he's nowhere."

" You don't follow me," said the Buddhist ; " I will make my meaning clear by a comparison. According to the Brahmanical doctrine, the fallen soul which repents passes after death into another and more perfect body, and goes on rising from body to body, it may be for a hundred or a thousand years or more, until it goes back to the Infinite, from whom it has wandered, and is re-instated in the position from which it has fallen. But I will ask you to look at the superiority of the system of Buddha :—by fasting, by praying, by solitude, by meditation, by keeping always in contrast the Infinite and the Finite, the Buddhist loses sight of self, until he becomes, as far as self-love or self-esteem is concerned, annihilated, and when self has gone, he is absorbed into the Infinite. The process is an easier and a much more sure one for the recovery of lost happiness than that of the Brahmans, and I take the liberty of recommending it to your earnest consideration—who have renounced Christianity, as I have been told."

" Does it come to this, Sir, that I am to annihilate myself?" said the Doctor.

" Yes, if you associate yourself with us."

" I have not at present an intention of annihilating myself," said O'Dowd. "There are, I hope, a few years in me yet, and I am disposed to enjoy them as much as my limited means will allow. Take yourself away, good Sir, and look for some fellow of softer brains to play upon. I have as much respect for Buddha as I have for Brahma, neither more nor less."

The Buddhist would have lingered on, and was arguing still, when he was cut short by O'Dowd, who said :

" I have an engagement which I must keep : I wish you a good afternoon."

The engagement to which the Doctor referred was entirely of his own making, nor would faith be broken with any one, if he failed to keep it, or postponed its fulfilment to some future day. It was, in truth, a self-imposed task,—to make a visit to Miss Ada Phlick, in return for that which

F

she had made to his surgery while he was away
in attendance on the dying pariah.

Now Miss Phlick, as we have said, had her own
ideal of Doctor O'Dowd. So when a comparatively short, stout, and ungainly man presented
himself to her and was received by her—Jumri
not being at home—and said that he came to
pay his respects in return for her visit the day
before, she regarded him as a messenger or a
friend of the Doctor's, but not as the Doctor
himself.

"I have called upon you," he said, "to thank
you for the visit you were so good as to pay to
the drug store yesterday, and to take your orders
for drugs."

"I thank you, but I am not in need of any of
the Doctor's good things at present. To be
candid with you, I went over yesterday to his
shop to remove from his mind a false impression
that was made upon it by a chattering Hindu
servant of mine. I hope he has not suffered from
his long stay in that malodorous Black quarter."

"It was not in the Black quarter that he came
to grief," said the Doctor smiling.

"No?" said the lady, "I believe it was in the
Ganges. His imprudence in going into the river,
while an act of Brahmanical worship was being
performed there has been misunderstood, and
taken to be an act of apostasy."

"Pardon me; I gave no ground for such a
fiction. My movements in the Ganges were more
like those of a prancing horse than of a worshipper."

" *Your* movements ! I spoke of Doctor O'Dowd."

" And I am Doctor O'Dowd, Miss Phlick ! Have you not seen me before ? "

" You joke, Sir : I have seen Doctor O'Dowd— a tall man, of shapely build and broad shoulders, and———"

" Ah, my dear Madam, you saw me, not as I am, but as I would have been but for the accident of being born in France."

" Are there two Doctor O'Dowds ? " hazarded Ada, musing.

" The O'Dowd is such a unique specimen of humanity that he could not be repeated," said the Doctor.

Ada thought so and smiled.

" I hope we won't be less friends on account of the accident," said O'Dowd.

" In the Ganges ? " said Ada.

" Oh no," said he, " in France."

Ada thought him funny and laughed.

" The heart, Miss Phlick—not the body."

" True—true ! " said Ada visibly thawing.

It was their first interview : they parted— already friends. Ada sat musing after he went away.

" Short or long," she said, " what's the difference ? A long body with a short heart ! A short body with a long heart. I feel disappointed that he is not taller, but he is not bad for the length of him."

CHAPTER VII.

THE JEWELLED ARM.

O'DOWD'S exchequer was hardly susceptible of further depletion, but every day diminished the stock of scented soap on the proceeds of which he had been keeping the spiritual and corporal together for a full calendar month. Now and again would the parable of Mohammed and the mountain flash across his mind like an inspiration, until he came to fear that in putting it aside he was losing a heaven-taught mode of extricating himself from his money troubles.

He was not of much repute in the city of Calcutta, but he was known to some few. When he appeared in the streets, walking with a solemn and sombre air in search of a summons to the sick, would those who passed him by, or those who saw him from their windows, know what he was aiming at? Would even the few whom he might name his friends suspect the object with which he went abroad?

There is but one philosophy for the hungry man.

There was the mountain—here was Mohammed! the mountain would not come to Mohammed—Mohammed must go to the mountain. This was the short and the long of it.

So a few days after his interview with Miss Phlick, he put on what he named his professional suit, which was dark in colour but of light texture, and left his house for a walk through the Black lanes of the city first, and afterwards through the White quarter, where Europeans and other strangers dwell. His appearance was not prepossessing: his coat was as long as a pilgrim's smock, and being buttoned all the way up, it showed a stout cylindrical form, moving along solemnly over a pair of short thin legs. Nor was the general dulness of the figure relieved, as sometimes happens, by the face, for he had put on a gloomy expression in keeping with his sable habiliments.

All the time he had an eye to business, though that eye was in hiding behind one of a pair of dark blue glasses: for though the optic in question appeared to be fixed on the ground, it rolled in a marvellous manner within its orbit, and took impressions of every bare foot that passed, every eye that sparkled like a star through the head-gear of the maidens that went by, soliciting in every direction a nod or a gesture that should tell him that he was wanted professionally.

He did not fail to create a sensation as he went along. Little rascals, the dimensions of whose clothing did not exceed those of a pocket-handkerchief, looked up at him and smiled, he thought, lovingly; little maidens of six years walked on at his right and left, or crossed from side to side in front of him—to have a good stare. Coolies, not paying to his dignity the respect that was due to it, jostled him as they went by. The only persons that gave him due deference were the ayahs and other servants who had for some time waited upon Europeans and habitually deferred to their superiority.

The place was nasty and poor ; the houses were but sheds ; crooked poles and matting met his eye on every side, and the flimsy tenements scarcely sufficed to cover the privacy of their occupants from the curiosity of the street. He had come near the end of the long and tiresome way, or, as he was calculating, he had drawn the cover to its last recess, when a baid, or town doctor, of black and forbidding visage, rushed excitedly out of a house, and right in front of him turned round and grinned in his face.

These marks of attention, kindly and coarse, came as a surprise to the Doctor, who received them alike with affability and smiles ; nevertheless, he would not, he thought, go home through the street, but make a circuit through one of the narrower lanes which debouched from it on every side.

Now the lanes in the dark quarter of Calcutta are not sweet-smelling, from various causes, and principally perhaps from the stagnant pools of water in which they abound. But the Doctor, in his airy mood, was not to be subdued by a stench. He warbled, under his breath, the strains of an old song, " Sweet Violets," as he went along ; and when any odour of unusual pungency struck his olfactory nerves, lightened the blow by repeating the names of perfumes with which he was well acquainted, such as frangipani! opoponax! white-rose!

He fought against the stenches, but they overcame him in the end.

"Pshaw," said he aloud, "it is unbearable." He took his snuff-box from his pocket and in his agitation missing the organ for which it was intended, scattered the powder over his portly person. He tried the snuff again; it missed a second time; and then he presented the appearance of a large cutlet—browned!

It was possibly this soiled exterior that attracted the eyes and the pity of Miss Ada Phlick as he entered his house to take rest, after his stroll. Perhaps, too, she was moved by an air of fatigue and languor that lay upon him.

However this might be, she sent Jumri hurriedly across the street to ask him if he would allow her to send him a cup of some soup made from a perfectly original receipt, and a glass of Rudesheimer, as he seemed worn out by his long walk under the fierce rays of the sun: she would deem it a great favour if he would accept this attention.

Jumri delivered the message in his characteristic fashion.

"Mistress have soap," said he, entering the surgery; "will Doctor have some?"

"If soap passes between us," said the Doctor, "I ought to be the one to supply it."

"I don't know," said Jumri, "Miss Phlick have nice soap—hot."

"Surely she can't be a soap-boiler in disguise," said the Doctor. "I don't take your meaning, boy; what are you trying to convey?"

"Hot," said Jumri, "and nice to drink."

"Nice to drink!" said O'Dowd. "Soap in solution, boy, makes, with water, a liquid named suds. Did you ever drink suds, Jumri?"

The boy hung his head.

"A little," he said, "when Miss Phlick was not looking, and wine with it."

"You could not have had a more powerful emetic; I wonder you survived it. Were you very sick after the dose?"

"I not sick; I very well and comfortable and jolly."

"You must have the stomach of a boa-constrictor," said the Doctor, "if you can digest suds and wine. Was your mistress laughing when she sent you with such a silly message to me?"

"She no laugh; she be very feeling for Doctor comin' home tired and hot. She drinking soap when she saw him."

"Whew!" whistled the Doctor; "how blind I am. Soup, not soap, you stupid! She was taking soup, made from flesh and bones, when her eyes fell upon me, and she thought she would share it with me. It is very kind. Tell her I will accept it gladly, and with thanks."

"And wine, too?" said Jumri. "Grand—Rudesheimer. I had a swig at the bottle—don't tell."

"Go now, boy, and bring the materials."

The Doctor, after consuming Miss Phlick's strong and delicious soup, and drinking two glasses of choice Rudesheimer, made his toilet, and went out to visit the White city, buoyant with hope and radiant with smiles. It was a stroll very different in its surroundings from that which he had made in the Black quarter.

He was, as before, grave and serious, when he entered the main thoroughfare. The smile had gone off his face ; his eyes seemed to be fixed on the ground, though one of them was rolling incessantly ; his pace was slow and solemn. He was like one who saw not. Ladies, in palanquins, passed over the retina of the wonderful eye. He saw them, but took no heed. Dusky lancers trotted by in troops ; he did not stop to look at them. Sepoys, in companies, with a band, went by on their way to a review ; they had no attraction for him. Up comes an elephant, with a cradle full of boys and girls on his back ; the glance of the man is on the the ground as the animal lumbers along. Rickshaws full of ladies are driven slowly past him ; they make no impression on the active organ. A jumble of coolies, with loin-cloths, and ayahs neatly dressed, and dark children in flimsy garb, are hastening on, but have no interest for him.

Will he not be drawn, against his resolve, to raise his orbs and look for a moment on the lovely houses that border the way ? Why, they are little less than palaces—red palaces of brick, with exquisitely wrought verandas painted in contrasted colours, beneath which families are seated talking and laughing, as they feast on some light viands and sip the juice of the grape.

A voice sounds in his ear—a voice which he has heard before, and he stops, for the first time, to break the silence. It is the voice of Major Staples, who is accompanied by Captain Halbot.

" Glad to meet you, sir," said Staples. " May I present to you Captain Halbot, of Ours, a very learned and devout son of the Church to which you belong."

O'Dowd bent his head.

" This, Captain Halbot, is a gentleman whose acquaintance I made casually; he hails from the sister country, and has been, if I mistake not, a good deal in the hunting-field, as he retains a title which he earned with honour at home."

At this remark O'Dowd seemed puzzled, but took the compliment in silence.

" This is the gentleman that Captain Stokes has been speaking of," said Halbot.

" The same," said the Major.

" He is a doctor of medicine ? " asked Halbot.

" A doctor," said O'Dowd laughing, " without patients or practice, I am sorry to say. Why, at this moment I am engaged in advertizing myself through the city."

" Effectively, by Jove," said Staples. " Anyone looking at you as you came up the street would be reminded of the end of all things."

" It is intentional," said O'Dowd ; " gloom put on for a purpose ! Seeing me passing, in the lowest depth of moodiness, people naturally ask : ' Who is that man ? ' the answer comes : ' He's a doctor.' The result : ' He's a grave and thoughtful man ; I would like to put myself into his hands.' "

" True, very true." said Halbot ; " count me among your first conquests. I will call upon you some evening after mess, late, and take your advice on a slight heart trouble."

They passed on, and O'Dowd lapsed into silence and seriousness.

So much gained, he thought ; Halbot will come and give me a fee, but when ? Meanwhile, unless Miss Phlick comes again to my aid, I will starve outright.

He was approaching the end of the street, when he looked round accidentally, and saw a man following him. He was a grave man ; he was full-bodied, and had thin legs; his dress was sombre, if not black, and he wore a pair of green glasses over a nose that might have been taken from the face of O'Dowd. It was perhaps his movement, more than his dress, face, or figure, that first attracted the gaze of the Doctor ; but as he continued to look at him, he was struck by his all-round resemblance to himself.

He was a mimic—a kind of actor that is often seen in India, whose delight it is to bring into ridicule, by imitating in public his mien and movement and copying his dress and figure, some chance wayfarer.

He had been walking after O'Dowd for some time, doing what he did, moving legs and arms as he moved them, stopping when he stopped, looking up or down or around in perfect imitation of his model, and rendering him, no doubt, a butt for the sarcasm and ridicule of the passers.

The Doctor turned quickly away, and went down a narrow passage, from which he emerged to find himself in a quarter of the city that was much less lively than that which he had left.

He turned to the right after he had gone a short

way, then to the left. He went in by one street, and out by another. Finally he strolled to a bazaar to inspect its wares, buyers, and sellers, but found it empty and deserted, except by a few coolie porters who were asleep.

No one stopped him ; no one addressed him ; no one even gave heed to him, as far as he could see. He heard an occasional laugh as he went by, and a smiling face passed across the vigilant optic now and then ; but laugh or smile were not for him— why should they be ? He was not, in his present guise, a man to make one merry, but sad.

Again he was near home ; but he would not enter his house for a while. He had done the two great divisions of the city ; but there was a section lying between them, sparsely peopled and with few houses, into which he now entered—to try what he should consider his last chance for the day.

"The O'Dowd's last pilgrimage ! " said he ; " if I don't meet with luck in this forlorn place I'll go home, and waiving the question of her nose, propose for the hand of the one who shared her 'soap with me."

He was attracted near the end of this route by the style of a large detached house. It was of brick, but not quite in the form of the mansions in the principal street, for it had no veranda ; while it was far removed from the neglect and squalor of the flimsy tenements in the Hindu quarter. It was not in the form of a European house, nor yet of the pattern after which the Mohammedans of India build : it was a native house, and, from its cleanliness, approach, blinds, shutters, and hangings, would seem to be tenanted by a native of wealth, if not position.

As he looked at it, half curious, half admiring, a rolling sash in a middle window was pushed back, and a coloured arm was thrust through the opening, encircled at the wrist by doubled bracelets which shone with gold and diamonds.

He started. Why did not its owner appear? Where were the eyes that directed its movement? He saw but the arm, which was firm and shapely, as if it had been cut by a skilled artist from a block of marble.

He looked more closely, and saw that its fingers were opening and closing, as if signalling to someone in the street. He could not take their motion as intended for himself; yet it sent a thrill through his frame, and kept him rooted to the spot on which he stood.

Could the signal be for himself? Was it frivolity, levity, even worse, turned upon perhaps the only man who had passed that house since early morning? Why should he not disregard it, and make haste to get out of a quarter that seemed a likely place for snares and allurements and the abode of gilded vice? But he could not go: the arm was before him, and the sparkling diamonds fascinated him like the eyes of a snake.

By a great effort he moved a little in a straight line to his right; but the loadstone in front brought him back to his former position. He then tried the opposite side; but the attraction was too great and he returned. It was in vain that he entered on a semicircular tour both ways: something always drew him to the apex of the curve, and kept him there. He did not attempt to advance, but he tried to retreat, and that he found impossible.

" I'm captured at last," he said in an audible tone ; " caught by an enchantress—a victim to the sorcery of one of those Indian snake-charmers. The worst of it is, that I will be held a prisoner here during the night ; for those cursed baubles on her arms would penetrate the darkness of the Black Hole of Calcutta. Woe to thee, O'Dowd ! before to-morrow's sun rises to be soaked with dew, poisoned by a snake, scratched by a wild cat, pecked by a vulture, or thugged by a drunken Chinaman."

His wailing must have been heard by the cause of his distress, for when he ceased to speak the jewelled arm was withdrawn and the sash rolled to. The strain upon his nerves thus relaxed, he proceeded on his way towards home.

He had not gone far when he was overtaken by a maid, who said that he was wanted by a lady in the house before which he had been standing.

In a moment he was under the porch, talking to a little portress, whom he recognized as the girl who had called some weeks before at his store to purchase gumra for her mistress.

" You live here, little maid ?" said the Doctor affably.

" How well you remember me !" said the girl, laughing.

" I could not forget the gumra," said the Doctor.

" Yes, gumra," said the girl ; and she laughed a

low pleasant little laugh. "I asked you for gumra, and you gave me soap."

Light as was the reminder, it made O'Dowd blush. How could he go into the presence of a lady with whose order he had so trifled?

"But Kèsur," continued the girl, "didn't mind; she be very sweet and generous; she was only glad that the Doctor kept the money, and she love soap."

"She is not, I hope, seriously indisposed," said O'Dowd.

"She be not sposed; she be sick," said the girl.

"You don't quite follow me. I meant to ask you if her sickness is of a serious nature," said the Doctor.

"Serious!" said the girl, "I don't know *serious*. She have big, big heart—too big for body; it be busting out."

This was enough. O'Dowd had spoken with the maid to give time to a little unmanly thrill to pass away.

"Now," said he, "my good girl, show me, if you please, into the presence of the lady."

CHAPTER VIII.

THE HEART OF KÈSUR.

As O'Dowd entered the room, a girl rose from a couch on which she had been reclining, and pointed gracefully to a seat, saying with a pure English accent:

"I have to make an apology for the homely manner in which I have summoned you to my house. May I hope that you will not attribute it to a want of respect for yourself or your profession?"

O'Dowd for a moment lost his self-possession, and muttered some words which were inaudible. His eyes were opened wide on the vision before him.

A tall, graceful figure, in a dress of fine white cotton, not quite, in make and form, like that he was accustomed to see on the streets, for it was looped up with brooches of costly gems on the left shoulder and at the waist, and hung over her like the drapery of a statue. Her long black and shining hair fell like a mantle upon her neck and back, and her rich anklets of the finest pearls mounted some inches above her embroidered slippers.

She wore no face-cover, as is the custom of Indian ladies in the presence of men; nor, in its absence, did she put on a mask of prudishness: but simple and natural in bearing and expression, she looked at the doctor with a pleasant smile, and a winsome twinkle of eyes that were full of varying light.

A glance at her would tell one that she was very young, though the lines of her figure betrayed the early maturity which is the gift of a tropical climate.

The ever shining sun of that gorgeous East had not laid too heavy a brush on her oval face, which was hardly darker than that of an Andalusian, while it bore no trace of a flatness which is rarely absent from Hindu features, however otherwise fair.

A poet of her country would compare her lithe form to the quivering stem of the lotus, as it rises from its lake bed, and her face to its flower when in full bloom.

Was she a sun-stricken dame, who was shut in this fine mansion with a number of maids, her keepers, who worshipped her for her simplicity and easy connivance at their doings? More likely she was a wayward woman, who had left her friends and cast aside the restraints of her rigid form of paganism ; else why was she showing her face ? Why was she betraying such levity ? Why did she call to her house a European doctor, while medicine men of her own race and colour were about, who would fly to her at a beck, and perceive at a glance the native ache that troubled her ?

O'Dowd gave a hitch to his blue glasses, and, with lower jaw a little fallen, was looking at her

G

now with a stare of curious scrutiny.   He was, in
truth, weighing her in a mental balance, and the
scale which was weighted against her virtue was
descending, when her sweet smile suddenly died
away, and an expression of care and timidity came
from her dark, shining orbs, which put a check
upon his rash suspicions, and carried him in
spirit to her feet, as a worshipper of truth and
innocence.

She was the first to break the silence which was
becoming strained.

" It was not a lady of the native race of India
that came before your mind as you entered this
house," said she.   " If you have resided long in
Calcutta, you must be aware of the objection of
Hindus to consort with the eaters of the sacred
cow."

" I thought of meeting here a lady of the same
hue and colour as the beautiful arm that was thrust
through the casement," said the Doctor, "and I
had wit enough to judge that she could not be a
European nor an African."

" You are an eater of flesh," she resumed, inquisitively, " as are all your compatriots ? "

" I *was*," replied O'Dowd with emphasis, "before
I came to this country."

"This is interesting," said she; " you have ceased
to contaminate yourself with the blood of things
that had life, and are now, in effect, a Hindu, as
regards diet."

" A Hindu in practice," he assented.

" In principle as well perhaps," she suggested.

" My principle," replied the Doctor, " is to eat

everything that is put before me, be it fish, flesh or frogs."

The girl was disillusioned.

"Do you not think it cruel, if indeed not wrong, to shed the blood of the creatures of Brahma?"

"Frogs—is it?" said the Doctor.

The girl smiled.

"All living things," she said, "are under the protection of the Indian god."

"Cobras and crocodiles? Mosquitos and man-eating tigers?"

"Yes!" she said "even these vermin, because they have life."

"Little care he is taking of them then," said the Doctor lightly, "while he is giving them free rein to rend and torture humanity."

Her fine Indian intellect recoiled, as if something struck it: if it was unlawful to shed blood the life of the cruel brute and reptile should be spared.

"I have been taught as a child," said she thoughtfully, "to love the bird, and lay no hand on the insect ; and, since I grew into womanhood, I have deemed it a duty to give honour to the sacred cow. Now I am confronted by a difficulty."

"And you feel yourself forced to admit that the life of noxious things should be taken, and your house of cards tumbles to the ground."

Giving up argument, she took shelter behind sentiment.

"Do you not deem it a little profane to partake of flesh that has been worshipped?" she said.

"Ready at all times," he replied, "to go with an easy conscience for a cut even off your pampered cow."

"Profane man," she said half-seriously; "would you not abstain from meat through respect for an Indian whim?"

"And get evolved perhaps," said he.

"Pardon!" said she, "the word 'evolved' is new to me."

"Turned into a lean coolie," he replied, "spontaneously."

A playful shadow passed over the girl's eyes: but it was only for a moment. She said demurely:

"You have found me in a cheerful mood to-day: and I could perceive that you were perplexed by my levity. I seldom smile and never laugh outright, nor is it, I think, pleasing to Brahma that I should be otherwise than grave."

"In this you are singular among your sisters," said the Doctor, "who are, as I see them, gay in disposition, and, in manner, bright and lively."

"Perhaps you might add, giddy," said the girl.

"No," said he, "not giddy, in any form, but playful, innocent, and natural."

"I," said she, laying emphasis on the word, "have been brought up in a rigid school."

"Which was quite unnecessary," said the Doctor, "and, with your permission, I will add, tyrannical."

"But it was at my own desire," she put in, "as a preparation for the great change."

"I too expect a change of place at the end of

life," said the Doctor lightly, "but carry the thought of it without sadness."

" I did not imagine," said she, "that you, a follower of Emmanuel, anticipated going to him by stages."

"Ahem," he ejaculated "there will be no stages or steps for me, but, I fear, a stop of some duration on the way."

" You believe then," said she, "in a transmigration of souls."

" I believe that the soul is immortal," he replied, "and that immediately after death it will go into the presence of God."

" Not so we," said she ; "our hope is, to wander from body to body, until we are cleansed of every stain, and thus rendered fit to go into the presence of the Pure."

" Have you ever," said the Doctor pointedly, " met one of these travelling souls that are going this pilgrimage, or anyone among your pious Hindus who remembers to have partially made it ? "

" It is puzzling," she admitted. It is a great mystery."

She was a thoughtful girl, shrewd and even critical without knowing it.

She revelled in the conception of a Being in himself and of himself perfect, without limit, pure, holy, present everywhere, eternal, all-powerful, the maker of the universe and the Providence of the world.

The idea of a Triad or Trinity, in which he is united with Vishnu and Siva, the preserver and destroyer, was not quite so pleasing to her, as it took from that abstract simplicity in which she loved to contemplate God. But she blushed at the notion of innumerable emanations from the Divine substance, falling always lower in the scale of existence, until they came to a stand in plant life.

All the same, she was docile in practice, and a faithful observer of the rules by which those of her religion endeavour to effect their sanctification, and make their lives pleasing to their divinity. She had made her pilgrimage to Hurdwar ; she was punctual at the sun-rise prayer ; she fasted and abstained from flesh meat ; and if she did not know of the ten great precepts of the law, a light shining in her soul told her that it is wrong to steal and be naughty and lie, and right to give honour to whom honour is due, to observe the regulations of caste, to say no word of anger, to inhale the odour of sweet flowers for the preservation of innocence, and to purify the soul from sin by frequent ablutions in the 'holy river.'

She was wayward in one respect. Though a girl of pure life and a modesty not begotten of paganism, she could not see the necessity for wrapping herself in that extreme seclusion which darkens the life of a woman in the East ; she did not think men so bad that she might not show her face to them at times, like a European, and she would not submit to the custom of wearing a veil at all times in their presence.

Her life, with its critical but sincere beliefs, its guileless and religious practices, its liberty of action and freedom from silly prejudices, was bringing her strength from a source that she did not yet recognize, and leading her on to a goal that she did not even dream of.

O'Dowd had been called to her house as a doctor, and not for a theological discussion ; he passed on to the object of his visit.

" Your little maid," said he, " whom I met in the porch as I entered your house, told me that you have been ill and complaining."

" Of palpitation," she replied : " my heart ever flutters, like that of a frightened bird."

"Love, or fear, or chili pods," he suggested. "Where shall I begin ? May I ask you to give me aid in a search for the disturber of your repose ? "

She seemed amused at his solemnity, as he moved his head from side to side, and peered at her through his dark glasses.

" If I said," she replied brightly, " that I was in love, you would perhaps advise me to put away or crumble my idol ; if I attributed my tremor to fear, you would probe my surroundings and delve into my hidden life to find the source from which it sprang. I will take your last alternative and say that I am not so far a Salamander as that I cannot be scared by a chili."

" Won't do," said the Doctor decisively : " if you wish a cure for your heart trouble, you must declare the source from which it comes. Candour, my dear young lady, is a condition of the doctor's prescription."

" Then I will be candid," said she, " as it is of such moment. Is it love, fear or chilis you inquire ?

All three, I reply. I have a lover, to whom I have been attached since I entered on my twelfth year. He is a passionate man, and has sometimes hurt me with his bitter tongue. I am a constant eater of rice, which I always season with chutney or chili."

"And, by so doing, lay the lines of a conflict between your heart and other internal organs, in which the former must come to grief; or, which is equally serious, you become, from the constant use of stimulated light food, anemic, in which state your dilated heart cannot pump its blood freely."

"What remedy do you suggest?"

"A change of diet," said the Doctor; "a more generous way of living for the present : meat, in solid or liquid form, and a glass or two of blood-making wine at dinner."

"Would you have me to become a renegade to my principles, or to join hands with one of those hated sects that wallow in sensuality? What would my old precepter, Gobiud Das, say, if he heard that I even listened to such advice?"

"What he might say or think matters little. He is, I dare say, a sour man, that has not yet risen above the prejudices of his training. In seeking a remedy for your heart trouble, the eye of your physician should be allowed to range freely over a wide circle of esculents as well as drugs, and his hand should not be restrained from offering what remedy he deems best."

She did not bend to his views.

"You must take me as I am, a Hindu in sympathy with the religion I profess, and remove my pain, if you can, by the use of simples."

The Doctor was at his wits' end : he was driven out of his own domain : must he again enter that of theology? He would make a little effort to open the eyes of this interesting girl.

"You will not, I hope, take it as an offence if I suggest a subject for your consideration," said he kindly. "You have heretofore taken your form of religion to be superior to all others, and looked upon it as the favoured one, alone true and sanctioned by God. I would ask you to look at it through my glasses, when you will see it as a picturesque from of paganism only, and a branch of the great Eastern superstition ; nor is it, in any point, superior to the system of Buddha."

She was struck with the full force of the Doctor's words.

"I think," said she weakly, "that my religion came from heaven."

"So say the Persians of their creed ; so say the Chinese of theirs ; so says more than half Asia of the doctrine of Buddha," said O'Dowd : he was amazed at the laurels he was winning.

"But Brahma is so wise," said she, "and Vishnu is so sweet."

"Faith, Madam," said he, "they are all learned and sweet if we take them as they are presented to us by their votaries, barring an occasional rake."

"What is a rake, Doctor?"

"A dissipated, dissolute fellow," said O'Dowd.

"You would not say, I feel sure, that any

divinity presented for worship in Asia was a rake."

"I might," said O'Dowd ; "and, as for the gods of the Egyptians, Greeks and Romans, who came from Asia originally, they were all rakes, including the ladies."

It was time to bring this interview to an end. It was embarrassing, while it was leading to no practical result. And yet the Indian girl was not sorry that she had called this European to her house. He was weak, she thought, and strong at the same time, and he was clearly a good-natured man who might be consulted in the hour of trouble.

He was the first that had partially raised the veil that shrouded her gods in a proud and egotistical isolation : and she felt a revulsion, while he ran on lightly, as if some cord that bound her to Brahma held her less tightly than before.

"I shall hope to see you again," said she, as they parted. "I need the advice of others more experienced, as I am alone for most of my time, and without many reliable friends in my caste. You are a Christian, it is true, and I have been taught to recoil from the name ; but I have thoughts and promptings. . . We must meet again. You shall come to me, or, better still, I may wander to your house some night, after the light has gone."

CHAPTER IX.

A MOHAMMEDAN LOVER.

As O'Dowd was leaving the house, a man brushed by him entering it. The Doctor turned quite round to look at him, as he stopped to speak to the portress. He was a tall, strong man, rather bronzed from travel than dark in colour, with piercing eyes, a firmly set mouth, hair and whiskers black as coal, and a cruel expression on his strikingly handsome face.

He made little delay in the entrance hall, but went straight into the house, with the ease and freedom of a frequent visitor, and entered the room in which Kèsur reclined, without giving notice of his approach.

She rose and received him cordially, thanking him for coming so soon again.

"Which," said she, "with your constant engagement in the courts of law, must entail a loss of time and money."

"Don't even speak of that," said he. "What are time and money, when compared to the pleasure of gazing on your beautiful face, and listening to the music that distils from your lips?"

"What a honey-bee you are!" said she, "and how generous of the sweetness that is in you!

May I, in return, give you joy on your freshness and strength, and express a fervent hope that you waste not your measure of health by over-attention to the affairs of your clients."

" All that will cease, Kèsur, when you are mine : then will I throw my law books to the winds, and live the easy life of a rajah."

" And leave this city, perhaps, to reside in a lovely mansion on the hills, in the high country ?"

" Or better still," said he, "alternate between your mansion here and some bungalow in the Hills."

" When shall that happy day come ? " said she, and she sighed.

" When you, beloved, remove the only obstacle to our union," he answered ; " but you sigh more than is meet when I come to you, which makes me fear that you have near your heart some trouble that is weighing heavily upon your spirits."

" Is it not," said she archly, " the right of lovers to sigh when they meet ? Or what other outlet can they find for the too great warmth that is consuming all that is within them ? "

" That is so like you, Kèsur ! Your quiet self-restraint brings to mind the delicacy that is attributed to the women of the Giaours."

To make a diversion, she said : " You met a man, of the sect so hateful to you, leaving the house as you entered."

" I thought so."

" He is," she continued, " a doctor of medicine. I called him to advise on the sighing."

" The sighing ! "

" The tendency to sigh, and the cause from which it comes."

" Then it springs not from love?" said he sharply.

" From love," she replied, " and another source beside it."

There was no necessity for a fuller explanation. He knew that it was love and fear arising from his persevering abuse of her religion, and his never-ceasing efforts to draw her within the fold of Mohammedanism. But fear or love, or whatever else it might be that agitated her, why should she bring in a third party to tell him of the secrets that were between them, and he even a Giaour, who would be only too glad to hear of the short-coming of a Moslem, and to send it abroad as a subject of laughter for the city.

His brow darkened.

We met the man already in the mess-room of the 4th Duffs.

His name was Akbar Yassov, a lawyer in a large practice in the courts. A plodding, stolid and exacting Mussulman, whose tyrannical manners and self-sufficiency were of themselves enough to spoil any romance in which he might be an actor, he loved the Hindu Kèsur with a devouring flame. He played with her, growling, as the beast of prey toys with the weaker animal he has taken for his morning meal ; and if the girl had not been so innocent and confiding, she could have read in the lines of his face a resolve to make her more his victim than his companion, a plaything—to be taken up at a whim, perhaps to be cast away in disgust.

That a woman of high caste, and of a race that is so gentle and tender, could bestow her affections on a man of this temper, seems strange ; yet Kèsur loved Akbar with a young and strong passion, which, in its unselfishness, made her ready for every sacrifice, and passed lightly over his defects, to rest with admiration on his proud mien, and handsome face and form.

It was now four years since he met her first. She was then but a child. He was called to her father's death-bed, to put his will in legal form, and witness the settlement of his entire estate, which was ample in land and money, on his only child. Akbar turned a speculative eye on the little maid, richly endowed as she was, and determined to make her his wife, when she should come to the marriageable age. He never lost sight of her, and watched, with warm interest, the fragrant bud expanding. In due time he proposed for her hand and was accepted only as a suitor ; but they would, no doubt, have stood in a closer relation ere this but for his aggressive and exacting Mohammedanism.

His brow darkened, and the girl's eyes sank under his frown. She saw that a scene was coming.

He smiled sardonically, as he said :

" I long to have charge of your patrimony ; cheats, I fear, and persons with sinister design, are ever around you, and preying on your credulity and good nature."

" I cannot agree with you in this view," said she ; " if I give to the poor and suffering, it does not seem to reduce my lacs much, and, if doctors come on invitation to cure my ailments, they receive only a just payment for their services."

" You require a guardian for your long purse," said he. " Do you keep too many in your service ? "

" My household," she replied, " is composed of ten girls and a porter ; and for my estates they need but one diligent and honest collector of rents ; for my ryots are attached to me as they were to my father, and would not, as they say, do an injustice to the daughter of a zemindar whom they loved."

" You know nothing," said he, " of the frauds and lying of ryots, who lounge in idleness, let their rice crops perish through want of tending, and then come to simple Kèsur, or a roguish collector, for a remission of rent, with a plausible story of losses by misadventure."

" Poor toiling ryots ! " said she. " Their rents are high and their honesty is proverbial. Would you have me to treat them as beasts of burthen, and, through tyranny, turn their thoughts to hatred, when a little consideration for their needs may fill them with love and gratitude ? "

" Oh," he said, " I forgot ; they are your own people. Hindus—upright Hindus ! devout worshippers of the sacred cow ! "

This was the first arrow from his quiver. She saw it fly, and knew its destination, but stood aside and let it pass her by.

"I am," she said, "as you should know by this time, a Hindu of the Hindus, who love my people and their ways, and would even throw a cloak over their shortcomings."

"I know it only too well," said he, with a grudging sigh; "but for that, I should have been long since the guardian of your substance and yourself."

"But you never will be," said she, inquisitively, "unless I give up my name and its religion and traditions?"

"Never!" said he, decisively.

"Then, Akbar Yassov," said she, "we had better go our divided ways, for I will not embrace the visions of your Prophet."

She had never before spoken so decisively on this subject; he even thought she was giving heed to his many warnings and loosing the cords that bound her to her early creed. He tried to subdue his rising wrath for a moment, but the savagery that was in him got the better of the attempt, and he said, raising his tone:

"I will not have it so; I will insist; I have been your guardian since your father's death; I can exact obedience to my wishes. Pardon," he continued, subduing his vehemence, "I am too impetuous, being used to appeal to juries in the courts of law. It is not anger that touches a heart like yours, but love. Love carries all before it, nor will it in our case fail to brush aside the only barrier to our union. As your ancient and faithful lover, I appeal to you, Kèsur—as your true-hearted adorer, who lives for you alone."

A short conflict between affection and principle in the girl's soul, and she rose superior to feeling.

" If I asked you, for love, to come over to my form of belief, would you not think me unreasonable ? Can I deem you just when you would do violence to my convictions ? "

" Don't talk so," said he, breaking into anger again, " or presume to compare a religion which says there is but one God to your wretched and demoralizing pantheism."

" Akbar Yassov," she replied, " you know that I have preferred you to many suitors for my hand and fortune : why do you speak to me in language devoid of feeling ? Know you not that your words pierce my heart, and would turn me from you for ever if I were fickle or selfish, or wavered in my long-cherished attachment to you ? Let us now and for ever waive this disturbing question of religion which may, in time, put us asunder, and enter on a course of mutual forbearance."

" Would that I could do so !" said he; " but I cannot. The early Mussulmans made converts by fire and the sword, and their spirit must animate every faithful follower of the Prophet."

" If a giaour," said the girl, " asked me to pass over to his form of belief, should I act against my principles to please him ? "

" The hated giaour !" he exclaimed ; " why do you bring him into our dispute ? You have not, I hope, been talking on religion with the insidious creature ? "

She remembered the fatherly, quaint and simple manner of her late visitor, and said :

H

" I have met only one Christian in my life, and if he touched upon religion in our interview, it was gently and without sinister aim."

" Just as I suspected," said he bitterly, " when I saw that lubberly fellow leave your house—he was here for something else besides medicine."

" I wish, Akbar," said she, intending to be playful and persuasive, " that you could imitate the delicacy with which Dr. O'Dowd treats the convictions of those who differ from him in religion."

This was enough ; it opened the flood-gate and let loose the pent-up fury of the Mussulman. He started to his feet and stood scowling at her in a savage manner. The girl shrunk from him in terror ; he had never before shown his character in so odious a form. All the beauty and manliness seemed to go out of his face ; she had stirred up the demon that was in him.

" A giaour ! " he shouted ; " an enemy of God ! You compare me to a miserable giaour ! Fie upon you ! I spurn your wealth—I spurn yourself. I go, never to return, unless you make a double promise most solemnly : never again to speak to a member of that hated sect, and to renounce your false Brahma for the pure religion of the Prophet."

She let him go without a word, and was, for the time, glad of the riddance.

Her affection for the Moslem had stood many shocks, but this was the greatest of them all ; still she could bear it, and overlook his tyranny if he would only cease to tease her on the subject of her religion. But if he went, as he had for some time,

on a line of ever-increasing rage and cruelty, she
felt that her patience must run out and her warm
regard for the man must give place to indifference,
if not to a feeling of dislike.

But it was a trial to think that Akbar Yassov,
whom she had known so long and loved so
tenderly, should pass from her heart without
evoking a feeling of sorrow or even an expression
of regret.

Seeta, a girl of her caste, but of much lower
social position, was announced. She shook off her
foreboding, and put on a pleased expression as she
received her.

"I have come, Kèsur," she said, "to tell you a
secret and to take your advice upon it. It is this.
I think very often of the Christians whom I met
when in Europe, and an inward voice tells me to
go over to them. I have called upon an Anglican
clergyman, and he has put me under instruction
for Baptism, which is the gate through which, he
says, one passes into their Church."

"Fie, Seeta! why have you delayed to tell me
of this great purpose?" said Kèsur. "You come
to take my advice when you have followed your
own whim. It is too late for me to raise an objection against a first step when many steps have
been taken."

"But it would bring me much comfort to hear
fall from your wise lips even one word of approval
of what I have done."

"If I gave you praise," said Kèsur, "it would
be of no value, as I know next to nothing of
Christianity; and if I gave you blame I might be,

through   ignorance,   depriving   you   of   a   great
good."

"It pleases me," said the girl, "to hear you say
that Christianity *may* be a boon.   Have you heard
even a little of it, and if you have, who might be
your informant?"

"A white doctor whom I called in for advice: he
is a Christian; he makes little of the religions of
the East, and he is a kind, good man," said
Kèsur.

"I think it is of him that my instructor has
been speaking.   His name is O'Dowd.   He is not
an Anglican Christian.",

"Are there other Christians, Seeta, that are not
Anglicans?   You are now an authority," said
Kèsur.

"Yes," said Seeta, "there are the Roman Christians, who form the largest division of all.   Doctor
O'Dowd is a Roman Christian, and so is an officer
named Halbot, in Fort William."

"Now," said Kèsur, argumentatively, "if the
Roman be the greatest of Christian sects, why
would you become an Anglican?"

"There is the difficulty," replied Seeta.   "The
Rev. Nethcoff Bingham, my instructor, would
probably say that the Romans have strayed from
the path of truth; but your Doctor, I suppose,
would answer that it is the Anglicans who have
fallen into error."

"I don't know, I am sure," said Kèsur; "but I
don't think it would be wise to go over to either of
them while you are in doubt as to their claims to
represent Christianity, for you would be giving up

a religion which represents Brahma for one that may not represent Christ."

"How my instructor will stare at me when I put this view before him. All the same, it is the correct view, and I will adopt it. I thank you much, Kèsur. I will call again upon you, when I shall have seen the clergyman; and if I succeed in finding the true home of Christianity, it may be that you too may seriously think of entering it with me."

The girl departed, leaving Kèsur in a very thoughtful mood, from which she emerged with a fixed resolution not to defer beyond the morrow her promised visit to O'Dowd.

CHAPTER X.

A VISIT TO THE DOCTOR.

HER thoughts that evening and during the next day were charged with perplexity: there were conflicts between love and hate—a flashing of new lights across her fancy!

The religious idea was passing out of the region of vision, and tiring her with its doubts and questionings; and the cruelty of her Mohammedan lover was calling for a quick judgment as to his claim to her hand.

The Doctor, on whom she thought of calling, was not a tower of strength—this she knew from her late interview with him; but he was kind and sympathetic, and she might expect from him, in return for her confidence, some advice, perhaps quaint, but certainly good-natured, in the trouble that had come upon her. She knew a secret pathway that led to his house; she would enter upon it, after sunset, and present herself at his door, not as a patient now, but as a friend in distress.

She waited hour after hour, until dogs began to bark and footsteps ceased to break the stillness of the street in front. Then she stole out through a postern door, and was lost to view in a dense grove of mulberries, creepers, and palms. A gloomy walk was before her, and a perilous one, if she made it in utter darkness, for creeping things were abroad, whose bite is poisonous, and stinging insects were buzzing in the air. Better, however, than a shining lamp was nature's provision for her safety—fire-flies on the wing, filling the air with a bright phosphorescence, moving about her in curves and broken lines, or resting in solid clumps of light on the trees that hedged the lane through which she went. Every mound and crevice of the ground was disclosed by these living sparks; and every vicious centipede that crept near her feet, and every snake that lay coiled on the verge of her path.

Slumbering birds had no welcome for her as she moved along. The parrot, awakened in his first nap, turned on his perch and croaked at her; and the Indian sparrow flew by her face with a shriek, as if he would resent being disturbed as he was settling down to rest, while the enormous moths of a tropical climate, and hideous beetles, as if it was their hour and privilege, came near and whizzed about her, and kept her company through the grove. But these sounds and grumbling mattered not to an Indian girl: nor did she take much heed even of the grating note of the mosquito that was seeking to effect a lodgment on her arms, which were bare beneath the folds of her loose robe.

She went on without fright or accident, and she was approaching an outlet when she heard the tread of some living thing moving through the bushes, and this made her quicken her pace. She seemed not to know from which side it came, for she directed hurried glances to the right and left, and peered in between the trees, wherever an opening occurred.

She paused before she passed into the open, and looked in front, and back through the winding lane, as far as her glance could penetrate. Failing to discover the cause of her momentary fright, she set it down to a nervous fancy, and went on, with easy steps, towards the house of the Doctor, which was quite near.

O'Dowd was at home, but not alone. There was a man—she could see by his bearing that he was a soldier—with him, in the room behind the drug-store, and they were talking with easy freedom when she entered. On seeing her, the stranger rose up, and saying, "Don't fail to present yourself," bade the Doctor a hurried good-evening, and went away.

She tried to utter some words in excuse for her late visit and for the disturbance it caused, but the Doctor would not hear her.

"My place, such as it is, is at your service always," said he kindly. "The soldier that was with me is Captain Halbot of the 4th Duffs, who called to leave a message from some men of his regiment, whom I met by chance a few days ago."

"I seem to know Captain Halbot," said Kèsur. "No longer ago than yesterday his name was mentioned in connection with yours, owing, I think, to the fact that he is a co-religionist."

"He is an Englishman," said O'Dowd, "and well informed on the theory of Catholicity, and its relation to other forms of belief. We were talking on the religious question when you entered, and I assure you, I felt very small and insignificant as a Christian in his presence. How is the heart?"

She was amused at the abruptness of the question, but pleased at the quiet familiarity of the man.

"The heart," she replied, "is neither better nor worse; but the mind seems now to keep pace with its movements."

"What? The mind disturbed as well?"

"It could not be otherwise," she said, "for besides the cruel words of my lover, of whom I spoke to you when last we met, another trouble has been sprung upon me."

"That man is, I fear, unworthy of you: but this is for yourself to consider; it would appear to me that grace and gentleness should not be mated to savagery."

How candid, she thought, but how vigorous!

"We will let him lie for the present," said she. "At another time I may talk at length of the cause of our disagreement. I left home this evening to crave from you just a little sympathy in another perplexing notion. A friend of mine has determined to become a Christian, and with that object she is at present being instructed by a clergyman. Out of this comes an idea, for I will not yet name it a conviction, that if she does right in going over to Emmanuel, I do wrong in remaining with Brahma."

"Logical!" said O'Dowd. "I am sorry that you did not put that poser before Halbot. I am but a purblind adviser in such matters, but I don't object to giving an opinion, which is that you are free to remain in your old religion until a new one has been preached to you."

"Who is to preach it to me, Doctor?" she inquired demurely.

"Your friend who is under instruction may do so," he replied.

"And she would willingly, I am sure, if I asked her, but she is only a novice in your doctrines."

"If I can give you any aid, I am at your service; but, I may tell you, I am an old-fashioned Christian, and have added very little to the modest stock of knowledge that I put up at school."

"You cannot be ignorant of the Christian's first principles," said she.

"Nor am I," replied he; "nor of many of his second and third principles. I can give you our teaching on the nature of God, the creation of the world, and the ten laws of morality; beyond these, don't count upon me."

The Doctor, at the request of the Hindu lady, gave a brief summary of the fundamental truths of the Christian faith and morality, and, when he had finished, asked her if she had in her Brahmanical religion tenets which could bear comparison to them for simplicity, beauty and self-demonstration.

"For," he added, "as I see your religion, in such figures of it as come before me, it is complicated, unattractive and unlikely. Your Divinities are hideous or grotesque—one of them riding on an ox, another on a flamingo, Shiva with a serpent

around his neck, Vishnu with many heads, Brahma
with four hands, I often stop before one of these
figures, when I am in low spirits, for a good
laugh, and pass away from him in the best of
humour."

"I have never loved the idols of my religion,"
said Kèsur, "nor believed in a multitude of
gods: my thoughts have been with a divinity
like your eternal, self-existent and all-powerful
Creator, and with one of those Emanations that
have come from him, Vishnu, the pure and
blameless; and for practice I have taken a
standard for the regulation of my conduct in
some ways like your rules of morality; for I
could not bring myself to believe that outward
observances alone could cleanse a sullied heart.
I had not even dreamed that your tenets were
so like those I had figured to myself. My want
is to rest in view of the simple truths you have
told me. How plausible they are! No soiling
of your Great Spirit with the things of earth!
No waste of His Divine nature! One, always
One! No union of God but with one sanctified
form of humanity—and this to regain for man
the position he had lost. You have put a picture
before me that has moved me much, and I think
that its effect on me is traceable, not to persuasion
or embellishment, but to the unstudied form in
which you have traced its outlines."

"For the present we will put this subject aside,"
replied the Doctor. "Christianity is best taken
in small doses. It may not digest if you swallow
too much of it together. You have not given a

direct answer to the question I put to you a while ago. How is the heart?"

" Still agitated and palpitating," said she.

"Rice and chutney?" said the Doctor.

"If you added the fury of a Mohammedan lover you would be nearer the truth."

"I don't love the Mussulman," said the Doctor very gravely; " he gives me the idea of a ferocious beast under a trainer's hands: he will lie down and fawn upon you as long as the whip is raised over him; when it is withdrawn, he will tear and devour."

" Have you met many of them?" said she.

"Their history and character are open to the world," he replied.

" Is it true, as he told me, that they are anxious to make converts to their system?" said Kèsur.

" So true," said O'Dowd, "that they will propose Mohammedanism or death to Christian nations whom they have overcome in war; and for their lying and cruelty, they are beyond telling."

" My lover then is a true Mussulman," said Kèsur with a sigh; "he proposes to me a change from Brahma to Mohammed; and because I will not make it, he threatens me with desertion, which is gloomy as the solitude of the grave."

" And cruel as he is, that faithful heart clings to him?"

" If I must admit it," said she; "but not so closely as before. I seem to see a growing wrath in him, which makes me fear even violence at his hands. But I would be steadfast and true to him always if he would allow me to follow my lights.

When he hears from me, as he must at some time, that I am drifting a little towards Christianity, he may spring upon me like a panther."

"Are you without a protector, child?" said O'Dowd feelingly.

"Absolutely," said she, "unless I call upon the police, or raise a storm among my Hindu friends. I will try to have patience and hope. If his love for me be like that which I have had for him, it will triumph in the end over pride and bigotry."

O'Dowd had heard enough to convince him that the girl had cause for the heart agitation of which she complained. He felt quite sure that her Mussulman lover would not change for the better, but becoming always more ferocious, might, in some fit of ungovernable rage, do her a grievous bodily harm; for he knew that a Mussulman is not one to pay respect to the immunity from violence which society demands for women. He believed that the girl should have a faithful friend to advise and take care of her; and as far as he, an old campaigner, with a large amount of worldly experience, and, for his age, a remnant of physical energy, might be found of use, he was ready to be her adviser and her cavalier; all the reward he would expect for his pains would be the gratitude of a child to, as he expressed it, "an old intermeddling fidget!"

The silence of her companion gave Kèsur a few moments for reflection. She thought of the lateness of the hour, which she had forgotten, and of the surprise that her absence at night would cause among her servants.

O'Dowd would have borne her company to her house, if she had allowed him : but she said that she required no escort, as the pathway by which she had come was a private one, on which few intruded, even by day. So he let her go alone, and stood looking at her retiring figure, well defined against the gloom around by her white robes, until she entered the mulberry grove and was lost to view.

She went along without fear, though with a thought of the noises she had heard in the place an hour before; and she had completed half the journey home, when she was startled by the opening of a festoon of creepers on her left hand, and her lover bounded into the path before her. He came like an animal that had been lying in wait for her, and. it flashed across her mind, with much of the ferocity of the brute beast.

She stood still. and gazed at him ; but her steady glance did not turn him from his design, which was to strike such terror into her in that lonely place that she would give way to his demand for a change of religion.

" I have been on the watch for you," he hissed, " but I did not expect to meet you here : nor could I dream that you would go out of doors at so late an hour, and, least of all, wander through a solitude like this."

He had scarcely concluded, when a third party appeared on the scene. It was Captain Halbot, who, after he left O'Dowd's, had lingered in the neighbourhood, attracted by the phosphorescent light, and hearing a movement within the grove had looked in, through curiosity, to see whence it came.

"Friends I presume, or perhaps more?" said he, addressing Akbar, whom he had met at the military mess.

"More than friends," said the latter: "she is my affianced, and would long since have been my bride, but for a trifling difference of opinion between us on a point of duty."

The soldier saw a suppressed leer in the eye of the Moslem, which made him resolve to linger near them, but out of view, until they passed out of that lonely thicket. He made some excuse for intruding on their privacy, and went away by the passage through which he had come.

Akbar saw him out of view, and then he turned savagely to the girl.

"Another hated giaour!" he growled. "They are now your common associates. You will be for going over to them one of these days, and embracing their religion."

She did not reply, but she was moving on her way slowly and in silence, when the Mussulman darted forward, and grasping her arm, drew her back and ordered her to remain and listen to what he had still to say. Gentle as she was, her high caste blood was tingling proudly in her veins, and her Eastern temper was rising into anger. She stood still, however, and listened to his abusive taunts, and when his fury was spent, she again attempted to move on, but he threw himself in her way and stopped her.

"Now you are in my power," he said: "I

will kill you if you don't come over to the Prophet."

"If I should ever change my religion," she said slowly and distinctly, " it will not be to Mohammed I will go, but to Emmanuel of the Christians."

She had scarcely uttered the last word when he sprang upon her and seized her by the throat, raising his right arm to strike her. She uttered a piercing cry of pain and terror, and in a moment found a strong protecting arm around her, and heard a commanding voice cry out :

"Away! Akbar Yassov : where is your manhood ? or is your love for this girl that of the beast for the lamb he devours? Away with you : I will hear no explanation : this lady is now in my keeping, and I will see her in safety to her house. You should blush for such conduct even though you are a Moslem. Away with you! Hands off! Relax your hold! Quick! Don't force me to take a course for which we may both repent when too late."

The Moslem, like a stricken mastiff, drew off growling.

CHAPTER XI.

A RESCUE.

THE contrast was striking. Light and darkness are not more opposed than were the two men that stood before Kèsur; one a swarthy Asiatic, the other a fair European; the first named of squat and muscular build, the latter, in form, compact and active, with all his thews and sinews developed by military drill; the Eastern a treacherous semi-barbarian, the Western a man with truth and justice written on every line of his face.

The races were on their trial before an unprejudiced child of nature, who looked from one to the other, scanning both face and figure, and gave her verdict, in no hesitating spirit, in favour of the British soldier.

"My hot temper got the better of me for a moment," said Akbar; " I make a humble apology to the lady,"—cloaking himself in stolidity.

Halbot awaited the lady's reply; then seeing that the expression of fear had not left her face, he said, addressing the Moslem, " You can go your way, this lady is in my keeping. I will, if she permits me, see her safe through the grove."

"There can be no peril but from me," said Akbar gruffly; "sleeping birds will not beset her, and she knows well that I would be the last in the world to do her harm."

I

"Please, Captain Halbot, don't leave my side," said Kèsur imploringly. "I tremble still under his terrible look and the cruel words that have fallen from him. See me safely into my own house, and I shall ever remember your kindness."

"Do, Captain Halbot," chimed in Akbar, "I unite my entreaty to hers. See her home; she is nervous and unstrung. The gossip of an old fool has brought her out into the night. She will forget this little scene to-morrow, or smile to have made so much of it."

Kèsur's lips shaped the word "Never;" but she left it unpronounced.

Halbot and she went on together through the illumined lane, strangers, but not without a longing to know something of each other. For Captain Halbot, this was the girl whose beauty flashed upon him one day, as he came upon her, unveiled, at a turning in a silent suburb; and for Kèsur, this was the soldier whom she had longed to meet, from having heard so much of his ripeness as a Christian scholar.

"It was but a sudden outburst of the Turkish temper," began Halbot; "you did not see it in the light of a mere change of mood?"

"I know I am timid," said Kèsur, "but I am not exacting. I have had to suffer from the harsh words of Akbar Yassov many times, and I have borne them without a murmur; but I never promised that I would be his bondwoman."

"Nor should you," said the Englishman—"if for no personal reason, because you are a subject of an Empire in which woman is the equal of man."

" Akbar," she said, " has the blood of the black race of Africa in his veins, and was, in early life, associated with his father as a trapper of slaves ; hence perhaps his tendency to crush the weak."

" A Turk," replied Halbot, " needs not to go to the Dark Continent to take a lesson in tyranny. We have the race in its highest bloom in Eastern Europe, and there it is both treacherous and cruel. Thank heaven that your lover has not come from Stambol !"

" No training ground," said the girl thoughtfully, " could be worse than the slave ship, and no school so bad as the slave market of Central Africa."

Halbot took some time to muse before he resumed the conversation. Was it not strange that this refined girl, knowing of his origin and early life, should have plighted her faith to the man ?

" Notwithstanding," he resumed, " you took him with confidence, perhaps, in the power of woman to subdue and reform ? "

" Not exactly that," said she : " I rather took him on trial ; and it was my knowledge of his early career that made me refuse to promise myself."

" It was well," said Halbot, " that you did not give away your freedom."

The words struck on the girl's ears with a peculiar sound. Had they a selfish meaning? She resumed more cheerfully :

" My physician has been prescribing for my soul as well as for my bodily ailments. Would you think it possible, that a Hindu could discover Christian promptings under her dark skin?"

"The surprise to me," he replied, "is not that these longings exist in one of your religious race, but that they are not found in many Hindu hearts."

"I cannot admit that the word 'longing' represents my mental struggle, it has not come to that yet; but an inward voice seems to give me warnings," said Kèsur.

"Might I ask you to let me know the form of these warnings?" said Halbot.

"Not to go over to Mohammedanism, as Akbar demands; not to remain with Vishnu if there be another God more holy. I introduced the topic of Christianity in a conversation I had with Doctor O'Dowd a while ago, after you left his house, and heard him, with much interest, expound the fundamental principles of your religion."

"And how, may I ask, did these principles agree with the promptings?" said he smiling.

"So, so," said she; "they were tending towards an agreement when other promptings came and put them apart."

"And these were?" said he inquisitively.

"Not to run the risk of losing caste; not to believe in the truth or purity of an unknown religious form; to make the best use of the present environment, and to remain in the creed of Brahma."

"Do you believe in the existence of two Principles?" said he.

"In opposition to each other?" she inquired.

"Yes," said Halbot, "a principle of Good, and a principle of Evil, the first named leading to God, the other away from him."

"I have felt suggestions in conflict within me," she replied, "but it never occurred to me to believe that they might come from an agent without."

"Yet so it is," said Halbot; "God and the Demon contending for the mastery in your soul."

"And who may the Demon be?" said the girl. "He is a new personality that I have not heard of up to this time."

"A hideous spirit that is ever striving to lead us to hell."

"And what is hell?" she asked, "or where is it placed? Your religion seems full of poetry."

"Did not O'Dowd tell you of the scene in the garden of Eden?"

"He told me of a fall of man from your God," she replied, "but did not name the place or manner of it."

Halbot gave her, in outline, the story of the position of Adam in Paradise, of his freedom from sin and care, his present happiness and his prospects, of the coming of the Tempter, the stolen apple, the eating of it, the discovery, the penalty; and when he had brought this narrative to an end, he bound up all that he had said with what she had previously heard from O'Dowd in a compact body of doctrine, closely knit in all its parts.

"It is wonderful," said she, "and puzzling, and

so large and wide that it cannot be taken in at
once ; but it is, all the same, of thrilling interest.
Your system appears to move so evenly : there
are no breaks in it ; one tenet follows from another,
and all together form a consistent whole. It is
different, I must confess, from the Brahmanical
method. That is broken and fitful : our gods
so opposed, in ways and morals ; their multipli-
cation so unnecessary and embarrassing; and
our rules for holiness of life so external and
undefined. I wish to be good—to shun what is
offensive to Vishnu, to believe in truth and to put
error aside. Ah, Captain Halbot," she continued,
" you cannot form an idea of the trouble that
seizes on me when I come to speak on the
subject of truth and error. It is a long way, I
think, from my position in the religion of India
to your Church, and a road beset with trials and
contradictions. It might have been better for
me if my convictions had not been disturbed.
for then I should be moving calmly under the
guidance of those lights, such as they are ; but now
those lights have been dimmed and I am only
dazzled and put off my track by what, I admit,
seems a greater luminary, which I am afraid to
approach lest it should draw me away from early
associations. Might I not remain, without qualms,
in my present position and withdraw my eyes
from the future ? "

" That would be," said Halbot, " to act against
conscience, which is not lawful. You must move
with your beliefs or you offend God ; but you
should, in an important matter of this kind, move

leisurely. You are not, in conscience, bound to rush on headlessly ; your convictions don't seem to me to be fully formed ; light is dawning upon you, but it has not yet filled your mind. Ask for more light. Your position is that of one of the greatest intellects of modern times, which, as it moved onwards towards a higher aspiration, prayed to be 'led on' in a stanza that has become immortal—

> Lead, kindly light, amid the encircling gloom,
> > Lead thou me on ;
> The night is dark, and I am far from home:
> > Lead thou me on !

Just as he was, you are wandering in a land where there is an uncertain glimmer appearing on the horizon towards which your eyes turn, though it is not bright enough yet to show the path you ought to follow ; and your wish should be that this glimmer should bring the day, which will enable you to steer your course towards home."

She looked at him with surprise and admiration. He had become animated as he spoke, and the cadence of his words was tender.

" Are all Christian soldiers like you ?" she said.

" I cannot answer for my companions in arms," he replied, " but I think that any Christian man, civil or military, should be moved to zeal by the silent appeal for help of one doing battle for truth and justice, as you are."

She saw her servants approaching. They had been disturbed at her absence from home at so late an hour, and had come through the mulberry grove in search of her.

" May I," said she, " before we part, say that I

am grateful to you, and shall always remember this
interview? May I hope that it may be repeated
on some future day?"

"At your pleasure," he replied, and they parted.

As Captain Halbot emerged from the grove to
go in the direction of Fort William, he met Akbar
Yassov again. The Mussulman had been waiting
for him with a view to resuming the conversation
and excusing his late violent words and conduct ;
but the soldier had had quite enough of him for
this day, and he went on in silence, hoping by this
means to shake off the intruder. But it was in
vain, for Akbar kept close by his side, speaking in
broken sentences in which he tried to throw upon
the Hindu the blame for the scene to which the
Englishman had been an unexpected witness.

Tired by the importunity of his companion,
Halbot at length said abruptly :

"I don't care to hear your excuses and explana-
tions, Akbar Yassov! Your language and action
were equally intolerable. You ask a defenceless
lady, over whom you seem to have assumed unjusti-
fiable control, to conform to your religious views,
and because she refuses you assault her. I stig-
matize such conduct as vile and intolerable."

"But, Captain," he pleaded, "she is only a
Hindu, and not much more than a child ; and you
know that innocents of the kind may receive a
stroke of the rod, and often do, to bring them to
obedience and discipline."

"You should know the law of the land, Sir,
better than others, and the rights and liberties
of every subject of the British Empire," said Halbot.

" Your slave-driving tendencies had been better left behind in another continent."

" Let that pass," said Akbar, annoyed : " my tastes and tendencies are my own : they don't hurt you, and you should not refer to them in language so offensive. I have been, I admit, exacting, perhaps imprudently and to excess, but it was with the object of forcing one who is dear to me as life to cease to be a polytheist."

" I think you would better express it, if you said—to force her to pass from an erroneous system to another not less devoid of truth or Divine sanction," said Halbot.

" That is your opinion," said the Moslem.

" Would you care to hear the grounds for it ? " said Halbot.

" I am very patient," sneered the other.

" Then I will tell them to you. Your religion has one truth—the unity of God, and two sound practices—prayer and temperance. But if it were a heaven-born system of religion, would it have let loose the demon spirits of lust and cruelty to torture and dishonour the people of every nation among which it has gained a footing from the time of its founder to the present day ? The peoples trained in it are like the sleeping beasts of the wild—always ready, when slumber has past, to rend and devour. I shall not irritate you further by saying what I think of your Prophet as a teacher of morals, nor of his mission, nor of his private life."

" You may say what you please of him," said Akbar interrupting; " I never cared much for him or his ways ; he is not to my taste, nor do I believe him to be other than a wild enthusiast and a clever organizer of predatory bands. You think I am a Mussulman. Pshaw! Outwardly, if you will, but in my heart and soul I am free of all such shackles."

Halbot looked with curiosity at the man as he spoke so enthusiastically. He thought, at first, that his paroxysm was a Turkish lie, told to deceive and ward off pressure; but as he continued to look upon his handsome but ill-omened face, in which there was not a ray of moral softness, he fully believed that he was the hypocrite he boasted himself.

"Akbar Yassovi" said he, "you surprise me for the second time to-night. From your training as a lawyer and your position in society, I took you to be an exceptional Indian subject of the British crown. Can it be that you are only jesting, and exhibiting yourself to me in false colours for a purpose that I cannot divine? When I met you among gentlemen you bore yourself as a man of breeding and culture; is it that you have one face for the public and another for your intimates?"

"Not exactly, Captain Halbot: I am simply a man of the world, dealing in externals, not in principles. I am outwardly a Mussulman, because it suits me, and I gain by it: I am a man of strong will, and I must attain my ends, if needs be, by force or by craft. Don't think the worse of me: it is the way of men of my class who have lost all faith in everything but place and money. My way, I may add, is the way of the world and the fashion of the hou

Halbot was moved with compassion for the lost man, while he was filled with a loathing for his bad morals. He said in a tone of some feeling :

" Akbar Yassov, we met accidentally to-night. It may be for the benefit of both of us. I have been taught a lesson which will make me trust less to appearance and profession than I have done, and you have received a warning to keep the law. At another time, I may express my opinion of the position you hold in the domain of truth and morals."

By this time they had reached Fort William, and Halbot saluting him abruptly, turned and entered the barracks.

CHAPTER XII.

O'DOWD IN THE JUNGLE.

THE conversation of O'Dowd and Halbot, interrupted by the entrance of Kèsur, as told in a previous chapter, calls for a passing notice.

The visit of the soldier was for consultation: on occasion of which he hoped to present the Doctor with a liberal fee for his advice, for he had heard of his poverty. He had come across him touting for business in the open street, and knew besides from the story of their visit to his drug store, told by Stokes and Staples, that the money drawer of that emporium was as empty of cash as its chests of medicine. He himself had a moderate income in addition to his pay, and being by habit a free-giver, thought he would make O'Dowd his banker to the extent of such money as he had no present occasion for. So when he had taken his views on a very slight ailment, he offered him some golden pieces of Indian coinage, suggesting, in an off-hand way, that they would cover the expense of such future consultations as might be necessary.

"No," said the doctor; "honour among professionals! Thanks innumerable! But I am not so poor as when I met you last. A high-class Hindu girl, daughter and heiress of a Zemindar,

who has money in abundance and overflows
with generosity, has taken me on as her medical
adviser; and it will take a lac of rupees to stop
the agitation of her dear little heart."

" I give you joy of your good luck," replied
Halbot. " May I add a suggestion—you have not
much. experience of life in India. Be careful in
your intercourse with the natives; they are
jealous of the white man—especially of doctors.
The women are under the influence of Brahman
priests, and they are intolerant fanatics."

" So far the sea has been smooth," said the
Doctor, "and I have been sailing upon it in
sunshine with my amiable patient; though I have, I
confess, noticed a caution and timidity in her
manner which makes me think that she would
conceal from co-religionists her intercourse with
the European."

" Be assured of it. These people hold a terrible
penalty over each other's heads: it resembles an
excommunication in our Church. They will, for
a cause which cannot be regarded as other than
trivial, deprive a member of their community of
the privileges of caste, which is equivalent to
social death."

" I think," said the Doctor, "that my patient
has a tendency to emancipate herself from their
tyranny. In conversation with her, I made a
passing allusion to the silliness of the religion of
Brahma, and my words seemed to carry a measure
of conviction to her mind."

" That persuasive Irish tongue of yours," said
Halbot—" I am not surprised to hear that the lady

fell under its influence; all the same, I fancy that you will find it very difficult to instil Christianity into the soul of a high-bred Indian."

" It won't be my fault if I don't heal the soul while I am curing the body of the darling ! "

" I forgot," said Halbot, changing the subject. " I was near omitting one of the objects of my visit to you. May I ask—have you ever been to a tiger hunt ? "

" There being no tigers in the mountains of Kerry, where my practice lay when at home, " said the Doctor, " I was forced to be content with a run after a jack hare."

" Well, we have a treat in store for you. A man-eating tiger has come up out of the Sunderbunds, and has been seen prowling in the open. Unfortunately, he has met his prey more than once in the form of a native, and carried him off; he has become reckless in consequence of his immunity, and now he threatens some villages. We are determined to bag him, and I have been deputed to ask you to accompany us on an elephant ride. We hope to give him a lesson in manners."

" Let me see," said O'Dowd, " I'm not much of a shot, nor am I swift of foot in case of a reverse ; I have, however, a vain fancy—I have had it from my youth—that I would be the deuce at a bayonet charge. I'll go. Arms according to fancy ? "

" You may arm yourself with a shillalah if you so desire ; but, as a matter of course, the company will see that you do not expose your life recklessly."

" Agreed ! I'm your man. Orphans looked to in the event of my death ? "

" Have you not your life assured against accidents ? "

" No," said the Doctor. " I had when in Ireland : I was like a twin brother to an evicting Scotch landlord in Kerry. We were the two ugliest men in the county. I insured my life against the accident of being mistaken for him, and shot from behind a hedge.

" We start from Fort William," said Halbot, smiling. " You will join our party there at sun-rise on Wednesday. Elephants will be provided, and the usual addenda. You will meet a pleasant company, and we shall have, I feel sure, a quite adventurous and most enjoyable day."

A faint twilight came creeping over the horizon forty hours later, and drifting slowly across the land, came in touch with the suburbs of Calcutta ; whence mounting some tall houses, it came down upon the Maiden ; and passing over its gardens, race-course and drill-ground, arrived at the gate of Fort William from which was issuing a proces-sion of men and beasts, equipped for the pursuit of the man-eater.

The officers of the garrison were abroad in force. Prominent among them were Staples, Halbot, Stokes and Scott, who, as they came into view, were joined by a man of homely figure, who emerged out of the mist. Shikarees were around, carrying spears and spikes. Beaters were in groups with gongs, bells and other instruments of discord. Mahouts, astride the necks of their elephants, were shouting and anxious to get under way. The howdahs were filled with hunters, ready to go forth.

A ride into the jungle, where the man-eater is known to dwell, must be at any time, exciting; but it becomes creepy when the brute is known to be at home and prepared to receive visitors. The thought of him, with his gleaming eyes, his fangs, claws, growl, spring, ferocity, great size and wonderful strength, has unnerved many a man of stout heart; and with the laugh of gay companions rippling around the hunter, he goes forth to his work seemingly indifferent, perhaps, but not without fear of a mishap or worse.

O'Dowd was the reckless man of the party. It was difficult to induce him to take a seat; he would have preferred to go on his legs, as he expressed it, or if that were not allowed, to mount a shambling pony that he sometimes borrowed for a morning ride in the Maiden.

He was talkative and amusing. "Give *me* the bayonet," said he. "You open fire upon a brute that is crouching or jumping, that does not rest for a moment; you miss him, or you hit him a surface blow which makes him more fierce and dangerous than before; he rushes at you—you miss him again; he is close to you; you club your rifle—it is too late: you cannot wield it so as to bring it down upon him; even if you did, it would not do him much harm; then, Sir, you are beneath his claws—mauled, because you have put aside the weapon of the British Infantry."

His concluding words were lost in a din of

shouts and noises—horns, gongs, cymbals, lusty throats all joining in a hideous concert. The jungle resounds. This is to wake up the enemy and drive him from his shelter into the open.

An animal rushes forth—but not the man-eater. He is allowed to go his way, without hindrance. The din rises again—dies away in an echo.

Voices have sunk to a whisper, and the wave of gaiety that had passed over the hunters has subsided.

And now comes the faint whisper of divided underwood; and a little later, the alarmed cry of some small animal, as it flies from something pushing through the tangled reeds. An easy breathing, not quite a growl, is borne upon the languid air.

These are indications that the game is near. The scattered beaters draw together, and the huge elephants raise their ears erect, lift their trunks, and already sniff the scent of battle. The hunters, seated on their backs, are on the alert, with their nerves tense and their eyes sweeping the fringes of the bush.

The rifles are already raised ready to be pointed at the quarry, when a voice is suddenly heard which breaks the silence and gives a farcical air to the procession :

" Let me down out of this confounded cage where I cannot bring my weapon into play, and I'll take my chance on the ground."

The voice was that of O'Dowd, who was struggling with an officer who was holding him by the coat-tails in his position on an elephant's back, from which he was trying to escape.

K

"Let me go, Scott!" he repeats, "if you don't want to see me dragged out of this crib and eaten before your eyes, without the chance of putting so much as a needle into the brute."

Down he went, for the coat-tails were giving way. The moment he touched the ground, he drew his bayonet from a side pocket, and fastening it on his rifle, advanced to the front of the party, and crouched in the attitude of a soldier prepared to receive cavalry.

Just then a loud roar is heard, and a mighty tiger jumps out of the jungle in front of the Doctor—not more than twenty paces away. A dozen bullets sing through the air, but not one of them touches the royal brute, whose gleaming eyes are fastening on the fat morsel before him. He crouches, preparing to spring.

"Back to the line, O'Dowd!"—"Heavens! he will be mauled before our eyes!"—"What an obstinate fool!"—such were the exclamations on every side.

But, not hearing or not heeding the cries of his friends, O'Dowd stood unmoved and with no apparent tremor, right in front of the tiger, with his bayonet fixed.

The impetuous spring of the savage beast was too high, and gave the Doctor a chance, which he seized with wonderful activity. The spectacle presented to the safe—because mounted—men of the party was so ludicrous that it elicited a loud burst of laughter: for while the tiger was in the air, the Doctor jumped at an angle of fifty to the right, and wheeled around, with his weapon still to the front.

Having missed his prey, the brute was carried forward by the impetus of his spring. When he alighted, he turned to the left preparing to throw himself upon a beater who had imprudently advanced beyond the line of mounted men.

Already he had his paw on the back of the poor fellow, when the word "Charge" rang out from behind. The Doctor was seen coming on at the double upon the prostrate beast. Pinned through the loins to the ground, the brute which had already received the contents of a rifle, turned upon his assailant a last lingering look of rage, and raising his enfeebled paw, struck him a weak blow, which fell on the throat and cheek, but did not draw blood. Then it fell back in collapse.

O'Dowd staggered, but quickly recovering his balance, took a pipe from his pocket, filled it, struck a match, lighted the tobacco, and was stooping to take a seat on the haunches of the dead beast when a great shout was raised and voices warned him to move away, until a few more bullets at short range should give assurance that all possible danger has passed.

The Doctor was at once surrounded by the members of the hunt, who have come down from their howdahs; and loud and hearty congratulations were addressed to him from many throats. He was the hero of the day, but seemed unconscious of having done anything to merit such attention.

"Now, Gentleman," said he, "don't. Keep quiet or you may wake the pet from his sleep. The only regret I feel is that I showed the white feather by jumping to the side, instead of standing like a British grenadier to receive him on the point of the bayonet."

"Not your first tiger-hunt, Sir," said Major Staples; "all your movements were those of an old sportsman. I give you joy on your knowledge of tactics."

"Oh"—from several of the officers—"he might have been mauled before our eyes, but for a fluke. Of his pluck there is no doubt."

"And of his skill, Sir, as a tiger-hunter," continued the Major lightly. "I have my own views of this game, and I may tell you, Gentlemen, I don't approve of the usual mode of attack. You take the animal at too great a disadvantage— safely seated on an elephant's back, out of reach of jaws and claws. Give me the man like our new friend, who tumbles out of his fortress, charges the enemy in the open, and is able, without a loss of honour, to retire from the field when the work is becoming too hot for him."

The Major's equivocal compliments were stopped by a catastrophe. The Doctor's cheek, ear and neck began to swell and change colour; and when he attempted to speak, his words were those of a man with a cold in the head. The tiger had struck a much heavier blow than he believed, and now its effect was showing itself in his altered visage and voice.

"Scott," said he, "you carried the bedicide chest od your brute: have you ba'dages id it?"

"I will examine it," said the lieutenant, "and report."

He went away, and returned in a few minutes with some linen, which O'Dowd cut into strips, and wound over the left side of his head. When he had completed his toilet, he mounted to his seat again.

Luncheon, which consisted of viands kept artificially hot, followed, and the exhilaration which arises from the removal of a strain showed itself in an exceptionally animated conversation.

Stokes was seen whispering to the Major, who, after a few minutes' consideration, rose to his feet, and spoke as follows :

" Much as we may regret the picture of woe reserved for the people of Calcutta in the person of our medical friend, as he rides through its thronged highways, we must congratulate ourselves on the widespread approval which his adventure, when bruited abroad, will elicit, and the lustre that it will shed over the members of this Hunt. That a man who has passed the prime of life, who is not light of body or swift of foot, who knows the delicate texture of the human frame and the liability of its nerves and tendons to snap asunder—that such a man should engage in what I may call single combat with a large and ferocious Bengal tiger, is a feat, Gentlemen, worthy rather of the old Roman amphitheatre, than of any modern arena that I am acquainted with. I have been deputed, by the Hunt, to felicitate Doctor O'Dowd on his bravery, and at the same time to present him with the skin of the animal which was, by his tactics, enticed into a position from which he could not recede, and in which he was brought within the line of fire of many rifles. I have much pleasure, Doctor O'Dowd, in presenting you this skin as a trophy, which I trust will be preserved amongst your relatives for generations, to keep alive in them a spirit, of—what shall I say—of—of—chivalry."

O'Dowd, from the elephant's back :

"Ge'tlebed! by ibperfect utterance will dot allow be to respo'd id suitable terbs to the coblibedtary words that have beed addressed to be by the Bajor. What have I dode to deserve theb? I charged upod a tiger, it is true; but he was dead. Would I have charged upod hib if he was alive? Yes, Ge'tlebed! I give beself the credit to say, that I would; because I did not kdow that a bullet had entered his body whed I thrust my bayodet idto his fla'k. I accept the skid of the brute. It shall be sedt to my sods in Australia, who will, I hope, treasure it, as a bebe'to of a bad who, u'der the peaceful garb of a hubad bei'g, codcealed a crocodile's heart."

Amid loud cheers, the Doctor concluded.

CHAPTER XIII.

MISS PHLICK DESPONDENT: KÈSUR HOPEFUL: " THE TIGER DIDN'T EAT HIM."

THOUGH Kèsur, as we have seen, was not observant of all the rules of caste, she passed for a pious Hindu, and as such was allowed to go her way without suspicion.

Her women servants, who had experienced her gentle rule, were loud in their praise of her, and would keep the secret of her harmless levity at any cost.

Even Gobend Das, the austere priest of her religion, the ascetic, who had known her as a child and watched over her as a girl, had no word of her that was not of praise; for she always came into his presence veiled, and left it demure and humble. But her character for steadiness and piety she put in peril for the pleasure of meeting and conversing with those friends from Europe whom chance had thrown in her way.

If a traitor had come upon her in her first interview with O'Dowd, when she met him smiling with her veil put aside, or if he had entered his house when she was there, after her midnight walk through the fire-flies, or had met her as she was flying in terror from Akbar Yassov under the protection of Captain Halbot, his report of her conduct would have stamped her as an evil doer and driven her forth an outlaw from her caste, to which she could never hope to return.

She was lucky: she had not been seen: no eavesdropper had been spying upon her. So she grew bolder. This day she left the house to pay an afternoon visit to her physician. Not finding him at home, she passed through the open porch of his neighbour's house and knocked gently at the door.

" Who is that ? "—from inside—" anyone there ? "

Receiving no answer, Miss Ada Phlick opened the door, and looked out. She saw a woman in white, calm, self-possessed and quiet, standing in a posture of expectancy.

" Surely you have made a mistake," said Miss Phlick abruptly: " there can be no one in this quarter whom you know, or who knows you."

" Pardon me," said the girl; " I have been here before to-day, to consult Doctor O'Dowd as to my health. Not finding him this afternoon in his office, I thought I might call on his next neighbour to inquire about him."

" I very much fear," said Miss Phlick, " that he is beyond the range of our solicitude: I feel, in fact, all but certain that he has been torn to pieces by a man-eating tiger, if not devoured outright."

The Hindu shuddered; and Miss Phlick went on: " I feel a presentiment—I have felt it since he left home—that I shall never see my friend in his integrity again. These hair-brained soldiers, with whom he went out to the jungle, may bring home a leg or an arm or a scalp of the dear man, as a memento, or, I might say, a trophy, but

O'Dowd they will never bring, if the tiger be hungry, as most of them are in such places as this, where there are no children to throw to them for the morning meal."

The Hindu seemed surprised at Miss Phlick's extreme view of the danger to her friend, and the strong language in which she conveyed it. She said timidly, but with a purpose :

" Who were his companions to the jungle ? There are so many officers in garrison ; and some, or at least one, of them I know to be not frivolous or heartless, but grave and most amiable."

" The usual set with whom he keeps company," said Miss Ada, giving no heed to the latter part of the Hindu's remark : " Major Staples, Captain Stokes and Captain Halbot, Mr. Scott, and as many more as you care to add."

" Sweet Halbot," muttered the Hindu under her breath ; but Ada caught the words, and said, with more haste than consideration for the other's feelings :

" Do you know of Captain Halbot ? He surely is not a man to wander much through the dark quarter of the city."

Kèsur, passing over with well-bred ease the taunt to her colour which lay under the words of her companion, replied :

" I have met Captain Halbot, and he has been, oh, so chivalrous and amiable. He could not, I am sure, be reckless of human life ; and everyone in his company will experience, as I did, the wisdom of his advice, and the strength of his protecting arm."

Ada did not love Halbot, but she was a white woman ; this *was* presumption.

" You must have mistaken a kind word for a special attention. Halbot is an aristocrat, and can afford to deal in general compliments."

" For me he did an act of knightly service, which if I forgot, I should be the most ungrateful of girls."

" You interest me," said Ada, who thought that she was descending socially in speaking so long to a woman of colour, " when you speak in this way. Pray, tell me, did Captain Halbot save you from a snake's bite ? "

" It was not a bite," said the Hindu, with much self-possession, " nor a snake."

" Perhaps," persisted Ada, " from the claws of a wild beast ? "

" No."

" High-caste Hindus," said the girl, who felt that she was being made light of, " do not run these risks. Captain Halbot's protecting hand was raised over me in a case of attack by another, to which any lady might be exposed."

" Do tell me the story, sweet Hindu." Ada's ice was beginning to melt.

" It would be telling you my life's history, if I did," said the girl ; " and you should not expect, as a newly made acquaintance, so great a confidence in our first interview."

" Look upon me as a friend of your friend, the Doctor," said Ada, whose curiosity was now thoroughly awakened ; " and for his sake—for the sake of one who esteemed us both, and whose memory we will ever cherish, if he has gone down in deadly conflict with the king of the jungle— let me hear the story of your rescue from the hands of a demon, for he must be such to assail so tender a creature as you."

The Hindu was silent, but moved her head in dissent. "Sweet Halbot!" she again murmured unwittingly.

"I admit to you freely," continued Miss Phlick, "that Halbot is all that you say and think of him, and more; and I will even join you in a hope that he may come to know of your kindly feelings for him and return them with interest; so now don't keep me in torture, for I long to hear of your adventure."

Kèsur did not reply, and Ada passed to another topic.

"You are, if I mistake not, a devotee of a being named Brahma," said she. "Was he a conjurer? or, if not, what was he?"

"He is a God," replied the Hindu, "or,"— hesitating—"he is believed to be one."

"You are, I perceive, uncertain about him," said Miss Phlick. "I do believe that Captain Halbot could tell you much regarding his pretensions, if you happened to meet him; which, I suppose, is now far from probable."

"Not by any means impossible," said the girl. "When Doctor O'Dowd comes back from the hunt, safe, as he is sure to be, in Captain Halbot's company, he will, if I ask him, bring that gentleman to his own house, and give me an opportunity of consulting him on my doubts."

"I wish I could share your hope," said Ada mournfully ; "my fear is, that while we are speaking, a considerable part of the substance of my friend is being converted into tiger's flesh and bone. Oh, how horrible is the thought that he, or any portion of him, may be lying in wait at some future day to surprise and perhaps tear and devour his fellow men, or even "—she added in a low voice—" the woman to whom he gave his heart ! "

The morbid state of sentimentality into which Miss Ada Phlick was sinking might have led her to even more gruesome reflections, but for a loud shout in the street, which drew her quickly to the window. On looking out, she saw an elephant bearing a party of the hunters who had gone away at day-break passing on to the White city. There were many men surrounding him, and she could perceive, from the motion of the crowd and riders, that an animated conversation was going on.

"Jumri ! "

The boy was at the door smiling.

"Jumri, go out quickly ; follow in the crowd that accompanies these gentlemen, who are coming from the tiger hunt, and be all ears until you hear some words fall from them that will tell of the Doctor's fate."

"Something is up with him," said the boy ; "if he ben't torn, he'd be back to tiffin."

"Go, boy ! " said Ada, "don't increase our gloom."

After the lapse of a quarter of an hour, Jumri returned, full of information, which was so closely crammed in his little mind that it came out both slowly and in confusion. All he was able to say, at first, was :

"He didn't eat him."

"Whom?" said Miss Phlick, sternly.

"The tiger," said Jumri.

"Who didn't eat the tiger, ridiculous boy?" asked Ada with dignity.

"The Doctor," said Jumri, quite satisfied with himself.

"Are you mocking me, lad?" said Miss Phlick.

"I no mock," said Jumri ; "I very glad."

"Very glad that the Doctor didn't eat the tiger? How could he? Have you any sense in that little brain of yours?"

"Ah, yes!" said Jumri ; "he only prodded him with a bayonet."

"Do you know the meaning of your words?"

"Yes," answered Jumri, cheerfully ; "I heard the talk of the people. They said—he didn't eat him, but he thrust a bayonet through his flank, and the tiger hit him a great blow on the jaw."

"Now," said she, "you are beginning to talk sense ; there was no eating, but a stand-up fight ; from which my dear friend came forth with only a damaged cheek."

"That's it," said Jumri ; "the tiger didn't eat the Doctor, and the Doctor didn't eat——"

"I command you to stop those silly remarks," said Ada very impatiently ; "I begin to think that you are more a jester than a fool."

And she had grounds for the fear that her words expressed. Jumri was probably not so innocent as he seemed. It was difficult to understand the boy : his knowledge of English was imperfect, but it seemed strange that his blunders in speaking it should be always in the direction of frivolity. Even now, though he had been severely rebuked, he turned to Kèsur, and said, with easy self-possession :

"Gunga was there too, and she was grinning up at the sahibs. She heard them tell of the eating and the prodding, and she won't keep it from you, when you go home."

Kèsur did not reply.

"Tell me, Jumri," said Ada, in a tone of conciliation, "was the Doctor much hurt ?"

"He have big head, they said, big cheek, big jaw, but no claws in him," said the boy.

"That is—he is not torn," said Ada.

"He be not torn, but, they said, *bulged*," said Jumri, smiling at the word.

"Ah—yes," said Ada,—"bulged—put out of shape! Though indeed," she could not but add, "the shape of him was not much at any time."

Kèsur rose to go ; but Miss Phlick asked her to remain until they should see the Doctor returning, which must be soon, as he would naturally desire rest and a compress of poppies to his swollen face.

Kèsur sat down again, and Miss Ada Phlick went to the piano, from which she elicited a number of sounds of a mixed character, not representing any known tune or melody : but an amateur could recognise in her playing an attempt to combine, in equal quantities, strains of the Dead March in "Saul," and the "Burial of Sir

John Moore," with the lively airs of the "March through Georgia," and the "Troubadour's Return from Palestine." The piano sang—it wept—it spoke—it scolded—it wandered, and finally became so hopelessly illogical that even Kèsur, who was no musician, became alarmed, and feared that there was something gone wrong with the player.

Ada, turning suddenly around, caught the expression of alarm on the face of her visitor, and withdrew her hands from the notes.

"I was trying," said she, "to express sympathy and joy at the same time : but your face tells me that I have not succeeded. Everything appears to mix but music—mixed flavours, mixed pickles—why, this dear man, who is coming home to us, was a mixer, or he was nothing ; and yet I cannot, without making myself ridiculous, make a little melodious medley in his honour."

"Pardon me," said Kèsur ; "I am a novice in your music, but I thought that it was played by a fixed rule."

"And so it is usually, but when pent-up feelings break their dam upon the pianoforte, what can you expect but the confused rush of many waters ? "

Kèsur could not see the connexion between turbid water and piano playing, and she gave up the contest.

A silence of some minutes followed, which was broken by the entrance of Jumri. He came to say that he had been down the street and seen the Doctor, who was coming, mounted on his elephant, and accompanied by two officers, between whom he was sitting.

" He be bandaged all over," said the boy, " very funny eye ! "

" Isn't this Jumri an unfeeling creature ? " demanded Ada, addressing her visitor. ." He is, I feel sure, laughing internally at our friend's mishap. He and that little huzzy of yours are turning everyone into ridicule : my eye is often upon them when they stop to have a laugh in the street."

" Gunga is a good little girl," said Kèsur, " but very lively. Why would you put a check to the innocent mirth of these young ones, who are only children in disposition ? "

" Perhaps I should not," said Ada. " I will confess to you that Jumri often amuses me very much, though, for discipline's sake, I feel bound to frown upon many of his pleasantries."

They went to the window, whence they saw three elephants approaching, surrounded by a large crowd. They carried the hunters, who had remained on the field to the end, and among them the Doctor, who was propped up between Scott and another subaltern, who sat on either side of him. In front of this party was the dead tiger, strapped on the elephant's shoulders.

O'Dowd was the hero of the hour : he was the only wounded man in the cavalcade : and the presence of the dead tiger so near him pointed him out as the slayer of the brute, and the bravest man in the party.

Shouts of a peculiar Hindu character were raised in his honour ; and every finger was pointed to him. The Doctor was the unmoved man of the procession.

" It's better thad the walk past," he said to
Scott, " as ad advertisebedt : they cad't say they
dod't kdow be dow.   The drugs I put id with the
bodey I lately received frob a patient will dot
beet the deba'd for theb that is sure to cobe frob
this bishap : a fortude, I feel, is id be grasp : they
will argue, the bad that could kill a tiger cad cure
a leper."

The Doctor was affability all over.   He smiled,
bowed, took off his hat : he assumed all the honour
of the day to himself.   When he came to his
own door, a hundred brawny arms were stretched
towards him, to help him to alight.   When he
went into his house and closed the door, boys and
girls lingered looking through the windows and
gossiping : but they wènt away when he appeared
again and asked them to disperse, saying that he
would be glad to see them to-morrow.

What was Ada Phlick doing all this time ?

Be sure, she was not an idle looker-on.   She
rushed to the piano and' played, by turns loud and
low, the strains of that martial but often mis-
applied anthem : " Hark ! the Conquering Hero
comes."   When she had satisfied herself that some
at least of her joyful strains had reached the ear
of the man for whom they were intended, she
opened a chest, and took from it some articles
of fine linen.   These she had wrapped in paper,
and having tied them with a cord, called Jumri,
and told him to take over and put into the
Doctor's hands these few little matters, which he
might find useful at present, and to say that she
had more at his disposal.

CHAPTER XIV.

KÈSUR'S NEW ROMANCE.

FOR the heroine of this tale, little more than a child in years, with few acquaintances and fewer sympathetic friends, the words and bearing of the British officer, with whom she had spoken so long and freely, were an experience not easily forgotten. She thought of them into the night hours, and next morning, when she woke, his name was on her lips.

Musing upon his words, she did not fail to take to heart the lesson they conveyed ; and then came on that conflict between interest and duty which ever accompanies the abandonment of early convictions.

A visitor was announced—the Reverend Nethcoff Bingham. Who was he ? She had never even heard of him. But Mr. Bingham had heard a full and graphic account of the scene in the mulberry grove, and the actors in it, the day before, at dinner, in the mess room of the 4th Duffs, and was just now under the influence of a vivid curiosity as well as a zeal for the conversion of a pagan. For Captain Halbot had embellished his story with a lively description of the graceful Hindu, of her intelligence and refinement, of her Christian tendencies, and of her gentleness and self-control under great provocation.

"I regret," he had said, "that O'Dowd is not with us to-day, as he could perhaps tell us something of the history of this girl, who is a patient of his—and, I am sure, a paying one, for her house, dress, retinue and all her surroundings point to wealth and high rank among her people."

"I wish," said Captain Stokes, "she would take me in and do for me; I would not mind her colour."

"Nor her form of religion?" said the Reverend Nethcoff.

"Oh, as for that," said Stokes, "we might make a compromise."

"No compromise could be allowable in the case," said Nethcoff. "The religion of Brahma is too far from Christianity for that."

"You make her a Christian then," said Stokes. "Halbot will give you an introduction: and you may tell her, as an inducement to come over to us, that you know a very devout soldier who is anxious to make her acquaintance."

"Will you present me to her?" asked Bingham, addressing Captain Halbot.

"I have not been presented myself," said Halbot. "I can scarcely be called an acquaintance. O'Dowd would be the person to whom you should apply for an introduction."

"Then to O'Dowd I will go to-morrow, and appeal to his good nature and Christian feelings; and I feel quite sure that he will put me on the way to the house of this fascinating damsel, and furnish me with a pass-word by which I may gain her presence."

Very early the next day the Reverend Nethcoff Bingham left his home for the residence of O'Dowd, dressed in a clerical garb adapted to the climate, and carrying with him all the appliances used in visiting, and notably a very glib and voluble tongue.

O'Dowd was at home, but in bed, where he made no figure to look at, for he was bandaged from the ear to the elbow, and his head was encased in a frilled night-cap, which had been lent by a sympathetic lady whose name need not be told.

He would see the visitor; he longed for someone to speak to; though his organs of speech were impaired, and words came from him in a thick and somewhat unfamiliar form.

The Reverend Mr. Bingham sped up the stairs to the Doctor's bedroom in three or four bounds, and he was inwardly much amused by the lady-like vision that came before him as he entered it. But, like a well-bred man as he was, he kept down his merriment, and gave expression to his sorrow at seeing the man so prostrate.

"Dot prostrate!" said O'Dowd, "but stiff—a flesh wou'd —dothi'g bore—ple'ty of vitality u'der a battered surface."

"You will be your old self in a few days," said the clergyman, in a kind tone.

"Id twedty-four hours," said the Doctor, udless I over-rate by codstitutiodal vigour."

"I have called upon you," said Nethcoff, "in

a partially selfish spirit. I have come to ask a favour of you. Will you be so good as to give me an introduction to a young Hindu lady, who is, I have been told, not only a patient of yours, but an intimate friend?"

"Why dot?" said the Doctor. "I will be odly too glad to add adother protector to the forlord creature. She is hudted like a hare by a Bussulbad hou'd."

"I thank you very much," said the clergyman, smiling: "I had much confidence in you, and I am glad it has not been misplaced. In what way shall we put our application for an audience?"

"A dote," said the Doctor; "give be the baterials. You will fide theb id the surgery: a'd I'll write a dote that will oped the door for you."

Mr. Bingham brought paper, pen and ink to the Doctor's bed-side, and arranging a make-shift desk in front of him on the coverlet, went to the window to look out while he waited.

Sounds of music were in the air; they came from the house over the way; they were neither sad nor sweet nor harmonious. They brought to mind the beating of a drumstick on a broken drum. The instrument from which they came was woody and sibilant, as if its heart's chords were broken; but the player touched it with a firm hand, as if it brought rest to a troubled spirit or called up sweet memories of the past.

The Reverend Nethcoff Bingham was, for once in his life, an unfair critic. Why did he mock at strains that he could not follow, or think lightly of airs that he could not connect? For aught he knew, the player might be producing the solemn movements of Mendelssohn or Beethoven, or the *Dies iræ* in the " Requiem " of Mozart.

More just was a dark boy on the door-step of the house, who with hands and feet beat time to the music within, and bent and turned his body to express the emotions which it drew from his soul. *He* could hear it well; and it seemed to be to him a cause of mirth and gloom in turn : for one moment he was at quick step, and the next he was wiping tears from his eyes.

The Reverend Nethcoff Bingham was a stranger in this part of the city. He had not yet made the acquaintance of Miss Ada Phlick ; nor was he aware that the actor on the step was a lad who was being evolved from a demure Hindu of Calcutta into the witty and often mischievous corner boy of an idle European town.

At the call of the Doctor, who had now finished his note, he turned from the window. He read it aloud, before giving it to his reverend friend. It ran as follows :

" I beg to present to you a friend of mine, who longs to know you. He calls himself a priest ; and he is, I suppose, a kind of one. He is, at any rate, a good man, and safe to receive in your house. Take him among the few friends that you have, and make him one of your body-guard : he is active and muscular, and, if needs be, you may call upon him to overawe that Turkish lover of yours, whom, I will confess to you, I don't admire. My dear young lady, I feel that you will not take this introduction as too great a liberty from your old physician, SEPTIMUS O'DOWD."

Nethcoff Bingham took the Doctor's note into his hand, read it, and demurred to one passage :—

"If I said, O'Dowd, that you were 'a kind of Doctor' would you take it as a compliment ? "

"As a very great ode," said O'Dowd. "I dever thought I was bore."

"Very well," said the clergyman lightly ; "the phrase will perhaps serve to amuse the lady, and put us on more easy terms."

"You're blind, Bighab, or you would have seen that this was the object aibed at."

The chaplain thanked O'Dowd and sped away, light of foot and spirits, towards the house of the Hindu. He had not gone a third of the distance when he met Captain Stokes, who had been on the watch for him, and now pleaded to be taken under his protecting wing and introduced to the lady.

"Impossible, my dear fellow," said Nethcoff ; "I could not presume so much : I go before the girl as a nondescript myself."

"How a nondescript ? " said Stokes.

"O'Dowd writes in this letter of introduction which I hold that I am, he supposes, 'a kind of priest.' "

"The bigoted old Papist ! His object is clear," said Stokes.

"Not to me," said Nethcoff. "I take it to be one of his whims—nothing more."

"Oh, it is more, and much more ! " said Stokes.

" He fears that you may endeavour to bring this woman over to Anglicanism, which must be distasteful to him, a Roman Catholic ; and to prevent this, he throws discredit on your ministry."

" I did not see it in this light," said Mr. Bingham ; " though, I confess, from what you say, a suspicion arises. What if I withhold the letter and introduce myself ? "

" Just what you ought to do. You and I go arm in arm, and as we pass her door, make a call on this little heiress, and say that we have come from ' Schloss O'Dowd.' "

" No, Stokes, that would be too crude. I go alone or not at all, and I promise that I will seek an opportunity of introducing your name."

" Thanks ! I am satisfied."

The reception of the Reverend Nethcoff by Kèsur was, as one might expect, formal. She did not quite see what might be his object in calling upon her. Could it be to impress upon her his form of Christianity, which, if Seeta was correct in describing it, differed from that of O'Dowd and Halbot ? She was on her guard from the beginning of their interview, and tried to keep the religious question out of view.

" You have come from Doctor O'Dowd," said she. " You are a friend of his : as such, I am pleased to meet you."

" We are acquaintances of recent date," said the Reverend Nethcoff, " and on friendly terms, though we differ in religion and in race."

" Are you not both English ? said Kèsur.

" No," said the clergyman, " I am : the Doctor

is of Irish blood, but not born in that country ; he has been given a perplexing name.   Have you not heard it ? "

"No," said Kèsur ; "in what is it perplexing ? "

"That it makes his nationality uncertain."

"Pray, what is this strange name ? " said she.

"French O'Dowd," said the clergyman smiling.

"It does seem a contradiction," said Kèsur.

"He is a Roman Catholic, of strong views," said Nethcoff Bingham.

"And a religious man," said Kèsur, ignoring the reference to the form.

"I will be candid with you," said the clergyman ; "I dislike his form of Christianity."

"And, I presume, he does not favour yours," she replied.

"No," said the clergyman, "he regards me as a heretic."

"All the same, you are on friendly terms : you have agreed to differ, and it is the more prudent course, is it not ? " said she.

"Courses which abound in prudence, my dear lady, are often lacking in zeal," said the clergyman.

"The Doctor is a zealous man," said Kèsur firmly.

"Zealous, I feel sure, for the conversion of the Hindu," said Nethcoff too eagerly. "There are others who would be equally zealous, and would lead their neophytes to a firmer shore."

"Have you made a study of the religion of Buddha ? " inquired Kèsur, to draw him from his subject.

He seemed perplexed.

"It is made a subject of study in our schools at home," said Nethcoff Bingham.

"Is it in favour among your co-religionists ? "

"It is regarded as a clever and attractive form of paganism only," said he.

"Only such ? " she questioned.

"How could we regard it otherwise from our standpoint ? "

"Your point of observation must be elevated,' said Kèsur.

"Would that you could raise yourself to it ! " said the clergyman.

"That would be difficult," she replied.

"Not so difficult as it seems to you. With a little friendly help and some instruction in our principles, you would soar above all the superstitions of Asia."

"Above the religion of Brahma amongst them ? " said she.

"As a matter of course," said Bingham.

"May I be candid and outspoken ? " said Kèsur.

"I shall esteem it a great favour."

"I have been born into Brahmanism," said she "and it may be a more difficult task than you imagine to withdraw me from it."

"I should so wish to put before you the claims of Christianity on the assent of all religious minds : I feel sure they would find an echo in your soul."

"I feel very grateful, and I thank you. I have been speaking on religious subjects with Captain Halbot. He is, I presume, an acquaintance of yours. He is full of zeal for the religion he professes. Do you know anything of his history ? He has quite as much of the clergyman as of the soldier in his manner."

"Yes," said Nethcoff ; "he was preparing for the ministry of his Church before he entered the army."

"This explains what has been a puzzle to me : he is full of information on all religious forms, but maintains the truth of his own with the enthusiasm of a priest."

"He is, in all directions, an earnest man," said the clergyman.

"He is charming in conversation," said the girl.

"You found him so ? "

"And so chivalrous," she continued.

"I heard him speak of having saved a lady from a coarse assault," said Nethcoff.

"I can corroborate what he said," she replied : "I was a witness to the attack and the defence."

"Is that so ? " said he.

"I was present on two occasions on which he showed himself a gallant knight."

"We were speaking of him as a Templar," said Nethcoff.

"I don't understand," said Kèsur.

"As a knight of the cross," said Bingham, "doing the work of a crusader."

"Oh, let us speak of him as a knight of the sword only," said Kèsur.

"I can infer, from your words, that his sermon made little impression," said the clergyman,

" Have you grounds for such an inference ? " said she.

" I think so—from your obvious disinclination to dwell upon it."

" I have dwelt upon his words alone and for hours together, and they have taken shape in my soul. This perhaps is the reason why I am not disposed to make them a topic of light conversation," said she demurely.

" I offer you an apology for having made light of a serious subject. I could not have supposed that you had taken so much to heart the words of a passing conversation, which is all that you could have had with Captain Halbot. My object in calling upon you was to hold out a helping hand to you, if you would allow me."

CHAPTER XV.

THE REVEREND NETHCOFF BINGHAM
TELLS HIS ADVENTURE.

THE Reverend Nethcoff Bingham, seeing very clearly that he could not bring his view of the religious question before the mind of the Hindu girl, who was obviously on her guard against its introduction, and feeling that he was on the losing side in the word-fencing that had gone on between them, bade her a polite and even cordial adieu, and left the house musing and amused, but with a firm resolve to repeat his visit on some future day.

She was a clever girl, he thought—a girl, too, of spirit and resolve, who could keep her own counsel, and was not to be led beyond lines she had laid down for her guidance. She may have been frank and out-spoken in her interview with Captain Halbot, as he told them at mess, but it was quite clear that she would not open her mind to the first-comer.

He suspected, though he was not sure of it, that the Doctor's note was of no profit to him. He had seen the girl smile as she read it, and look at him with curiosity, as if trying to find in his dress or bearing some indication of the ambiguous position assigned to him among the clergy.

He did not meet Stokes for some days. When he came across him for the first time after his visit to Kèsur, he underwent a rigid cross-examination at his hands.

" Is she gullible ? " said the soldier, without preface.

" Now, Stokes, pray don't ! She is charming in mind and person—not one of your vain fools, who will throw themselves away on a red coat or a fair skin ; a self-possessed young dame, who abates nothing of her rank, and, I think, puts herself on a line of perfect equality with an English lady."

" I was prepared, from Halbot's narrative, to hear of her beauty and refinement," said Stokes ; " but I thought that the softness of her race would remain with her ; for it is not often that a girl of her blood asserts herself."

" I cannot say that she asserts herself: she is simple and very gentle, but feels that she is a gentlewoman, and does not strive to conceal her feelings."

" I have no prospect then of getting into her good graces."

" You may : I see no unsurmountable obstacle, if she becomes a Christian," said the Reverend Nethcoff.

" Which may or may not be ? "

" Precisely."

" Did you bring the subject of conversion before her ? "

" I did not get even a chance of doing so."

" Marvellous ! Did she refuse to hear you speak on the subject ? "

" No ; but like a skilled tactician, she manœuvred to prevent my introducing it."

" Did she foresee that it was the object of your visit ? "

" I must think so."

" Then, believe me, it was O'Dowd's letter that put her on her guard."

" It may be so ; though I suspect she may have been arrayed against me by another."

" Who could it be? Do you suspect Halbot ? "

" My suspicion does not fall upon Captain Halbot. He is incapable of underhand dealing."

" I agree with you ; but it must have been some one who knew of your intended visit to the girl, and pointed to a possible pit into which she might be drawn."

" Might it not be a priest of Brahma that told her to be reticent in her converse with Christians ? "

" True ! " said Stokes ; " these Brahmans are, I believe, full of craft. They argue like Old Nick and close their eyes to evidence. If ' coached ' by one of these Sophists, she would try to carry you into her own superstition."

" And she seemed disposed to do so, but in a half-jesting way. I was quite unprepared for her home thrusts : she used her foil with the skill of a trained fencer."

" If you have fared so badly at her hands, she would turn me over, no doubt, if I presented myself to her as a suitor."

" I fear so."

" One word more," said Stokes ; " did you

introduce my name, or say I was anxious to know her?"

"Not the latter certainly: I merely said that I had been conversing with you before I entered her house, and that you accompanied me to her door."

"You could not have said less about me. I thank you all the same: you were put in durance like a naughty child by this vestal, I can see, and there remained until she set you free. Was it not a spectacle for men and angels—a learned Divine of the Christian Church silenced by a girl with no learning but the fables and follies of a visionary system of Paganism!"

"You take pleasure in my downfall," said the clergyman.

"It amuses me immensely," said Stokes.

"Put your hand in the lion's mouth—do, Stokes! Call and leave a card, and say that you will return the next morning to pay a formal visit. You may be better received that I was, as you don't go in a religious guise. Run the risk of being, as you express it, 'silenced,' and then come to me and report progress."

"I shall sleep on the matter," said Stokes. "Who knows what I may do? You have excited in me a great curiosity to see this strange girl, who seems to be so immensely above her sisters of the Hindu race."

They parted; and Mr. Bingham, who felt somehow that he wanted relaxation and news, bent his steps in the direction of the house of Ada Phlick, of whose presence in Calcutta he had heard some days before.

He found the lady at home : she was always at home since the return of O'Dowd from the tiger hunt. She was pensive and evidently in want of someone to cheer her. The Reverend Bingham saw this at a glance, and determined to raise the spirits of the lady, while eliciting from her the gossip of her neighbourhood.

" I hope I find you at peace with the world, as well as with yourself ? " were his first words.

" I was fretting a little," said she, " and felt worried by an accident that has befallen a friend."

" O'Dowd had a wonderful escape," said he mischievously.

" I have not heard the particulars of his adventure," said she, " except in a rambling way from my boy, Jumri."

Mr. Bingham told her of the bayonet charge, and how the Doctor had faced the enraged beast.

" Is he all there, think you ? " said she demurely. " I sometimes fancy that my neighbour is more than eccentric."

" He is sane as most men," said Nethcoff, " and even shrewd : his levity of manner is put on to amuse himself and his friends ; if indeed, it does not come from his Celtic temperament."

" Is Doctor O'Dowd, I wonder, a Frenchman ? He poses as such, but I seem to find traits of character in him which are too soft for the Gaul."

" He is as much a Frenchman as you are, Miss Phlick ! It is a part of his comedy to pretend to the name : he is Irish of the Irish, and by no means a bad type of that bright and humorous race."

M

" Whatever he is," almost sighed Miss Ada, " he has a kind heart for those who are in trouble."

" Have you been the recipient of his attentions ? " asked the Reverend Bingham.

" Not beyond some little neighbourly civilities," said the lady demurely ; " in truth, such acts of benevolence as have passed between us had their origin with me : I thought the man neglected, and I did him some little kindnesses."

" It was easy to see that, on entering his sick room. His head-dress, Miss Phlick, which I gazed on with admiration some days ago, bore evidence of a lady's thoughtfulness ! "

Miss Phlick flushed slightly. Could it be that he had not removed the frilling ? She had sent an express order, through Jumri, who bore the article across the street, for the removal of the borders before use, which that ingenious youth had turned into a command for their retention.

" His appearance," continued Bingham, " was womanly—that of an elderly and well-nourished female, whose features had been knocked out of place by a toothache or a visitation of mumps."

" I should have thought that the slap in the face dealt him by the tiger would not have had a refining effect, but the contrary," said Ada.

" Nor had it a refining effect on his features. I did not say, Miss Phlick, that he looked lady-like."

" ' Womanly,' I thought you said. What could have given him the air or pose of a woman ? "

" Come, Miss Phlick, be candid : you know as well as I do what it was that unsexed him."

" Could it be ? " said she. " No—it was not :

I took care of that. I am not in any way account-
able for the eccentricity of his head-dress ; he must
have been perpetrating a joke."

" That may be ; but who supplied the material for
it ? Some lady must have had a hand in the pie."

Did Doctor O'Dowd wear a frilled night-cap
when you saw him ? " she asked nervously.

" Frills, and borders, and strings !—and all the
other characteristics," said his Reverence.

' Then there was betrayal somewhere," said she.
" You would not think me capable of setting a
face that I respect, if not admire, in a frame-work
that must make it ridiculous."

" I shall be happy to set aside the suspicion if you
tell me of anyone else who may have done so."

" It is not for me to suggest. He has, I dare say,
a washerwoman ; and he is on friendly terms with
a lady of colour," said Miss Phlick.

" I will defer to your superior knowledge. I
should have thought, in my simplicity, that Hindu
ladies did not wear frilled night-caps," said Nethcoff archly. " But enough of the subject : let it pass.
I am not sorry that you have introduced Kèsur's
name to my notice : I have called upon you to-day
for sympathy in a let-down I have experienced at
the hands of this lady."

" Had she the presumption," said Ada, " to speak
to you on equal terms, forgetting the disparity of
race ? "

" She is a Zemindar's daughter, and rich," said
Bingham.

" All the same, a mere woman of colour," said
Ada.

"She is of the highest caste," said Bingham, "and her colour is both rich and ripe ; her manners, too, are playful and agreeable; but she will not give heed to you, if you speak to her on religion. My grievance is, that I called at her house to convert her to Christianity, and that she did not allow me even to introduce the subject of my visit."

"I do," said Ada, "sympathize with you, on having to endure the rudeness of the woman."

"She was not rude, Miss Phlick, but adroit, She did not close her ears to any words of mine, but she gave me no choice of a topic, and carried me from subject to subject, as if I had been a child."

"I do believe," said Miss Ada, "that the native races of India are being spoiled by their rulers, who, instead of keeping them in their places as hewers of wood and drawers of water, are giving them higher education and drafting them into society."

"I don't quite agree with you, Miss Phlick. The Hindu race, especially the women of it, have learned but little from books, and cannot go into society while caste restrictions prevail : and surely you would not deprive so gentle and lovable a people of the advantages that Western civilization brings into its train ? Let them gather all the fruits that spring from their position as British subjects, but——"

"Allow me to finish for you," said Miss Phlick, "let them be, at all times, humble and patient listeners to the words of wisdom that fall from the lips of their white masters."

" Thank you," said the Reverend Bingham, " but I should be sorry to express myself so. My hostess of an hour ago would have been nothing as a listener but a demure school girl : as a speaker, she was lively and attractive. My complaint is, not that she opened her own mouth freely and often, but that she closed mine in part."

" Why did you not force your subject on her attention ? " said Ada.

" Which, pardon my saying so, is the same as if you asked—Why did you not forget that you are a gentleman ? "

" You might, I think, without impropriety, have made the woman understand that she was speaking to a superior," said Miss Phlick.

" How could I, when I had serious doubts on the subject ? "

" It is your humility, as a minister of the Gospel, that suggested these doubts. It seems to me that a Hindu huzzy should not stand in the presence of one like you, and reply to your words in monosyllables."

The Reverend Nethcoff Bingham was gradually approaching the object of his visit ; which was, be it candidly admitted, to elicit, for his own amusement, some of the peculiar views of Miss Ada Phlick on persons and things ; so he continued, in a lighter tone :

" I fear I have been representing this Eastern siren as an ogress or a sphinx. I feel that, before we part, I should make amends to her, by saying emphatically that she is a perfectly

charming type of that class that many won't have
—the lady by nature, without artificial training."

" I am not, Mr. Bingham," said Ada, " a
believer in the existence of such a class : the hot-
house plant will not grow in the cold earth outside,
or, if it springs up for a while, it withers."

" There are ladies who are geraniums," said the
Reverend Bingham, "or orchids, if you prefer it,
who require a peculiar atmosphere to mature
them, and the hand of a skilled gardener to keep
them in bloom. They are, at the best, of sickly
growth, and in freshness and vigour much inferior
to the flower that blooms outside with but little
culture and no unnatural forcing. Of the latter
class is this Hindu—like a white man that, by
a freak of nature, is born of dark parents—this
girl, among the lively but not vulgar sisters of her
race, has absorbed the hues and tints of our
modern civilization."

" She did not impress me much," said Ada
Phlick.

"Come now, Miss Phlick, you are a judge of
beauty. Is not the girl an Eastern rose, fragrant
and sweet ? "

" For her race and colour, she is not unattractive."

" Was she veiled when you saw her ? "

" At first, when we met : afterwards she let
down the face covering."

" And you were dazzled ? I confess I was."

" No ; " replied Miss Ada, indifferently : " I was
rather puzzled."

" Puzzled—how ? "

" I wondered where she could have got a skin so tinted and a nose like that of a Greek statue."

" I fear, Miss Phlick, that you took a hurried and partial view of that fair face. Still I won't charge you with prejudice : you were pleased, I feel sure, with her manners."

" Her manners are soft enough," said Ada, "if not somewhat simpering, which does not prevent her from looking longingly towards a higher sphere : she is a lass of ambitious aspirations."

" I should not have thought so," said the clergyman.

" Oh, yes, indeed ! 'Sweet' "—she hesitated— "I must not betray her by going farther—'sweet'— let me say—'Staples' were the words I heard from her lips. I had scarcely patience with her, and felt quite relieved when my door closed behind her."

" Have you ever heard, Miss Phlick, that a jury composed of men and women never agree to a verdict when sitting on a woman's charms ?"

" I should deem it . not unlikely," said Ada Phlick.

" It is a puzzle in the present case," said Nethcoff, rising to go."

CHAPTER XVI.

CONDIMENTS AND A NIGHTCAP.

O'DOWD was still in bed nursing his jaw, and being nursed. Especially the latter; for there was a sympathizer over the way whose thoughts were ever upon him.

Jumri could not, had he wished, be blind to the fact that his mistress was developing a taste for cooking since the day of the Doctor's return. He came upon her with frying-pans and saucepans, omelette-shapes and gridirons in her hands; and he caught her unawares over the stove one day, enveloped in an apron, with work-stained fingers and heated brow, coaxing a kidney that refused to fry.

But the fact was brought home to him in another way—he was bearer of sundry dishes across the street; now it was the half of a peacock that he carried, now a mango just brought in from the Ganges, again an indescribable mixture of sundries and rice, and occasionally one of those little sweet dishes, in coloured condiments, which the ingenuity of a well-trained cook will devise.

The ever-vigilant eye of this boy detected another practice—that of reading—to which Miss Ada Phlick gave herself over at this time. Heretofore her leisure hours—and they were many—had been devoted to the piano; but now a book was ever in her hands. And the guileless youth took note that the book she held was always the same, and concluded that she was learning from that book something which she had not known heretofore.

" She be learning to dance, may be," soliloquized the bright lad, " or to speak Bengali: anyhow she'll go cracked over this book, if she go on like that. I'll steal it from her if I can."

He did so. The very next time that Miss Phlick went out for a walk, he made his way into her parlour, and had no difficulty in coming across the volume to which he had taken such a dislike. It was lying open on a table. Having secured his prey, he strolled off with it to a barber, who was a friend of his, to submit the capture to his inspection, and ask him the nature of its contents.

It was a cookery book—neither more nor less. When Jumri learned this fact, he whistled, and hurried back to put it in the place in which he had found it.

We have said that Miss Phlick was reading when she was not cooking: but, in saying this, we had not told the whole truth ; for there was another work to which she devoted her evenings when the mental and bodily strain of the day was over. It was knitting in thread and worsted what seemed to the vigilant eye of her boy to be a neck-muffler, a pair of socks, or a night-cap.

Jumri deemed the last-named a necessity. He did not admire the Doctor in a frilled head-dress.

" He be as ugly as Buddha almost," said the lively boy, " with his nose, eye and ear all in one lump, wrapped in a crumpled border like a plum-pudding; and his other eye winking, as if he'd say—' This be the work of Ada.' "

Jumri might jest at her expense ; but Ada's course was clear before her, and she followed it with unflagging assiduity. When she was not cooking, she was reading or knitting; when she was not reading, she was knitting or cooking ; when she was not knitting, she was cooking or reading ; and all for—" Ah, the dear man ! "—she could never do enough for him.

Miss Phlick laid down her needles, and, folding in paper the textile work upon which she had been for some days engaged, said :

" Jumri, take this to the Doctor, with my compliments."

There was not a smile on the face of the arch youth as he took the parcel in his hand. He was all gravity until he got to the porch, where he raised an end of the covering, and took a peep at the contents. Seeing a blending of bright colours, he put aside the cover and held between his eyes and the sun a gaudy night-cap of the old stereotyped pattern—funnel-shaped, with a crimson tassel and a border of bright green.

" I'll have a try on," said he, laying down his turban, putting the night-cap over his head, and pulling it down until it covered his ears. Just at this moment Miss Phlick was heard approaching the door. Jumri was so confused that he mechanically, and without looking at it, seized the turban, and crumpling it into the paper cover, marched across the street with the night-cap on **his head.**

By this time Miss Ada Phlick had gone back
to her old favourite seat near the window, and was
looking down on the street. There she caught
sight of her boy, in the night-cap, crossing to
O'Dowd's. If a galvanic battery had sent a current through her frame, she could not have received
a greater shock; for, apart from the utter levity
and impertinence of her servant, which the vision
betrayed, there was the revelation of that work of
love and compassion in which she had been so
long engaged.

What would the public say? What would the
loiterers and strollers on the street, who saw Jumri
and his head-dress, say? Would they believe that
the night-cap had been bought in Calcutta, or
knitted by a native of the country? Obviously,
no! It was a foreign night-cap; coming from the
house of a foreigner, going to the house of a
foreigner. It was a male night-cap, coming from
the house of a lady, borne on the head of that
lady's servant! There was only one explanation
that must strike the most indifferent gazer—that
this night-cap was a love-token, woven by the deft
fingers of Miss Ada Phlick for her compatriot
over the way, to shield his wounded head from
draughts and insects, and infuse into it that even
warmth which is necessary for the removal of
swellings and the dispersion of angry humours.

For a moment—it was a moment of weakness
and fear—Miss Ada Phlick forgot the proprieties,
threw open the casement, and in a shrill and angry
voice, shouted—yes, shouted—the name of " Jumri "
across the street.

" Jumri!" she cried, "come back. How dare you——?"

The sentence was never finished, nor does the writer of this record presume to say what might have been the ominous ending of it. Jumri did not come back : he may not have heard the angry call of his mistress, or he may have heard it as one deaf of both ears. He was near the door of the drug store when the alarm was sounded, and he passed in without giving heed to it—leaving Miss Phlick in a state of mental horror not far removed from frenzy.

He entered the chamber in which O'Dowd lay on his bed, less swollen than when we saw him last, but lady-like in what appeared of him over the bed-clothes, as before. He looked at the boy ; he looked again, and smiled. This Jumri took to be an expression of greeting, or joy for the gift he was to present to him.

The unsuspicious lad laid down the little parcel that he carried, within reach of O'Dowd's hand, and said :

" This be with Miss Phlick's compliments."

" What is it, Jumri?" said O'Dowd, looking archly at the boy.

" Miss Phlick don't tell Jumri what she sends," he replied ; " she be very cunning."

" And Jumri never tries to make it out," suggested the Doctor ; " he is such a faithful boy."

" May be he does—sometimes," he answered.

" Could you even guess what's in this parcel?" said O'Dowd.

" 'Tis fish, I tink," said Jumri.

" It feels too soft for fish, and too dry," replied the Doctor ; " try again."

" I don't know," said the boy, " if it's not a night-cap."

" It's not a night-cap, Jumri : it doesn't feel like one : 'tis too big and too crumpled."

" 'Tis a night-cap," said Jumri : " I had a peep."

" You *are* a precious youth," said the Doctor. " Miss Phlick has a blessing in you."

" She has," said Jumri, " and she tinks so : I be playing pranks always—to keep up her spirits."

" Your present prank isn't a bad one," said the Doctor, " but you should be more careful crossing the street."

" I be very glum in the street—never a laugh or a jump, and my clothes nice and clean, and my face washed."

" And never go out without your turban ? " inquired the Doctor.

" Never ! I wear it all the time."

" Go back to your mistress now," said the Doctor, " and give her my compliments, and tell her that I am thankful for her thoughtfulness."

" Open it," said Jumri, " it be grand—like a green and red parrot."

" Go now, boy," said O'Dowd ; " I'll open it later on."

" Open it now," he persisted, " and put it on : you be like an old woman in that nasty thing."

" 'Tis very comfortable and cool," said the Doctor ; " I'll wear it for a few days longer."

" Don't," said the youth, " 'tis horrid : your face be like a pudding in a pan."

"Come," said the Doctor decisively, "off with you : and tell Miss Phlick that you gave me the night-cap, and that I said it was worthy of her deft fingers."

Jumri saw that the Doctor was determined, and he departed gaily and without suspicion.

Miss Ada Phlick lay in waiting for him, and her excited feelings prompted her to make a bodily assault on him then and there ; but she curbed them and listened, without sign of emotion, to the glowing words in which he described the gratitude of the Doctor for the timely gift and the beauty of the article.

"It be like a number of sun birds all rolled up together," said he, "with their colours melting into each other like anything : the Doctor am beautiful in it."

"Did he try it on?" said Miss Phlick sternly.

"Not quite," said the truthful lad, "but it was the same as if he did."

"Did he take it in his hand?" said Ada.

"Oh, yes! I put it on the bed near his hand : and he took it, and felt it, and said that it wasn't fish at any rate."

"What put fish into his head?"

"Twas I," said Jumri, hanging his head, "for fun."

"You knew it was not fish?" said Ada.

"I knowed it well," said Jumri. "May I go now? I be off to Fort William to see the soldiers drilling."

"I think you would do better to go to bed : you are more in trim for it," said Ada wrathfully.

"I go to bed?" said the boy in surprise. "I no

go to bed and the sun shining : I not a lazy little fellow."

" Jumri," said Miss Phlick seriously, " I must part with you, for you are an absolutely incorrigible lad."

" I don't know *corrigible*," said the boy.

" You have spoken the truth at last : you don't know what it is to mend your ways, and you never will."

" I have no ways to mend," said the boy ; " I have only my clothes, and my mother mends them, when they are broken."

Ada was provoked. The suggestion to charge upon the boy, and demolish him, entered her mind again ; but she brought her temperament down by a vigorous rubbing of her nose, which Jumri, in his airy mood, could not pass over.

" Miss Phlick," said he, " be giving herself big red nose ; can't she let it alone ? "

The climax was coming : this remark was unbearable.

" She be always a-rubbing it : consequence, it's growing as long as a horn," he continued.

Miss Phlick breathed a prayer for patience.

" Jumri tinks the Doctor won't love her," he went on, " if she don't keep her hands off."

Her patience, at this piece of impertinence, ran out. She rushed at the boy, seized him by the shoulders, and pushed him before a mirror. Then, for the first time, he became conscious that he was bearing O'Dowd's night-cap on his head. The effect, however, was not what Ada Phlick anticipated. The boy was neither over-awed nor frightened, but amused to such a degree that he broke into an uncontrollable fit of laughter. He laughed from the highest hair of his head to the soles of his feet: he wriggled, writhed, all but danced. If he checked himself for a moment, it was to break out afresh louder than before. It was in vain that Miss Ada Phlick shook him, at brief intervals vigorously: her frequent cries, " Jumri, have you gone mad?" produced no effect beyond making the scene more ludicrous. In the end it was brought to a close by the boy himself, who ran out through the door, saying, "I am off to the Doctor's for my turban."

After his departure, Miss Phlick sat down to ruminate. "I have somewhere, in my French reading," she said, "met the expression, 'enfant terrible': this is truly a dreadful boy, and so different from other lads of his race and training, who are humble, silent and respectful. He pretends to simplicity, and he is cunning as a—wolf-dog. He would even rule the house, and take its mistress under his command. Such ideas!—such squeamishness! Even a loved and precious feature cannot change its colour for a moment without attracting his attention. He is more like a *gamin* from the streets of Paris, or a wag from the slums of Edinburgh, than a Hindu."

She felt it a duty incumbent on her to wait on Dr. O'Dowd and dissociate herself from this late escapade of her boy. What must the "dear man" think but that he was made the victim of an unkind jest, prompted by the mistress, and carried into effect by her confidential servant?

She crossed the street—Jumri had left the Doctor's house—and with some timidity and much delicacy made her way to the bedside of the invalid, who had now put aside her frilled night-cap, and was beaming with smiles and amiability under the little bright canopy she had provided for him.

"I would have waited your perfect recovery to present you with my felicitations, but for the outrage just done you by my insolent boy," said Ada.

"Pray, don't mention it, Miss Phlick. "It did not hurt me in any way. I saw through it the moment the lad came before me: he had been peeping at your work of art, for it is no less"—touching the cap—"then put it on his head and laid down his turban. Some one coming in suddenly had startled him; and in his confusion, he rolled the turban in the paper cover and forgot that he had put the night-cap in its place."

"I wish, Doctor, that I could think that it was a mistake on his part, though he could not be deemed blameless, even then; but he is such a comedian that I am always in doubt as to his motives."

"Don't give yourself a moment's trouble on the score of this little incident. It has been to me a source of amusement only; and I can assure you, it has had the effect of a refresher on me—nothing more."

"You are so considerate, Doctor!" said Ada, tenderly.

"Allow me, dear Miss Phlick, to seize on this opportunity—our first meeting after my recovery—

to thank you most warmly for the delicate and seasonable attentions I have received from you during my recess. Poor Jumri—though he slipped a little to-day—carried out with much grace and kindness all your wishes, and loaded me with all sorts of things fair to the eye and agreeable to the taste, and by his prattle made me quite joyous while consuming them."

" He can be a good boy sometimes, Doctor," Perhaps said Ada. " I expect too much gravity from one of his years; but you would pardon my complaint of him if you were a witness to his constant restlessness."

" He cannot I think, be other," said O'Dowd; " his nervous system is easily thrilled. Sparks are flying through him and from him, which he does not voluntarily give out; they spring not so much from his will as from his nerve centres."

" I have thought of something of the kind," said Miss Phlick, " when viewing him in motion. He is more like a machine than a man. To be candid, it has sometimes struck me that he is a victim to some malady that rules him. What might it be? I have asked myself—might it be tic-douloureux? But no—there is nothing dolorous about him. I am strongly of opinion that it must be St. Vitus' dance. If I am right, Doctor, what remedy would you recommend?"

" Ahem !" coughed the Doctor, " if I were you, I would have him shampooed without delay."

Ada did not see proportion between the disease and the remedy. She went away trying to discover it.

CHAPTER XVII.

THE DOCTOR MEETS TWO BROWN FRIENDS AND VISITS A WHITE LADY.

THE Doctor grew better rapidly.

The swelling went down : the obstacle to correct articulation was removed. Miss Phlick's head-dress was sent home—the one with the frills—and the other was put aside. O'Dowd rose from his bed none the worse for his late mishap, and went into his drug store to take up the thread of his suspended business.

The said business had not been at any time lively ; but it had been growing steadily since the date of the Doctor's call at the house of Kèsur who had given him liberal fees, which enabled him to replenish his empty bottles and jars. Now there was quite a hum of life in and about the shop. Maidens, from the native quarter of the city, came to buy draughts as dark or blacker than themselves. Elegant ladies of Western blood drove to the door in their carriages, and sent in their footmen to purchase scents and toilet requisites. Shaving materials were often asked for, and a general washing seemed to have set in, so great was the demand for soap. " All this," thought the Doctor, " is the outcome of my triumphant return from the tiger hunt."

And it was so : people of all classes were anxious to see the hero who had met the man-eater in single combat, and made him bite the dust.

" You are a brave man, sir !" said a commissary of police, over the counter ; " it is not every day that we hear of a fencing match like that you were engaged in. Your name will live for ever in the annals of Indian sport."

" Well, Commissary," replied the Doctor modestly, " it was my first outing in the jungle and——"

" I hope it won't be your last, Doctor !"

" And, I was going to add," continued O'Dowd, " I was desirous to give the poor beast a chance."

" A noble thought, Sir," said the commissary : " it does you credit : it is not thus that your countrymen are inspired, when they draw around their game a line of fire that would put a company of soldiers to flight."

" My blood and breeding, Commissary, would not allow me to be a party to such mean tactics," said O'Dowd.

" You don't look quite English," said the policeman.

" I have not a drop of English blood in my veins," said the Doctor. " I'm a hybrid French-man."

" Good Heavens !" said the officer, " that is a queer title—half-breed, I suppose."

" As thorough-bred, Sir," said the Doctor, " as a prize greyhound or a winner of the Derby."

The commissary was thrown off his mental rails by this answer, and dropped the subject of nationality.

By degrees the enthusiasm went down. As the various classes of the population had a look, at close quarters, at the hero of the hunt, they began to suspect a mistake or a *ruse* : they were quite disillusioned by the shape, age, and bearing of the tiger-slayer. He was but a heavy, elderly, matter-of-fact little man, much more likely to kill a patient than a beast of the jungle. It was a shave of those military barbers of Fort William ! After a few days the calls at the drug store began to decline ; and at the end of a fortnight business went down to the low level from which it had so suddenly started, and O'Dowd had plenty of time in which to pay a round of visits to those who had called upon him or left their cards, during his illness.

Kèsur was the first to be thus honoured. The girl had not seen him during his retirement, but he knew that she had been anxious about him and had made many inquiries as to his state at Miss Phlick's and among their common acquaintances.

She had much to say to him. She told him, first, of the visit of the Reverend Nethcoff Bingham, and of his vain attempt to draw her into a conversation on the religious question.

" He was most agreeable," said she, " and very friendly : I was attracted by his fine person and refined manners, but I kept him, all through our interview, in a state of mild torture."

" How cruel ! " said the Doctor.

" I thought," said she, " that if I allowed him to run on, he would efface the impressions made on my mind by Captain Halbot, whom I had met two days before, and I would not have his words even blurred for worlds."

"Very nice!" said O'Dowd lightly: "you have been in gay society during the absence of your guardian."

"Who is my guardian?" said the girl innocently.

"A man known to the marines as French O'Dowd."

Kèsur laughed lightly.

"I did not flirt while you were away," she said, "but, I admit, I saw more company than usual."

"So it appears," he replied; "Nethcoff, Halbot —who else?"

"Akbar Yassov," she replied: "but I did not see them all at my house."

"You saw Halbot at home," the Doctor ventured.

"No, indeed," she said; "I met him in a mulberry grove."

"Quite romantic," said the Doctor.

"Was it not?" said she.

"Thrilling!" assented the Doctor.

"You have used the correct word," said she, "it *was* thrilling."

"Were you quite alone with him?" said O'Dowd.

"I met him twice," said Kèsur.

"Twice, in a mulberry grove, alone?"

"I did not say alone," said Kesur.

"I am puzzled," said O'Dowd. "Who could be with you?"

"Who, indeed!"

"Was it Captain Stokes?"

" No ! You could not think so."

" Miss Ada Phlick ? "

" That serious lady does not wander through woods at night."

" Your frisky little maid, Gunga ? " suggested O'Dowd.

" No."

" Do tell me : I am curious to know who it was."

Kèsur told him the story of her meeting Akbar, on her return from her visit to himself, of his strong language and violence, of the sudden and unexpected appearance of Halbot on the scene, of his intervention, and of the retreat of the Mussulman.

" And then," said O'Dowd, " you had the Englishman to yourself, and you put him in the place of the discarded Turk."

" Would that not have been presumption ? " said Kèsur.

" You might," said the Doctor, " and I think you did."

" *I* am not so sure," said Kèsur, thoughtfully. " I am a girl of Indian blood, and you know what that is in the eyes of a European."

" Bother colour," replied the Doctor ; " you are not a black nor a mulatto : I'd prefer the shade of your countenance to that of a pink and white European posy."

" No, Doctor," said she continuing, " I did violence to the longings of my heart, and kept out the idol which would take possession of it, if allowed."

" Well, well ! " said the Doctor, assuming a serious manner ; " you acted best for your own peace of mind, and I congratulate you on your firmness."

Just then he saw, for he sat near the window, the Buddhist who had called to speak to him after his dip in the Ganges, passing along the street, and, saying a hurried good-bye to Kèsur, went out to meet him.

The man came along solemnly, his eyes rolling over such objects as he encountered, but furtively, like one not at home with his company. His features seemed more distinctly Chinese than when last we saw him, and his pig-tail was more in evidence, as if he would shelter himself under the flag of the Celestial Empire, while he dared to be the advocate of Buddhism among the Brahmans.

He opened his almond orbs to their utmost capacity when O'Dowd stood before him, and, without preamble or apology, lightly said :

"The early and late rains to you, John Chinaman."

His mouth opened with his eyes. Was it at the easy freedom of the Doctor ?

"I am a Buddhist priest," he said with dignity.

"You were, when you called on me, some months ago : rumour has it, that you have since faced about," said the Doctor.

"My face is, as it ever was, turned to Lhassa," said the Buddhist piously.

"Is it turned from Pekin, nearer home?" said the Doctor. "I was under the impression that the Emperor of China is as good a Lhama as the creature that sits cross-legged on the holy mountain."

"They are both blessed," said the man, " and dear to Buddha."

"Ahem!" coughed the Doctor wickedly.

"They live apart from the fading things of earth," continued the Buddhist.

"Ahem!" repeated the Doctor.

"They are hidden in a mist of sanctity," said the grave one.

"How many of them have you, all told?" said O'Dowd.

"Need I say? The world knows," said the Buddhist.

"I have a doubt about one of them," said O'Dowd.

"Which?" asked the Buddhist.

"The Emperor of China," said O'Dowd.

"He too is a Lhama in spirit, if not in name. There are three Lhamas making Buddha manifest to man : the Dalai-Lhama in Lhassa, the Lhama of Little Thibet, and the Lhama of Mongolia. The Emperor of China is as closely identified with the Divinity as any of them."

"Ahem!"

"Our emperor," continued the Buddhist enthusiastically, "lives in a hidden away palace, amid spirits of light—"

"Stop, man," said O'Dowd, "you are talking nonsense. The spirits that surround your emperor are of the flesh—fleshy."

The Buddhist turned his eyes up to heaven ; and O'Dowd, feigning not to see his look of horror, went on :

"Now, Mr. Buddhist, you are a man of common sense ; answer me a plain question. Is the

Emperor of China of the same calibre as the Dalai-Lhama ? "

" As a Chinese Buddhist, I am forced to say that he is."

" That will do," said O'Dowd ; " don't say another word about them."

" I cling to them," said the grave man, " as the baby clings to its mother."

" And yet you are preparing to turn your back upon them."

" Who says so ? " demanded the priest, angrily.

" Oh, come ! " said O'Dowd : " as if the whole city was not saying so."

" Buddha forgive the city ! " said he, piously.

" Amen," said O'Dowd, as he turned away to suppress an outburst of laughter.

He was doomed to meet all his casual acquaintances this day. Up the street, looking, if possible, more grave and sombre than the Buddhist from whom he had parted, came the Brahman priest, whom we met in his drug store a few months before.

" Another of those pleasant fellows ! " soliloquized the Doctor. " I'll stop him, and give him a wrench. " Your reverence," said he, " I suppose you are in pursuit of your friend. I have been speaking to him : he is straight before you. If you quicken your pace, you will overtake him."

" To whom do you refer, Sir ? " said the Brahman.

" To the Buddhist—who else ? " said O'Dowd.

' I have no Buddhist friend," said the priest bitterly ; " I hate the false god and his followers, without exception."

" Isn't Buddha as good as Brahma ? What's the difference ? " said the Doctor.

" Buddha as good as Brahma ? " echoed the other bitterly, dwelling on every word. " Is darkness as precious as light ? Is sickness equal to health ? You should measure your words, Sir ; your utterances are silly."

" Thank you," said O'Dowd : " I meant a compliment for your divinity. From my point of view, Buddha is to Brahma as four to two."

" He has, I admit, a larger following," said the priest, " but what is that ? "

" Everything," said O'Dowd ; " in a contest between rivals for popular favour, the leader of the minority is nowhere."

" You don't seem to understand us, Doctor O'Dowd. We don't take pride in numbers, but in learning and science : the Buddhists have no books and no tradition worth speaking of."

" They tell the story of Buddha, as you do of Brahma ; and it is as likely to be true. Of what use are books when no one knows who wrote them ?"

" Oh, profane man ! Hast thou not heard of the Divine Vedas, that were written in Sanscrit, at the beginning of the world ; of their elegant diction and profound philosophy, and of the legal code of Manon, the first man ? "

" No, Sir ! I am a plain person : I don't deal in fables. Who, pray, is Manon ? I hear of him for the first time."

" He was the grandson of Brahma."

" I have you, Sir ! Manon was a man : may I ask was his grandfather a man or a god ? "

"He was the Creative Principle," said the other wisely.

"If he was the Creative Principle, he was not, in the ordinary way, the grandfather of Manon, and should not be named such. Good-day, Sir —merely a little nut to crack—crack it at your leisure."

"Now," said the Doctor, "I'm for Ada Phlick. By the way, what a name—*Phlick*! Poor girl! she should get rid of it as soon as she can. Shall I help her to do so? No—emphatically, no! Turn it, as you will, it would not consort with my Celtic patronymic; the firm of O'Dowd and Phlick would be sure to come to grief. And yet she deserves much of me: she is a kind creature, and she is lonely. I'll pay her a little attention, call on her occasionally, and be to her an adviser and a friend, as she has been to me."

Miss Ada Phlick sat at home in state, expecting the Doctor's visit, and when his genial voice was heard outside in converse with Jumri, a slight spasm interrupted the beating of her heart.

"Come in," she cried faintly, in response to a gentle knock at the door; and when the Doctor appeared, she added, "You are very welcome."

"To thank you," said O'Dowd, "for your great attention during my illness, and to offer my service in return. Command me, as a trained spaniel, to run your errands and carry your parcels."

"Ah, Doctor," she replied tenderly, "you must have known and experienced a mother's love."

"Not at all, my dear lady. I was, so to speak, born an orphan."

" I would have been more than a mother to you, if I had known you early in life," said Ada tenderly.

"Never too late to begin," replied the Doctor; "let us stand *in loco parentis* to each other."

"What is that, Doctor? I don't understand Latin."

' If you be a mother to me," said he, " I will be as a father to you."

"Kind man!" said she; "you will be everything that is thoughtful and amiable, I am sure: and I will not fail to consult you in all my troubles. You shall be henceforth my medical adviser, and my counsellor. You may, I fear, find me sometimes importunate, as I am subject to nervous seizures, but I will trespass on you—on you alone and above all others—in all the trials that befall me."

They were on friendly terms at last; but it must be said that they regarded each other n a very different light. The Doctor's feelings in regard to Miss Phlick had not the slightest tinge of romance in them; they were simply the outcome of gratitude; but the lady——. Well, ladies will be peculiar, especially if they have facial defects that more or less isolate them; and being lonely they will have their likings, irrespective sometimes of age and shape.

CHAPTER XVIII.

A CRY FOR HELP. IMPRISONED IN A CELLAR.

A STRAIN was put upon the new friendly relations between Septimus O'Dowd and Miss Ada Phlick the next day, but the Doctor was equal to the tension.

From the lady came a hurried message. " Will Doctor O'Dowd call upon me with the least possible delay? I wish to consult him, above all others, in a trouble that has come upon me. Have unbounded confidence in his advice."

" The climate of India again!" murmured O'Dowd. " What is the nature of the disturbance, boy?"—to Jumri, who stood waiting. " But how should you know? Go, and say that I will not wait to clothe myself as a gentleman, but will fly to her abode in my shirt sleeves, collarless, tieless! Poor old girl! Bile!" he added privately.

He went across the street with a rush, and found himself in the presence of a lady *en deshabille*, who had forgotten to remove her morning papers, and to put in position her teeth, which lay forlorn and neglected on the washing slab, and whose dressing gown and the wraps that it covered brought to his mind the kirtle of a Tyrolese maiden.

If he was inclined to smile at her appearance, he was pulled up quickly by the wild manner in which she received him.

"Doctor, I have become a pagan!" were her surprising words.

"Be calm, my dear," said O'Dowd. "Hallucination! Delusion! I knew a lady who fancied that she was a turkey, and believed that she would be quite well if only she could gabble."

"Don't trifle with me, Doctor! I am serious, sensible, and in possession of all my faculties. I have become a pagan, and I lay my misfortune at the door of a little brute."

"Of a little brute?" said O'Dowd, menacingly. "I demand his name: he shall hear from me. It may be an officer from Fort William will take my message to him. Pistols or swords—I care not which: but he shall answer to me, with his life, for the enormity of having seduced a compatriot of mine from the Christian faith."

"But he is invisible, my kind, my chivalrous friend," she said, with grateful tenderness.

"I will bring him out of his lurking place, by the collar if need be, the skulking hound," cried the Doctor fiercely.

"You cannot: he may not be touched; you cannot even draw near him, for he lives far away in the land of emancipated spirits."

"He is dead—the little ruffian?" demanded O'Dowd.

"If he ever lived," she replied, "which I doubt. Such a monster could scarcely be born of woman, however degraded."

"Your imagination is excited, Miss Phlick! What is your trouble? You must know you are talking nonsense."

" Oh, little Dicky ! " was her reply. " Wicked little Dicky ! I admired—I all but loved you ; I stood by you with glistening eyes when you drew the divine form of Friby's foot ; I followed you up the hill to fame ; I gave you my heart-felt sympathy in your love troubles—grieving when you failed in your suit, and rejoicing when you seemed to reach the goal of your desires ; and I went away with you from Paris in despair when your mistress disappeared, and all was over, and your life was a dreary blank. I even condoned your little foibles ; I looked upon you with tenderness when you came home to your lodgings a little sot, and spoke foolish words, and, for aught I know, fell asleep with your head in the coal-scuttle. The Bard admired you, but not so much as Ada Phlick. Muffy loved you, but what was his love compared to the tender emotions of a woman's soft heart ? Deceptive little Dicky ! Unfeeling, ungrateful little Dicky ! You had hidden under a guileless exterior a corrupt heart—under a boyish playfulness the ferocity of, what shall I say, Doctor ? "

" A roaring lion," suggested O'Dowd at random.

" No, no ; that is not the word : the poor little plaything was incapable of roaring ; and as for resembling the king of beasts—he was more like a little purring cat. But no matter. Let the simile pass ; let the sentence remain for ever unfinished. Where was I, Doctor, when I broke off ? "

" In the moon," said O'Dowd wilfully.

" Ah, Doctor, you should not be frivolous, when our highest interests are at stake ! " said Ada, moving her head gravely and thoughtfully from side to side. "I have been calling up the image of my destroyer before his fall: I have not been allowing Bengal lights to fall upon him, and change him from green to red or yellow, but I have been turning upon him a pure white light, in which his youth, his beauty, his sweetness, his genius, his all-round attractiveness have been shown forth and all for the purpose of a contrast."

"I see," said O'Dowd, "I understand it all. Don't distress yourself by continuing the story; allow me to fill in the picture. This little chap, whom you name Dicky, you have found to be a double-dyed scoundrel. You thought that he was innocent, and all the time he was a wicked wretch. You believed him sincere, while he was in reality a hypocrite. You looked upon him as a Christian, but discovered, to your horror, that he was an unbeliever. But, bless my soul, madam," he continued, looking straight into her face, "what have his antics to do with your becoming a pagan?"

"Don't, I pray you, Doctor, try to come between me and my fatal purposes. It is too late. The poison has been already swallowed; the deadly drug has killed the germ of spiritual life within me; I am a pagan for good and all. You ask what have his antics had to do with my change of belief? It is not his antics that have made me a pagan; but the words, the arguments of one whom I looked up to as a model of truth and discretion—they have driven out of me the

o

spirit of Christianity, and when this spirit was gone, what was to fill my soul but paganism, pure and simple ? "

" I differ from you," said the Doctor. " I think you need not have gone so far at a bound. There is a half-way house here in India, at which you might have stopped on the way from your Christian home—not that I would recommend it in any other form than as a temporary asylum, but if——"

The Doctor's remarks were cut short by a loud knocking at the outer door. He started, looked hard at his companion, and she returned his stare. For the first time they seemed to realize the oddness of the situation. There was O'Dowd, with bare neck and no coat, his shirt-sleeves tucked up, like a porter prepared to lift a sugar barrel or to carry a bale of cotton on his back ; and here was the lady, toothless, hairless, and, in her short skirt, looking like a ballet girl run to seed. The knocking was repeated. What was to be done ? Another loud blow on the bronze, dealt by a strong hand ; and then the bland accents of the Reverend Nethcoff Bingham were heard in the passage, asking for Miss Phlick and expressing a hope that he had not called at too early an hour.

Ada rushed for her teeth, crunched them between her jaws, drew a dress over and about her, and backed upon the door until, with strings, hooks and buttons, she produced the usual effect of cohesion ; but she had not time to touch the curling papers, the result of which was, that her head bore the appearance of a potted pineapple, with the brown and white colours reversed.

O'Dowd looked around him for a mode of exit, and seeing a small door in the wall to his left, drew it back, and precipitated himself through the opening, falling down a few steps into a cellar, into a congeries of household odds and ends, including tin or metal canisters, fire-wood and a large collection of empty bottles, whole or in fragments.

He was on his legs in the twinkling of an eye, had drawn the door to noiselessly, and with his ear to the key-hole waited for the conversation of the desponding lady and her spiritual adviser.

" A hundred thousand apologies," said the Reverend Bingham, not without a ring of pleasantry in his tones, " for having come upon you so suddenly. This Hindu boy of yours muttered some words which I took to be an invitation to enter, for, I assure you, I understand the language of these people very imperfectly."

" I make no stranger of you," said the lady. Besides, as a clergyman, you have a right to call upon every member of your communion at all times."

"But, I can assure you, Miss Phlick,"—looking at her imprisoned tresses—" I make a point of never calling upon a lady, however urgent my business with her may be, even if she be '*in extremis*,' until I have satisfied myself that she has made her toilet as well as surroundings may permit."

" My poor imprisoned ringlets ! " said the lady archly. "Let us suppose that they are flowing freely over my neck. You would not have found me in this state but for the early visit of a friend— I might even say, confidant—who is good enough to advise me sometimes in my money matters."

" A falsehood ! " muttered O'Dowd in the closet —" a wilful perversion ! "

" My dear young lady," said the Rev. Bingham, " my visit is a pastoral call. I have not for some time seen you at church, and this is a spiritually dangerous country."

" Coming to the point," said O'Dowd, under his breath.

" I do not for a moment waver in the hope that you are, in belief, a firm Anglican, and that you rate at their proper value the vagaries of the followers of Buddha and Brahma ; but the pageantry of these Eastern beliefs is, to the newcomer, dazzling, and may—I regret to say, often has cooled the religious fervour of people from the West."

" Buddhism and Brahmanism have nothing in them to attract me," she replied ; " I have not even thought them worthy of a passing glance or a moment's consideration. Indeed, if I were tempted to leave the religion of my youth, I should not stop at them on my way down the hill, I should sink instead into bare paganism."

" She's coming near," said O'Dowd. " If she tells the Reverend Bingham what she told me, he'll have a fit ! "

" There should be no danger," continued the

clergyman, " for a well-instructed Christian, in the glamour of these Eastern superstitions. If you have ceased to attend church, it is not, I am glad to believe, because you are travelling to Benares or Tibet. Now I must touch another point. It is a delicate topic to broach; but as a clergyman, I have a duty to perform. I trust you to give me credit at least for a good intention. You have lately—haven't you?—made the acquaintance of a gentleman dwelling in this neighbourhood, who is commonly said to be an emissary of the Pope?"

"Oh, Lord!" sighed O'Dowd in his closet. "That's me, as I'm a Frenchman."

"I will be candid with you," he continued. "The person I refer to is a certain doctor. He may, or may not, be a successful healer, but I am old-fashioned enough to mistrust the honesty of papists. I prefer a man whose mind shews in his face; and for my medicine I think *aqua distillata* more wholesome than *aqua lustralis.*

"The heathen!" commented the prisoner.

"Is not your language rather strong?" said Miss Phlick with dignity. "It is not generous, it is hardly just, to bring charges against the absent. I confess I have made the acquaintance of Doctor O'Dowd; I am glad to include him in my circle of friends. I don't know whether the Doctor is an agent of the Pope," continued Ada with spirit : "but if he is I think the Pope has chosen a very nice one—there!"

"Well said, Ada!"—in the closet.

"It is in our human nature to cherish our own idol," replied the chaplain, apparently rather nettled, " and I sincerely hope that you may never find reason to regret the confidence you so generously repose in the honour and honesty of this person. For my own part——"

At this moment the conversation was interrupted by a roar of anguish from the cellar.

" My carotid artery is severed ! " proclaimed an agitated voice. " I am bitten through stocking and pant. Poisonous fangs have penetrated the flesh. The virus is running through my system. Help! help ! "

Why he did it was not obvious ; but whether from fear of the snake or because he discerned a similitude to the voice of the man whose reputation he had been engaged in poisoning, certain it is, that Mr. Bingham bolted. Yes, that is the word. He did not retire, he did not withdraw from the room in the manner of visitors, but he ran. He slammed the door behind him, and was already well on the way to his house before his hostess had recovered from the shock of the words.

When presently she recovered, she went anxiously to the closet, and opened the door. Looking in, she saw the Doctor seated on an up-turned tin bucket, nursing his left leg, which was covered with blood, that still flowed from a wound in the calf. His first words surprised her.

" Has he left the house ? " he inquired. " May I come out of this dismal hole ? It is no less than a miracle that I have not been fricasseed by the jagged ends of broken bottles, or my breath taken from me by the choke-damp that fills the place.

I have been breathing through the key-hole for half an hour or more."

" I am so sorry for you," said Miss Phlick in a tone of sympathy. " I was longing for the departure of my tedious and prying visitor ; but, Doctor," she continued anxiously, " what can I do for you ? Is it dangerous ? "

" I hope not," he replied brightening. " I feel that I shall live, if we can only staunch the wound."

" But the snake, dear friend," said she : " the virus —the poison—how can it be driven from the system ? "

" Faith, Madam," it has not entered the system at all. It was a bottle that did it, with the teeth of a cobra on its broken edge, and the shining coat of the same on its round and smooth surface ; but 'twas lucky all the same that I cried out."

" Then fly," said she, "—or rather creep—to the surgery and apply a styptic ; and I will follow you across, when I have made myself presentable."

" Ahem ! " murmured the Doctor as he looked at her retiring figure.

CHAPTER XIX.

THE TRAGEDY OF LITTLE DICKY.

THE native of the New Hebrides, sitting on his upturned boat, consumes with relish his "long-pork" chop. But even this sable epicure would probably reject with repugnance the suggestion to kill and cook a venerable relative. Which is an example of the fact that in everyone, if you search deep enough, you will come upon a conscience.

Infinite are the degrees between the cannibal and the well-instructed Christian ; and between Christian and Christian, too, the difference is enormous. But among those who, in fact as well as in name, accept the Christian revelation, none is to be found who does not venerate the Bible as the word of God, and read with reverence the mystic records of the creation and fall of man, the great tragedy of his redemption, and the assurances of his immortality, fraught with tremendous consequences of joy or sorrow.

Miss Phlick was no saint, but she had been well brought up, and her conscience, at the time of the interview narrated in the last chapter, had suffered a severe shock.

She had heretofore taken for granted all that she had heard in church and at school, or read in her Bible ; and now, for the first time she was told that there is no Providence on earth and no justice in heaven, and this by a lad of blameless life and great ability, and otherwise of charming personality. She felt herself quite overpowered by the sophisms of Little Dicky.

It would be better for her to rise, she thought, and send at once for a friend before the light of reason was put out, or a seizure of some kind stopped the working of her system.

She did so. The friend came. But he was not equal to the occasion ; or, at least, untoward circumstances, as we have seen, prevented his tendering advice : and Ada Phlick, when she passed across the road an hour later in the day, to inquire for the Doctor's wounded limb, was in as parlous a state as when she first summoned him to her house.

" I find *you* better, thank Heaven ! " said she, as she entered his scantily furnished day room ; " but, alas, *I* am still on the downward path."

" Retrace your steps," said O'Dowd. " Have courage : all cannot be lost for you, because a little idiot spouts a stream of nonsense."

" If it be nonsense," said Ada thoughtfully, " but it seems to me dreadfully convincing : I am swept away."

" With the stream," said O'Dowd abstractedly. " If I were you, I would ply the oars against it."

" I am a terribly poor sculler," said Ada dolefully.

" My dear lady," said O'Dowd, " even the babes of Christianity have force in them to grapple with the sceptic, if they have courage and faith. The best thing is not to argue or dispute with him ; let him say what he likes, then out with your *Credo*."

"Like a life-preserver. But, dear Doctor O'Dowd, where can poor weak I find the strength—even if I had heart enough to strike ? "

"In your soul you will find it, as I did, in plenty —buckets full. I make it a point of duty never to allow a profane theory to enter my mind. I know that there are sceptics abroad ; modern society, they say, is full of them ; they assail all the old beliefs and mock all the old moral practices. They hold up for our admiration glowing pictures of the advance of science, and tell us that 'as science clears the way, religion steps aside.' When they talk like that to me, I up with something heavy : I tell them that lunacy was never so prevalent, that idiot asylums overflow, and that common sense is leaving the higher levels, where theorists and dogmatists abide, and making her home among trusting and simple folk."

Ada Phlick looked dissatisfied.

"If Little Dicky," she said plaintively "said to you, as he said to his dog Bounce, 'The God of your belief is not mine, and never will be,'—how would you reply ? "

"Ahem !" said the Doctor, "I'd advise him to have his temperature taken."

"If he said, 'Christian beliefs are no better than bread and butter'?"

"Really," said O'Dowd, "I think I'd whistle and look out of the window."

"And if he said——"

" Pray, don't. If he said another word of that ribald nature, I'd tap him on the nose, and ask him to come on."

" Ah, Doctor," she said, half-smiling, " you are happy, and I almost envy you in your pugilistic confidence. But my mind is of a different temper : I must have argument for argument ; if the reasons of the Unbeliever are to stand, the faith of Ada Phlick must go under."

" How long do you think you'll take to arrive at paganism ? " said O'Dowd.

" Did I not tell you that I have arrived there already ? "

" You did. But your conversation shows that you are only on the way. Step into a Buddhist temple before you go any farther, and amuse yourself by looking at Buddha here, Buddha there, Buddha standing, Buddha sitting, Buddha lying. Bury yourself in flowers and incense ; and before you have risen out of the stupor brought on by the quaint ceremonial, I will be at your side with a plaister that will heal all the wounds inflicted on your soul by the little pagan rascal."

Ada Phlick laughed, but the Doctor's well-meant raillery left her still inquiet.

The Doctor was his old self after two days of treatment, and to celebrate his convalescence donned his gala suit the third day after his mishap, and issued from his house, singing :

> " Comme je suis sorti au clair de la lune,
>   Gai et chantant un chant commun,
>   Qu'est-ce que je verrais, mais un babou brun,
>   Assis sur une grille."

—a translation, as he would lightly say, from the Sanscrit. For, anxious to keep himself *au courant* with the language of his ' mother-land,' he occasionally perpetrated translations into French, such as the above, not always of classical accuracy, but touched with a certain humour, in which the Doctor took a pride, as a *vivacité* derived from his place of birth.

He is remarkably jaunty to-day. It is his desire to let off a ttle of the mirth that is in him, in the French verse, that makes him avoid the streets and people, and pass into the suburbs on leaving his house. But whither is he going? Has he not made a promise to Miss Ada Phlick that he will ' heal the wounds of her soul,' or, in other words, supply her with an antidote against the irritant poison which the Agnosticism of Little Dicky has poured into her system?

Though light in manner, and seemingly forgetful of his promise, the Frenchman has an eye to business. He is going in search of an acquaintance, whom he knows to be read in controversial literature, and able to defend Christianity against the attacks of all comers—Jews, Mohammedans, Buddhists, or Agnostics—and whom he has found on all occasions ready to lend his aid to the side of truth and morality.

He met him after a short time just as he had expected ; for he knew that at a certain hour of the day he walked through the avenues of luxurious growth that run out from the city to the west and north-west, and give shelter from the fierce rays of the afternoon sun.

" As usual, Doctor ; in good humour with yourself and the world ! But why do you expose your precious person to the danger of sunstroke ? " said the new-comer.

" In the cause of chivalry," said the Doctor. " I sometimes feel that I was called by nature to be a Knight Templar, but did not respond, as I should have done ; and now I endeavour to make amends for my cowardice by being the champion of women, whenever I get a chance."

" Is it so ? I give you joy on your calling ; it is a noble one. Would it be impertinent to ask for particulars of the case you have now on hand ? "

" An old maid ! " said the Doctor—" but no, I will not spoil the poetry of my story by introducing it in this way. A girl—no, that is not the term. A matron !—no. A damsel—no—*hé, voyez-vous* (permit me to put it in French), a *demoiselle aînée* has fallen into paganism."

" You don't say so."

" Stop—hear me out. She has collapsed into unbelief, she says ; though I think she is only sliding down the hill towards it. No matter—she is in a sad plight. She has met, or heard of, or read of one Little Dicky, who seems to be a mischievous little ass, who cannot keep his foolishness to himself, but must make to himself a following of weak-kneed bachelors and susceptible old maids. She has listened to his words, and fallen under his influence, and, against her grain and inclination, has been driven from her early faith and forced into unbelief. She is absolutely unable to give any reply to the specious arguments by which he supports his profanity."

" If I mistake not, the lady has been reading ' Friby,' " said Captain Halbot, for it was he.

" Who the deuce is ' Friby ' ? " said O'Dowd.

" Have you not even heard of ' Friby ' ? " asked the officer.

" Bedad, not I ! " said O'Dowd.

" Then you are behind the age," said Halbot.

" I am—I admit it. I have had the realities of life to think of and provide for : a man does not dine off a novel or drink romance.

" True, Doctor," said Halbot, with a touch of pity in his tone. " I should have remembered that you have had to swim against the current. All the same, you have not lost heart, and you will reach the bank by-and-by. 'Friby' is a tale, written by Blanco, the well-known artist. It has had a tremendous run—everyone reads it. Little Dicky is a leading character in the story, and he is made to talk, in a singularly offensive form, the language of the Agnostic."

" May I ask, Captain Halbot, if you have had a tussle with this imp ? Do you feel yourself able to enter the lists with him ? For if you can put him down in argument you might come with me to the modest house of Miss Ada Phlick, the *demoiselle aînée* of whom I spoke, and give her a helping hand—lift her out of the slough and set her up again as a Christian."

" I am in your hands," said Halbot, " but I confess to a feeling of timidity. The lady may not care to discuss her scruples with a stranger."

" No fear," said O'Dowd. " She has no rooted objection to the service, though in these days she is glad to make a friend of a thickish, out-of-shape, little hybrid medicine-man. Come along, and I will present you to her ; afterwards, in conversation, I will find some opening for the subject that now weighs so heavily upon her spirits."

Halbot offered no further opposition, and they went through the shady pathways of the suburbs, towards the house of Miss Phlick. On arriving at the place, O'Dowd entered alone, to prepare the lady for the visit of his friend.

A copy of " Friby " that lay on the table at once provided an opening. Miss Phlick found the passages which were the cause of her trouble, and asked the Doctor to be good enough to read for the stranger the soliloquy of Little Dicky and all that he said for the information and edification of the dog Bounce.

It was not without a struggle that O'Dowd waded through the stuff; and when, after curious comments and many profane expressions, he laid down the book, he professed himself ready to follow Miss Phlick into the land of darkness, if Halbot did not smash to dust the bulwarks of unbelief raised against the ways of Divine Providence.

" Mr. O'Dowd is all the time, like most of his compatriots, an unwavering believer in revelation," said Halbot ; " I therefore brush aside his last remark as dust thrown without the intention of blinding."

" And forget that I was born in the land that gave birth to Voltaire," said the Doctor.

" Forget it, in recalling the fact that you are the present living representative of an old Popish Irish Clan."

" Go on, Captain—put me out of view : I am not for discussion at present."

" It is the Doctor's inborn politeness that spoke in the remark with which he ended his reading," said Miss Phlick, feelingly. " I verily believe that, in his goodness of heart, he would escort me whithersoever I go."

" On with you, Captain Halbot ! " repeated O'Dowd ; " don't mind me : I can take care of myself."

" I feel somewhat embarrassed," said Halbot ; " I don't very well know what I am expected to say. It is a strange position for a man like me to find myself in—the rôle of an apologist of the Christian religion. But if," he continued, with a smile, " our friend believes that I shine in controversy, perhaps you will give me a line."

" Well," said Ada imploringly, " why did Little Dicky call the narratives of the creation of the world, and the flood, and of the sun standing still at the command of Joshua—' *old comic tara-diddles* ? ' "

" Faith ! I can answer that myself," said O'Dowd ; " because he was a scurrilous little scoundrel."

" Pray, don't, Doctor," said Ada pouting, " throw ridicule upon a subject of such vital importance."

" Pshaw ! Of what importance to soul or body,' said O'Dowd, " can be the balderdash this lad talked to his dog ? "

Ada turned to Captain Halbot.

"The Doctor is right," said he; "calling names (as the children say) does not advance a cause: and in controversy on topics bearing on religion or unbelief the practice is a sure sign of weakness."

"And what precisely," said Ada reflectively, "is a taradiddle? It sounds rather scientific—they are always coining new words."

"More likely connected with dancing," said the Doctor; "there is a ring in it which reminds me of a Scotch reel or an Irish jig, and makes me inclined to name the lad that applied it to so sacred a subject, a contemptible little piper."

Ada looked reproachfully at O'Dowd.

"Forgive the learned Æsculapius," said Halbot, "he is dreaming of the tarantella. The word is surely a familiar enough nursery word. Of course no serious person, whatever his views, would apply it to the venerable traditions of the Hebrew people. But I think I must not off-hand attempt to discuss these things. Perhaps when we meet again, if you still find Little Dicky troublesome, I may try to exorcize him."

Ada accepted the suggestion cordially, and Halbot departed with O'Dowd.

CHAPTER XX.

PLACE FOR THE GOOD SAMARITAN.

WHEN the Reverend Nethcoff Bingham had expressed so unfavourable an opinion of our medical friend, more than hinting he was no better than a secret agent of the Pope, he was perfectly aware that the Doctor was listening to him ; for he had caught a glimpse of his notable figure, as it abruptly retreated into the secret chamber of Miss Phlick's domicile.

That evening he dined at the mess, and gave the company a graphic description of all he had seen and heard in Ada's parlour, and a very vivid picture of the lady's head-gear and the Doctor's costume and performance. But when a few days later he came across O'Dowd at the early bazaar, he saluted him with cordiality, as one might salute an acquaintance whom he has not seen for months.

But the Doctor was cool : he had not forgotten, the chaplain's unkind insinuations, and was disposed to have little to say to him in the future. After a few remarks, the parson was turning on his heel, when O'Dowd said pointedly :

"There is an English lady, who is, I presume, a member of your Church, residing near my bungalow. Have you called upon her ? She is alone and needs a friend."

A smile stole over the handsome face of the Reverend Bingham as he replied :

"You give me welcome news. I am always glad to add to the number of my congregation. Pray, what is the name of the lady, and where precisely does she reside ? "

"As if you did not know it already ! Why, bless my soul ! " exclaimed the Doctor, unable to restrain himself, "you were seen going into her apartments last Tuesday forenoon."

"Not seen by you, Doctor," replied his Reverence, equal to the occasion. "I called at your house at twenty minutes after eleven o'clock on that day, and I was told by a coolie, who was standing near your door, that you had rushed across the street half an hour earlier, dressed in a paper cap, a pair of shoes and a bed-gown."

"Blessed is the tongue of the liar ! " said O'Dowd, quoting what he supposed to be a proverb from the Vedas. "How could a man like me, depending for his bread on the public, and debtor alike to Christian and Hindu, appear in the streets like a buffoon in a circus, unless he was mad or drunk."

"I don't venture even to guess : I simply repeat the words of the Indian. I supposed that you had been called in haste, and had not had time to put on your usual out-door dress. I took it for granted that you had been luxuriating in a loose and flimsy garment, and that, in your zeal for a patient, you had spun out of doors regardless of appearance."

"I give you my honour," said the Doctor, "I

wore no bed-gown on the occasion, but a pair of loose white ducks and a jacket. I certainly had on my boots. Not being a paper-maker, I have never used a hat or cap of that material in my life, even in private."

"But the fact remains," said the Reverend Nethcoff, "that you did leave your house hurriedly at eleven o'clock last Tuesday, and remained away from it until one o'clock; from which I infer that you could not have seen me if I had entered Miss Phlick's house any time within an hour before midday."

"Might I not have heard of your being there?"

"Who could tell you?" said Nethcoff. "There was no one abroad in the heat."

"Was not a coolie abroad, by your own admission?"

"Yes; one, I suspect, that was hurriedly summoned by yourself to protect your property while you were away."

"Bother it all!" said the Doctor. "It is a deceptive world—you can trust no one in it. Even those whom you believe to be friendly to you are only too happy to cast a stone at your good name, if they get a chance of doing so out of your hearing."

"Now, Doctor," said Nethcoff, laughing; "in this remark do you refer to me or to the coolie?"

"I will be candid: I refer to you."

"Then in reply," said the parson, "I assure you, on my solemn word of honour, that I never, except in jest, spoke lightly of a friend in his absence."

"Examine your conscience, good Sir," said

O'Dowd ; "and you will find that on one occasion, at least, you suggested unkind suspicions of an absent man with whom you were outwardly on friendly terms."

The Reverend Nethcoff Bingham suddenly resigned his magisterial tone, and looking pleasantly at O'Dowd, asked :

"What the deuce took you into the cellar, Doctor ? "

"What cellar" said O'Dowd in amazement.

" Miss Phlick's cellar : whose else ? "

" I, in Miss Phlick's cellar ? "

" You, amongst the bric-à-brac of that gay closet."

" The D—— ! Pardon me,—— "

" And why, Doctor, were you eavesdropping when a clergyman was speaking to a member of his Church ? "

" Ada, you deceiver ! You betrayed me ! I'll never trust a woman as long as I live ! "

" I assure you, Doctor, that the lady never hinted at your being in the cellar," said the Rev. Nethcoff, " nor, as far as I know, let drop any word from which this fact could be inferred. I have not met her for a length of time."

" Ideas," said O'Dowd, " of length, breadth and thickness are different in different men. What do you call a length of time ? "

" Well, I would say, that five whole days may be fairly so designated."

" You are a clairvoyant then, Bingham ! For if Ada Phlick did not tell you that I lay among the broken bottles and buckets of her recess while you were lecturing her on neglect of her Christian duty, you must have come into knowledge of the fact by magic."

" I heard a faint rolling and rumbling in the cellar all through my interview with the lady."

" I don't know how you could."

" And a roar of pain and anguish at the end of it, that made me decamp."

" A cowardly proceeding on your part ! "

" For I felt sure of the source from which that cry came, and did not wish to compromise the lady by stopping to see the bursting out of a half-dressed man from the hiding place."

" Bah ! " shouted O'Dowd ; " how could you know that I was without a coat or shirt-collar ? "

" I knew it for a certainty."

" You must have seen me retiring."

" Not retiring—diving head-foremost into the well."

" Ada again," said the Doctor. " She let you in of a purpose ; she was backing on the door when I turned to fly."

" And would have covered your retreat effectually, but that I took the liberty of driving in the door—and, I fear, the lady—by a strong push of my shoulder—not knowing, of course, what was there—when the vision of a trussed navvy was presented in all its comic bearings."

" Would you care to know why I was *en deshabille*? "

" No, the coolie explained that sufficiently."

" Enough of this untoward adventure," said the Doctor. " It has, however, a moral : it illustrates the story of the man who fell among robbers."

" Minus the Good Samaritan ! " said Bingham.

" Ada played the part," said O'Dowd.

Having by this time arrived at an understanding, they walked amicably along through the stalls of the early market.

The scene was a lively one, and, for such as saw it for the first time, attractive and picturesque; but for O'Dowd and his companion it had lost the charm of novelty. They looked listlessly at the wares set out for sale. They bowed to an acquaintance now and then, but they did not stop to converse. They laughed lightly at the squeamishness of the worshippers of Brahma, who turned with horror from the side of the market where the flesh of the cow was exhibited.

With a pang, O'Dowd saw attractive baskets of mixed provisions carried off in panniers on the heads of dusky boys, and thought of the skilly and rice, the plain bread and coffee, which made his daily meals at home, and longed for a " pillau " or a " tiffin " of hashed or curried flesh.

The Reverend Nethcoff Bingham stopped before a stall over which a girl presided. She was weaving a coarse texture of hard cords and humming in her throat a gurgling ditty, for her mouth was busy with a cigarette. Addressing her as Seeta, he congratulated her on the joyous freedom with which she set aside the restraints of her pagan superstition. We have already met the girl.

She had been in Europe as an ayah, with an officer's widow, where she imbibed certain notions of liberty ; and after her return to India, had made herself remarkable among the girls of her caste by setting aside or treating with levity many of the proprieties of the Brahmanical religion, which she professed. She even thought seriously of throwing over the worship of Brahma for the Anglican creed, and some time previously had waited on the Rev. Mr. Bingham with a request that he would give her instruction and fix a date for her admission into his Church.

She was a pert and lively thing, neither pretty nor ugly, with an easy, familiar manner. Her reception of the clergyman on this occasion was neither humble nor deferential. She was evidently much taken by his handsome face and figure, and took no pains to conceal the impression they made upon her.

"Behold me," she began: "I am still as free as the birds of the air. You thought you had taken me captive, but I must think long and seriously before I go over to your people. I find that Anglicanism is only a form of Christianity, and not Christianity itself."

"Which," said the Reverend Bingham, "is an objection more specious than solid. Christianity has indeed various forms; but beneath its outward shapes there is essential unity: it is not an abstraction but a reality."

"I can understand," said the girl, "how it is that Christianity must exist in one form; but I cannot see how it can accommodate itself to more forms than one, any more than I could admit that true religion may assume the shape of Brahmanism and Buddhism."

" Well said ! " broke in O'Dowd. " You have put a poser to the parson ! "

" Not so fast, O'Dowd," said Nethcoff, a little nettled. " The girl has only stated a truism. It is, as a matter of course, admitted that if the forms of Christianity were as wide apart as those two leading creeds of the East, they could not each embody the teaching of the Redeemer ; but as the difference in the Christian forms is but trivial, Christianity may reside in any of them."

" What do you say to this ? " said O'Dowd, looking to the girl.

" I have been told," said she, " that the religion of China is not more different from the religion of Persia, than the religion of England is from that of Rome."

" In this you have been misinformed," said the clergyman. " The fundamental tenets of Anglican and Roman Christianity are the same ; but you look in vain for a common basis in the systems of Buddha and Brahma."

" Do they not both demand a faith in a First Principle ? " said the girl firmly.

" And if they do, in a distorted way, what will you make of it ? " asked the clergyman.

Instead of answering the question, the girl continued :

" Do they not both affirm that the soul will never die ? "

" Perhaps so, confusedly," said Bingham.

" And do they not admit of an eternity of woe or joy ? "

" I am not clear on that point."

"And do they not, in common with all the religions of Asia, teach that some actions are right and some wrong?"

"And if I admit all your postulates," said the clergyman, "what will it avail you?"

"You will have admitted," said the girl, adroitly, "that the religions of Asia have a basis of belief in common like the divided branches of Christianity; and," she continued, knitting her brow, "if the religions of Asia, agreeing in so many doctrines, cannot be all true, why should you say that Anglicanism and Catholicity are equally the religion of Christ?"

"Christ," replied Bingham, "is the Head of every sect in Christendom. Not so Buddha. Not so Brahma. They do not claim allegiance outside their respective followings. If Brahma were the god of the Persians, the Chinese, and other nations of the East, they would all represent him equally; but outside the peninsula of India he is repudiated, and regarded as little better than a myth."

The Reverend Bingham was now speaking over the girl's head. His eloquence did not affright her. She repeated again what she had said in substance before—that Anglicanism had no special claim to represent Christianity, in face of the fact that the Roman Catholic was a wider and older Church.

"All the same, it has a certain right to stand sponsor for it," said his Reverence; "and this ought to be enough for you."

"By no means enough," said the girl argumentatively. " It seems to me that if I am to abandon the religion of Brahma for that of Christ, I ought to enrol myself, not in any Christian sect that professes to hold and teach His doctrine, but in that sect in particular which He has appointed to represent His views."

" I agree with you, my girl," said O'Dowd. " You ought to make sure of your foothold before you take a step on slippery ground."

Mr. Bingham seemed to be annoyed again at O'Dowd's obstructive remark, but he bit his lip and remained silent.

The Hindu continued :

" You are, I am sure, Sir, surprised and annoyed at the change that has come over me within a short time. When we met some months ago, I was quite ready to pass to your religion ; I knew no better course to take ; but since then, I have been talking long and often of Christianity, and the result is that I am doubtful as to the form of it that I ought to adopt."

"Some one," said the parson, " has been tampering with you ; some busybody—some mischief-maker —has been trying to hinder you from grasping the fruit that was at your hand."

" I have only talked the matter over with a dear and faithful friend of mine, and received her advice as to the step I was to take."

" And who, my pretty one, is this friend of yours ? " asked Mr. Bingham ; "and on what grounds does she presume to come between a clergyman and one who was on the eve of becoming, by adoption, his spiritual daughter ? "

"She is," said Seeta, "a great lady, owner of extensive estates, and she is as good and true as she is rich. She is wavering as to the truth of Brahmanism, but she has been meeting an instructor, whose views are different from yours."

To create a diversion, Mr. Bingham remarked:

"I was under the impression that the castes among the Hindus are kept so much apart that their members may not converse or even meet."

"But, Sir, Kèsur is of my caste, which is of the highest, though I am poor: and she does not disdain to talk with me, who am in all other respects so much her inferior. She is looked up to with much affection by us all; and her words are wise words."

"Notwithstanding which, she has been a crude reviler of the Anglican Church," said the clergyman, drily.

"I assure you, no," said the girl. "Her language is never even tinged with bitterness: she merely thinks it wise that those who meditate a change from the religion in which they were reared, should put to the test the claims of rival churches which invite them to pass through their doors."

"I cannot linger for the present," said the parson. Another day we will resume this talk. Meanwhile I leave you in the hands of my friend, Doctor O'Dowd, whom you will find to be as learned in theology as in physic."

CHAPTER XXI

AN AGNOSTIC RUN TO EARTH.

WHAT do our sages mean? Whither would they
lead us? Not into the paganism of Nineveh and
Tyre, or into the temple of Isis, or the glorification
of sensuous beauty which was the religion of
Greece, or the confused mysticism of India, or
the prostrate repose of the Buddhistic cult in China
and Japan; but into a land untrodden, unexplored
—where there is no moral discipline, because no
system of eternal reward and punishment; no
supreme judge to deal impartially with immortal
souls, which must give an account of all things
done in the body.

Science, using its admirable discoveries for the
subversion of faith, is a canker that eats into the
heart of society, the destruction of hope and love—
more mischievous than blindness or ignorance.

Captain Halbot was a man of a type not often
met among the combative officers of the British
army. He had been a student for the priesthood
in the "Accademia" in Rome; and his early
training clung to him like a well-fitting garment.

He was surprisingly well-informed, therefore, in
all matters connected with the tradition and history
of the religion he professed; and, whether from his
any visits to the Propaganda College when in

Rome, or the long hours he spent in the Vatican Library, had imbibed a thorough knowledge of the religions of the East—indeed, of all the paganisms of ancient and modern times.

But when O'Dowd asked him to combat off-hand the agnosticism of Miss Ada Phlick, he had shown too much confidence in his preparedness. To meet such an advocate of unbelief as Little Dicky, who disguised his fallacies with words of seeming sincerity and candour, was not the work of the moment. Hence it was that, in his first interview with the distressed lady, Halbot did not enter fully into her difficulties, but reserved for some future occasion a full discussion of the profane monologue addressed by the youth to his dog.

He had made use of the respite to look into the question. He had opened " Friby." He had read the profane passages. He had thought the difficulty out, and he was now prepared, when called upon, to cross swords with the Agnostic.

Miss Ada Phlick had been anxiously expecting him since the day he called upon her with O'Dowd, and he had been putting off his visit to her for one reason or another. But an urgent message from the Doctor summoned him upon a certain day to her house ; whither he went, accompanied by Captain Stokes.

Stokes, who was a graduate of Trinity, Dublin, was in ignorance of the object of this visit, and thought merely of the fun of eliciting the views of an eccentric lady, who had a delusion, a small income, and prospects of a tidy inheritance.

They arrived at the house.

" Miss Phlick at home ? "

" Yes,"—from Jumri, who added confidentially that " he thinks she is either going crazy or is on the way to join the Mussulmans."

She received them pensively, and complained mildly of the long time she had been left to struggle alone with the enemy.

" I will make atonement," Captain Halbot said, " for the time I have kept you in suspense, by entering at once upon the combat with the disturbers of your faith and principles."

" This lady," he added to Captain Stokes, " has been reading ' Friby,' and her convictions have been shaken by the agnosticism of Little Dicky as expressed to his dog Bounce."

" I remember the passages," said Stokes : " they are convincing and misleading at the same time."

" If you said ' misleading ' only, it would be more correct," said Halbot.

" I am not so sure of that," said Stokes. " I think that the argument against the justice of Providence, running through this monologue, might lead a well-read priest astray."

" Just what I have been thinking," interposed Miss Phlick, " and if Little Dicky's shafts might find the way through the armour of a professed theologian, what shield is an unlearned woman to oppose to them ? "

" There," said Halbot, " I must beg to differ from you both. And, in general, it is my firm belief that agnosticism is the outcome of intellectual pride, and that the rank and file of agnostics have more vanity than reason."

" Is not this language too strong, Halbot ? said Stokes. " Surely there are among agnostics plenty of well-stored and highly cultured minds."

" Of course ; but all the same I hold most firmly that the foundations of agnosticism are laid in pride and self-conceit."

" Agnosticism is so much the fashion at the present day," said Stokes.

" So is moral degeneracy," said Halbot.

" And," continued Stokes, " if it be the philosophy of the navvy, who crunches his bread and cheese on the road-side, of the merchant in his office, of the professor in his study, and often even of the fresh, wholesome-minded girl, it must have in it something that makes a wide appeal to human nature."

" Pardon me," said Halbot; " say to human depravity ; it will be nearer the truth. Human nature, unspoilt, does not rise in rebellion against a religion that has raised the world's standard of love and purity. But to come to Little Dicky's complaints of the ways of Providence. Here, Miss Phlick, is one of the passages you marked, page 134—' It is very wicked and most immoral,' it begins ' to believe——"

" That is it," said Miss Phlick.

" The speaker goes on," continued Halbot, " to suggest that ' the Unseen Immensity made us for a freak, designed us for a fall, turned us adrift, and damned us from the beginning—keeping in reserve for us a hideous hell if we are bad, and a tiresome heaven if we are good, and meanwhile watching our movements through every keyhole, and taking account of our smallest shortcomings.'"

"Well, after all, that is very like what the Bible teaches."

"Surely not," said the Captain. "You have read the Bible to little purpose if you allow that to represent its doctrine. This is a mere caricature —and a very dull one."

"Well, Captain Halbot," said Ada, "it is all very well for you to pooh-pooh it; but, seriously, why were we not so made that we could not sin? And why has Providence, if it be good, exposed us to the danger of falling into hell?"

"Well," said Halbot, "I will give you as well as I can the explanation of the schools:—'Existence' is God's free gift. He need not have created man. The world might have been left as it was at the end of the fifth day. But if having chosen to create man, God had denied him liberty of will, or had bestowed upon him free will but not the power of using it, man indeed would have been unable to do evil, but equally unable to achieve moral righteousness. Man, therefore, endowed with reason, would still, without free will be something less than man. So, also, if instead of an immortal soul he were a mere ephemeral creature, his spirit would be mortal like an ape's.

"Man, being an immortal soul, must be created for an end; which end, as Aristotle, by the unaided light of reason, rightly discerned, is Happiness. And happiness must be defined in relation to his nature as a free moral being. It could not be a temporal happiness: that would not be in proportion to the wants of an immortal soul. It must, then, be eternal, and might be of two kinds: it might arise either from enjoyment of creatures or from enjoyment of the Creator. It is revealed that nothing less than the latter is the destined end of man.

" If he miss this, it will be through his own fault, for God gives to every man grace sufficient for him. To some He gives more, to others less; to all He gives enough. On many, He bestows it in mysterious ways, not manifest to the on-looker. There are men and nations whom He seems to forget in his distribution. Does He leave them, like unbaptized infants, in Dante's first circle ?

" Whether God scatters his gifts among men with a liberal or sparing hand, man's responsibility is proportioned to what he has received. The degree of responsibility grows steadily through life with every new gift of grace. From no two individuals is the same debt due. The waif of the slum, who has never heard the name of God pronounced, except in blasphemy, whose ears have been defiled by cursing and foul talk, and whose heart has grown callous in an atmosphere of vice and violence, till he has grown up a moral monster and a danger to society, has less responsibility than the cultured and respectable professor, who, born of Christian parents and enjoying a reputation for purity and honest living, has in truth made light of the revealed word, and has undermined Christian beliefs and led a revolt against God. While he dies with a curl on his lip, the outcast of the slums has—who can tell ?—received as the first heavenly gift of his sad life the grace to say from the depths of his heart, 'Lord, be merciful to me, a sinner,' etc. And he has gone down justified to his house rather than the other.

"The day of account is a day so wide and liberal as to make every allowance for poor stumbling humanity. Then the little account of the untaught savage, containing but a few items, may be received and marked 'paid'; and the 'Remember me, Lord, when Thou shalt come into Thy Kingdom' of the home heathen shall out-balance the filthy record of his crimes. Alike the soul that has preserved its purity, and the soul that was ever falling and ever rising again, shall be tenderly judged, and the troubled consciences of some shall rejoice when the ingenuity of Divine mercy shall show how some limited freedom or partial advertence has mitigated the malice of their transgressions.

"For God condemns to endless woe only the wilful sinner—the man, that is, who, knowing the law, is equipped by grace and nature to observe it; who is not dozing or absent-minded, but with full knowledge, and full liberty, and full strength, and full advertence, rebels; who puts aside the Creator, and chooses in his stead some created trifle. Is it possible to deny the justice of condemning such an evil doer to eternal separation from the Infinite Being he has rejected?

"These facts and inferences are not exclusively Christian property : they were, in part, anticipated by the great moralists of antiquity. The infidel of our own day is their principal and most virulent opponent. He will not have a man responsible for the use of his reason to his Maker, but demands freedom from all duty to God, substituting for that some nebulous altruism in which the race, or society, or the 'overman,' takes the place of 'the Eternal, the Immortal, the Invisible.'

" You are, I hope," he continued, turning to Miss Phlick, " now satisfied that a good picture has been daubed over by an unskilled hand in the passages from which we started, but that the picture underneath remains a beautiful work of the Great Master. In modern authors, you must expect to meet with sentiments like these, sometimes expressed in language of satire, sometimes cloaked with the charm of poetry, or the grace of classical prose."

Captain Halbot broke into a little laugh as he concluded. " You will think, Miss Phlick," he said, " that I ought to be wearing a black rather than a scarlet coat. These religious questions carry me away. I do hope that my sermon has not tired you ? "

" No ; I have been pleased—more than pleased. You have made it plain that Providence did not create man 'for a freak,' did not destine him for a fall, but gave him a free will by which he might avoid a fall. If He has created hell, it is for those who will go there by their free choice. If He has His Eye on the works of man, it is with a view to giving a heavenly reward to those that are good. But, " she concluded, in a lighter tone, " I do not quite see but that a city of gold, as heaven is described to be, would become, as time went on, monotonous and tiresome."

" It is not gold, but God, that fills to the brim the cup of everlasting content ! " said the soldier gravely.

CHAPTER XXII.

THE HOLY BIRDS OF INDIA : THE MOTIONS OF THE HEART.

AFTER this visit of Captain Halbot, Miss Phlick found herself at peace ; and now that lady, in the spirit of thanksgiving for her rescue from the hands of Little Dicky, was prepared to put aside the pride of race and colour, and to leave her home on a visit, on equal terms, to a girl whom she had heretofore regarded as an inferior.

We have already had a glance at Miss Ada's toilet, and we shall not again intrude on the privacy of that mysterious and complicated process. Let it suffice for the present that she went in *en deshabille*, and came out from the process robed in light.

The word is appropriate. Dressed fashionably in white, she passed into the street, going in the direction of Kèsur's house, and her face bore traces of the powder-puff.

She met no acquaintance on the way, nor did she take much heed of the crowd that passed her by. At Kèsur's door Gunga received her.

" Kèsur is feeding birds," said the little maid ; " but you won't mind : they are nice little things and very friendly."

Ada pouted. She hated pets ; she would not

suffer the atmosphere of her rooms to be polluted by so much as a butterfly.

"I shall call later in the day," said she, "when these things have taken flight. They are in their place outside the house; I never allow them to enter my windows."

"They are always here," said Gunga: "in and out, as they please. If you wish to see Kèsur in her own house, you will never find her without the holy birds."

"Holy!" said Ada. "Don't say 'holy,' girl! No living thing can be holy that is not rational."

"The birds of India *are* holy," said the girl, "and the cows and all the animals. They may be out-caste with you, but in Hindustan every native house is open to them."

"More is the pity!" said the Englishwoman. "Air cannot be pure, nor the carpets free from dust and vermin, where these intruders are allowed to enter."

"Shall I tell my mistress that you are here?" asked Gunga, who appeared to be annoyed at the attack on the birds.

"Yes; and please add that, if she is now too busy to receive me, I will call upon her again later in the day."

Kèsur did not wait for Miss Phlick to enter, but came out to receive and conduct her into the house. Her reception of the English lady was kind and friendly. But Ada's face fell, and her nose rose in rebellion against the state of things that she saw on entering the room. Right before her, on guard, as it seemed, strutted a large and soldier-like bird. He seemed to salute her as she passed in, and moved on by her side until she took a seat, when he turned majestically and walked back to the spot on which he stood before. Seeing an expression of surprise and alarm on Ada's feature, the Hindu laughingly said :

"This is my master of ceremonies: 'the Adjutant,' we call him. He is a kind of heron, that courts the society of man, and is a terror to noxious things, such as lizards, toads and serpents ; he devours them in quantities."

"I should have thought," said Ada, "that the grove where reptiles abound should be his home, or the banks of the river where frogs may be had for the searching."

"He will not remain in those haunts," replied Kèsur. "Poor argill! Come, you can see he is a sociable bird,"—patting his head ;—" he is loving and faithful, and would, I feel sure, protect me from aggression, and, if need were, die in my defence."

Ada looked unconvinced.

"And these other smaller pets," the Indian lady continued, pointing to minnows, kites and sparrows that were hopping about the floor, " are they not nice company for a lone girl ? "

"To me, they would be unbearable pests," said Ada.

"Surely not," said the Hindu. "Habit would make them dear to you. You would revel in their little pranks and soften to their loving approaches ; their pleasant chirping would be music to your ear."

She made a sweeping gesture, whereupon all

the birds flew around her, and perched, some on her shoulders, others on her outstretched arms or on her head : one tiny thing lighted on the bridge of her nose. The last performance Ada resented. She rose to depart, leaving untold the story of Halbot's visit, which she knew would give much pleasure to Kèsur. But the Hindu, divining the cause of her hurry, clapped her hands together ; whereupon all the smaller birds flew out through the open windows and the argill stalked solemnly out of the room.

"You will not leave me so soon," said Kèsur, "now that the pets are gone. Those sacred birds ! Ah, if you could understand how dear they are to Vishnu ! But you don't like them. You have not, perhaps, been long enough in India for that : their company would while away an hour agreeably for you, who, living alone like me, must have many wearisome days."

"Our ideas are different," said Miss Phlick ; "our tastes have little in common. Our hearts may, I admit, respond to the same note, for we are alike human : but these common birds as pets !"—with a lift of the nose—"if you made nightingales your companions, or even canaries, but——"

"Well, let them be for the present," said Kèsur courteously. "I may bring you to love the bird as a favourite of heaven, apart from his colour and music. Let us talk on some other subject."

"It was not of birds that I called to speak to you to-day," said Miss Phlick ; "but to tell you of my escape from a great calamity, through the intervention of your friend, Captain Halbot."

" You have seen him ? " inquired Kèsur, eagerly.

" And enjoyed a most interesting conversation with him for some hours," replied Miss Phlick.

" He is bright and clever, isn't he ? " said Kèsur.

" Yes ! " rejoined her companion ; " and he has read so much ? "

" Did you talk about religion ? "

" Yes !—and irreligion," said Ada.

" But surely not in praise of it ? " queried Kèsur anxiously.

" No. He is a strong believer and a good man."

" Isn't he handsome, too, and manly ; and so chivalrous and gay," cried Kèsur with enthusiasm.

" I was so taken up with his words that I forgot his face and figure."

Kèsur sighed. " I must confess," said she, " that in my only talk with him, which was quite accidental, his words fell like music on my ear, while his presence and manners made me tremble."

" You were not afraid of him ? " said Miss Phlick.

" It was not the tremor of fear, but a thrill of interest that I could not control."

" I wonder whether you tried very hard ? " said Ada archly.

" Indeed, I did," said Kèsur. " Why should I give away my heart without a struggle to one who would set no value on its vain throbbings ? "

" How sensible you are, Kèsur ! You are a model

and an example to many girls—who thoughtlessly squander their affections on men who don't care for them." Becoming confidential? "Dear Kèsur," she continued, "I called to talk to you on my escape from Agnosticism, but I think this is much more interesting. Let us have a nice cosy chat."

"I don't think I quite understand," said Kèsur.

"Oh, but you must—any girl would. Tell me all about Captain Halbot. You are in love with him—you know you are."

"I cannot say that I am in love," said the Hindu, simply. "I admire Captain Halbot, and his image comes before me rising and lying down. I can hear the echoes of his voice as if he had just spoken, and I see him driving off the man who was springing upon me like a leopard, and I murmur his name. That is all."

"Is this the love of an Eastern girl?" said Ada.

"Call it love, if you will," said Kèsur; "I call it gratitude and admiration."

"You heartless little pigeon!" said Miss Ada Phlick. "I thought that the children of this sunny land were more ardent; but there is no impulse where there is no freedom."

"I am not one of the enslaved, Miss Phlick!" said Kèsur, "and now that I have dismissed my Mohammedan lover, I shall never marry unless on equal terms with the man of my choice. But Captain Halbot I cannot aspire to ; he must be to me a dream in the present, and in after years a memory."

" How unpractical ! " said Ada. " It is not so
that we manage our love affairs. If we give our
hearts, we expect a heart in return."

The Hindu girl did not at once reply ; but
when she spoke it was in a tone of cheerfulness.

" I have told you of my romance," said she,
" and now I expect your confidence. You have
an admirer, I feel sure, who woos you and has
given you proof of his liking. I think I already
know him, for I am not blind, but I shall not
venture to pronounce his name unless you give
me permission."

" It is but a short name, and a homely one,"
said Ada Phlick. " Let it be understood. We
can talk of the bearer of it with less reserve and
without a blush."

" It is a harmonious name," said the Hindu,
" and it sounds of high birth and good breeding."

" You think so," said Ada, " because it is not
familiar to you. In the British Isles, the name
of my lover would not be counted distinguished."

" I have heard many British names," said Kèsur,
" but few that impressed me so much as that of
the man of whom we speak."

" What's in a name ? " said Ada Phlick. " It
is not the name that makes the man, but the man
that ennobles the name."

" But if the name and the man be equally noble,
how happy for the admirer of both ! '

" True ! " said Ada, tenderly—" quite true ! You
are a sweet girl, Kèsur ! "

" The tall lithe figure and the aristocratic name
match each other," said Kèsur.

"Do you think him tall? I should have said of middle height," said Ada.

"He is as tall as a Sikh," said Kèsur.

"Hardly," said Ada, in some surprise.

"And so well proportioned!" said the Hindu.

"Is he not a little too stout?" said Ada.

"Not to my taste," said Kesur.

"I have confidence in your taste," said Miss Phlick.

"Because you know I am not an interested party."

"Yes, and because in this lightly-clad community you learn to judge," said Ada.

"But they are so slender," said Kèsur; "living, as they do, on rice and vegetables."

"Well," said Ada Phlick, "the man to whom I have given my affections has been, I fear, living much on slops, and it is not from high living that he is so well filled out."

"He is," said the Hindu, "however fed, a figure for the sculptor to take as a model."

Ada Phlick was a trifle bewildered.

"He is not young," she said hesitating; "but for a man of his age he is well preserved."

"I begin to see through your remarks," said Kèsur: "you are fishing for compliments for this friend of yours. Notwithstanding, I will be outspoken. Your lover is, in my judgment, quite as young, if not a little younger, than yourself, and surely you are not old."

"You are paying me a 'Jumri' sort of compliment. My bright boy has told me that I am as old as my chosen one, and that he is as old as Buddha 'a'most.'"

"I should have thought," said Kèsur, "that you were in every respect well matched; even in religious profession you do not differ."

"You think so, because all forms of Christianity are for you the same. Ah, that I could convert him to my views!"

"Are you not of the same sect?" said Kèsur.

"Would that we were!" said Miss Phlick.

"He visits you to speak on religion, does he not?"

"Hardly of religion: he is not much on that line. He has visited me very seldom, and then his talk was frivolous!"

"I could perceive," said Kèsur, "that he is of a very bright and cheerful disposition. I now confess to you, for the first time, that he paid me a visit some weeks ago, and amused me very much by his playful and wise conversation."

"I knew that he called upon you, and was well received: he could not, if he had tried, have concealed it from me. I know all his movements," said Ada.

"Pity you do not attend his church," said Kèsur; "it is there that you would find him in his best form."

"To whom do you allude?" inquired Ada, at last grown suspicious.

"The Reverend Nethcoff Bingham," said Kèsur.

"I feared that there was a mistake somewhere," said Miss Ada Phlick.

"And is there?" said Kèsur. "Am I wrong in believing that he is the man of your choice?"

"You jest surely, or you are amusing yourself

at my cost. I could never love a clergyman—
with his stiff collar, his black clothes and his
sanctimonious tone. He would take away my
spirits, or give me the blues."

" You were so gracious to him in my presence,"
said Kèsur.

" As my adviser in matters spiritual," said Ada
Phlick.

" If he be not your chosen one, do let me into
your secret."

"Not for worlds, now," said Ada Phlick.

"Never mind," said the Hindu slily. " I will
trace your lover through a common friend."

" If you can," said Ada.

" And I am sure I can, for he is a newsmonger,
and generous of his information."

" Who may he be ? Do tell me, Kèsur."

" Only my physician, Doctor O'Dowd."

CHAPTER XXIII.

HOW THE DRUG-SHOP WAS REPLENISHED.

O'DOWD had been often invited to dine at the mess of the 4th Duffs; he had refused, but without giving any reason.

A letter from the Colonel, a verbal invitation from the Major, a deputation from the Subalterns, all had been received with courtesy; but the bidding was still declined.

Skirmishing parties crossed from Fort William to take him by surprise, and wring consent from him—in vain! Like an oyster, the more he was tickled, the tighter he jammed his shell.

He was grateful, profoundly so, for the attention of the warriors. He was sorry that he could not meet their wishes. He loved their society. He was nowhere so much at home as when with them, but——

Halbot was his favourite, possibly because the Englishman was, in manner, the opposite of himself. They met, smoked, and talked much; but even Halbot was not made aware of the cause that kept him from the mess, until one day, finding him unusually confidential, he drew it from him by a direct question.

"Tell me," said he, "Doctor O'Dowd, why is it that you will not come to our mess?"

Ahem!"—the Doctor, hesitated; "*pour vous dire vrai*, the sun of India has spoilt my wardrobe, which at this moment contains but two threadbare coats. One of them is as gloomy as a funeral pall, and the other as faded as a girl of fif—— ahem!"

"Graphic!" said Halbot, smiling. "Is this candour French? Once before, Doctor, I ventured to offer myself as your banker. May I venture to do so once more, at least to the extent of a new outfit?"

"Thanks innumerable! I prefer to wait on fortune. I would be now well above my calls, but for the attentions of a rogue, who helped himself to a large sum which I had put away in my belt on the day I left Southampton for this country."

"How much precisely did you lose?" demanded Halbot.

"Two hundred pounds," said O'Dowd.

"To get at your belt, he must have attacked you."

"No—I was the aggressor: I put temptation in the man's way, by hanging a coat, to which I had transferred the coin, on a hook in an open cabin."

"Marvellous!" said Halbot, who seemed to be following a clue. "Did your suspicions fall on any one?"

"Not on any one in particular. I thought that the thief might be one of the cabin servants, and I did not wish to involve myself in the risk of making a general charge against a respectable body of men such as they; so I ate my garlic in silence, and did not even mention the loss to the officers of the ship or the passengers."

" When did you miss the money ? " asked Halbot.

" It was taken during the night," said the Doctor. " I realized my loss in the morning."

" Was it taken early on the voyage ? " inquired Halbot.

" No, we had been twelve days at sea before I missed it."

" Could it, by any possibility, have been stolen a week or even some days before you became aware of the theft ? " demanded the soldier.

" No, I took the money from a pocket the day before it disappeared, counted it, and found that it was all there," said O'Dowd.

" Excuse my prying so much into the details of this theft : I have an object in doing so. Look upon me, for the moment, as a detective officer trying to trace a fraud. May I ask you—it will be my last question—if you made the acquaintance of any stranger on that voyage ? "

" I did—of a good-natured fellow who was bound for the gold-diggings at the Cape."

" This suggests to me one more question. Have you an impression as to the day of the month on which the money was taken ? "

" It was on the 21st of March, the night before we cast anchor in the harbour of Capetown."

" Allow me to put together in my own way the information you have given me, and to submit it for your correction. You were robbed of a sum of two hundred pounds at sea, on a voyage by steamer, from Southampton to the Cape of Good Hope. The money was taken during the night; you missed it on the morning following. The theft took place in a cabin in which you were sleeping; you had no suspicion of the perpetrator of it; you made no inquiry about it on board, and no complaint to the officers of the ship. The date of your loss you fix as the 21st of March, the night before you entered the harbour of Capetown. Are these items correct?"

"Perfectly correct," said O'Dowd; "and it just occurs to me to add, that the name of the steamship was the 'Ganges,' and the name of the Captain was 'Bowles'; and that we left Southampton Water in February, two years ago."

"I will say to you, Mr. O'Dowd, pending the arrival of our common friend, Captain Stokes, who has, as lawyers would put it, the carriage of this case, that I believe you are in luck, and that your lost money has been traced and will be given back to you unconditionally and undiminished, within a short time. It will be only necessary for you to tell my brother officer what you have told me, without taking from or adding to the narrative."

"I have had a feeling for some time," said the Doctor, "that something would turn up for me, and it was the strength of this presentiment that kept me from an act——ahem!"

"I should regret very much to think that you contemplated self-destruction," said Halbot.

"The immolation of O'Dowd!" he replied. "I all but resolved on it, Sir!"

"Not deterred as a Christian by the enormity of the crime?"

"No, Captain Halbot. The hurt would not have been to heaven or earth, but to Septimus O'Dowd only."

"I am not quite with you," said Halbot.

"No wonder!" said O'Dowd; "but you would be if you had been a witness to the kindness of a fair lady, living not far away, who has been very gracious to me since she came into this neighbourhood. Bedad, Sir, I was near offering to share my poverty with her."

"Don't tell me the name of the lady," said Halbot.

"Why not?" said the Doctor. "You guess it, if I mistake not, already. Phlick is her name, Ada Phlick, to whom you gave your lecture on Christian evidences. That she would take me for her lord and master even my modesty cannot doubt. My own attitude is less forward."

"Miss Phlick," said Halbot, "seemed to me a woman of some principle and of amiable temper."

"And," said O'Dowd, "of very kind and generous impulses. I give her credit for all womanly qualities, including a desire to consort for life with an eligible partner. But, hang it all! I dislike her taste. Would any woman with an eye for proportion look a second time at such a——a pigmy as your humble servant?"

"Your objection to Miss Phlick seems to arise from the fact that she has shown a liking for you. I believe that her having too frankly shown her liking for you is the one principal obstacle to your union with her."

" No, Captain ! Your inference is not quite justified by any words that have fallen from me. If a woman with a nose of ordinary dimensions had taken to blushing and bridling, I might have borne it with patience, perhaps even have returned it—even though I could not approve her taste."

" Well, then, it seems," rejoined Halbot, " that your objection to the lady is rather of a whimsical character. Her nose is large, I admit, but her other features are regular ; her figure is correct and her disposition is kindly. If you are in the matrimonial market, Doctor, you will hardly do better ; for I must confess the justice of what you have said of your physical self : you are a man of years, and a little tarnished by the hand of time."

" I am glad that we have turned this subject over and seen it in different lights, for who knows but some day I may be forced to come to a decision upon it abruptly, without getting time to balance the nose against the pose. I fully agree with what you have said. Miss Ada Phlick even with the appendage, is too good and nice for me ; and yet, I tell you candidly, I am not likely to propose marriage to her while I retain my proper senses."

" I now go," said Halbot, " to search for Captain Stokes, who may or may not be in barracks ; he and Major Staples, who are close friends, are often away when off duty. It might be as well if you were to remain in or near your house for a few hours, on the chance of receiving a visit. I believe and hope that it will be agreeable to you."

O'Dowd, left alone in the society of his drugs and bottles, became speculative, and, for the first time since he lost his money, suspicious of a fellow passenger. His suspicions, however, did not fall on the man who had stolen it, but on a red-haired, ferocious German, who had occupied the berth over his own in the cabin.

His meditation was cut short by the arrival of Captain Stokes, who came to look into O'Dowd's claim to the stolen money. From what Halbot had told him he believed that O'Dowd was the owner, and his last lingering doubt was removed by the Doctor's full and straightforward statement.

"What a simple man you are, O'Dowd!" said the soldier. "If you had made a complaint to the Captain the morning after the robbery, you would have had your money in your belt long before the end of the voyage."

"It was a piece of strategy on my part," replied the Doctor. "I waited on fortune and she was true to me."

"Your tactics were peculiar," said Stokes; "would any sane man, I ask you, expect to recover stolen money unless he took means to trace it to a thief?"

"I have not moved through life on the lines of worldly prudence at all times," said O'Dowd. "I have had a way of my own that I followed, for whim sometimes, oftener to avoid trouble."

"What trouble would it have given you to make a simple statement of the loss?"

"It would have been," said O'Dowd, " like casting a shell into the middle of the ship's company. Suspicion would have fallen on every side: the innocent and the guilty would have been confounded, and many a fair reputation might have been wrecked. The guilty party would have slipped my money over the side of the vessel; and while my loss would have been irretrievable, my story would have been only half believed."

Stokes nodded his head several times, as he weighed the Doctor's words, but he did not reply until he had thoroughly considered them.

" If your object in keeping it dark was to search for threads of evidence noiselessly, you were walking in the way of our best detectives."

"That is as it may be," said O'Dowd; "you are, I think, giving me credit for an amount of shrewdness to which I cannot lay claim; but clever or stupid, my plan has succeeded, it would appear, in bringing the offender to terms."

"I hope to have your money within a month," said Stokes. "When I touch it, I will send for you."

They parted. The Doctor was amazed at his good luck. "That a robber should offer evidence against himself was a subject for romance! What a story could be woven around it! If he knew what a poor duffer I have been," he reflected; "if he knew the depths to which I have had to descend to keep myself afloat! One would be inclined to think that he was a frequent visitor to the drug store, and on friendly terms with the empty bottles! It comes to this : there are men who steal by design and others who steal by accident. Accidents will happen! Hang it all! Sure I was born by accident myself!"

The chemist's store was presently seen to wash its face, as it were, and put on a gala dress. All the dust and dross that had been accumulating upon it and sinking into its crevices, began, after a stout resistance, to give way before a coolie's brush and bucket. Cranks and crannies in the walls were filled in with stucco. The sign-board was taken down to be re-lettered ; but somehow the Doctor was so pleased with the mutilated " D " that he gave orders to have it retained and even improved into an unequivocal " F " and the little " h " to be enlarged.

Mysterious boxes came to the door, and were allowed to remain on the threshold unopened for some days. Jars of a gigantic size, encased in wicker-work, were taken from cars and laid down by the boxes. A furniture van was pulled up in front, and gave out its contents in the form of a cullender, a coal-scuttle, a frying-pan, a dresser, stools, a fender, and a kitchen table.

The Doctor was determined to make a good use of his recovered wealth, and now or never to make his business pay.

A large quantity of water from the Ganges was run in somewhat mysteriously, to reappear in in a day or two in the forms of " aqua pura," " aqua frigida," " aqua calida," " aqua rara," that might be used for outward or inward application, according to the whim of the customer, without doing the slightest mischief to body or soul.

Mysterious sounds came from the store. Now it was the chopping of some hard substance ; now it was a grinding of pebbly ingredients ; now the saw was at work, now the pestle. The outer door was kept closed, but anyone looking into the store from the living room behind might see a stout man enveloped in a voluminous grey apron, with bare arms, as busy as a bee, storing in crocks and bottles against the ills of life, sweet and bitter essences, mild and pungent extracts, with compounds innumerable, to be wrought into medicines by the skill of a practised hand.

O'Dowd was in his glory.

"Now or never!" said he ; " my last effort to wake up this drowsy city to a sense of its folly in neglecting to take the advice of one of the most eminent—ahem !" he added, by way of finish to the sentence. " Brahmans and Buddhists and Baboos and Boobies—my hand to you. If I catch any of these worthies coming to my store for medicine or consultation, I'll give him a dose that he won't forget to the day of his death ! My day has come at length."

"You are going into a new dress, Doctor," said Stokes, as he entered the drug-store a few weeks later, bringing with him the money that had been stolen. "You must have a generous credit in the town to be able to effect so much without capital."

" I am going into a dress coat and its trimmings,

as I am pressed to dine at your mess, and have heretofore declined the invitation on account of the defective state of my wardrobe. As to those adjuncts to the store, they are mere trifles."

"In your eyes—not in those of an observant public."

"If the public would look behind the scenes— but I must not betray professional secrets. Bulk, Sir, and worth are different things. The drugs, as raw material, are mere straw; it is the touch of the alchemist that turns them to gold."

"And you are the alchemist?" said Stokes.

"That is understood," replied O'Dowd; "and in truth, Captain, I should require to be one, to prepare these medicines for the Indian stomach."

"You find the constitutions of these people different from those of Europeans, I dare say?"

"Different! You may as well apply a blister that would tease and burn the flesh of a European to a mahogany table as to one of these dark people; and the Eurasians are not much better!"

"Oh, Doctor! The Hindus—the gentle race among whom you have found your greatest friend!"

"Don't think I mean to speak unkindly of them," rejoined the Doctor; "for the sake of one, at least, I am bound to treat them gently."

"Our next meeting will be at mess," said Stokes, as he rose to go.

CHAPTER XXIV.

THE DOCTOR DINES AT FORT WILLIAM AND MAKES A SPEECH.

THE Doctor's first act after receiving his lost money was to call upon a fashionable tailor and give orders for a brand-new suit of clothes of the latest fashion. And his second act, worth recording, was to sit down opposite a dim, cracked and patchy little mirror, looking piecemeal at himself, encased in these habiliments.

If he could but have taken in the whole figure together! But a disjointed trunk, disconnected legs, and above all, what he quaintly named the 'burst,' seen by halves, were not reassuring ; and without a little vanity and the self-satisfaction springing from it, he would be nowhere among the smart men at the mess-table the next day.

He looked serious and sighed. He was tired by his efforts to focus the whole picture.

"Still," said he aloud, "the clothes are not, as I can see them, baggy, owing, I daresay, to the symmetry——ahem ! "

For a moment he thought of crossing the street and bringing himself under the critical eyes of Ada Phlick ; but he refrained.

Our readers will already have taken note of the Doctor's manners and antecedents. He was not a refined man, in the sense in which the epithet is applied to many inane drawlers of the present day—he was not a " society " man. A country doctor in Ireland, with a small income and a large family, is scarcely looked at outside the circles that his professional duties touch. He was only a middle-class Irishman of the old school, with possibly some good blood in his veins and the instincts that follow good breeding, however remote ; but his native wit, his good-natured disposition, his tenderness for those in pain or trouble, his genial uprightness, made ample compensation for defects which, if many, were only surface-deep.

He was not conscious of a kind of fascination that drew others towards him ; but the 4th Duffs —men of exceptional opportunities—saw in the old Irishman an independent type of manhood, with the freshness of earlier and less conventional times about it, and took to him with a wonderful unanimity of approval.

The scene that met his eye as he entered the mess-room the next day was not of a nature to give him confidence. It was brilliant and dazzling, in striking contrast with the plain equipage of his home.

The uniforms made him dizzy. There were officers in mess-jackets of scarlet, naval men in blue with stiff golden epaulettes, and grandees of the country in the flowing robes of that picturesque Oriental land.

The room was gay with festoons of evergreens mixed with natural flowers, hung upon the walls and around the windows ; beautiful exotics adorned the tables in clumps and tiny sprigs, while orchids in richly enamelled pots occupied the spaces of the room that were outside the track of the waiters.

" Colonel Baily—Doctor O'Dowd ! " said Major Staples. " Doctor O'Dowd — Bomsary Butle-buoy ! " said Captain Stokes. " Captain Uniake—a countryman of yours ! " said Captain Halbot.

O'Dowd was simply amazed at finding himself equal to the occasion : he bowed and smiled—he was neither timid nor embarrassed.

" I salute you all, gentlemen," said he, with a courtly sweep, worthy of a French aristocrat. " I am glad and honoured to make the acquaintance of each and every member of this distinguished company."

" Doctor O'Dowd is of French origin, Colonel Baily," said Captain Stokes, "though he bears an Irish name, and is, I believe, quite at home in the language of both nations."

" A member, I presume," said the Colonel, " of one of those families who sought refuge abroad at the time of the Revolution ? "

" No, Colonel," said the Doctor ; " I was born quite accidentally in France."

" By Jove ! " said Major Staples ; " I thought we were all born by design ! "

" I take it that this gentleman's mother was passing through France when the event took place unexpectedly," said the Colonel.

" It was so," said O'Dowd.

" You speak French ? " said the Colonel.

" I lisped it in my infancy," the Doctor replied.

"Where did you take your degree, Doctor?" said Stokes.

"In the hunting field," interposed Major Staples. "Mr. O'Dowd is not one of your quacks who assume, without right, the title of Doctor in Medicine and put the letters 'M.D.' after their names, but a genuine cross-country Irishman, who drops the 'D' for an 'F.'"

"You are enigmatical, Major!" said Colonel Baily. "Pray, what suffix does Mr. O'Dowd assume?"

"'M.F.,' Colonel—'Master of Fox-Hounds,'—slightly abbreviated."

"Is that so, Doctor," said Colonel Baily.

O'Dowd was an indifferent horseman; but the title was an honoured one at home, and he must not refuse it when offered.

"Take it," he said, "on the authority of the Major."

"You were a seventh son, O'Dowd?" said Captain Stokes.

"Not quite," said the Doctor,

"If you were not absolutely the seventh son, why were you named Septimus?"

"A whim of my father's. He was in some ways a strange man: he began everything, even a story, at the wrong end; he thought he would have at the least seven children, all sons; and he intended to name them backwards."

"What an idea!" said Stokes. "Then your youngest brother was named Primus?"

"I had no youngest brother," said the Doctor. "There was only one blossom blown after me, and he was named Octavus by a mistake."

" By Jove! What a family history!" said Major Staples ; " all at sixes and sevens!"

" I must protest against farther questioning," said Colonel Baily. " I invite you, gentlemen, to fill your glasses. I have a health to propose, which, I am sure, you will not dishonour. You anticipate me : it is the health of the guest of this evening, a scion of an ancient race, a member of an honoured profession, a man who is, I am told, as capable in the field as in the cabinet—Doctor Septimus O'Dowd. ' The O'Dowd ' I will take the liberty of naming him, for he is the sole living representative of the chieftain, who, let us say, carried that name to Palestine in the days of the Crusaders." (" Hear, hear!" on all sides.) " I am not a man endowed with descriptive powers: if I were, I would paint our distinguished guest in very bright colours. It would be my wish to do him justice all round, but the task is too great for my powers of conception and expression. I seem to discover in him a type of manhood, very interesting, very fresh, and very different from that to which we Englishmen are accustomed. He seems to me a genuine representative of a race that held its own in wit, music, and book-learning amongst the ancient peoples of the West : and a very distinct charm in Doctor O'Dowd is that he is as genuine and unsophisticated as if he had lived in the age of our George the First instead of that of our reigning Sovereign.

" I ask you to join with me in wishing him length of days, success in his efforts to check the diseases that periodically stalk over this Indian

country, and the results of a successful professional
practice—an honoured old age, surrounded by the
trophies he will have won."

The Colonel sat down and the cheering was loud
and long continued.

O'Dowd rose to return thanks. Placing his
right hand open upon the board and his left under
the tails of his dress coat, he compressed his mouth
and glanced up one side of the table and down the
other. Then he commenced :

" I would be able, under ordinary circumstances,
Colonel Baily and gentlemen, to take a man's part
in what you will allow me to name 'after-dinner
manœuvres ; ' but I confess that I am unnerved—
all but shattered—by the brilliancy of the company
surrounding this board. I am not an orator : I
would probably have been endowed with the gift
of speech, but for an accident which happened at
the time of my birth. But though my lips cannot
give utterance to the sentiments of gratitude with
which my heart overflows for the honourable
position I occupy to-day, in being the guest of a
body of officers who are ornaments to the military
profession generally and to the British Army in
particular, my silence on this head will speak with
the force and volubility of one hundred, or I
would say, double that number of loose and silvery
tongues.

" Gentlemen, you are all, or nearly all, Englishmen : I am a Franco-Irishman. I go, heart and
soul, for the prosperity of the dear little Island,
out of which I was born by a freak of nature ; but
I believe that this prosperity will be attained by

her through incorporation in the Empire on equal terms. My wish is to see the sisters similarly decked, wearing the same boots, hats, coats, gowns, jewellery, with as much coin in the pockets of each as is wanted to provide for all her needs. This is, I believe, the aim of recent legislation; and this is the only method by which the Empire can be knitted together, and its bone and sinew developed for the industrial works of peace, and the fighting operations of war.

"Colonel Baily and Gentlemen, I thank you and I subside."

All this time, champagne of the best brands, followed by Chambertin and El Madeira, had been flowing freely. The Doctor was as an old oak in thirsty ground, which sucks up the moisture about its roots to the increase of its beauty and strength.

He was beaming and blooming when he left the dining-table for the ante-room, but not a shake had been taken out of him; nor was his utterance either thick or impeded.

The ante-room of a military mess is believed by some nervous persons not to be so proper as the mess-room, and for a sufficient reason—the drinks are more decidedly alcoholic.

The Doctor took his brandy and soda, and repeated the dose; which notwithstanding, he was well-balanced on his feet when he started for home just as the clock struck twelve.

He met with no accident on his way, nor any object to arrest his attention, until he arrived under the windows of his friend, Miss Ada Phlick.

S

He looked up ; there was light. He listened ; there was music.

"She's at it," said he. " Shall I steal upon her? She will be delighted to see me—in my robes. And, for all her nose, there are uglier women in the world than Ada Phlick—and less affectionate!"

CHAPTER XXV.

IN THE SPIDER'S WEB.

HE went to her door—knocked. Jumri was inside, asleep; but he started from his slumber at the sound, and stood before the Doctor, blinking and rubbing his eyes.

"I am glad you come!" he said. "She be waking the street up with her music, and keeping Jumri out of bed. Pull the door after you, when you're goin' out—I'm off to my mother."

"Announce me before you go," said the Doctor, so thickly that the boy looked into his face.

"You been dining out," said the bright youth. "May-be drinking Rudletimer (Rudesheimer). You're fluffy."

"What an imp you are, Jumri," said the Doctor. "Tell Miss Phlick that I am here; and then you may go to Jel-e-le-bad, if you are so minded."

The Doctor took Ada's hand when he entered the room, and held it for a long time in his addressing her as 'Miss Phleeky,' and protesting that he had not seen her for an age, and that he had been longing for an opportunity to open his mind to her, on a subject of equal interest to them both. Ada felt that a crisis in her life was coming, and she prepared for it as a woman of spirit. The Doctor went on:

"Long years are past and o'er, since I parted—

—did you ever part, Miss Phleeky, with a toy that you cherished?"

Ada deemed it unnecessary to reply to this irrelevant question.

"*I* did," continued the Doctor. "I parted with my heart's treasure, and since then I have been a lone bird."

He was coming, she thought, to the point.

"I can feel for you," she said. "I, too, have been a solitary. Sit down, Doctor! I pity you."

"You'd weep for me," said O'Dowd, "if you knew all."

"And not to have even a pet dog or a parrot to be fond of you!" said the lady. "Ah, Doctor, but for Jumri, bad as he is, and the piano, I should have long since gone off my head."

"We are so near," sighed the Doctor, "and yet so far."

"It is, I admit," said Ada, "sad to be alone, even with the piano and Jumri."

"Can Jumri, or the piano, or both of them together, fill the heart?" said O'Dowd. "I put it to you as a proposition, and I demand an answer."

"They cannot: I must be candid," said Ada.

"Then if Jumri and the piano cannot fill the heart, what can fill it? There is the poser," said the Doctor.

"Perhaps memories," said Ada discreetly.

"Oh," said O'Dowd. "You surprise me."

"Perhaps hopes and longings!" she added. "You can tell from experience, Doctor; your heart has already overflowed."

" Hopes and longings can never fill the heart of man, nor wallflowers," said the Doctor, decisively.

She looked closely at the man to see if he were all there.

" Nor wallflowers," he repeated. " You look surprised : you are mentally asking yourself, What is a wallflower ? Ah ! is it necessary to explain ? "

" No," said Ada Phlick. " I think I understand."

" You can't but understand," said O'Dowd ; " you would not be a woman if you didn't."

" A wallflower cannot fill the heart," she said, " because it is too young and has too much of the spring of life about it : it is the autumn bloom that can do it."

" The autumn bloom—you are right !" said the Doctor. " The matured fruit ! Would you be disposed to fill a vacancy, dear Miss Phleeky ? "

" In the heart of only one," said she, " in the wide world."

" Is that one, may I ask, near or far away ? " said the Doctor.

" Beyond the seas," said Ada, tentatively.

O'Dowd groaned. " I envy him," said he.

" If you knew him," said Ada, " you wouldn't."

" I wish he were dead," said the Doctor.

" Fie, Doctor !" she said ; " you would not mar my happiness ? "

" I wish he were dead," repeated the Doctor, thickly. " He has no right to be in the way of another."

" Poor dear ! " said she, " he wouldn't hurt a fly."

" But he would, Miss Phleeky!—he'd hurt me. He has hurt me already : he comes between me and the apple of my eye."

After this declaration, Miss Ada Phlick began to think that the Doctor should be in bed, as his mind was evidently astray.

" Go home now, dear Doctor," said she ; " the hours run on, and you require rest. We will renew this dialogue to-morrow, when perhaps we may find a way to remove this obstacle to your happiness."

" To-night or never, Miss Phleeky! Remove him this moment ; put me in his place ; and then I leave you the happiest of men."

" Oh, Doctor ! "—sighing—" it has come upon me so suddenly. I tremble like the leaves of the aspen. Can it be possible that you want a help-mate—you who are so self-contained ? I cannot believe it. I cannot think that one so happy in his isolation is about to throw himself into the tempestuous sea of matrimony."

" All for you ! All for you, Ada ! All for your sweet society ! I'll risk it. Will you take me off the shore into your saving bark, and we will sail together down the river of life ? "

" Could I refuse you, if I would ? "

" Then you are mine ! " said the Doctor, rushing forward and falling into the stove.

She helped him to his feet. He was not embarrassed.

" I was hastening to seize your hand," he said, " for the ratification of the contract, when I lost

my balance.   Let us, Miss Phlick, by anticipation,
' plight our troth.' "

She extended her hand to him ; he took it
and said :

" I, Septimus, take thee, Ada,"—adding : " etc."

" Is all this serious, Doctor ? " said Miss Phlick,
with an eye to business ; " and are you sufficiently
clear to see through the obligation you are con-
tracting ? "

" Dreadfully serious ! " said he.   " Grimly grave !
There may be an opaque corner in the mind still ;
the fumes of a prolonged carouse may not have
gone off entirely ; a little note of warning may
be trying to make itself heard.   Notwithstanding,
being owner of Septimus O'Dowd in *fee*, and
being also, with some slight drawbacks, ' of sound
mind, memory and understanding,' I give him to
you ' to have and to hold, from this day forward,'
etc., and I wish you luck in the possession of such
an old trump."

Ada Phlick thought it useless to continue the
dialogue.   The Doctor was not rising in sense or
wit.   What he had said he could not recall.   She
would hold him to his engagement, and should he
later on, endeavour to retract the words he had
spoken, she could remind him that they had been
repeated after she had warned him of their serious
and binding import.   She bade him a friendly
good-night, and after he was gone, went at once
into bed, but not to sleep.

O'Dowd   went   out,   whistling—the   horrid
practice !—and a little later, as Ada turned on
her pillow, she heard the strains of a song coming

up from the street, under her window. Was it
a serenade? She stole to the casement, pressed
her ear to the glass, and heard:

"Why am I here at so late an hour, singing—
My notes on the night air so recklessly flinging,
  Under the dew?
Reckless of night-birds and gnats that are stinging—
Drops of cold sweat from my tangled hair wringing—
  Ada, for you!"

"Ah! the dear man!" she said, as she turned
from the chilly night.

Was O'Dowd in these silly proceedings a responsible agent? He was not, obviously, as clear as
usual: he was not so cautious and guarded as was
his wont; he had in his manner a fire and a dash
which had left him since he came to India. We
already know that he was on his guard against
the fascinations of Ada Phlick, and that his last
thought would be to ask for her hand, or to take
it if offered to him. Under the influence of a
temporary aberration he had forgotten all his
cautious resolves, and he was now like a large
fish hooked, powerless in the water, waiting for the
gaff and the last strong pull—to be landed, high
and dry, on the bank.

And, be sure, Miss Ada Phlick was not quite
an innocent. She had long cast her line across
the street, and baited it with dainty morsels, and
she had watched her Irish salmon nosing it, and
even nibbling it a little sometimes; but she had
been, up to this night, disappointed, for he had
always sailed away when she thought he was going
to swallow.

Now that she had him hooked at the moment when she least expected it, if he escaped from her it must be by some plot or evil chance entirely out of the common course.

Miss Ada was building castles for hours continuously ; for this night brought her no sleep. Should she go into the surgery, and settle down for life amid the bottles, amid the odours of drugs and scents, some of them sweet and soothing, others suggestive of cuts and bruises and swellings —stealing a glance, through a chink, at the shortcomings of human nature, and listening (by accident) to doleful tales of aching teeth and pinching corns, and stomachs unworked and unworkable ?

Or should she—ah, she would—bring the dear Doctor into her own fragrant little sanctum, as into a villa, a country-house; it would be delightful —a house of business and a home. The former a grimy place, if you will, but a little mine in which nuggets of precious metals may be picked up ; and the other a little palace of light, with pictures, ornaments, soft couches, music, and—she was going to add—Jumri, but she changed it for "a fairy Queen."

In years to come, she might return to Europe, on a visit to relatives ; or she might go home for good, laden with the spoils of the land of gold ; and then—then for the first time, she could present *him* to her friends. Some might turn up their noses, and others turn eyes askance, and a few might have the bad taste to titter, and some brutal girl, through pure jealousy, might say : "You fished for a shining salmon and caught only a skate ; " but her mother—ah !—her sensible mother, if then alive, would take a practical view.

She felt that she was illogical, but she could not help it. Why take him home at all, if he was to form a subject of merriment, nothing more ?

Did she love him ? Well, she had thought up to this time that she did. Now she feared she did not. She had wrestled with him and brought him down ; but now that he was at her feet, she valued him only as a conquest. He had never been handsome ; and he looked particularly ugly when proposing for her hand. She never saw his feet so distinctly as when she was forced to seize upon one of them to pull him out of the fire-place. It was large and misshapen. There was in fact nothing to admire in the outward man : he was a perfect fright in a dress coat, and his patent-leather boot was as big as a coal-box.

But he was her own Doctor all the time. Away with beauty and symmetry ! He was her own witty, quaint, good-natured little jester ; upright and well-principled, who never, she was convinced, had given one fibre of his heart to anyone but herself—was always thinking of her, sighing for her, dreaming of her ! This she was prepared to assert solemnly before a magistrate or a commissioner of oaths.

She would come to love him, if she did not at present : but it would be his mind, his soul, that she would love. Yet she might come in time to admire his roundabout figure, his solemn face, out of which a gleam of fun was ever ready to break—even his little legs! She knew that among dogs certain breeds were valued for their short legs and out-turned paws.

There was a certain appreciation of realities in the wandering thoughts of Miss Ada Phlick that night ; and when she tried to warble, " Ever of thee I fondly am dreaming," the words died on her lips.

As for O'Dowd, he had but a blurred idea of the important step he had taken : nor indeed was he very clear as to the flight of time. He remained for an hour singing under Ada's window, and thought, that if he had had a guitar, or even a banjo, he would have remained there until the dawn. Snatches of " Cooling my fevered brow " came from him, and he gave *fortissimo* the refrain " Ada, where art thou ? "

There were but few passing on the street ; and the Doctor had wit enough to suspend his musical performance every time that he heard footsteps approaching. He was unmolested and unmolesting, until he fell under the eye of a Chinaman, who came rolling out of a night house in the Black quarter, half - recovered from the opium trance. His unfocussed eyes saw in the Doctor a statue of Buddha, and he salaamed profoundly before him.

" Up with you, for a fool," said O'Dowd. " What do you mistake me for ? I'm none of your idols, but a plain Christian man."

The sottish fellow mumbled in Chinese ; and the Doctor understood him to address the word Buddha to himself. He moved away from him, but the man crept after him, always on his knees, and when he came near, bent forward and touched the ground with his head.

"Do you mistake me for a heathen Chinee?" said O'Dowd. "You drunken sot!" moving away again.

"Buddha! Buddha!" said the Celestial, seizing him by the feet and twining his arms around his legs.

"Buddha! Buddha!" repeated the Doctor, in mockery; "take off your hands, or I'll—I'll go for your pigtail."

The fellow ran his hands up the Doctor's legs, endeavouring to fold him in a religious embrace.

"Hands off, you grimy thing!" roared O'Dowd. "Do you mean to sully my——" he tried to say dining-out suit, but in his flurry he let fall the words "bridal robes!"

The Chinaman took no notice, but was sticking to him like a fly-blister, when a policeman came by, and seeing the struggle, seized the assailant by the shoulders and dragged him off, saying to the Doctor:

"This fellow has come out of an opium den: leave him to me. How did you come across him?"

"He mistook me for an idol of his," said the Doctor; "and came licking the ground at my feet. When I spurned his vile flattery, he tried to seize me in his arms."

"To rifle your pockets, Sir!" said the officer, "and then, perhaps, garrote or stab you to escape discovery. You have had a providential escape, for he is a strong brute, with no more conscience than a jackal. Let me have your name and address : I will have him before the magistrate in the morning for assault and intended robbery. The slums shall be, for some months, empty of one night-bird."

The Doctor gave his name and address and turned into his house, struck a light, passed into his bedroom, said a few hasty prayers, thanked God that he was neither Buddha nor a follower of his, and went into bed. He sung in a low voice before he went to sleep :

" It was not for me that I heard the bells ringing ! "

CHAPTER XXVI.

BUZ-BUZ ESCAPES.

HE woke the next morning from a long sleep, in a state of tremor. He had been dreaming a bad dream, in which he was carried through a number of blood - curdling adventures, in swamps and jungles, amid cobras, alligators and panthers, and left swimming over a deep hole near the sea coast, where he was caught from below by an octopus, which closed its tentacles upon him and was drawing him slowly to the bottom.

The hideous monster seemed to have a nose of great length, which came up with the claws, and sniffed at him, and even nibbled him as if with small teeth, and knocked him about as a young cat does a mouse which she plays with before devouring it ; and slowly the waving tentacles relaxed their hold of him, and the water receded from him and left him standing on dry land ; but the nose, which never abandoned him, took up a position in a human face, which he thought was the face of a lady he had met somewhere, though he could not say who she was or think of her but as a stranger.

" Heigh-ho ! " sighed he, as he opened his eyes ; " I must have had an indigestion to dream such a dream ! The viands of that mess dinner and the wines ! "

Memory was beginning to act, and the scenes of

the night before were emerging from a haze, and he seemed to see a connection between his dream and something beside the dinner of the 4th Duffs.

" It was Ada's nose," said he, " and no other, that was my nightmare ; and the claws were Ada's ; and the tightening and the squeezing were hers and the dragging into the depths of the ocean. A miracle — I escaped from her — ahem ! "

When all the mists were gone off bis brain, and he realized the follies of last night's movements, he became the most despondent of men, and angry—very angry—with Miss Ada Phlick for having entrapped him. For what was her action in playing love-tunes on a piano after midnight, but a snare laid to catch a wary old fox !

"Old butterfly that I am !" said he, mixing his metaphors ; " flying and flapping my wings around a light, and not satisfied until I touched it and got singed !"

He left his bed after a while, and dressed carefully, giving more attention than usual to his shaving and general adornment, and then crept noiselessly into the drug store, as if he feared to be observed from the other side of the street. Having locked the outer door he put the key in his pocket, and returned to partake of his breakfast.

Such a desponding man was he that he sighed at intervals during the meal, and so absent-minded that he put a sugar-tongs into his mouth for bread, and swallowed the contents of a mustard-pot, which he poured into his tea.

He had, he felt, put his foot in it and taken a step which must either bring him to a premature decay, or close his career in the capital of India. For Ada Phlick !—he never loved her. How could he, unless he loved her nose, which was impossible? Even if he could find it in his heart to tolerate that monstrous feature, he would not lay down his liberty at her shrine unless forced to it by a sense of honour and a feeling of strict obligation. Here was the point : he had proposed for her hand and been accepted. Was there any door left open through which he might escape from her, without a violation of all the proprieties ?

He could find no answer to this question, though he put it to himself in every form.

" A man who makes an offer of marriage is bound to it in law and honour, if it be accepted. I have offered my hand to Miss Ada Phlick. She has grasped it. Can I withdraw it ? Spider-like, she has been fascinating me with a wicked eye, while weaving a web around me. When I least expected it she sprang upon me, and infused a poison into my frame. Did she give me a fair chance to fight for my liberty—buz, buz, buz— like a captured fly—ahem !"

He dropped out, unobserved, through a door in the back of the house, strolled among trees and trod little pathways, lone and hidden, that ran in curves and zig-zags towards the bank of the great river. Arrived there, he paused, looked round, and satisfying himself that there was no one near or approaching, he beat time with his feet, while he emitted strains of plaintive melody from his throat and lips alternately. This over, he went on, keeping near the Ganges and shunning the society of man. He even turned from the river after a time to find a greater solitude, and wandered through a scrubby waste, becoming always more wild and dangerous, until he arrived at the bank of a creek, where he stopped, and unfolding a parcel that he carried under his arm, took from it an old pair of shoes and laid them down on the bank.

He turned to retrace his steps ; and now his movements became those of a loiterer bent on killing time. He poked at large lizards with his walking-cane ; he trampled small snakes under his big shoes ; he stooped for a handful of stones and took pot-shots at every brilliant bird that passed him on the wing ; he gathered bunches of wild flowers, to look at them, smell, and throw them away ; finally, he took a seat on a jutting rock and fell into deep meditation. But strange! his thoughts were not of Ada Phlick or of his entanglement with that lady, but of a loved one gone for ever, and of dear old times in the distant past—of a little sylvan cottage buried in creepers, where birds sang all day, from early morning in spring, though their colours were dark and sombre ; where wildflowers, of less pretensions than those around him, perfumed the air ; and of the prattle and laughter of little ones that rippled through the shrubs and hedges, and of the love and union that breathed in the atmosphere of the place.

He thought of the trials of that remote time, too, of the narrow income and the want of many

T

comforts ; and then a sweet and patient face, always lit up with a bright and cheering smile, came before him ; and he could have cried like a child in the presence of that vision of bygone days.

As it was, he looked very sad and was sinking every moment deeper into despondency, when the sound of familiar voices approaching struck his ear. The speakers were hidden by a natural hedge of low mulberries, and talked loudly, not suspecting that there could be an eavesdropper in such a lonely place. The voices were those of Staples, Halbot and Bingham.

"I have it," said the parson, "on the authority of her Hindu boy."

"By Jove!" said the Major ; "hooked at last!"

"I know, as a matter of fact," said Halbot, "that O'Dowd did not—could not—love the woman."

"Then," said Staples, "he must have seen double when he proposed for her hand."

"Did you observe him as he left the mess? said Halbot.

"Yes," said Staples, "and put him on his way home."

"Was he excited ?"

"I would rather say 'exhilarated' from champagne."

"Was he," interposed Nethcoff Bingham, "capable of taking care of himself when you left him ?"

"And of another," replied the Major, "as the event proves."

"No badinage, Major, pray," said the Reverend Bingham ; "I have a motive in asking if O'Dowd was a responsible agent when he left your mess. Miss Phlick's boy asserts that he was 'fluffy' when he arrived at that lady's door."

"He was, I should say, clouded to some extent," said Staples.

"I can fully accept Major Staple's pronouncement," said Halbot. "If O'Dowd was mentally clear he would not have committed an act which I know he regarded as suicidal."

"Think you, Halbot, that the man is bound in conscience to carry his unlucky promise into effect?" said Staples.

"Put the question," said Halbot, "to the professional interpreter of the law of morals."

"What think you, Bingham?" said Staples.

"I should think," said Bingham, "that O'Dowd would be free to reconsider a promise which was made in semi-consciousness."

"Such, too, would be my decision," said Halbot.

"Would you declare him free in honour, as well?" said Staples.

"Most certainly," said Halbot.

"O'Dowd's responsibility is but one branch of this muddle," said Mr. Bingham. "Miss Phlick's requirement is another. She will hold him to his promise if she can. If her boy is to be believed, she is already putting her trousseau together."

"So soon?" said both, in surprise.

"When I called this day at her house, to pay a pastoral visit, Jumri told me that she would see no one but 'milners' and 'costumers.' 'She be getting grand clothes,' said the boy; 'she be going to marry the Doctor.'"

"Did you ask him for his authority?" asked Halbot.

"Yes. He said he had been eavesdropping upon them—his eye at the keyhole of the door and his ear on a chink—and that he heard every word spoken, and saw every movement of the parties from the moment O'Dowd entered the room."

"By Jove, Sir;" said the Major; "O'Dowd is in a tight place. If the boy should appear as a witness to the promise, the law will take hold of the old romancer. If I were in his position, I would scamper!"

O'Dowd heard no more: they had passed on. It was of moment to have the opinion of two honourable men that his engagement to Ada Phlick might be set aside without a violation of conscience or honour. Should he take a hint from the concluding words of that quaint but sometimes practical jester, the Major of the 4th Duffs?

His thoughts were upon this dialogue as he strolled slowly back towards the city. He had been now many hours from his house. The sun had approached the meridian and passed it, and gone down far on his journey to the horizon, and was already hoarding his light for a world below; and, though the air was still sultry and the earth like the floor of an oven, a light breeze was coming in from the sea, which in its passage fanned the aching brow of the Doctor, and even acted medicinally on his gastric juices.

The animal man had been neglected: it was

rising in rebellion. No food had passed his lips for the nine hours he had been wandering, and he deemed it absolutely necessary that he should find some quiet and retired hostelry, where he might treat himself to some substantial viands before turning his face towards home.

What had come over him? Why was he so anxious to keep out of view? What was he meditating?

He was still a long distance from the city; there were few houses on his way, and these were far asunder, and none of them sold meat and drink. He jogged along wearily until a constitutional reaction set in, and then he conversed with himself brightly and almost audibly of the perils and gains of a prospect that was before his mind. All this time he was drawing nearer to the immediate suburbs of Calcutta, and when he entered them he found a tavern wherein the weary traveller could have food and rest.

He passed in; ordered a substantial dinner to be served in a private room; swept away an enormous amount of vegetables, fruit, and beer, and then fell asleep in an easy-chair, and sang nasal airs for some hours.

It was midnight when he woke. He pulled himself together and went out into the streets, where all was silence and solitude. There was no conveyance to be had in the outskirts of the city at that hour, so he started on a brisk walk towards home. He had not gone far on his way when he saw a covered palkee approaching, borne on the shoulders of four strong coolies.

The Doctor stepped off the pathway and went to meet them. When they came up, he said: " Anyone within ? "

" No," said one of the men. " We come back from the hospital, whither we have taken a sick man."

"What sickness ?" said O'Dowd. "Not cholera?"

" No, nor fever," said the man. " A sunstroke, I think, for he could neither speak nor move."

"Would you take a fare across the city if you were well paid ? " said O'Dowd.

" Yes, or to Joinagar Backergunge," said the man.

" Draw the curtains," said O'Dowd, "and let me enter. Carry me down towards the Black city, keeping on by the suburbs, and drop me on a spot that I will indicate."

" You're a pretty heavy weight, Sahib," said the principal bearer. " I shall expect four rupees for carrying you."

" You shall have them," said the Doctor. " Don't answer questions on the way."

They moved along briskly. The Doctor was a good deal shaken, for his bearers were not quite sober : his currents of thought did not flow as freely as they might ; notwithstanding which, his head was out of the litter every five minutes, in mild protest against the motion or giving directions as to the route. They met very few on the way. O'Dowd heard a horseman pass and rein in his steed as they went by, but he did not try to stop the palkee or address himself to the men that bore it. On arriving near the

entrance to the mulberry-grove that has been
so often written of in this record, there was a
halt. The Doctor alighted, and after paying
his bearers, went noiselessly through the trees of
the thicket, arriving after a smart walk at the
postern door of his residence.

He entered, struck a light, and prepared to
retire for the night. But first he went through
the house bearing a small lamp in his hand, to
satisfy himself that no one had entered during his
absence.

There was a vigilant eye over the way that had
been set upon the house from early morning : it
now saw for the first time signs of life flitting
across the windows. He was there still : he had
taken rest all day after his night's carouse, and
would come forth with the sun in the morning !
The dear man would cross the street assuredly,
and come to renew, in serious sobriety, the proposal
he had made in—oh !

But the Doctor did not open his door in the
morning, nor flit across a window, nor pass over
the street to visit his affianced, nor was he seen
to leave his house. The surgery was silent as the
grave : knocks at the door were left unanswered,
and Ada Phlick was in a state of nervous
tremor.

All this day O'Dowd remained in bed, living on
the simplest fare, and taking at intervals fluid
magnesia and other equally inflating draughts,
until, by evening, he was as light and buoyant as a
balloon. Then he rose as darkness set in, and
observing the same mystery in his movements as

the day before, slipped silently into the mulberry-grove, going in the direction of Kèsur's house.

He stopped on the threshold to gaze on an object that was crouched near the door, and, showing neither life nor motion, seemed more like a statue than a man. It was a fakir.

The fakir, in India, is a being of more than doubtful reputation. While pious Hindus look upon him as an ascetic given over to prayer and mortification, independent observers of his ways and manners describe him as a vagabond in a state of semi-nudity, pretending to live upon alms, but in reality stealing, murdering, and committing every act of obscenity and violence.

What brought this wretched man to the door of a lone and defenceless lady O'Dowd wondered, as he called to him to rise and move away. But the hideous fellow, whose face and as much of his body as could be seen were daubed with mud and yellow paint, pointed to a poignard and a flask of poison by his side, to give the Doctor to understand that he was sitting in *Dharna*, that is, that he was prepared to take his life if the inmate of the house did not comply with some request he had put before her. He had been sent there by the Mussulman Akbar Yassov, to tease and frighten Kèsur, who had ceased to receive his visits since the day he had assaulted her in the grove.

But the ruse was not successful. Akbar had lost for ever his place in the heart of the girl, and another image had taken his place. She looked with perfect indifference, as she went out or entered her house, at the foul mendicant, who raised the dagger to his breast and the poison bottle to his mouth every time that she approached.

O'Dowd passed in and was shown into her presence. He conversed with her long and earnestly, but in so low a voice that if there was anyone listening outside the door of the room, he could not hear a word that fell from either of them.

It was a mysterious interview, but it seemed to end to the satisfaction of the Doctor, who, however, bade his companion a rather pathetic farewell and sighed as he left the house.

CHAPTER XXVII.

THE DRUG STORE CLOSED: EVASION
OF THE DRUGGIST.

DID he return to his home that night? No one met him going towards it; no human eye saw him lingering near it or passing through its door; no light or noise from it hinted his presence within.

Dark and silent as the grave was the drug store, and the rooms above and behind it. They were wrapped in that mysterious gloom which always follows and often shrouds a tragedy in which human life has been taken.

Persons living hard by passed the deserted house without comment. But as days grew into weeks, and the doors in back and front were not opened, they saw a mystery in the case and made it a subject for gossip.

Had the inmate committed a crime and fled from justice? Had he got into debt and given his creditors the slip? Was he alive but hiding? Was he dead—the victim of some prowler of the night who shrouded his deed in darkness? No answer coming to any of these questions, the thread of the case was taken up by the police. But as in British India every man's house is his castle, which may not be broken into without a grave and sufficient reason, a month was allowed to pass before the executive officers of the law were given a warrant

to act ; and when they did move and entered the
store by the window, and passed through the day
and night rooms, and looked into the closets and
yard, they saw no trace of the late inmate nor
any clue that would help them to account for his
disappearance.

The bed was there—not much disturbed—as
if he had slept a sound and unbroken sleep the
night before he went away ; and the time of his
departure might be fairly guessed from a discovery
made in the parlour. The remains of an unfinished
meal were on the table, and that this meal was
breakfast and not dinner was clear from the nature
of the fragments. The police came to the conclusion that Septimus O'Dowd had not been
attacked or wounded in his house, but that on a
certain day in the forenoon, after sleeping in his
bed and commencing, but not finishing, his breakfast, he went forth—whither they could not say :
only from the confined, almost stifling atmosphere
of the place and the decomposed state of the
crumbs and fragments on the table, they inferred
that he did not return.

A question that naturally occurred to the heads
of the police and called for an answer was : Could
any person residing in his neighbourhood throw a
light on the character or habits of the missing
man ? One of the first questioned on the subject
was Miss Phlick, because her modest dwelling lay
nearest to the Doctor's, and its windows commanded a full view of the door by which he
commonly passed in and out.

Miss Phlick knew nothing—had seen nothing

If anyone could have seen him it was she, for she confessed that she had often watched his movements. But on the forenoon of the day on which he went way she did not see him leave his house at all; and if he did leave it, which she felt herself unable to deny, he must have gone out through a window or a door behind, and have had a solid reason for so doing, which she, above all others, could not and would not attempt to penetrate.

" Please," said the officer, " do not search for a reason : we are not making inquiries into motives, but facts. I would ask you, Miss Phlick, to say if you looked upon this missing man as a whimsical person, who, to create a sensation in the city and to give food to its gossips, would be capable of going off in a tragic manner and hiding himself from the public view."

" He was light and airy in manner generally," said Miss Phlick ; " and sometimes forgetful of the proprieties : but I should not call the dear man whimsical, for I think he had always an object in what he did."

" What, may I ask, do you mean by the words ' light' and 'airy,' as applied to him ; and in what way did he forget the proprieties ? "

" When at home he was often whistling and singing French songs," Ada replied ; " and I have seen him even dancing in his shop, which practices I regard as light and airy, and even improper in a man of his age and figure."

" His figure, I presume, was thick and bulky ? "

" Clouded, I should say," said Ada Phlick : " he gave you the idea of a man seen through a mist,"

" Yes, I think I understand : he may have been of lighter build than he seemed to be, and taken pleasure in hiding an agile frame under a heavy swathing of clothes."

" Such was my fancy," said Ada Phlick.

" Then on the whole, Miss Phlick, though the man was of cheerful temperament—and despite his age and ' clouded ' appearance, rather frivolous—he was, in your opinion, incapable of leading the inhabitants of this great city on a fool's search, merely to satisfy an insane impulse ? "

" That is my belief," said the lady.

" Had Doctor O'Dowd, as far as you know, many friends ? " said the officer.

" He was forlorn when I first came to reside here ; and I had much pity for him. It was his loneliness that made me take an interest in him, and help him in some little domestic ways. Later on, he made the acquaintance of some military officers, and they were frequently with him."

" You say he was alone. Did he keep a servant ? "

" No ; he could not, I believe, afford the expense."

" Had he not a medical practice ? "

" Very little, as far as I could see."

" Did he not sell drugs ? "

" Yes, he was prepared to ; but no one seemed to buy them."

" How, then, did he keep soul and body together ? "

" He must have had a friend who supplied him with money, or he might have lived on small loans."

" There must have been someone in the background, then, to keep him in funds. Who could it be? Have you any idea on the subject ? "

" I have an idea, but I should not wish to make it known. In honour, I should not feel myself permitted to do so."

" Now, Miss Phlick, I am going to take the liberty of making an inquiry to which you may or may not respond. The question I feel bound to put to you—you are at liberty to leave it without an answer—is this : Was he, to the best of your belief or within your knowledge, a romantic person —a man, I mean, apt to fall in love and give his heart away without hesitation to members of your honourable sex ? "

" I should think," said Ada, a little embarrassed, " that he would bestow the affections of his heart on one only ; while, in his light way, he might say sweet and tender words to many."

" Then you regarded the man as a flirt ? "

" Not exactly ; but as a gallant member of society."

" Let that pass," said the officer. " You think that while he could joke and laugh and pay compliments in ladies' society, he would not be found to throw himself away on girls indiscriminately ? "

" I go much farther," said Ada, suppressing a sigh ; " and I give it as my deliberate opinion that Doctor O'Dowd would be, in all circumstances, faithful to his first or his last love, as the case might be."

" Had O'Dowd a sweetheart ? " asked the officer pointedly.

" One that loved him ? " said the lady.

" No, one that he loved."

" I cannot say with certainty," said Ada Phlick.

" Can you surmise on the point ? "

" I can ; but I should not like to do so."

" I shall feel very much obliged if you will have the great goodness to state your opinion ; for on this point much depends—in fact the case hinges upon it. For if Mr. O'Dowd was in love, he might, in his anxiety to gain the object of his affection, perform very strange antics—or perhaps I should rather say, act a farcical part in a comedy in which, for aught we know, he might be abetted and assisted by the lady, who would all the time conceal a purpose of moving herself and her belongings secretly to some distant town of the peninsula ; to rejoin one who would be regarded by the public as dead."

" If a statement of my view be of such vital importance, and may tend to dispel the mystery in which Dr. O'Dowd is involved, I will not, even at some cost to my feelings, withhold it. I do believe that he loved and was loved."

" It only remains then, to ask you to give fuller shape to your statement by making known the name and address, or the name without the address, of the lady on whom he bestowed his heart."

" Oh, don't ask me," said Ada, in a fright. " I could not do so : I would not for worlds. That secret is buried deep down in my soul, and may not see the light. No ! " she continued enthusiastically, " not to bring him back, not to save his life from the jaws of the crocodile or the fangs of the tiger, could I be so far forgetful of the obligations of friendship as to reveal the workings of that heart that loved him unselfishly—that sounded an assembly when he drew near, and almost ceased to beat from the day his presence was withdrawn."

"We cannot, as a matter of course, madam, ask you to betray your friend, though it would seem to us that she would be a gainer by aiding the police in this inquiry. She is, we hope, above suspicion of conspiracy to cover the retreat of O'Dowd; and if this be so, would it not be to her benefit to come forward and state what she knows of the man's character and tendencies—for no one can be so fully acquainted with them as she—and enable us with this information to get on his trail, run him into the open, and finally bring him back to his friends, among whom, it is to be presumed, the lady holds the first place?"

"All, perhaps, very true," said Ada. "She would give worlds to see him again; but her heart could not endure the torment of a cross-examination, and the publicity which would follow on the avowal of her love for the Doctor would overwhelm her with confusion, and might even inflict serious injury on her health."

"As the consequences might be so serious, we will not press the question. Before leaving, we thank you for the valuable information you have so freely given us. We must, at the same time, tender you an apology for an intrusion on your time altogether out of proportion to the interest you could take in an elderly and misshapen stranger of whimsical habits and childish susceptibilities; whose presence in your neighbourhood, far from being a source of pleasure to you, must sometimes have annoyed you and distracted your domestics."

"I confess to you," said Ada, rising, "that I in common with his military and other friends, am much pained by the tragic fate which, I fear, has befallen my neighbour."

"That we cannot doubt, from the kind and almost affectionate terms in which you have spoken of him."

It was quite true, as Ada Phlick told the police officers, that O'Dowd had few friends or acquaintances in Calcutta. Hence these functionaries, on leaving her house, knew not in what direction they should turn to gain further information about him. They knew enough now of his disposition, manners and habits to make them believe that he had not taken his life, or run away of set purpose, and they strongly inclined to the opinion that he had met with foul play at the hands of someone jealous of him, or whom he had offended, or that he had fallen a victim to a wild beast or perished by an accident.

The few inquiries that they made as they went along the street added very little to their knowledge of his movements on the day of his disappearance, which was the point on which all their questioning now turned; and they were going in the direction of their quarters disappointed when they were met by a Hindu lady, who stopped before them, and asked, in a somewhat shy and

U

anxious manner, if any light had been thrown on the disappearance of the "eminent French surgeon."

Here was another lady friend, thought the officials—perhaps the loved one of whom Miss Phlick spoke.

No, the mystery surrounding his disappearance remained. Perhaps the lady knew something of the man, and would allow the police to put a few questions to her regarding him? She might rely on their assurance that they would not be too prying, and that they would not press for information on any matter that she might wish to withhold.

She beckoned to a large house of brick at the end of the street, and went towards it in silence, followed by the officers, whose hopes had revived.

Our readers will have identified the Hindu lady as Kèsur, who had been sincerely depressed by the news of her physician's sudden and mysterious disappearance.

The officers of the law found her in tears when they entered her house; and when she composed herself and sat demurely to hear their questions and give them an account of her relations with the missing man, they could see that she was labouring under a very keen sense of bereavement. They began with the usual formula:

"You were acquainted with the missing man?"

"Yes."

"And perhaps stood to him in the relation of a friend?"

"I cannot say. Friendship must be on both

sides. I had very much trust in him as my medical adviser; and finding him at all times very kind and sympathetic, I was attracted to him and held him in no ordinary esteem."

"Pardon me for suggesting that perhaps a warmer feeling than that of esteem grew out of the attitude in which you stood to each other." The officer thought it just possible that this might be the lady-love to whom Miss Phlick had obscurely pointed.

"You surely cannot think," said the Hindu with spirit, "that an honourable physician of sixty years would declare himself the lover of a patient who had not yet seen her sixteenth summer."

The Hindu had scored, and the policeman must be more guarded in his suggestions.

"I should have seen that: pardon me. I withdraw the words. Your feelings for O'Dowd were of the kind that commonly exists between physician and patient; but if I mistake not, as they were warm and trusting, they brought you often together."

"This I cannot deny," said Kèsur.

"Then may I ask when you met this man for the last time?"

"On the day before he disappeared."

"You conversed with him?"

"For some time."

"Did he on that occasion tell you of his intention to go away, or even hint at it?"

"He did not."

"Was his manner the same as usual?"

"Not quite."

" Were his words on the ordinary lines ? "

" For the most part ; he, however, made a very singular request of me."

" Can you tell me what the request was ? "

" I cannot."

" You complied with that request ? "

" I did."

" Might it connect itself in any way with his flight ? "

" I don't know."

" This is critical," said the official. " Would any consideration induce you to reveal the words that O'Dowd addressed to you on the occasion ? "

" I shall not reveal them to mortal, unless the movements of the Doctor make them manifest."

" Did he bid you good-bye when he was leaving ? "

" He did not."

The officers dropped the conversation, and went away.

CHAPTER XXVIII.

A REWARD OFFERED.—FEMININE TEARS.

SUICIDE, murder, a ruse, a flight from debt, the bite of a poisonous serpent, the claws of a hungry beast, and the old story—a lady in the background—and no one to offer a clue !

Consultations between the heads of departments were numerous and prolonged ; detectives were sent through all the quarters of Calcutta and its suburbs and up and down the Ganges ; telegrams sped away to the most distant cities of the peninsula : suspicious houses and rowdy lanes were visited by the police ; but no answer worth recording came to inquiries, and no clue was found that might lead to the solution of the mystery.

Finally there appeared posted by the doors of all the police stations of the city the following proclamation :

"FIVE HUNDRED RUPEES REWARD.

"Whereas, one Septimus O'Dowd, doctor of medicine and compounder of drugs, a man who, under an Irish name, was fond of posing as a Frenchman, has disappeared mysteriously from his house and place of business, which lies between the Black and White quarters of the city of Calcutta ; and whereas there is no blood sprinkled on

the floor or furniture of said house, nor other
indication of a struggle which might induce the
belief that he was wounded or assassinated within
that building; and whereas it is believed and
said by those acquainted with the missing man
that he was not a person likely to take his own
life by the use of the rope or the knife; and
whereas he was known on some occasions to ride
recklessly into danger of tigers, leopards and
panthers; and whereas the whole community of
this city and the districts surrounding it is much
exercised and agitated by this sudden vanishing
of one of its citizens: Notice is hereby given that
anyone who shall produce the body of the said
Septimus O'Dowd, alive or dead, or shall give
such information as shall lead to its discovery,
will receive the above reward.

"The following may be taken as a fairly correct
delineation of this missing man :—Height about five
feet and five inches. Trunk long and cylindrical,
without any perceptible waist. Legs short and
thin, ending in a pair of large feet, somewhat out
of the usual line, turning a little to the left. His
face is grave and lively by turns; puffy, but
without any mark or sign of dissipation. His
movements vary according to the business he has
in hand—slow when on professional duty, rapid
and jaunty when on pleasure.

"Dress varying between white and sable black ;
often wears green glasses, but whether for the
protection of his sight or to conceal a pair of
leering and twinkling eyes his most intimate
friends cannot say."

The official signature was attached.

The population of Calcutta—white, black, and bronze—read the proclamation; and the reading of it brought crowds to the neighbourhood of the house from which the missing man had disappeared: some to gratify a morbid curiosity, others to make merry over the personal peculiarities of the departed doctor.

Timid, gentle, and, in their way, charming little boys and maids, dark and fragile as reeds, clustering like purple grapes on the branches of some bamboos that stood to the rear of the house, surveyed the building with brilliant, sparkling eyes; half-caste girls, stately damsels carrying on their shapely heads pitchers balanced with unerring poise, stopped on their march past to have a look through the windows at the dreary deserted rooms. Suddenly, out of the crowd of spectators, comes an African giant with the face of a baboon, and long bare legs of polished ebony, to stand behind the girls and look over their shoulders, making his own hideousness more remarkable by contrast with the beautiful flowers of the East.

Everyone had a theory to account for the strange and sudden flitting; and while one would have it that he burst asunder and was blown away by a high wind, another was positive that the evil spirits took him—and why not, for what was he but a benighted pagan from the West?

Miss Ada Phlick, over the way, has her visitors, who, though few in comparison and absolutely select, are quite as prying and talkative and given over to speculation as the gossiping and chattering boys and girls on the street.

The first to arrive at her apartments was Kèsur, who come ostensibly to return the visit paid her a week before—in reality, to inquire if O'Dowd had been traced or heard of.

At another time and under different surroundings Miss Phlick would have received her coldly, but, a common affliction is a bond. If the truth must be told, Ada was jealous of Kèsur; for she thought, from certain words that had fallen from her at their last meeting, that she discerned in her a possible rival. But what difference could it make now? He was lost to both of them; and there could be no sacrifice of feeling in allowing their tears to flow together over his grave.

The young women sat down in silence, looking at each other; neither of them seemed to find words in which to convey her thoughts on the sad event that brought them together. They sighed. Kèsur let a tear fall, and Ada coughed.

"You have no doubt come to make inquiry about this great calamity," said Ada at length, "and to express your sorrow at the loss of your medical adviser?"

"He was more than a physician to me," said Kèsur, thoughtfully; "more like a father or friend of long-standing, who could not do what he deemed enough to promote my happiness as well as my health."

The irritation of Ada's throat returned, and she coughed again, this time a significant cough.

"He was friendly, I believe," said she, "to all alike who came within the range of his professional eye; but outside that circle—ah!"—and she sighed.

"His regard for me," said Kèsur, innocently, "was special, for he could not have found time to linger with his other patients as he did with me—speaking on the highest interests of the soul."

"Poor dear man!" said Ada, ignoring the latter part of Kèsur's remark. "He had very few patients to talk to, and I am forced to say that he was fond of gossip when he could find a hearer."

"I can assure you," said Kèsur feelingly, "that his talk with me was often very serious, and had for its subject religion."

"He spoke of your religion?" said Ada, inquiringly.

"And of his own," said the other.

"He was a *Roman* Catholic," said Ada, laying stress on the word.

"He was a Catholic, he said," replied Kèsur, "and a member of what he named the Old Church!"

"I am a Catholic," said Ada Phlick, "and belong to an older Christian Church than that of my lost and much regretted friend."

"He often told me," said Kèsur, "that your Anglican Christianity is an up-growth of modern times."

"Poor dear old Irish prejudiced Papist!" said Ada. "He knew little of controversy and less of history; and, I am quite sure, never read a chapter of the New Testament in his life."

Their conversation was interrupted at this point. The Hindu boy come in to announce the arrival of Captain Halbot and the Reverend Nethcoff Bingham, who had come to express their sympathy with Miss Phlick on the violence done to her nervous system by this shocking occurrence in her neighbourhood.

The Reverend Nethcoff Bingham had not been in the rooms of Miss Ada Phlick since the well-remembered day on which he had seen Doctor O'Dowd taking what is named in the phraseology of bathers a "header" into the bric-à-brac cellar of that lady; and now, as he entered her apartment, his eyes instinctively turned to the door of that closet. His glance in that direction was not lost on Miss Phlick, who raised a handkerchief to her eyes and moved her head solemnly, as one struck by a painful memory.

"Yes," she began tenderly; "it was there that he was imprisoned: there he lay patiently for an hour, in the heat and choke damp, amid broken crockery, without a word of complaint, until a deep gash on the lower part of the leg forced a cry of agony from his lips. Little did I think when he emerged from that cellar, wounded but not overcome, that we should have so soon to mourn his utter disappearance.

A deep sigh escaped from the Hindu, which made the Reverend Nethcoff turn towards her and say, in words of kindly sympathy: "You, too, are one of the bereaved."

"Yes, up to the day of his withdrawal he was taking a lively interest in my welfare, which I shall ever bear in grateful memory."

The clergyman seemed puzzled by the breadth of the girl's reply, and looked to Miss Phlick for its interpretation.

" He was striving," said that lady, " to withdraw her from the worship of Brahma ; and by an argument the force of which we were discussing when you entered, to guide her into that form of Christianity which he professed himself."

Bingham smiled : was this reconcilable with the light and frivolous habit of the Doctor ?

Divining the cause of his amused surprise, the Hindu girl intervened.

" He could be very serious at times," she said, " and seemed to me to be stirred by a strong emotion when speaking of the antiquity of the faith which he professed. It was the faith of the sacred writings, he said, taught by a Church that never changed."

" If he meant to convey by these words that his church was the Primitive Church of the Scriptures, he made a very great mistake," said Mr. Bingham.

" I was telling her so," interposed Miss Phlick ; " and at some cost to my own feelings, throwing a quiet ridicule over the poor man's pretence of Scriptural knowledge, when you were announced."

" Did the Doctor then deceive me ? " said Kèsur.

" He certainly misled you, when he said that his church was the primitive church, but not wilfully, I would venture to say, for in his ignorance he thought so."

Up to this Captain Halbot had been a close and attentive listener ; now he spoke for the first time : " If your church," said he, addressing the clergyman, " be the same as the Primitive Church, how will you fill the gulf of centuries that yawns between them ? "

" I will leave it open," said Nethcoff coolly ; " or if you will, cram it with superstitions, unscriptural practices and errors."

" I thought you claimed for Anglicanism," replied Halbot, " absolute continuity."

" Some do : I do not. For me the Church has, as it were, dived into the great ocean of time, and remained submerged from the fourth to the sixteenth century of our era. Then it emerged in its primitive truth and beauty."

Kèsur intervened.

" If I was obliged to believe," said she, " that the religion of Brahma disappeared for centuries and went to sleep, even on the bed of the Holy River, I would long ago have abandoned it, for I should have lost all faith in its divine origin. What keeps its followers together is the conviction that it has never changed and is unchangeable."

" Which I accept as an intimation that you will not embrace the Anglican form of Christianity, in the event of your abandoning paganism," said Bingham.

The Hindu seemed to reflect, but she did not reply.

CHAPTER XXIX.

NONE the less friends for the divergency of their views, Captain Halbot and Mr. Bingham left Miss Phlick's house together ; while Kèsur remained talking to that lady without aim or spirit, until she also rose to leave the room. Then the Hindu wandered forth with no settled purpose, taking no heed of the route she was following, until she found herself on the bank of the Ganges.

The mighty Ganges ! The " Holy River " of India ! Through what alternations of gaiety and sadness does it follow its long course between its cradle in the ice-bound slopes of the Himalaya mountains and its grave at the mouth of the Delta : tripping gaily by great cities of Moslem architecture, crawling sluggishly between treeless banks in the long reaches of the wilderness, listening by turns to the croaking of the vulture, the bleating of the elk, and the growl of the king of the jungle ; giving shelter beneath its yellow surface to the harmless mango fish and the armoured crocodile. What sorrows and what secrets you have carried to the sea, O mighty stream !

The great river was gay and full of life. The Maiden was crowded with loungers, some of them still as statues, others moving slowly along, and not a few sitting or lying prostrate on the reddish

burnt ground. Shipping of heavy tonnage lined
the banks of the stream. Monkey-faced boatmen,
gibbering and chattering for a fare, put out to
meet the steamers that went solemnly by ; barges
and grain vessels, rafts and sand-tubs went up
and down in slow procession. But the most
attractive and the strangest side of the picture
was that of the bathers, some of whom were just
leaving the water and some on the point of entering it, while others were immersed in its yellow
flood.

The scene was too much for Kèsur : she closed
her eyes to it and moved along the bank until she
passed away from the crowd. She went on, turning
neither to right nor left, without looking behind or
straining her eyes on the long pathway before her,
until her footstep alone broke the silence of the
still air, until the throbbing of her heart told her
that she had travelled too fast and wandered too
far from home.

She stopped.

A voice seemed to come up from the river at
her side like a siren's, singing and calling by
turns. She drew nearer to the edge and listened.
Eddies and ripples were speaking below, and the
burthen of their talk was, "Come." She turned
from the bank and was stealing slowly away, but
the voices followed her, saying, " Come in from the
broiling heat, and stretch your parched limbs in
this cool current, and turn its refreshing spray
over your tired and aching head."

Again she drew near the bank ; but this time
there was no murmur from the water, only a wide

and still surface was before her, reflecting the flags and scrub that grew above, and the shadows that passed slowly over the face of the heavens.

A water-fowl was sporting in the middle of the stream, diving and rising and skimming along the top of the water with flapping wings, showing by his every movement the pleasure he received from his bath. She followed him in his flight, and envied him his joy. He was chirping, and in his own way speaking. She bent her ear to catch the sounds that came from him, and again she seemed to hear the invitation ; but now the word was not " Come," but " Follow."

A thrill of fear ran through her frame, but her resolve was not shaken. She would not enter the water in a place such as this, where its depth was not known, and where under-currents might prevail ; and yet, she could not leave the treacherous river-side, for a strange and strong fascination held her. She moved forward, until she came to some disused stairs, which went down from the bank to the pebbly river-bed ; and here the suggestion to enter the water became more instant : seeing that bathers had gone down here, the place must be safe.

Still she stood hesitating and undecided. She would go in, and she would not. Who was to save her if the current should carry her away? Meanwhile, in her state of doubt, it would not be amiss to remove her armlets of gold and unclasp the circlets of fine pearls that were holding her lower limbs in captivity. This done, she approached the brink, and looking down into the water was caught by a fairy hand that drew her on with a strength that was irresistible.

She unloosed her outer robe and laid it down; for a moment, she flitted in a long and narrow dress of crimson silk, as perfect as any piece of statuary the soil of Greece ever gave up from its classic depths; then she went down the steps slowly, until her feet touched the bed of the river. She did not rest when there, but went out into the stream, wading along and testing its depth, until the water rose about her, and her head and shoulders only could be seen above the surface.

She knew the whims of the Ganges, and how to keep it in good humour. She swept the water with her outstretched arms and came back, creeping up the incline until she arrived in a shallow spot; there she bathed, after the manner of the Hindus, noiselessly and with much grace, until cooled and refreshed, she continued her course towards the stairs.

Her foot was on the first step; she was loitering —perhaps, too, taking breath after her exercise— before mounting to the bank. She was looking upwards and was not conscious of a danger that was coming from behind in the form of a rolling wave, that had been set in motion by a steamer. It struck her unawares, carried her off her feet, and bore her along by the bank into deep water, where after a short struggle, she sank drowning. Once she came to the surface, and, raising her arm to heaven, cried out in a voice rendered strong by terror, " O, Christ, save me !" Then she sank, without further struggle, to the bottom.

The words had scarcely passed her lips, when a form leapt out from the bank, and a strong man had plunged in. With powerful strokes he made for the spot where she had disappeared. There he dived, and within a minute he came up, with his arm about the inanimate form of the Hindu girl. He struck out for the bank, where a man in native Indian costume was waiting to receive and help him up with his burthen.

After a while, Kèsur, limp and still, with sunken eyes and mouth partially open, her straight black hair falling over her back and breast like a veil, was lying on the bank between the two men, who were chafing her hands and feet and moving her gently to and fro as on a pivot, to encourage respiration.

As they looked on the expressionless face the Indian gave a sudden moan, and speaking in tones of strong motion, said :

"It is Kèsur : don't you recognise the dimpled chin and broad intelligent brow? See, here are the pearls she always wore at her ankles. My Kèsur! I always loved her, though she put me aside, and now I claim her as my own."

"This is not time for a rhapsody, Akbar Yassov!" said the other man. "The girl is in my keeping, as a pearl brought from the depths, and shall not leave it, dead or alive, until she is given over to the care of her relatives."

"But she is living," said the Moslem, pointing to a throbbing vein on her temple ; "and no one has so good a right as her ancient lover to carry her off and nurse her back to health."

" You rave," said the other. " That would be to take advantage of the powerlessness of a girl in order to compromise her. Away with such ideas ! Better go, if you know her friends, and summon them, that they may take her over and keep her with them until she recovers from this shock. Or, stay,"—as the other was preparing to go—" hasten to her house, and order her servants to come here at once with a closed litter, to bear her away."

The fierce Moslem raised no objection, for he had reason to know the strong will of his companion ; and he moved away so rapidly that he was soon out of view, leaving Captain Halbot, for it was he, alone with the now awakening Hindu.

She opened her eyes and gazed curiously at her rescuer.

" I am a stranger to you in this mud and slush costume," said he.

" Your face was so lately before me," she answered feebly, and stopped.

An awkward silence followed, which was broken at length by Kèsur.

" We are destined," she said, " to meet in woeful straits, and always with some third party spying upon us. I seem to have seen through my eyelids another man standing near you, and to have heard his words."

" And well you may," he replied. " It was the Moslem, Akbar Yassov, that helped me to carry you up the bank ; and, with a lover's instinct, was the first to say your name and catch the dawn of your returning life."

The girl shuddered and looked all round with a dazed and timid stare, fearing to be confronted by a man whom she now thoroughly distrusted.

"Do not be uneasy," said Halbot. "He is not here; I have sent him away, a willing agent, to procure assistance. You will be in my keeping for an hour or more, when he may return, it is true, but with your servants, bearing dry clothes and stimulants, and a covered palanquin to carry you home unobserved."

"Do take me away," said she, imploringly, "before he comes back. I am too weak to meet him now; the very thought of him sets my nerves throbbing."

"We are not just now in suitable trim for the streets of Calcutta," he replied, with a light laugh; "and even if we were properly robed, the vision of a Hindu lady tottering along with a British officer by her side, might create an impression of opium, or something worse."

She was gaining strength: she smiled.

"What *shall* I do, if he comes before me?" she said.

"Trust in me," said Halbot; "I will send him away, on some pretence, before he has time to cause you the smallest unrest."

"I am so thankful," said she, fervently.

"Are you strong enough," said the soldier, "to hear me speak on another subject?"

"On any subject," said she, rising to a sitting posture.

"What shall it be—religion or city gossip?" asked Halbot.

" Is not religion the more natural now, seeing that I have been saved by Christ ? "

" Then you called on His name in consciousness ? "

" Dim, dreamy ! " she replied. " I was looking for some prayer in my struggle ; and finding none in my own religion, I cried out a Christian ejaculation."

" Learned from poor O'Dowd ? " suggested Halbot.

" I think it was an inspiration of the moment. He never spoke to me of prayer. The words came of their own accord : I could not have arrested them, even if I had wanted to."

" And I was brought on this way to hear them, and driven by an impulse to act in the name of Him whom you had called to. All this betokens the existence and presence of a benign Providence —of One whose sleepless eye is on the ways of man—who is always ready to hear the cry of those who call upon Him in the hour of trial or death."

" How happy you are in the Christian religion ! You seem to live and breathe in God. With us it is so different. The god whom we should respect is taken from us, and we are left to the care of lesser divinities that are more of earth than of heaven. Even our solemn prayer at the dawning of the day, led by a grave and austere priest, who with up-lifted eyes raises his hands in blessing over the multitudes who enter this river for the morning purifying ablution, is spoiled because it goes not to the all-seeing and ever-present Being, who made and preserves the world."

She seemed to tire and droop after she had finished these words, which were spoken with much spirit and feeling, but she raised herself at once, and supporting her head with her arm, went on :

" Those promptings and warnings, of which I spoke to you in our first interview, have taken a new shape in my mind, and I am now hoping to worship Christ and Brahma together ; to borrow your precepts and act upon them, and continue by profession a Brahman."

" Who puts his hand on the plough," quoted Halbot gravely, " and looks back, is not worthy of the Kingdom of Heaven."

The girl started to her feet : she did not expect such a reply.

" Am I such a criminal ? " she exclaimed in alarm. " I did not dream of profanity or dis- respect to Christ : I only thought of an easy way to escape from the difficulties by which I am beset."

" I merely cited the words of Him whom you venerate—words which He addressed to those who came to Him and were falling away from Him again."

" But I will not fall away, Captain Halbot. I will never leave the Christian God that has been preached to me ; and if I cannot have Him with Vishnu and Brahma, I will let them slip from my memory."

" If you take Him as your God, you must bring

no strange gods into competition with Him. He, with His Father and the Holy Spirit, must alone receive your adoration. He is a jealous God, and will have no rival."

"Then I must abandon all my beliefs, if I become a Christian?"

"No less than your worship and practices," he replied.

"Are you not too severe and exacting?" said she. "May I not go to the sun-rise prayers in the Ganges, whither I have daily turned since I could first think and speak?"

"If you become a Christian," he replied, "you must profess Christ before the world."

A perceptible tremor passed over the girl; the struggle was too much for her then. She would have fallen to the ground if Captain Halbot had not come to her support.

"It was not the time for this grave discussion," said he. "I should have remembered that your strength was not equal to it. You will, I hope, excuse my unwise zeal; but it occurred to me that the moment had come to put before you, in all its fulness and austerity, the claim of Christ on your allegiance, now, when He has saved you from death, and to ask you to become His disciple."

"Not yet," she replied; "not quite yet! Later on, when I see more clearly the light that attracts me, more fully recognise the voice that invites me: but I will pray to Christ more earnestly than before, and ask Him to lead me on gently to the truth,"

Captain Halbot bent his head in meditation. His deepest sympathy was with this tender Oriental plant, and he thought that it might wither if touched by any but gentle hands, for it seemed to be not yet strong enough for transplanting.

" Then pray to Christ," said he, " and in the very words you spoke when death was at hand ; they are, in substance, the same as those addressed to Him by a body of His disciples in danger of shipwreck when He was on earth, and now, as then, they will be heard."

Servants and bearers were seen approaching ; but to the great satisfaction of the Hindu, Akbar Yassov was not with them. He had pleaded fatigue and gone home, but said that he would return to her house later on, to felicitate her on her escape from death.

The girl entreated, and Halbot promised that he would call upon the Mohammedan, and take him for a walk in the suburbs, and carefully avoid, while in his company, every approach to the district in which she lived. He should be told in plain terms that she must not, for the present, be disturbed by the visits even of her truest well-wishers.

CHAPTER XXX.

THE MYSTERIOUS PALKEE.

THE placard offering a substantial reward for
such information as should lead to the discovery
of Doctor O'Dowd, living or dead, was extensively
posted and eagerly read, and bore fruit of a very
varied and curious character, but of little value to
the authorities.

In came a coolie the next day after its appearance to the police barrack, carrying in his hand
a large and much-worn pair of shoes, which he
had found on the bank of a creek, and which, from
information he had received of the size and form
of the Doctor's foot, might well have belonged
to him! The man was of a speculative turn of
mind, and gave it as his opinion that O'Dowd,
having taken off his shoes to cool his feet, had
been caught by a crocodile, drawn into the water
and devoured.

A very hideous and squalid Hindu woman had
a statement to make in confidence to the police,
but would not give her name or place of residence.
She was bewailing the sorrows of her lone existence, she said, on a spot far down the Ganges, and
hoping that some prowling beast, from the not
distant jungle, might come that way to carry her
out of the troubles of her dreary life, when she
heard the voice of a man calling, as she thought,

for help. She went towards the spot from which the accents came, but, when she arrived there, she heard no more than an echo, faint and very sorrowful.

She was turning to retrace her steps, when a shout came up from the same direction, followed by the din of angry voices in a hot dispute. She feared to draw nearer in the open, and entered a brake, where she lay hidden for some time listening with all her ears to the noises. Then she discovered that what had seemed to her to be a quarrel was a melody sung in a cracked and shaky voice by a man, who immediately came into view. He was a heavy man, elderly, and dressed in black ; and from the movements of his lips and feet she believed him to be insane. It was her deliberate opinion that he threw himself into the river—though she did not see the act—and was carried out to sea and drowned.

The Department dismissed this creature with contumely. Why should she attribute the crime of suicide to a man because he was of a joyous temperament ? A prisoner does not dance at the foot of the scaffold, nor whistle when he is led out to be shot !

A traveller, who had just arrived from Delhi, came before a magistrate and testified that he had seen in that city a passenger whom he now suspected to be O'Dowd, dressed in the Chinese costume and wearing the pigtail ; but on being closely questioned as to his features, this witness was forced to admit that he had the almond-shaped eyes of a Chinaman ; whereupon he was seized by an officer of the court, at his Honour's command, and thrust without ceremony into the street.

Another outsider came to say that he had been in Allahabad, and that he had met in a street of that city a religious mendicant who could be no other than the Doctor in disguise, for he was fat and jolly and a stranger, and had a name for charming cattle and giving simple remedies to the sick. But the Department demurred to the inference, and thought it highly improbable that the lost man would, at great pain and risk, effect his escape from Calcutta, where he was known and respected, to throw himself on the streets of a provincial city in a state of semi-starvation, unless he had committed some crime (which was not suggested) and was fleeing from justice.

A hawker who had, at very great risk, escaped through the beasts and serpents that infest the swampy country below Calcutta, had met, as he came along, a fakir who was not like the fakirs one meets every day, who take sorrowfully to their lives of mendicancy, but a burly, blustering fellow, who was clearly a new-comer, and clearly had torn himself away from a city life for a freak, rather than from an awakened sense of religion. Might not this be the missing man? Might he not have chosen this life for a while, as the one above all others in which he could most effectually lie concealed?

The police told this man that he should consult a Doctor as soon as he could on the state of his mind, which seemed to be unhinged.

And just as the authorities were getting heartily

tired of the silly evidence that was coming before
them, a sepoy of high caste entered their office
and volunteered a statement, which he gave for
what it might be worth, though he did not presume
to say that it dispelled the mystery connected with
the disappearance of O'Dowd.

At or about the time that Doctor O'Dowd was
first missed, according to his account, he had
happened to be sent from Fort William, where
he was stationed, across the city on military duty
as an orderly, at one o'clock in the morning.

He had passed, on his way, a party of four
men who were bearing on their shoulders a palkee.
He had not looked closely at the bearers, nor
could he point them out among a number of men,
for he had been gazing with curiosity on the litter.
And yet there had been nothing quite uncommon
about it; it was merely closed and its curtains
drawn. Nevertheless he had begun to speculate
about it as it passed, and his thoughts in connection
with it resolved themselves into an alternative:
they were either carrying in that litter a lady
gagged, or removing the body of someone who
had met with foul play. These had been his
thoughts at the time, and he could not, if he would,
divest himself of them. He had almost forgotten
the event before many days had elapsed, or, if it
had come before his mind since then, as now and
then it had, he had smiled at the impression made
upon him. But he thought it a duty now, when
the authorities were so taken up with a suspected
murder or suicide, to give it for what it was worth
to the police, who, no doubt, would decide whether

it might possibly throw some light on the puzzle they were trying to solve.

The respectability of the man, the moderation of his language, and the event itself as related by him, made an impression on the authorities. In the absence of any other clue to the solution of the mystery, they would take up this one and follow it as far as they could; and they thought it not improbable that it would lead to some discovery. What more likely than that the removal of the body of a murdered man should be accomplished in this way, and under the cover of darkness ?

Another proclamation appeared the next day, for the police thought that a reward should be offered which might induce some one of the carriers of the mysterious palkee to come forward and betray his companions :

" Whereas a palanquin, borne on the shoulders of four men, was carried through the streets of Calcutta some time after midnight on or about the 16th day of last August, or some days before or after that date ; and whereas the said palanquin was closed and its curtains drawn ; and whereas there are grounds for believing that the body of a murdered or gagged man or woman lay hidden therein :

" This is to offer a reward of one hundred rupees to anyone who will come forward and give information as to the contents of said palanquin, whither it was carried, and where its contents were laid.

" BY ORDER."

A week elapsed—another week—a month—
and there was no answer to this invitation: no
one came forward to claim the proffered reward.
This silence was the cause of official and non-
official discussions. The police argued thus: If
the bearers of the palanquin carried an ordinary
burthen inside, such as a man who had dined out
and taken more wine than was good for him, or
a lady who had been taken with a fainting fit in
the street or in the house of a friend, or a person
sick of a contagious disease, whom it was deemed
prudent to send to a hospital at night, some one
of them would have come forward to state the
fact and relieve the pressure on the mind of the
public. If, on the other hand, they carried a
drugged or gagged or murdered man, one of them,
assuredly, tempted by the reward, would have
made a report to the Executive, which would
save his own head while consigning his accom-
plices to the gallows. But no one coming forward
to give evidence in the case, the department was
baffled and must leave the farther investigation
of the mystery to an interested public and an
ingenious press.

Civilians argued like the police, and it became
a general belief among all classes that a crime had
been committed and that all trace of it had been
lost.

The news of the calamity spread far and wide
along the Ganges and through the towns and
cities, and penetrated even to the hamlets of
Central India. The press took it up and discussed and dissected it, and blamed the police

and abused the detectives and found fault with
the authorities for not offering a larger reward for
the discovery of the perpetrator of this odious
crime.   *The Putna Times* made itself remarkable
among the leading newspapers by the view it
took of the tragedy, as follows :

"REVIVAL OF THE THUGS.   MYSTERIOUS
VANISHING OF A MAN AND WOMAN."

"At a time when we believed that life was exceptionally safe throughout the peninsula of India,
two events have occurred which have sent a thrill
of alarm, and even of horror, through the community, and which, as we write, are shrouded in
the darkest folds of mystery.

"One is the disappearance of a medical Doctor,
well-known and in large practice in Calcutta ; the
other, the sudden vanishing—the word is not too
strong—of a Hindu lady in Putna.

"Here, near our own doors, almost under our
eyes, a lady of the highest caste enters an hotel,
takes possession of a room, comes down to her
dinner, eats a temperate meal, mounts the stairs
again, going apparently to her bed-room, vanishes,
and is never seen after, either inside or outside the
hostelry.

"In Calcutta, the eminent physician alluded to
above was seen in his surgery, let us say, to-day ;
is known to have eaten his breakfast this morning ;
but on the morrow, he is not seen.   And on that
night late, after darkness spread its pall over the
city, a gloomy litter is seen stealing through the
streets on the shoulders of four miscreants, which

is supposed by the Intelligence Department of the city to have contained, in a whole or crushed state, the mortal coil of that harmless man, whose mission was entirely for good, especially among the native population.

" It is not many years since human life in India was practically in the hands of a number of ruffians who were known as Thugs. The question we have now to ask ourselves, is : Has that horror revived amongst us ? Have the Thugs come back again ? It would seem to us that they have, and therefore we would warn the public to be on its guard. Let no lady travel by herself without a protector, if she would avoid the risk of being spirited away, goodness knows whither; and let our men too, especially our Britishers, be cautious. Let them not go out alone at night or into solitary places ; they know not who may be lying in wait for them, with murderous intent.

" The police will, there is no doubt, do their duty in connection with these horrible tragedies ; but for the public there is but one word for the present —*Caution.*"

Jumri, Miss Ada Phlick's boy of all work, took a somewhat whimsical view of the situation created by the Doctor's disappearance. He was reading the proclamation at the door of a police office when a Hindu girl came up and stood by his side, and, without speaking, looked at the page and read.

Turning half round, he recognised Gunga, with whom he had often a passing word on the street.

" Is it you, Gunga," said he, " coming to groan ? "

"I am not coming to groan," said the girl; "I come to laugh loud."

"Fie, Gunga!" said Jumri. "The Doctor is gone; I cry, and Miss Phlick cry, and the piano cry, and everything cry," and he raised his arm in mock solemnity, to wipe away a tear.

"And my mistress cry too," said Gunga. "She be in love with the Doctor."

"She ben't," said Jumri; "no one love the Doctor but Miss Phlick."

"Ah!" said Gunga, "if you saw Kèsur when she first heard of him blowed away!"

"What — blowed away? He be not blowed away; he be carried on back of argill—up—up into air, and dropped down into the sea and drowned."

"Who said so, Jumri?" asked the girl.

"Jumri said so,"—stoutly.

"Jumri be a fool," said the girl. "No big bird take fat Doctor on his back. He be as heavy as a small elephant; but a wind come and blowed him into nothing."

They both laughed loudly and long, and turned to walk together in the direction of Miss Phlick's abode.

"Mistress at home, Jumri?" asked the girl, as they went along.

"She be always at home now, playing music," said the boy.

"Oh, you story-teller!" said the girl. "Didn't you say she be always crying?"

"Yes!" said Jumri, roguishly; "she be always crying, she and the piano together."

" Does your piano cry, Jumri ? "

" Oh yes !   It be always crying since the Doctor was taken up," replied Jumri, " big tears, as round as an egg."

" You be a nice joker, Jumri," said she.

" I be no joker ; I tell truth : jum ! jum ! jum ! say the piano ; quite sad, as the band plays when they be burying a soldier."

" A dead march, Jumri ? " she said.

" A dead march. "

They walked on in silence for some time, when the girl took up the broken thread.

" Kèsur love another now," she said, stooping confidently : " she often say, when she thinks she's alone, ' Sweet Halbot ! ' "

" What is sweet Halbot, Gunga ? " asked Jumri, " Is it a thing to eat ? "

" You be a wise one, Jumri ! " said the girl. " Could you eat a man ? "

" I could," said Jumri, " if he were made of sweet stuff ! "

They were now arrived at Miss Phlick's door, and the girl told Jumri that she had a message for his mistress, which she was to give, in person, to that lady ; she would remain, she said, outside and have a look at the Doctor's window, while he went in to tell of her coming.

" That little thing over the way ? " said Ada, in reply to Jumri's announcement.

" Yes," said Jumri, looking out ; " that be she."

" What can she want, the little hussy ? " inquired Ada.

" She be good little one," said Jumri, chivalrously.

Y

"Go away, you pert boy," said Ada ; "send her to me."

"Gunga told her story, which was a request from Kèsur that Miss Phlick would bear her company on the Ganges steamer the day following, on a trip down the river, where they might enjoy the scenery of the Sunderbunds, and make inquiries as they went along regarding their missing friend. But Miss Ada Phlick would not go ; she feared the Thugs, who, she believed, were now abroad.

CHAPTER XXXI.

A THRILLING EXPERIENCE ON THE GANGES.

THE next morning, at an early hour, when the sun was already shedding his first rays over the plains of Bengal, Kèsur, seated under an awning in a steamer on the Ganges, was by turns musing and reading as she waited for the departure of the boat.

She was alone, having failed to induce Miss Phlick to bear her company. Her little maid, Gunga, was seated at a respectful distance, with one eye on her mistress and another on the passengers of various hues that were coming on board, and the motley crew of loungers on shore who were waiting to witness the departure.

Among the last of those that crossed over the gangway, was a Guroo, or high Brahman priest, of thoughtful mien. He did not raise his eyes from the deck as he passed along it ; but, notwithstanding, found his way to the place where Kèsur was seated, where, taking a chair, he drew it to her side and sat down for a talk. He was more than an acquaintance of hers : he was a friend ; and she had, in earlier days, hung with delight on every word that fell from his lips, as a teacher of morals and expounder of the doctrine of Brahma.

A recognition, a salutation—and they spoke

familiarly. The usual topic—the disappearance of O'Dowd.

"I cannot," said the grave man, "bring myself to believe that he was murdered and carried away a corpse in a litter ; I think that he went away of his own accord, and will reappear when least expected."

"I hope it may be so," said the girl. "What do you think could be his motive for a flight so sudden and mysterious ? "

"To advertise himself," said the Brahman. "He comes to us, a stranger, to make a livelihood by selling drugs and tendering medical advice. No one knows him ; he has no practice in his profession and little sale for his wares. He sends a thrill through the population of the city and the towns of the province by disappearing suddenly and leaving no trace, no indication of the manner of his flitting. Now his name is on everyone's lips ; and when he resumes his interrupted business, the public will flock to him in thousands."

"You have, I think, drawn upon your imagination," said Kèsur, "in attributing such a design to the absent man. He was neither artful nor deceitful, but simple and straightforward, and, as I believe, quite incapable of planning or carrying into action such an unworthy plot as that which you so confidently conjecture."

"Do you speak of him from knowledge, or from hearsay ? " inquired the Brahman, turning sharply upon her.

"From knowledge," said Kèsur, composedly.

"Were you acquainted with him ? " said the priest.

Yes," said Kèsur ; " he was my physician."

' I take the liberty," said the other stiffly, " justified, I hope, by our long intimacy, of saying that I regret to hear of your calling to your house a white unbeliever while you had within reach medical advisers of your own race and religion quite as competent as he."

" You are free to lecture me as you did when I was a child," replied Kèsur, " but I feel that you have not in me the docile hearer of those days. I now follow my own judgment, and think that I am experienced enough to direct my steps in any course that I may think fit to enter upon."

" I regret to hear you speak so," said the Brahman : " the liberty you take to yourself is full of danger. You are letting loose the cable that binds you to the shore, and you may find later on that you have drifted out to sea and are beyond hope of rescue."

" I cannot see my position in that light," said Kèsur. " You seem to me to make much harm out of an indifferent act, such as everyone is free to perform."

" The act of calling in a Christian physician is not, I admit, criminal in itself, but beneath it lurks a danger," said the Brahman.

" That is from your point of view," said Kèsur ; " but from mine, it seems so trivial, that it creates in me no apprehension."

" But you are still a true follower of Brahma, I feel sure : and would not run the risk of putting his claims on your service in comparison with those of the Christian God."

"Don't be too sure of me," said Kèsur. "I claim full and perfect liberty in religious matters too."

An indignant expression came over the face of the priest; he scowled upon the girl as he answered:

"Shame upon you, for a renegade Hindu! I believe you will be turning your back on Vishnu by-and-by, and rushing, with blinded eyes, into the arms of the new superstition."

Kèsur seemed shocked by the vehemence of the man, but controlled herself to answer: "You march to conclusions too fast, Gobind Das! Does it not strike you that it would be more mannerly and less unkind to teach me, if I am going wrong, than to heap upon me words of rebuke, which the words I have spoken have not invited?"

The quiet self-possession of the girl drew a clumsy apology from the arrogant ascetic; but he took advantage of the permission she gave him to propose a serious discussion on the claim of the Brahmanical creed to allegiance, and he settled down in better temper to a lecture on its position.

"The Brahmanical religion," he began, "is the oldest in the world, as is proved by the text of the Vedas, written in Sanscrit, a language that for countless ages has ceased to be a vulgar tongue."

"Do not the Buddhists lay claim to as great an antiquity?" said Kèsur.

"If they do," said the other, "their claim is not supported by existing documents."

"I cannot quite see," said Kèsur, "why it is that

a document proves the truth of a religion more than a verbal tradition, or why it is less likely to be fabricated."

The Brahman was simply amazed by this reply coming from a girl whom he supposed to be unfamiliar with the subject. He said : " You have been comparing creeds, I can see, and putting their rival claims to a test ? "

" Not," she replied, " on the score of antiquity ; nor, indeed, have the claims of the Buddhists had any part in such discussions as I may have been engaged in."

" Perhaps," said he, " it is Christianity that you have been weighing against the religion of Brahma ? "

" And if it is ? " she replied.

" I should regret it much," he said gravely.

" But why ? " said Kèsur.

Because it is a Western religion," said he, " and not suited to the tastes and habits of Orientals."

" If it be the true religion," said Kèsur earnestly, " the peoples of the East should conform themselves to its beliefs and its code of morals."

" That is so," he admitted grudgingly ; " but it is not the true religion, as is proved by the facts that truth has been always in the world, and that Christianity has not been always there ; for a period of two thousand years is but a brief day compared to the untold ages that have revolved since the birth of the sphere on which we live."

" Might not a similar objection be urged against the truth of Brahmanism ? " said Kèsur. She thought that she was making a point.

"No," said the Brahman decisively; "because Brahma, with Siva and Vishnu, represents the creative principle as well of truth as of the world."

The girl had exposed herself to a fatal thrust, and she had received it. She writhed for a time under the pain that it caused, as it went tingling through her nerves and telling her that her vision of Christianity was but a dream picture.

Could it be that Captain Halbot was ignorant of the claim to antiquity put forth by the Brahman? Might he have erred, and in erring deceived her, when he urged her so earnestly to enter the Christian Church as the home of truth? That he would not wilfully lead her astray she felt sure; that he was more learned than this pretentious Brahman, she had no doubt. She would take heart. She would consult him on the difficulty that had been sprung upon her; for the moment she would cease to argue.

But her astute companion, seeing the advantage he had gained over her, resolved to push his victory home.

"Have you computed the number of years," he asked, "during which Christianity has existed as a religion?"

"I have had no thought on the subject," said Kèsur.

"But you have heard of the Christian era?"

"Yes."

"And never inquired the meaning of the words?"

"No."

"If you go back to the beginning of a period of 1860 years, you will find the birth of the Christian era."

" Which means, I presume," said she, " that this epoch is the date of the appearance of Christ on earth ? "

" It means also," said the Brahman, "that Christianity, as a religion, is not yet two thousand years old."

" And is not two thousand years a large part of the world's life ? " said she.

" Absolutely," said the Brahman, " it is a long period of time, but it is short compared to the long ages that have passed since the religion of Brahma began to shed its light over the peninsula of India."

Kèsur was silent : in truth she could not find a reply. She was shrinking in spirit from the confident man with whom she had been speaking, and thinking of some excuse for leaving him, when a thrilling struggle in the water brought all the passengers to the side of the boat.

Their voyage was down the Ganges, and they were now entering one of the channels of the Sunderbunds. The land on both sides, and far over that region of creeks and swamps, was in a state of nature, covered with forests of ancient growth, and given over to savage beasts and to animals of gentler type that fell to them as their daily prey. The tiger, the leopard, and panther were at home in these solitudes, and roved unmolested over the land ; while the waters were alive with crocodiles of all sizes—some could be seen on the banks basking in the sun.

The commotion in the water was extraordinary. A beast of the jungle had pursued an elk from the interior of the forest to the river bank, from which both animals, unable to check their wild haste, dropped into the stream below. The runaway struck out for dear life, but its pursuer stopped, and sent up a growl of rage and pain that made the forest around ring. The passengers on the steamer were gazing earnestly to discover the cause of the animal's trouble when, as he rolled himself on his side in his agony, the head of a crocodile appeared above the surface of the water, holding in his iron jaws a foreleg, which he had caught just above the paw.

The efforts of the struggling brute to shake off his assailant were piteous to behold. Writhing and plunging, he strove to catch and rend his tormenter. He struck at him with his paws, but the blows, enfeebled by the fluid through which they passed, produced little or no effect. Then he sprang out of the water, drawing the crocodile again to the surface, but not shaking him off. Finally, losing heart, he stretched out his limbs to their full length, and seemed to turn a distressful appeal to the passengers clustered along the steamer's bulwark.

The fight appeared to them to be drawing to a close, and the victory to be with the reptile, when the panther put forth all his strength for a last effort to save his life. Turning his face to the shore, he struck out for it vigorously, and succeeded in dragging his invisible assailant with him into shallow water, and even pulled him on to a low bank. There he pounced upon him, with his jaws apart and his terrible teeth bared ; but they could not penetrate the matted coat. He then struck him on the side of the head with such force that he broke the connection between them, leaving a part of his foot locked in cruel jaws. Then falling on him again, he ripped him open and left him for dead, with his entrails falling out on the ground. Seeing his victory complete, he uttered a loud howl of defiance and limped away painfully into the bush.

Kèsur had been watching this exciting struggle, and she turned from the river when it came to an end. The Brahman had left her, and she was glad, for in his absence she could give attention to the object which brought her into this vessel ; which was to make inquiry among its officers regarding her lost friend, the Doctor. She thought that he might possibly have got away from Calcutta by the river, and have been seen, though not recognised, by someone on board the boat.

It was easy to introduce the subject, for it was still a common topic of conversation.

" Have you," said she, addressing the captain, " had on board at any time the man who is missed from his home in Calcutta ? "

" I think so," said the captain, " for short trips ; the description given of him would point to one of my occasional passengers."

" Might I ask," said she, " if you observed that this passenger was reckless and careless in exposing himself to danger of death ? "

" The man I have before my fancy," said the captain, " asked to be put off in a boat on a part of the shore that we did not regard as safe, owing to the presence of beasts and serpents."

The Hindu shuddered. She had got, she feared, a glimmer of light by which she might read the Doctor's fate.

She thanked the captain, and returned, agitated, to her reading.

CHAPTER XXXII.

KINDLY AID, BUT UNAVAILING.

O'DOWD was gone, and with him the heart of Miss Ada Phlick. The little angle, at the meeting of the White and Dark quarters of Calcutta, would have been a sombre spot then but for the antics of the Hindu boy, Jumri. He may or may not have been kept in check by the presence of Ada's friend over the way; or he may have missed, in the Doctor, a butt for his sarcasm and an outlet for his merriment. Certain it is that after his disappearance he became a free jester, and put no bounds to his freaks, which were often at the cost of his mistress.

Look at him at Miss Phlick's door. He has gone outside and roared in an inhuman manner; and then he has slipped into the house, thrown the door wide open, and in a voice so loud that he can be heard by his mistress, has ordered the brawler to be off and not to dare to disturb the family.

Or he has knocked loudly and rung the hall bell, and passing quickly in and closing the door, has opened it again with much clatter and called out, " What a noise you make ! He never lived here. Go across the street and kick the door, and don't cease to kick until he comes out to you : he be a heavy sleeper."

Or he has run round the corner and shouted, "Big Buddha," after a fat man going down the street, and then walked solemnly out of his hiding place to meet him when he turned back in a passion, and to assure him, in the blandest accents, that the scamps who called out after him, who were *white-guards* only, have run off by a lane, and are not worth looking after, as they are always in mischief.

Miss Phlick, from her window a witness of these performances, at last addressed a letter to Mr. Bingham, requesting him to call upon her as soon as possible, as she wished to take his advice on the mode of dealing with a very troublesome servant.

At the end of an hour or so, the Reverend Nethcoff arrives, light and cheerful as usual, at the modest house of his countrywoman, and immediately Miss Phlick entered on her complaint.

"I am," she said, "the most tried of women. I have in my employment a little jester, who, I fear, is drawing all eyes upon me, and making me the butt of scandal-speaking tongues."

"The seclusion of your life makes you nervous, my dear lady!" said Mr. Bingham. "What has the lad been doing?"

"Dreadful things," said Miss Ada. "Shouting, dancing, charging down the street—and, to speak generally, all the business of a paid buffoon."

"It is, I admit, inconvenient. Boyish humour, however, cannot be kept under; and to be candid with you, I think it is better to let it evaporate in even troublesome freaks than to suppress it, when perhaps it may explode in downright mischief."

"Ah," she rejoined, "you could not speak thus if you had been, even for one day, a witness to the sayings and doings of Jumri."

"Pardon me, Miss Phlick, I would. You are alone; as a consequence, depressed—I might even say, sad. Might you not raise your spirits by taking a wholesome view of the pleasantries of this lively youth?"

"Pray, what do you mean to convey by the words 'wholesome view'?"

"Perhaps I should use the word 'healthy' instead. Nothing contributes to the ruin of health more than fretting; nothing more to its preservation than receiving events as they occur, in a cheerful spirit. Why, my dear lady, a century and a half ago, when life was duller than at present, every court in Europe had a Jumri to keep its royal head in good humour. May I suggest that your boy be summoned before us, when we can put some questions to him, with a view to discover the motive that compels him to act so whimsically?"

Jumri was called in, and entered the room all smiles and innocence, in apparent ignorance of having given cause of complaint to anyone.

"Well, boy," said the English chaplain, "what is this you have been doing?"

"I been doin' everything," replied Jumri. "I been answering calls at door, brushing the Mem-sahib's boots, cookin' breakfast and dinner, carryin' messages, drivin' thieves away, rubbin' chairs and tables—I be boy of all work."

" Is this all ? " said Bingham.

"That's all," said Jumri.

" Nothing else, you're quite sure ? "

" I be crying for Doctor," said Jumri, passing his sleeve over his eyes.

" Oh ! " said Miss Phlick, "did I ever——"

" Pardon, Miss Phlick ! Leave the lad in my hands. You mean to tell me that you have been grieving for Doctor O'Dowd ? "

" Oh, yes ! " said Jumri. " I and Gunga."

" Crying ? "

" We be all crying here : Miss Phlick crying, the piano crying ; Jumri keeping company."

" But you have been, I am informed, laughing too."

" Not much laugh," said Jumri.

" Well, if not laughing, you have been cheerful and noisy."

Jumri hung his head.

"Yes, I have been told that you have been calling loudly at the door and chasing children through the streets."

" For fun," said Jumri, raising his eyes.

" But your fun is not wanted," said the clergyman, " and is very offensive to your mistress."

" I not know," said Jumri, with an expression of perfect innocence.

" I think," said Bingham, " that your look of innocence is put on for a purpose. You are, I fear, Jumri, a very bold boy ; and you know very well that you are doing wrong when you make all this noise and clatter. I would advise you to enter on a different course, to keep your tongue silent and your feet still, and to reserve your merriment for some other place, far away from the house of your mistress."

"And if Miss Phlick die of crying," said, the boy, "'tis her own fault, because she wouldn't let Jumri cheer her up."

"You may go now, lad, " said Nethcoff. "I shall hope to hear a good account of your conduct on my next visit."

Just then a scraping at the door was heard, and in response to a "Come in," uttered by Miss Ada Phlick, Kèsur, calm and gentle as usual, entered the room and held out her hand.

"It is not necessary," said Miss Phlick, looking to the clergyman, "to introduce this lady to you. You have met her before : you have lectured her on the error of her ways, and tried to withdraw her from paganism."

The Reverend Nethcoff·was hurt by this candour. He said gravely, "I have had the pleasure of meeting her here and in her own house. A dawning of Gospel light has been upon her for some time, in which she begins to see the shortcomings of her form of Eastern mythology."

I fear," said Kèsur, with an expression of care, "that this vision has passed away, leaving me more a disciple of Brahma than I was when it first rose before my fancy."

"I am very sorry, indeed, to hear you speak so," said the clergyman. "It is seldom that a soul begins a journey out of darkness without a strong

z

and wise motive ; and I think that a return by the way passed over can only come from whim or weakness of purpose."

" I have had a long and trying conversation with a learned Brahman," said Kèsur, "and he has suggested what I cannot but regard as a great obstacle to my reception of the Christian belief."

" Should I be intrusive if I asked you to mention the obstacle to which you allude ? "

" No," said Kèsur, thoughtfully ; "I see no reason why I should make a mystery of it. I thought, previously to my conversation with my co-religionist, that the Christian was a very ancient creed ; but he assured me that it is a new and modern form of belief compared with that of Brahma."

" And you believed him ? " said Nethcoff.

" I did. He spoke with such confidence and sincerity."

"You won't, I trust, think me narrow-minded when I say that his words expressed what is now regarded by the scholars of Europe as a fable."

"Which is the fable ? " said Kèsur. " Is it the oldness of the creed of Brahma or the newness of that of Christ ? "

" Both," said the clergyman, " are false as he put them before you ; but the Brahmanical account of the age of Brahma is not only fabulous, but universally rejected by the learned."

" Brahma, you think, is not older than Emmanuel ? " she asked.

" I waive that question for the present," said Nethcoff, " and I affirm that the religion of Brahma does not go back more than three thousand two hundred years."

" But the religion of Christ," said Kèsur, interrupting, does not go back more than about eighteen hundred years."

" Let us," said the clergyman, " first determine the date of Brahma's alleged revelation, and afterwards we can make comparisons. Brahma was said by his learned disciples to have revealed the Vedas, or sacred books, at the beginning of the world—that is, as they put it, twenty-six million years ago. In proof of this wonderful antiquity of creation, they brought forward astronomical tables showing the state of the heavens at various periods from that remote date to modern times. These records were received as genuine for some time by many learned but hasty critics ; but later on, and on closer examination, they were rejected as pure fabrications, drawn up to deceive, some hundreds of years after the birth of Christ. With the authenticity of these astronomical tables went the antiquity of Brahma and the Vedas."

" But still," said Kèsur, " you allow an age to the Brahmanical creed which is greater than that of Christianity ? "

" I have said that it may, and probably has been, in existence for a period of three thousand and two hundred years ; and I have allowed you to say, without contradiction, that Christianity does not date back farther than one thousand eight hundred and sixty years. From these admissions you have naturally drawn a conclusion in favour of Brahmanism. And now I have to ask you if you are quite sure that the older system must, of necessity, be the true one."

" Is it not evident ? " said Kèsur.

" By no means evident," said the Englishman. " Error may date back to any period, no matter how remote, if it does not touch the time of man's creation ; and, by a parity of reasoning, truth may appear, in a new dress, at an age comparatively modern. We have displaced Brahmanism from its vaunted antiquity of twenty millions of years, and forced it to place its origin after the date of the Deluge. What guarantee have we that it was not set up by an impostor ? Or why should its assumed age make it more credible than Christianity ? Hence I say that the argument of your learned Brahman, which has been such a puzzle to you, and driven you back into a system of error from which you were emerging, has no force, is captious and deceptive, and, while calculated to mislead, cannot bear the test of inquiry."

"Your mode of disposing of the argument for truth derived from antiquity would apply to Buddhism as well," said Kèsur, listlessly.

" And to all the religions of the East, which are ever boasting of a fabulous antiquity."

Kèsur thanked the clergyman for his explanation, and having saluted him gracefully, bade good-bye to Miss Phlick and passed out of the room.

As she was leaving the house she met Jumri, who was standing outside the door. He seemed inclined to speak to her, but she passed him by, as he was not of her caste, and proceeded in the direction of her home.

Miss Phlick and Mr. Bingham had something to say of her before parting, and they said it. The lady thought that she was "daft already, or, at the very least, approaching that state," which the clergyman could not admit, for her intellect had grasped his argument with singular readiness.

"She is the most charming type of an Oriental lady that I have met," said he; "and her graceful person is under the control of a rarely gifted spirit. She will, I trust, find the truth, for I cannot think that it will be refused to one who values it as she does."

CHAPTER XXXIII.

SEETA PUTS ANOTHER OBSTACLE IN
KÈSUR'S PATH.

In his conversation with Kèsur, the Reverend Nethcoff Bingham did not dwell, at sufficient length, on the unique antiquity of revealed religion as proved by inspired writings ; while some of the sentences he used, such as that " truth may appear, for the first time, in a new dress, at an age comparatively modern," were too obscure to be convincing.

He would have done better if he had put in contrast the age of Moses with that which is fixed for Brahma by modern scholars, and the date of the Pentateuch with that which they assign to the Vedas. This would have set aside the claim of the religion of the Brahmans to truth on the score of antiquity.

Though Kèsur thanked him for his efforts to enlighten her, she left his presence in a maze of doubt. And she stood, like so many others, on the brink of the river of life, drawn towards it by a strong attraction, but held back by fear and self-interest, seizing, meanwhile, on any straw to save herself from falling into the stream, and thankful that it gave her a moment's breathing before making the fateful plunge which would carry her to a distant shore from which there was no return.

She was followed into her house by the market girl, Seeta, who brought her a new trouble. She came to tell her of a talk she had overheard in the Bazaar, between Captain Halbot and Mr. Bingham.

" It is not the old story again," said the girl, " but something quite strange, which, I think, should be weighed well by us both, before we leave our early home for the Christian temple."

" Weary — weary ! " sighed Kèsur listlessly. " Will there ever be an end to surprises? I am farther from Christianity now than when we last spoke of it. A Brahman priest has thrown across my way a barrier which I have not been able to pass over ; and a Christian minister, whom I invited to give help, has failed to turn it aside : and you come now to add to the pain and doubt which the words of both have left in me."

" Then I had better be silent," said Seeta, " and leave the words of even Captain Halbot unsaid."

" Crafty Seeta ! " she replied. " You know I *must* hear *his* words : they rang in my ears when I heard them for days and days, like the fall of music."

" But I cannot give you his words unless I give you also the words of his companion, and tell you the subject of their conversation."

" For Halbot's sake, I shall be a patient listener."

" Of whom do you think they spoke ? "

" How should I know ? Of Brahma perhaps— the old, tiring subject."

" It was not of Brahma they spoke for once," said Seeta, to excite curiosity.

" Oh, then; of Emmanuel ? " inquired Kèsur.

" No."

" Then I am glad that they spoke of neither of them, for their words can only add to my difficulties."

" Don't be so sure of that," said Seeta. " They spoke of Buddha ; and one of them told of his standing in the way of all who are moving towards Christianity."

" Buddha is of no interest to me," said Kèsur, with the strong repulsion of a Brahman. " His distaste of the religion of Emmanuel would be for me a motive to embrace it."

" I think you would take a lively interest even in that strange god, if you heard what Mr. Bingham said of him," put in Seeta.

" There is little to be said in his praise," said Kèsur ; " but if he is accurately represented in such figures as we see of him, he is uncommonly fat and stupid."

" He can be lively too, and inventive," said Seeta, provokingly ; " but I am speaking to you in riddles. You can form no idea of the relations of Buddhism to Christianity unless I give you the whole dialogue of these men."

" Then give it."

" Well, how shall I begin ? " asked the girl, taking a seat for the first time ; " and when shall I come to an end ? It is a long tale, and is all crowded in my head together. Yes—it began in this way : They had been telling me that the religion of Emmanuel is a very old system ; that it changed, in form only, after Emmanuel came

and that Emmanuel was promised long before ; and
I had taken my lesson, and was thinking it over,
when the clergyman gave me quite a shock by
saying that Buddhism is much more a subject of learned comment just now in the schools of
Europe than the religion of Brahma, because of
its resemblance to Christianity. ' The followers
of Buddha ' said he, ' use bells to summon to
prayer, in the same way as the Christians. The
Buddhists make long fasts like the Christians, and
some of them live apart from the world like monks
and nuns of the Christian Church. The rosary
beads, which are so largely in use among the
followers of Emmanuel, are likewise in the hands
of the disciples of Buddha ; and the Buddhist
service, accompanied as it is by music, incense
and flowers, and conducted in the dim light of
closed and curtained temples, is not unlike the
solemn Mass as seen in the churches of Italy."

" And so ? " said Kèsur.

" Captain Halbot," went on Seeta, " did not deny
that the Buddhists use a beaded string in their
devotions, but said that he attached no importance
to the custom : the practice of employing bells to
summon to public worship was, he said, of world-
wide usage ; and at the most, the resemblance
was only on the surface. But I am puzzled : I
cannot go farther : I tried to keep in my mind,
by repeating them often, the very words used by
Captain Halbot and the clergyman in this dispute.
I have told you some of them ; all the others have
dropped from my memory."

" You have told me, I fear, too much for my

peace of mind," said Kèsur. "This day has brought me more than its share of troubles."

"Which," said Seeta, "will all be removed in your next interview with your wise military friend."

"Would that such an interview were within measurable distance ! But I very much fear that I may not meet Captain Halbot again, as his regiment is in daily expectation of an order to return to Europe. Nor should I feel quite satisfied to hear him discuss these points with Mr. Bingham. His opponent should rather be a Buddhist priest, who would say all that can be said in favour of his religion earnestly and from conviction ; but I cannot hope that such a privilege will be given me. I know not a priest of Buddha, nor could I, with propriety, invite a British officer to the house of a solitary Hindu maiden."

"Allow me to be your agent in this delicate matter," said Seeta. "I am a girl of experience. My travels and residence in England have taken from me the timidity and reserve of a Hindu woman. I have met and spoken to men of different ranks and classes, of various hues and many nations ; and I shall not be abashed by a Buddhist, whom I do not yet know, and a soldier whom I have already met. Have trust in me : I will call upon Captain Halbot and tell him that a lady of my nation craves his advice in a trouble that has come upon her, and I will stop in the street the priest to whom I have referred, and tell him that a British officer wishes to learn the nature and grounds of the religious system of

Buddha. When I shall have induced both to consent to a meeting, I will appoint the day and place of it, which will be in your house, at a time that you may deem most suitable."

" You are a wise little fairy, Seeta ! " said Kèsur. "I put the case entirely into your hands. If anyone can bring it to maturity, you can. Meanwhile I will live in hope that this new obstacle to Christianity may be removed by an eloquent and clever advocate, and " she added, smiling, "in anticipation of renewing my acquaintance with Captain Halbot."

Seeta laid her plans wisely, and carried them into execution without unnecessary delay. Both Captain Halbot and the Buddhist were taken by surprise at the very unusual request she put to them ; but after some hesitation and inquiry, they consented to meet on the morrow of the day upon which they were addressed, at the house of Kèsur, at sun-down.

Kèsur received due notice of the hour, and was prepared to receive them. They arrived separately. Captain Halbot was the first to appear : he was wearing his uniform and sword, and looked all over a brave and gay cavalier. While waiting for the coming of the Buddhist he entered into a lively and friendly conversation with Kèsur, to which the arrival of the priest put an end.

CHAPTER XXXIV.

THE PRIEST OF BUDDHA.

THE Buddhist was the same who had called upon O'Dowd after his dip in the Ganges, and argued with him on the claims and attractions of Buddhism, as compared with the religion of Brahma. He was a ready and well-informed man, a good linguist and an artful disputant; but, like a true disciple of the fat god, he was self-sufficient, even arrogant, and not to be convinced of error.

He saluted the Hindu more heavily than deferentially, as he took his place opposite Captain Halbot.

" If I were not convinced of the truth of the creed of Buddha," he began, " its universality would make me believe in it."

" It commands the assent of, I fancy, four hundred millions of men," said Halbot.

" Not so many," said the Buddhist. " More likely three hundred or two hundred and fifty millions."

" In either supposition," said Halbot, " it is a vast following, greater than that of Brahma or of Mohammed."

" You might add," said the Buddhist, " greater than that of Emmanuel."

" And if I made this admission," said Halbot,

"which I am far from making, it would be little loss to me, and no gain whatsoever to you."

" A singular opinion," said the Buddhist. " I wonder that you commit yourself to so rash a saying."

" Shall I explain ? " said the officer.

" If you can," said the Buddhist.

" I see no difficulty," said Halbot. " Your Buddhism was a small religion previously to the twelfth century, when it was driven out of India by the followers of Brahma. Since then, by bending and crouching and accommodating itself to other forms of belief, it has spread itself over vast regions to the North and East of India : its displacement of T'ien, the god of the Chinese, alone made it dominant in the most populous empire in the world."

" Does not its success in propagating itself say much for its vitality ? " said the Buddhist.

" Against other forms of paganism," said Halbot ; " and you will please remember that vitality and truth are not convertible terms. Mohammedanism has shown a vigorous vitality for a thousand years, and you will not grant it the attribute of truth."

" Whatever view you take of the means by which Buddhism spread itself over the earth," rejoined the other, " you cannot deny the antiquity of this creed. If the multitude of its adherents can be explained by a human accident, its immense, its immemorial life carries us back to its origin in the Eternal."

" How old do you make Buddhism ? " inquired Halbot.

" As old," replied the Buddhist, " as the religion of Brahma."

" Which is," said Halbot, " about three thousand two hundred years from our day."

" Oh, much more !" said the Buddhist. " It is not by thousands but by millions of years that we compute the era of Gautama."

" Indian fables, my dear Sir," said Halbot. " You have not been reading, but living in a poetic past. The schoolboy of our day knows that the astronomical tables which the Brahmans used to prove that their religion was founded twenty-six million years ago were drawn up in the eighth century of our era."

The Buddhist was silent, and Halbot followed up his point.

" Indians, Chinese, Cingalese, Siamese—it is the same story with all the peoples of East Asia : you all claim for your traditions the sanction of an extravagant antiquity for which you have no evidence that might convince an unprejudiced inquirer, and in this way you actually bring discredit upon whatever in your institutions is really venerable."

" Now, Captain Halbot, listen with attention to what I am to say in reply to your repudiation of our claims to antiquity. What evidence, I ask you, had the civilized nations of the past but assertion ? What else have the civilized nations of our day ?"

" I will answer you briefly," said Halbot, "*written records.* The Christian nations of the world have sacred books that tell of the origin of their

creed, and fix with accuracy the date of its introduction. The Mohammedans do not try to go
behind the age pointed out in their Koran ; the
ancient Greeks and Romans were content with
Homer and Hesiod as the authors of their mythology ; and it is only you in India and China that
have gone into the clouds, where all is obscurity
and doubt."

"Do you know the tenets of our venerable
religion ? " said the Buddhist. "Are you acquainted with its forms and practices ? "

" To some extent," said Halbot.

" Then," said the Buddhist, " you know the
story of Gautama's life and death."

" And that he left no writings," said Halbot,
" to prove that he is not a myth."

" Left no writings," the other assented, " but
introduced a new civilization and a religious creed
without rival."

" Do you think so ? " said Halbot dryly.

" Confine your view to his religious tenets for a
moment. First, an abstract idea of the Divinity."

" A relic of the original revelation made to the
first man," Halbot replied.

" Secondly, an infinite space filled with creative
atoms," said the Buddhist.

" An idea," said Halbot, " shared with Epicurus
and Lucretius."

" Thirdly, a Divine spirit animating matter in
its various forms and working through them,"
said the Buddhist.

" Pantheism," said Halbot, " however derived."

" You will at least," said the Buddhist gravely,

"give their full value to our doctrines of the liberty of man for good or evil ; his responsibility to an invisible judge ; his reward with God, if he walks in the way of virtue ; for these are, if I am not mistaken, Christian doctrines as well ? "

" They are Christian doctrines, without doubt, and, as such, entitled to my respect : but you will pardon me, when I give it as my opinion that they are a later addition to Buddhism."

" How could that be ?   What do you mean ? "

" This," replied Halbot, slowly and with emphasis : " it is not possible to say with certainty, what was the first form of Buddhism, but it is probable, that it was a simple affirmation of the existence of God, and of Buddha as His messenger. The restless intellectuality that introduced Buddha to the world found for him a code of belief and morals, by borrowing largely from contemporary philosophies. From Epicurus it took the atomic theory of creation ; from Brahmanism, the idea of a multitude of gods ; and from Christianity or Judaism, the sublime doctrines of moral responsibility and a future happy life."

" Christianity ! " echoed the Buddhist, scornfully. " Why do you introduce it in this connection ? What has Christianity to do with India ? It is an extern and distant creed, of which Buddhists could have known little, even by hearsay."

" Pardon me," said Halbot, "your predecessors in the profession of Buddhism must not only have heard of Christianity, but seen it at work in the conversion of the unbeliever : for one of the associates of Christ, its founder — Thomas the

Apostle — preached it to the Indians eighteen hundred years ago, and in the fourth century of our era travelling teachers from Persia founded many Christian communities through this peninsula. Besides, the contention of the Roman Empire with Christianity and the victory of the latter, and the diffusion of the Christian Faith over Western Asia, and up to the gates of Hindustan, could not have escaped the notice of its adherents. I admit, that the Buddhists might have derived their doctrines of liberty of action, responsibility for its use, and a future state of rewards and punishments from the primitive revelation given to the predecessors of the human race in common ; but certain religious rites and practices that I see among your people make me incline to the opinion that you borrowed them from Christianity."

Kèsur had up to this time listened in silence to the arguments of the two men ; she now intervened with a spirit and intelligence which took Captain Halbot by surprise.

" May not the beliefs and practices of Christianity have been taken from Buddhism, as it is the older religion ? " said she thoughtfully.

" Your question is too wide," said Halbot. "Confine yourself to the practices."

" Pray, why ? " said Kèsur.

" Because, the beliefs of Christianity come from its sacred books and traditions," said Halbot.

" Is that so ? " said she.

" Yes," said he ; " and some of these books are the oldest written records in existence."

"Then," said Kèsur, "I withdraw the word *'beliefs'* from my question."

"And you ask whether the practices of Christianity may have been a re-hash of Buddhism?"

"Yes," said the Hindu, "served in a more piquant sauce."

"We must thoroughly understand each other; let us come to details," said Halbot.

"Then I will mention, one after another, the practices I have in view."

"I am all attention," said the soldier.

"To begin with trifles," said she, "bells are used in common by Christians and Buddhists."

"Certainly," said Halbot, "what then?"

"You puzzle me," said she. "It seems strange."

"Why should it seem strange that a simple and natural instrument for calling men to public worship should be used by different and opposed religious communities?"

"Perhaps," said Kèsur," the Christians learned the use of bells from the Buddhists."

"And perhaps," Halbot replied, "the Buddhists took the custom of using bells from the Christians."

"Incense is used in worship by Christians and Buddhists," said Kèsur.

"Yes," said Halbot, "and was used by the pagans of Egypt, Greece, Rome, and by many other ancient nations."

"It is, then," said she, "a pagan usage; and, if this be so, how did it find its way to Christianity, and when?"

"Excuse me," said Halbot. "Incense, in the worship of God, is not a pagan usage only; it was

used also by the Jews, who were the chosen people
of God from the beginning. They introduced the
censer in religious functions, and it was from them
that Christians learned to use it."

" They tell me," said Kèsur, " that you and
the Buddhists alike employ strings of beads for
the purpose of telling the number of prayers
you have said."

" If we do," said Halbot, " what follows ? "

"·Why should they be used by both?" was all
she could say.

" May I give you a little history of the introduction of beads to the Christian Church ? "

" I shall feel obliged."

" In early Christian times there sprang up
a custom of laying down pebbles to account for
the number of prayers recited. An anchorite, for
example, proposed to himself to repeat the Lord's
Prayer one hundred times a day, and, to save the
distraction of keeping account of the number
said, laid down a little stone at the end of each
recital. In time, these pebbles came to be bored
through and hung on a string, and carried about,
and ultimately took the form of what are now
named rosary beads."

" That is interesting," she replied, " but whence,
pray, did the Buddhists derive this practice ? "

" Presumably from the Christians," said Halbot.
" They have been notorious plagiarists and
borrowers on all sides."

" Or they may, surely, have evolved the practice
like the anchorites of whom you have spoken ? "

" Very possibly."

"Now," said Kèsur, " I have put before you the difficulties against Christianity that have been suggested to me. I leave you in the hands of this grave man, and listen."

The Buddhist eagerly entered the arena.

" This lady," said he, "made allusion to the style and form of our public worship, but lost sight of the argument she intended to found upon it. Our beautiful worship," he went on, " so soothing, so absorbing—have you ever, Sir, stolen into one of our temples and reposed there, while the voice of prayer, on the breath of living flowers, went up amid incense fumes before the shrine ? "

" I have been in your temple during worship," said Halbot.

" Moved, I would say, by sympathetic emotions ? " said the Buddhist.

" Moved by curiosity at first," said Halbot, " and by pity as the service proceeded."

" By pity ? " said he, in surprise.

" I felt," said Halbot, deliberately, " a pity for your worshippers akin to that which, if you will allow the comparison, I underwent when I visited an opium den."

" Oh, Sir," said the Buddhist, " the comparison is unjust. How can you compare a profound religious rite to a debasing practice that no good man applauds ? "

" I judge by effects," said Halbot, coolly. " You seem to me to lie in your temple, during worship, as powerless as the consumer of opium in his fetid den, and to come forth from your service as enervated."

"That is the result we aim at, Captain Halbot," said the Buddhist : "we mean to lose ourselves in the intoxication of music, flowers, perfumes, shadows, motionless forms and deep gloom—to quit, as it were, our narrow confines of self and so to anticipate the bliss of absorption."

"You have expounded your doctrine candidly," replied Halbot ; perhaps I may as well leave you in possession of it without comment. I must, however, say, that it seems to me extraordinary that men of acuteness in religious matters, such as the Buddhists unquestionably are, should attribute a supernatural result to a perfectly natural process."

"But what you name a natural process—that is, destruction of self by surroundings of sweetness and gloom—is the last step in a life of preparation. Who, Sir, fasts so rigorously as the Buddhist ? Who so heroically withdraws himself from the pleasures of life ?   Who is more earnest in prayer ? His life is a journey toward that absorption which shall make him one with God."

The earnestness of the man moved Captain Halbot.   His strange fanaticism, and the blindness with which he clung to it, made him anxious to open his eyes to the unseen world of faith.   He must talk with him again, and show him how all that was good and true in his belief and practice came from God, through Jews or Christians, and that all its defects and shortcomings were traceable to human perversity.   He bade him farewell, expressing some such hope.

For some time he lingered with Kèsur, who

confessed to a growing conviction that whatever was good in Buddhism was derived from external sources.

Too much has been made of this Oriental superstition by certain decadents of the West, who have even taken in hand a propaganda, and have won a temporary vogue for a system which they imagine reflects the esoteric doctrine stripped of its popular trappings. But, as it is found in the lands of which it is indigenous, Buddhism is a jumble of borrowed beliefs and practices. If it had come into Italy in the days of Nero or into the Grecian peninsula two centuries earlier, it would have placed Jupiter or Zeus on a pedestal by the side of Buddha : if it had been in Egypt in the age of the Ptolemies, it would have modified its ritual to meet half-way the enthusiastic crowds that gathered in the temples of Isis.

Modern travelling scholars who have lingered to gaze on the yellow robe of the Buddhist priest, and descant in glowing language on his silence, his seclusion, his recollection, his grave and pious bearing, seem to have forgotten that the pagan priest of ancient Rome was in dress and movement quite as imposing as he, and in public worship, quite as rapt and sanctimonious : and when they write of the Buddhist monks and monasteries as something distinct from heathenism, they have surely for the time lost sight of the convents near the temples that gave shelter to the priests of Minerva, and the Virgins who guarded the Sacred Fire,

CHAPTER XXXV.

THE DOCTOR'S TESTAMENT.

PENSIVE and pale, thinner than when we first made her acquaintance, Ada Phlick sat at the piano playing something out of Beethoven that wailed and shrieked.

Jumri was outside the door, with his ear to the keyhole; and he too was showing symptoms of unrest, but not in the direction of grief. He was accompanying the music with suitable gestures and grimaces, when a postman's knocking put a sudden stop to his performance.

He went quickly to the door and took from his hands a registered letter for his mistress. He carried it in to Miss Phlick, and laid it on the table before her, saying :

" Dis be news from someone in Benares ; maybe the Doctor, I tink."

" You *are* a forward boy ! " said Ada, not ill-pleased however ; " you have been spying on the stamps."

" I always spy," said Jumri, cheerfully ; " I be a curious little fellow."

" Stop these remarks," said Ada. " There, take this slip to the letter-carrier. Close the door, and leave me alone."

Jumri went out, closing the door after him ; but he did not leave Ada Phlick quite alone, inasmuch as he substituted his eye for his ear at the keyhole, and took note of the ardour with which she seized upon the letter, the haste with which she broke the seals, and the rapidity with which she turned the pages, until her eye lighted on the signature. Then the boy, unable to overcome his curiosity, opened the door and walked in without notice.

Miss Ada Phlick was still absorbed with the document, when she looked up accidentally and saw the irrepressible standing near. She would have extinguished him there and then, but he retired to a position near the door, the handle of which he held, and backing through the opening, until only his head was visible, said :

"There ! I knowed it was from the Doctor : now you be happy, I'm off ! "

The letter was indeed from the long-lost Doctor, and, as Jumri had said, bore upon it the Benares postmark.

And such a letter ! So quaint, so characteristic of the man ! And yet it was not without feeling, evinced in the desire to make amends for his sudden evasion of the consequences of his precipitate offer.

"Ada, sweet daughter of my heart and home ! (see Byron's *Childe Harold*)"—so it began, " you little thought that I would, that I *could*, bring myself to fly so soon after I had ' plighted my troth ' to you. The words are solemn ; they form a part of the nuptial contract ; but, alas ! they do but represent the purport of the little speech I made to you that sombre night in October, when

I called at your house, as I was returning from dinner at the hospitable mess of the 4th Duffs.

"But I ask you to go back in spirit to that evening, and ask yourself if I was a responsible being while the words above referred to flowed from my lips—frankly, did I know what I was saying? I was not, to put it in pure Saxon, drunk: I believe I kept my legs fairly, though I have a dim recollection of having put my hat over one of your lamps and extinguished it—but let that pass; my utterance was not very thick; my eye was not quite dim; and yet I ask you again, did I know what I was saying, when I asked for your heart and hand?

"Ah, Ada, say no! Solace a troubled conscience by admitting, 'No, Doctor! You were in the moon that night, and your words were but the babbling of a babe.'

"So they were; they could not have been otherwise. Could I ever, while in possession of my senses, have consented to throw upon your hands a burden like that of my ignoble self? Just think, to have and to hold me for life—that is, to feed and to dress me, to house or to lodge me, to drive me in a coach or to row me in a boat, to carry me from city to city in the peninsula or perchance across the seas to the home of my boyhood, and all at your own expense! Yes, to expend your whole income on an old frump without means or practice, whose pleasantries, neither elegant nor refined, would have been the sole return for the devotion of a self-sacrificing wife!"

At this point, when the disinterestedness of the Doctor came to light, a tear that had been trembling on Ada's eyelid overflowed down her cheek.

"The dear man!" she said tenderly, "I would have taken him joyously 'for better or worse,' or altogether for the latter." She read on :

"I could not—you are woman enough to know—have any repugnance to take you as my wife, if I were a marrying man ; and I have fled from you notwithstanding, and with no ordinary flitting. Forgive me, Ada, if I have refused the golden egg that was laid for me, if I have declined to pluck the apple that was at my hand, if, in a sense, I have preferred the companionship of sacred cows to that of one of the most cosy and attractive women that the capital city of Bengal contains within its wide area—which leads me to give you a short description of this 'Holy City,' in which for the present I have pitched my tent.

"This is a beautiful, but an unsightly city. When you look at it from the river, it is a series of ghâts—handsome flights of steps leading down to the water's edge—temples, minarets, lofty houses, parapets, buttresses ; when you penetrate to the interior, a labyrinth of narrow crooked streets and a medley of abominable odours!"

Miss Phlick laid down the letter, and cried, "Jumri!" in a clear voice.

The boy appeared.

"Jumri," she repeated, "I go up the Ganges to-morrow, and may be away for some days. You may go home to your parents until I return."

" Oh, no ! " exclaimed the boy, " I go up the Ganges too : I go all the way to the ' Holy City.' "

She looked at him steadily, expecting to trace an incipient smile. Seeing none, she asked :

" What ? "

" I go," he repeated, " to be a big brave bully, and pull her away from Thugs, if they be carrying her off."

" Who ? "

" Miss Phlick, surely," said Jumri.

" You ridiculous lad,"—but she thought that this gave evidence of some character—" go ! "

She resumed her reading.

" You will be naturally anxious to know how I left Calcutta, and by what route and mode of conveyance I came to Benares. I cannot, I regret, satisfy you on this head, beyond saying that I made use of a heretofore untried, but very simple device, which I could not reveal more definitely without compromising one who shuns publicity and whose wishes I feel bound to respect.

" Don't, I beg of you, fly to the conclusion that I have had an accomplice in the planning of my flight : I had not. I let no one into my secret, and if there be any cleverness in the thing, you must attribute it to my French elasticity.

" When you receive this letter, I shall have entered upon a new stage of my roving, but whither I shall wend I cannot now say."

" Jumri ! " almost shrieked Miss Ada, " come here, good boy ! My voyage up the Ganges cannot for the present be entered upon. It would be, in fact, without an object : the bird has flown."

" The Doctor am flown," inquired Jumri, " the same as he flown out of Calcutta, and was dropped in Benares? He be goin' to be dropped in the sea, may be, the next time."

" Now, go away, boy, and don't let me hear you run on in that foolish line of talk again ! "

Jumri retired crushed.

The letter became absorbing.

" Ada, ' sweet daughter, etc.,' I feel that I am in your debt, and, as a man of principle and honour, I recognise the bond.

" Ada, I would not put your feelings to the cruel test of appearing in open court, and avowing your love for a useless old hulk. Rather, I have sat as a jury upon myself. I have presided as a judge at my own trial; have brought in my verdict and pronounced sentence; and now, in the form of a will, send you the finding of the court as regards damages, which I trust may be some slight compensation to your outraged sensibilities and act as a salve to your riven heart. Thus:

" I, Septimus O'Dowd, of Benares, formerly of France, Ireland, and Calcutta, being of sound mind, but of body somewhat emaciated by the use of flimsy food—I will avow it even in this city of sacred cows — will and bequeath to Miss Ada Phlick, of Calcutta, in lieu of my heart, which is not worth her acceptance, a large quantity of shaving materials, which lie in my shop in Calcutta, with tooth-picks and brushes, scents, soaps, and razor strops, sponges, air-cushions, pills, draughts, drugs of various kinds (begging her to

beware of such as are poisonous), bandages, and
elastic stockings ; together with such crocks,
bottles, jars, cases and boxes as she may find
scattered through the surgery or other rooms in
the house. I put emphasis on the *shaving
materials*, inasmuch as they are in much demand
among a population that has a great tendency to
sprout, and therefore command a quick sale. At
the same time, I would not so concentrate her
thoughts on these articles as to make her overlook
the perfumes, for example, that are so much
needed in the native quarter of the city in which
she dwells, or the brushes of various kinds that
are indispensable in a land of dust and insects,
or the balsams and plasters that alone can heal
the wounds of the human body arising from
bumps, or bruises, or the bites of mosquitos.

" And it is my wish that the lady above mentioned may see her way to a quick sale of all the
articles put forth in this my Will and Testament,
as now, while the mystery of their recent owner's
disappearance is table-talk throughout the peninsula they must go up in value as the relics of a
remarkable man.

" Signed, sealed, and delivered as the last will
and testament of Septimus O'Dowd, Doctor of
Medicine and Chemist, in the city of Benares,
on the sixth day of October, eighteen hundred
and —, in the presence of Jumpsy Jegirif and
Jernky Jersum, &c."

Miss Phlick laid the letter on the table open
before her, leaned her chin on her palm, knit her
brow, and slightly bit her lip. A glimmer of new

light was dawning upon her, in which she saw O'Dowd no longer in the light of a "dear man." Perhaps it was her Scotch thrift (for she came from beyond the Tweed) that made her balance the legacy against the regard she had had for the giver of it, and finally come to the conclusion that it was for the best that he went away. She would offer the contents of the store to the public by advertisement, but would not appear in the business or allow her name as legatee to be known ; and when she should have received the proceeds, she would wind up her affairs in India, dismiss Jumri, and start for the "Land o' Cakes."

CHAPTER XXXVI.

ADIEU TO THE LOTUS FLOWER.

IT was quite true that the 4th Duffs were to leave Calcutta soon, and with them Captain Halbot. They were under orders for Hyderabad, in the Madras Presidency; whence they would, after a few months, proceed to the coast and take ship for England, on the expiry of their term of foreign service.

The state of Captain Halbot's feelings for the Hindu girl whom he had striven to bring over to the Christian Faith, could not well be gauged by another, nor were they quite measurable even by himself. That he regarded her with much interest was obvious; but that his interest in her rose to a warmer feeling was not proved by word or act of his, during the few months of their intimacy.

Now he was to leave India, with no prospect of returning there for years, if ever; and a question occurred to him which he could not evade : Should he see the girl and bid her good-bye, and for the last time ask her to abandon the superstitions of her youth, and enrol herself among the followers of Christ ?

There were reasons for this course; there were reasons against it. It seemed to him a duty to bring to completion, if possible, the good work in which he had been engaged so long; but he thought it desirable to avoid a pathetic parting scene, which might raise vain hopes in the breast of a woman whom he knew to be deeply attached to him, and perhaps shake, if not shatter, the resolve he had made to regard her in no other light than that of an interesting, erring sister.

It required all his strength of will to refuse the appeal of a tender little missive that he received :

"Would Captain Halbot, always so kind and patient with his humble Hindu friend, grant her one last interview, as she is sorely troubled with new doubts, and feels that they can be solved by him only, who has so often come to her aid in the hour of trial ? "

"Would Captain Halbot grant her one last interview ? " He sat down to reply, but could not for a long time find words in which to clothe his refusal.

"Would Captain Halbot grant her one last interview ? " How, as a Christian, could he refuse it ? How, as a man, could he turn away from this tender pleading of a woman ? Why should he, as one capable of loving, reject the cry to him for succour of the only daughter of Eve that he was ever tempted to love ?

And yet he would refuse the interview and reject the cry for help, and turn from this pleading, because a new spirit was to give shape to his future destiny.

He took up his pen and wrote :

"Child of the East,—

"In your abiding patience and goodness, forgive me; do not think less of my devotion to you, because I decline, reluctantly, to see you before I leave Calcutta for good. It is difficult to refuse your last request. If it gives you some pain, be assured that it gives me no less; let us bear the burden of it together and find solace in community of suffering.

"My sympathies are with you in your struggle between Vishnu, the god of your fathers, and Emmanuel, who calls you away to follow in His footsteps: and I write this letter in the hope that it may be of some assistance to you in making the right choice.

"Vishnu or Emmanuel!—that is the issue that is before you! The religion of which the former is the only tolerable representative, or the religion of which the latter is the founder. I would not ask you to resign your ancestral religion if I did not know it to be erroneous; I would not invite you to enter the Christian Church if I were not certain that it is the home of truth. Nevertheless, I do not wish that you should base your conviction on my bare word; but I hope in this letter so to put in contrast the evidence of Brahmanism and Christianity that you may see the paramount claim of the latter on your assent.

"I will begin by paying a deserved compliment to your religious ceremonial. Your mode of worshipping God is both solemn and picturesque. Outside Christianity and Judaism, there is no public form of worship to compare with the Brahmanical for persuasiveness. It seems to an outsider to meet the religious wants of a simple and confiding race, whilst its ablutions and open-air meetings are well in accord with the demands of a tropical climate.

"The spectacle of your men and maids in the 'Sacred River,' at the rise of the sun, praying with their priest, in rapt attention and a fervour that falls but little short of ecstasy, is a picture that must impress itself on the mind of the religious man whose privilege it is to see it.

"The disciplinary side of your religion is not less worthy of admiration; for while it has taught a vast community of probably a hundred millions of souls to be tender to each other and gentle in their treatment of all living things, it has led a number of its professors into solitudes, to practise there the severe virtues of silence, recollection, and mortification.

"Such being your religion, such being its worship and practices, such being the fruits of its teaching, we seek the source from which its spiritual energy springs; for it must be admitted that the ancient paganisms of Egypt, Babylon and Assyria, of Bactria, Greece and Rome, produced no such flowers of piety and charity as the system in which you have been reared.

"Why is it so? Why is it that Brahmanism, as a religion, has accomplished what no other pagan system has well begun?

"I might reply to this question by saying that Brahmanism is not only a religion, but a system of philosophy as well, and that therefore it acts upon its votaries with a twofold influence; but as even in ancient Greece, where philosophy was more general and dominant than elsewhere, its teaching did not reach the masses to any appreciable degree, I will leave this answer for your consideration, and go on to indicate a more potent factor in the success of Brahmanism as a teacher.

" Ages before your Brahma, or the reformer, Buddha, was heard of, there appeared, among the captive Jews in Egypt, a man who was neither a myth nor an impostor, but a seer, taught by the Most High, and sent by Him to unfold to the wondering eyes of his nation the history of the creation of the world and of man. He gave a guarantee for the position he assumed as a messenger from Heaven by stopping the working of laws that regulate life and motion, and producing startling prodigies by the utterance of a word.

" He gave to the world, through the Jewish people, a true record of the nature of God, of His rewards, His punishments, His laws, His dealings with man, His requirements of man, the virtues He expects man to practise, the vices He wishes him to avoid. In a word, this envoy of Heaven, in books of entrancing beauty, written under Divine impulse, poured forth a torrent of light over the world in which can be seen the solution of all the problems which are ever agitating the human mind and leading unbelievers to despair.

" Your Brahmans have drawn largely on this record of Moses, and here we discover the source and foundation of any and every good they have achieved as teachers of religion and morality. From Moses they filched the conception of a self-existing Being, infinitely perfect, pure, holy, one, eternal, all-powerful, omnipresent. The idea of a Trimurti developed itself on the analogy of the Christian Trinity. From a like source come the doctrines that man has fallen, and of the necessity of a return to God, of the utility of penance and the advantages of fasting and prayer, of the religious peace of community life and retirement from the bustle of the world. These beliefs and practices lingered among the descendants of a people who brought them from western Asia.

" It is matter for surprise that the Brahmanical religion has accomplished so much, even with the aid it has received from the record of Moses ; for, with all its pretence and activity, it is more than tainted with immorality. It degrades the Divine Nature by supposing it to assume, not one stainless body, like Christianity, but countless human forms infected with every vice : nor does it rest here, but it goes on to say that the Divine, so united to man, becomes the slave of human passion and riots in the commission of every forbidden lewdness.

" It is reckless of the character of its Trimurti. At least, in its popular form, it gives up two of its members to nameless vices which throw into the shade the licentious excesses of Jupiter and Alcmene.

" Is not the contrast marvellous ? First, a Divinity, spiritual and pure as a ray of white light : side by side with Him, a divinity carnal and sullied with all the mire of earth ! A system of rigorous ethics for the rule and guidance of man, no ethics for the divinity, and no barrier even of shame to keep him within the limits of decency!

"It is a system of pantheism as well. According to it, the Divine Nature is ever descending, ever diffusing itself into earthly forms, sending forth from it emanations to grasp and inform matter, until it becomes in the end the soul of the universe, and breathes and acts through matter.

"Man himself, in your system (so far as I understand it), is but a phantom through which the divinity gleams, a machine on which it operates, an instrument through which it speaks; he loses the power of directing himself and is driven forward, to the negation of free will, by a blind fate, which pushes him on as a being without light or strength. From which it follows as a consequence that, in your system, man has no responsibility, and that he may not expect a reward for his good deeds nor dread a punishment for his sins.

"The Brahmanical religion seems to be full of inconsistencies. It is sinless and sinful, sensible and silly, learned and ignorant, purifying and defiling. It teaches by precept the mortification of the flesh, and by example, the indulgence of every evil proclivity.

"It has been the rôle of your apologists to pass over the sensual side of Brahmanism, to cast a veil upon its profligacy, puerility, and irreverence, and to dwell only upon its unique claim to be the first among systems of pure spirituality.

"When looked into, it is found to be, like the religions of Buddha, Zoroaster and Confucius, one result of man's blind reaching forth into the

unknown. Its characteristic doctrines are but con-
jectures, backed by no testimony of the Divine
Wisdom.

" Nor have you a monopoly of sacred volumes
whereon to found your tradition. The writings
of Confucius for the Chinese—for the purity of
the morality they inculcate, if not for style or
diction—are fully equal to your Vedas ; and the
Avista of the Persians, named ' the divine and
living word,' is a thesaurus of doctrines, political
and religious, quite as practical as those proclaimed
by your sacred books.

" Nor is your idea of a fall and a redemption
private property. All the religions of Asia tell
us of a wandering of man from a heavenly home,
and insist on the possibility and necessity of his
return to it, differing only in their conception of
the means by which this home-coming is to be
effected. In this connexion, I feel bound to assure
you that the worshippers of T'ien and the followers
of Zoroaster have much more elevated notions of
the machinery of man's restoration than your
teachers ; for my part, I find it impossible to put
on a level the Indian dream of a return to God by
migration of the soul and the sublime doctrine of
salvation through a mediator that is found in the
traditions of the Persians and Chinese.

" I feel, somehow, that you might expect from
me a more homely treatise than this, and that you
may think that more of feeling and less of controversy might meet the needs of a half-convinced
soul like yours. But if I have addressed you
almost as a stranger it is because I have seen in

you, side by side with strong Christian proclivities, an ardent attachment to the ideal of the Divinity presented through your Brahma, Vishnu and Siva, and a lingering love for practices of devotion which, though harmless and soothing under one of their aspects, are of unmixed pagan texture under another.

"Shortcomings, I know, you will pardon. Callousness, I trust, you will not suspect. Zeal for your conversion, a sincere wish for your peace of mind, are the motives that have carried my pen over these pages.

"Finally, let me exhort you, Child of the East, to turn from a system which strives to hide its grossness under a mask of austerity, and to cloak its idolatry and worship of evil spirits with shallow sophistry.

"But while Brahmanism is inconsistent and based upon no secure testimony, how different it is with that sublime code of creeds and morals to which you have been drawing near but too slowly. Here every claim is orderly ; at every stage there is evidence. Judaism stands sponsor for Christianity. The great lawgiver of the Jews, Moses, to whom I made reference farther back, is an impartial witness to the expectation of a great deliverer by the Jews, and the longing of extern nations for His coming. He carries back the tradition of Christ to the garden of Eden, which was man's first dwelling-place on earth ; and from the age of Moses down along the centuries stands a cloud of witnesses, uttering in prophecy the events of the life of the Redeemer. Minutely they tell of His

birth, His sorrows, His death, His burial, His
resurrection. They point to the hermit of the
desert that was to announce Him, and to the
Virgin that was to usher Him into human life.

" But I feel that I am treating unworthily the
religion I profess, when I put it side by side with
a mysticism which has sprung out of human whim
and passion, even though it be shaped, to some
extent, by relics of primitive revelation carried
over the earth by wandering man. I will therefore
bring this long letter to an end in a few practical
remarks.

" I cannot be mistaken in you, Kèsur ! I seem to
look into your soul, and to see its workings and
longings, its yearning after virtue and its desire to
please God.

" Where can you find the discipline that you are
seeking but among Christians, where you will find
well-defined rules for the regulation of personal
conduct and bearing towards others and God ;
where nothing is left to whim or prejudice ; where
those ten rules, which you have heard and admired,
form the character and make it all-round virtuous,
with a virtue most attractive and undeniable, which
purifies the soul to its very centre and makes it
equally pleasing to God and man.

" I have done. I have written enough to one who,
I trust, has already entered on the journey from
the service of Vishnu and kindred deities to the
God-man, the Saviour of the world.

" I bid you farewell. It was a hope of mine, long
cherished, to see you within the fold of Christianity
before duty should call me from India. I feel

confident, however, that your change of religion is
only a question of time. You won't, I trust, think
that I mean to flatter, when I say that you are too
good and pure for the sensuous divinities that
claim you—too clear of mind and clever for the
sophisms by which they ask you to be convinced.

"May I, in conclusion, let you know why it is
that such a priestly zeal for your conversion has
shown itself in my intercourse with you? It is
because I too have been meditating, for myself, a
change to a higher spiritual level. The novelty
of military life has for me passed into monotony,
the glamour that surrounds it has gone into colour-
less mist, and I already foresee a severance of ties
that hold me in bondage to its maxims and
pleasures. But a pleasing reminiscence of my
military career will ever remain in my intercourse
with you and the hope that in some measure I
have helped you to direct your steps."

When Kèsur had read this long and argumenta-
tive letter, she pressed it to her lips, and, holding
it in this position, weighed its arguments. Doubt
as to the claims of Emmanuel soon gave way to
certainty. And with a smile she laid the precious
letter in the white drapery of her bosom, close to
her heart.

Her dream of humble love had passed away,
and she must henceforth try her very best to
reconcile herself to the inevitable.

It was well that she had trained herself to
patience: a spirit of fatalism, derived from her old
superstition, helped to deaden the weight of the
blow that had fallen so suddenly upon her.

In child-like submission, soothed in her sorrow
by the simple device of making a treasure of his
last written words, she went about her home
occupations, thinking much and often on the
religious question, seeing no visitors and going
forth in the early morning or late in the afternoon
to wander over ground hallowed by the footsteps
of the friend she was to see no more.

Sometimes it was by the Ganges that she
lingered, looking across to the spot where she had
sunk into the water—drowning ; sometimes she
stood musing on the bank where she had lain
insensible after being brought ashore, thinking
how he had watched over her, chafing her hands
and gently moving her frame, until her heart
began to throb again. Or she strayed away into
the mulberry grove, where Akbar Yassov, like a
beast of prey, had sprung upon her and frightened
her, and might have done her irreparable wrong,
but for the timely coming and brave intervention
of the noble British soldier.

The struggle in her mind between Vishnu and
Emmanuel was now virtually at an end, and she
no longer doubted as to the path she ought to
follow : but the shrinking timidity of her nature,
with an ever-abiding sense of racial inferiority at
the back of it, kept her from seeking a Christian
priest to prepare her for entry into the Church.

Other sacrifices rendered necessary by a withdrawal from Brahmanism she was prepared to
make without complaint. The loss of caste would
be easy for her, and the severance of old ties of
friendship would be no obstacle. To be frowned

upon as a renegade and an unbeliever was more serious ; but this too she would bear. The difficulty to her conversion lay not now in the trials surrounding it, but in a lack of courage to go forward and ask to be admitted among the catechumens preparing for Baptism.

CHAPTER XXXVII.

CAIRO : THE LOST FOUND.

THE days were passing rapidly, and the society in which we have been living for twelve months was gradually breaking up and disappearing. The time for the departure from Calcutta of the 4th Duffs had come, and that distinguished corps, having marched to Hyderabad, had passed on to Madras and embarked for England ; but, in consequence of troubles in Egypt, a detachment had received orders to disembark at Alexandria and was now in quarters in Cairo.

Halbot gave his idle hours to the old monuments of the place and to a study of its religions and superstitions ; while Captain Stokes and Major Staples were often on a tour in the suburbs, taking stock of the humours of the place.

One evening they had walked further than usual and were lounging back to barracks, tired and heated, when their eyes fell upon a man in front, who, like themselves, was out for a stroll. There was something in his build that was not common ; some peculiarity in his dress ; he carried himself rather heavily, but with an evident aim at lightness of step and bearing. He appeared to know everyone ; and while he raised his hat to persons of position that passed, he had a pleasant word for the fellaheen he met and was particularly gracious to the native children and women.

"By Jove!" said Staples, whose glance was fixed upon him, "this old chap is an institution; let us not let him get out of view."

"He must be," answered Stokes, "the Mayor of the town, if they have such an official here. What a pompous old bashaw! He seems to be basking in the moonshine of his innate self-sufficiency."

They followed him unobserved and without inconvenience, as he was going more or less on their way, until they came to a square of the city, where he escaped from them, entering a large house and remaining there.

They forgot the incident in the pleasantries of the mess dinner, and the next day, after parade, they left the barracks again to continue their inspection of the "lions" of the place, for Cairo is well worth examining in detail; and the 4th Duffs were not to spend much time in the city, as they expected any day to receive orders for a march to the Soudan.

Going down by the Khalig, where the best houses of the city give life and beauty to the banks of that canal, they saw their man of yesterday passing in a barge with a number of fashionable ladies. He was almost hidden from view by parasols, which the girls laughingly held over him.

"By Jove!" observed Major Staples, "what a family he has! All these girls are, I suppose, his daughters. They don't appear to differ much in age; there must be more than one pair of twins among them."

"One, two—seven!" said Stokes. "He is a happy man to be surrounded by such sirens; they are fanning him, I think."

"Fanning, by Jove!" said the Major. "If we could follow, we would see them hugging 'papa' before long. Shall we take a boat and start in pursuit?"

"I thought you were in command of a detachment," said Stokes.

"Heaven help the detachment," said the Major, "but I am not on duty at this moment."

"All the same," said Stokes, "let us leave the old coxcomb to his happy fate, and pass away from him without envy. I feel sure we shall come across him again, for he is in his way a feature of the society of the place. Have we not been speaking of going towards the desert, to inspect the tombs of the caliphs?"

"Yes, to be sure; let us go at once. Good-bye, Daddy!"—waving his hand vaguely.

They took a carriage and drove out of the city and were not seen again until seven o'clock, when they turned into the mess-room, full of the beautiful specimens of Saracenic architecture they had been for some hours inspecting.

There is in the centre of the city of Cairo a garden, named, in the language of the place, Esbekiyeh, where bands play and people assemble in large numbers to eat and drink and be merry, for, besides the music, there are restaurants there and a very attractive theatre.

Into this Elysium came Stokes and Staples the next day, at the hour when it was most full, and seated themselves on chairs outside a ring, in which a number of gentlemen were walking slowly around a band-stand, chatting, smoking, listening to the music and casting discreet glances on the specimens of English and native beauty that were to be seen all around.

In the ring, and right on a line with the officers' position, a group of gentlemen halted—among them the man whom they had seen in a boat the day before. They had now an opportunity of looking into his face. They had no doubt as to his being "made up" to a very unusual degree. His hair was abundant and as black as a night in Algiers; he wore no beard or whiskers, but a large moustache of a rather fierce form, curled up at the ends and slightly tinged with gray; in his left eye he carried a single glass, and he wore quite a profusion of chains and trinkets.

They listened. He spoke in a loud voice and with much confidence, and in a strain of English which some would not consider Attic; he used much gesture, and threw himself into dramatic attitudes; and, in his whole get-up, appearance and manners, realised the word "bashaw" which Stokes applied to him when he first fell in their way.

"I have a delicious hunger on me," said the Major, "impelling me to follow this spotted pard, and trace him to his lair—to make sure if he is, as I suspect, a member of the community that deals in risks and chances at the cost of old maids and other innocents."

"He does excite a longing, I confess," said

Stokes, " and a thirst which must be hard to bear, unless it is drowned in discovery."

They rose and strolled along indifferently, but with an eye on the portly man, who had become for them such high game. He turned to go—they prepared to follow him at a discreet interval; he sat— they sat at a distance, with their eyes seemingly turned from him. They saw him go to the band and speak to the conductor, join some ladies who entered the ring, and take a round of it with them ; go into a café and have some wine ; come out, hesitate, and finally move away towards the entrance of the garden. Then they rose and followed him slowly out into the street.

He went along, as on the first evening they saw him, receiving the attention of the passers and returning it with much affability ; but, as if he had a suspicion that he was being watched and followed, he turned occasionally and looked behind ; and it was only by a series of subtle devices, such as entering shops, going off the street by one passage and returning to it by another, stopping to gaze at monuments and public buildings, and loitering to speak to vendors of curios, that they were able to follow him without drawing his eyes upon them.

He stopped before a showy mansion, and drawing out his keys, opened the door and let himself in. The officers, who came up a short time afterwards, read on a plate of polished brass: " Monsieur le Docteur Septime."

They rang the bell :

" Is the Doctor at home ? "

" Yes, he has just come in."

" Take him these cards."

" Be seated, gentlemen."

Without a moment's delay, the man they had seen in the garden entered the surgery and bowed like a Parisian.

" Your business, gentlemen ? " he said in an affable tone of voice.

" An infernal nervous attack," said Staples. " I feel both seedy and shattered. By Jove " he added, " I fear I am coming to that state of body which is aptly characterized by the word ' tottering. ' "

" You return, perhaps, from active service ? " said the Doctor.

" And a good deal of inactive service too ! " replied the Major.

" What might be, as far as you can see, the immediate forerunner of the present nervous seizure ? "

" I come from India," said Staples, " a land of lively sensations ! The last shock I received there came from one of your profession."

" What did he do ? "

" Disappeared, Sir ! Vanished !—and left all India gaping ! "

The Doctor looked at him and smiled.

" You require a double dose of saline, Sir ! " he said ; and changing his high tone and accent to one which seemed familiar to the officers, he shouted :

" Adèle ! bring in the saline and glasses. Ayala, 1846, *sec.*"

A voice came from inside: it was not French; it was not English or Scotch.

"Pardon her accent, gentlemen," said the Bashaw; "she is a Frenchwoman, born in Kerry."

They had him at once: it was O'Dowd.

"By Jove!" cried the Major; "By Jove!"— and he collapsed.

Stokes was more self-possessed, and thought of saying a few nice things on their reunion, but was not allowed by O'Dowd, who waxed quite eloquent.

"How did you leave Ada Phlick?" were the first words he said. "Not dying, I suppose, of a broken heart. And poor little Kèsur, who so often kept the wolf from my door, and who so fondly loved —but I won't betray her confidence. Did you see the creature after I left? I'll never forget her: it was she that sent me out of Calcutta. Take the saline, Major, and pass the wine to Stokes. Your health, gentlemen! I am more than glad to see you under my roof."

"By Jove, Sir," put in the Major, "it's a dream."

"No—faith!" said O'Dowd, "it's a reality, but a little dim. I am master of the situation here: fawned upon by the rich, adored by the natives, surrounded by a galaxy of beauty whenever I appear in public. Patients?—as many as I can take under my care: liberal fees. Every comfort and even luxury. Called in to prescribe for the Khedive—admitted to court! It's a dream in the sense of Moore's touching song. 'It is all but a dream at the best, and yet when happiest seems o'er,'—but all the time, it's real, tangible."

"You must," said the Major, who was regaining

the use of speech " have used some very infernal means to escape from Calcutta."

" Kèsur put them into my hands," said O'Dowd.

" Dealt in the Black Art, eh ? Indian sorcery and that sort of thing ! I thought that girl might be a necromancer."

" No, Major, no, but the dearest little lamb I ever met in my chequered career ! She put certain appliances between my hands, at my own request, without knowing what they were wanted for, and by means of using them, I vanished."

" Mysterious, Sir ! I should feel inclined to say if in order—demoniacally mysterious ! Is it a locked up secret, or shall we go away moon-struck ? " looking at his watch.

" Adèle ! Bollinger !" said the Doctor. " This is my French maid," when she entered.

" Don't mind him, gentlemen," said a fresh, cheery voice ; " it is part of his fun. French indeed ! the widow of John Moloney, of the ' Fighting 5th,' at your service."

Mrs. Moloney looked all over a Hibernian, and a fine, handsome type of the race.

" Let it pass, Bridget," said O'Dowd. " Cut the wire : now—thanks !—you may go. I have a long story to tell these gentlemen."

Bridget shook her head slightly at the Doctor, whose back was turned, winked mysteriously at the officers, and went out.

" Gentlemen," said the Doctor, " as I was saying, it was that tender Hindu girl that gave me the means of escape from Calcutta and from Ada Phlick. I called upon her late in the evening of the day before I disappeared. I asked her to give me a full suit of her clothes, which I wanted for a person in distress. 'Loose,' I said, 'and roomy, as they have to cover a big, full body.' I would take, I added, some ornaments—spurious, if she had any—in the form of anklets, bracelets, and clasps. All that I asked for she gave me freely and cheerfully, and I carried them home in a hand-bag, which I had brought for that purpose ; but I did not go into the garments for an hour or more, but sat thinking and occasionally laughing heartily at the project I had taken in hand. Can you understand my feelings, Major, on the eve of passing into the semblance of a black woman ? "

" No, Sir," said the Major, " creepy perhaps, with a trickling down the spine."

" Possibly a sensation of burning shame," said Stokes.

" Neither the one nor the other," said O'Dowd, " but a feeling of mirthful awe : it was a terrible risk for an old, out-of-shape fellow to attempt to pose as a woman, and this in the midst of a sensitive and observant people, who might easily find me an impostor, as I did not know their language ; or convict me, on my tone of voice, even if I did ; but the venture was so intensely funny that the thought of it made me laugh until I was well-nigh sick."

" Your state of mind does you credit, Sir ! " said the Major. " If I were entering on such a course, I should be in an infernal funk."

" I had," continued O'Dowd, " brought home a

pot of copper paint the day before, and a fine brush with which to put it on ; and I then sat opposite a mirror, tinting and dying until I brought myself to the proper shade, and looked really very like a Sepoy. Then I put about me the loose drapery that I had brought from Kèsur, covered my arms with bracelets and my legs with anklets, and drawing over my forehead and the lower part of my face the usual integuments, I stood on my legs, a Hindu woman all over, of a matronly and imposing aspect.

"The sequel is not long to tell. I left Calcutta in my disguise, and went up the Ganges by steamer all the way to Benares, but in a tremble, because I had much trouble to keep out of view my big feet, the sight of which would have been fatal to my project ; I kept them well covered, however, by letting my wraps down till they swept the ground. Another cause of fear was my tendency, contracted by long habit, to break out into a French song."

"I should have thought," said Stokes, "that your ignorance of Hindustani would be your greatest obstacle."

"I had made provision for that," said O'Dowd, "by pretending to be dumb; so when anyone addressed me I answered by gesture, putting my hand to my mouth to indicate that I could not speak. I need not continue the tale of my subsequent movements : I have said enough to dispel the mist hanging over the O'Dowd tragedy, and to prove to you that the detective system and its theories can be, in some cases, a huge sham and swindle."

" By Jove, Sir ! " said the Major, "you are an acrobat : you would make a fortune in a circus. You have told us, in graphic language, of the evolution of O'Dowd into a Hindu woman ; you won't surely leave us in ignorance of the rest of the adventure."

" True.   Thanks for the hint: the Bollinger ! The final act is the plot of the whole movement. In my ramblings from city to city, I was laying down the lines of a second metamorphosis, and I fixed on Delhi as the spot where it should take place.   Arrived in that fine emporium, I entered a large hotel, with many doors and passages ; asked, by signs, for a bed-room ; took possession of it, locked the door, washed the paint off, divested myself of Kèsur's trappings, put on my own clothes, which I carried in my hand-bag, and came forth from that room as you now see me.

" By J—" began the Major.

" The mess waits for us," said Stokes, looking at his watch.

CHAPTER XXXVIII.

FIFTEEN YEARS LATER.

FIFTEEN years have passed since the ripple, of which we have been writing, passed over the stagnant life of Calcutta—fifteen long years! Long enough to break up a family circle, and scatter its members in exile over the wide surface of the globe—long enough to pilfer one by one the pearls that glittered on the roll of friendship, and leave one only behind to tell of their value and signalise their loss—long enough to make the young man middle-aged, and break asunder the silken cords that bound him to the *deliciæ* of life— long enough to extinguish the hopes of the ambitious, and bring to naught the ambitious hopes of the struggler for wealth.

What has become of the actors in this our little drama during these fifteen years? Whither have they gone? Have they passed over to the majority, or are they still among the seething crowd that is ever pressing onward?

Miss Phlick, for one, is alive; not only is she alive but blooming.

She is mistress now of a manse of modest pretensions, away up in the Highlands of Scotland, where, having no outlet for romance, even in the diluted form in which it sometimes abides with a matron, she has turned from herself and is wholly occupied with plans for the culture of the dark races of our globe. She has put herself to much trouble in organizing a society for the better clothing of the Hindus ; but it has not hitherto been a conspicuous success, as she would have no model for the new apparel unless it should take the form of the kilt of her native land, the merits of which her protegés are slow to recognise.

Captain Halbot has carried into effect his resolve. He has retired from the military profession, has put aside the scarlet coat, taking in its place the sombre habit of a priest. He resides near a well-known church in London, where he bears a well-earned reputation of a friend to the poor, a consoler to the sick, and a staff to the frail and weak.

He is seen of an evening, sometimes, on the Thames Embankment, walking with a clergyman of the Established Church, whom, though now a little aged and not so handsome as in earlier life, we have little difficulty in recognising as the Reverend Nethcoff Bingham, sometime chaplain to the garrison in Calcutta, and now rector of an important parish in Essex.

Akbar Yassov may be, for aught we know, still living and practising in the courts of law. He ceased to be a guest at the military mess in Fort William. His moroseness was ever increasing after his rejection by Kèsur, and he presently ceased to veil his contempt for Europeans, to whose meddling he attributed his loss of her love, and, what he valued more, her fortune. He lost his temper at table often, and quarrelled at a jest whereto another would have found a jesting repartee. Men of cultured habits would no longer have him as an associate, and so he passed out of the privileged circle into which he had gained an entrée.

Jumri and Gunga are now man and wife, according to Hindu law and usage. They have retired into the Black City, where they keep a little store for the sale of Indian curios. They are blessed with only one child, a bow-legged little fellow, to whom they have given an orthodox Hindu name ; but in the privacy of their little home, where they often revive their scant knowledge of English, they speak of him as " The Doctor," and he seems to like the name.

When we last heard of O'Dowd, he was resting on his laurels in Egypt. He had climbed the hill, arrived on the summit, and was now a star in his profession ; but as in adversity he was hopeful and resourceful, so he was neither dazzled nor overmuch elated in the time of his success. He now thought often of his sons in Australia, and felt a longing to share with them the modest competence acquired in the Egyptian capital.

But should he not, before putting himself under the Southern Cross, explore a little the fine continent to which a lucky chance had brought him ? He thought he would like to go up the Nile, but the Dervishes were on the warpath. Vistas in other directions opened before his fancy. He looked through them, but found, to his chagrin, that they were blocked by lions, serpents, or cannibals. Finally he determined to go down the

Red Sea, put up at Suez for a while and wait for developments.

It was in Suez that he heard, for the first time, of a strong nation of mixed Dutch and Huguenot blood that was carrying everything before it in South Africa, and was so bubbling, restless, and aggressive that it might fairly be deemed a subject for sedatives.

It was enough. He would go down to them —not as a mercenary, but as a benefactor. He arrived in Durban, then a slimy place, and with none of those attractions which British skill and labour have since given it. He went on shore. He looked around. He spoke to everyone he met. In his hotel he made enquiries as to the sanitary condition of the town. Then he entered a lumbering coach of ancient type and started for Boerland, intending to give gratuitous advice to its people on the whims of the nervous system.

"Why," said he, "the very names of these people are stony. It's not sedatives they want, but blood-letting and bringing down." He opened his medicine chest, and waited for customers. They came, dropping in by units. They asked for strengthening medicine.

"It is too much strength you have," he ventured, "and, as a consequence, too much cheek. You are not Dervishes of the Soudan that you should push the world before you, nor cannibals of the Congo that you should make a meal of your fellowmen, but the descendants of decent people in Europe, who kept their constitutions in order by pills and good behaviour."

This language gave offence to the modern Israelites. They shook the Bible in his face. How dare he insult the Chosen of the Lord? Guns were pointed at him. He turned and fled, and as he lumbered down to Durban, he made this prophetic reflection : " This people will not be brought round by pills, with whatever coating : it must be by pellets of another kind."

This visit was the last act in O'Dowd's African comedy. He took steamer at the Cape for Australia, or rather the first of a series of steamers that were to bear him to that sunny land. He was returning as the Prodigal Father—to throw himself into the arms of his long-neglected sons. He thought he would abandon the medical profession, and take rest—perhaps to solace his declining years with music.

He arrived in Melbourne in due time, and, in pursuance of his dominant idea, sought and found a seller of musical instruments ; but it must be confessed, he entered his shop somewhat timidly. He wished to purchase — he could not name it — a flute or a piccolo, or a clarionet, a reed, in fact, that would give forth the sound of all these instruments combined.

" You may as well," said the vendor, who was amused by the Doctor's words and manner, " add a 'cello and a violin."

" You don't gauge my want," replied O'Dowd with dignity. " My desire is to purchase an instrument that will reproduce the music of the shepherds of Ancient Rome."

The man looked closely at him, as if questioning his sanity.

"Our instruments," he said, "are for modern times. If you want an old Roman reed, you must look for it among the sheep-skinned peasants of the Roman Campagna."

O'Dowd had gained information. The pipe on which Virgil's shepherd played was still in existence. He would order a few of them through a broker, and then he would present them to his sons, who would awaken the echoes—"Ahem!"

The three officers of the 4th Duffs, whom we have so often met—Staples, Stokes, and Scott—have retired from active service with their regiment, to devote themselves to those semi-civil, semi-military occupations which are reserved for those who have done their country's work with credit to themselves and advantage to the public service.

Such is the glimpse at the subsequent history of the leading characters of this tale which has been granted to their biographer, and is now communicated to those who have followed this story; for in Calcutta, where they abode for a time, it would be idle to speak of them. They have lapsed from the memory of the public, like the vision of an uneasy dream.

Who in that City of Dreadful Night remembers O'Dowd and his whims, or has ever heard of him or them? Who is there that saw Miss Ada Phlick in her window watching his movements, or gave heed to her, or took pains to guess at the cause of her patient and prolonged vigils? Who was a witness to the silly pranks of the Hindu boy Jumri, or who gives a thought to the prattle of little

Gunga, as she lingered on her way to gather up
the news of the quarter?

Military records, preserved in the archives of the
British Army, will tell of the sojourn of the 4th
Duffs in the capital of British India, and will set
forth a list of the officers who then commanded
this regiment, from its colonel to its most callow
subaltern; but the quaintness of Staples, the
loquacity of Stokes, and the seriousness of Halbot,
were scarcely known outside military circles.

And yet, notwithstanding this general oblivion,
there was one in Calcutta who lived in the past,
and whose every thought went back to one
whom he saw in the period embraced within the
limits of this story. He had grown to a man of
thirty-three summers, but was a stripling of
eighteen years when the events of this tale were
enacted. He was of little account, for he was poor
and clad in rags. He was even repulsive, so that
passers-by carefully guarded against the smallest
contact with him, and even left the pathway to
avoid meeting him directly. But he did not court
their respect, and seemed to believe that contempt
and the lowest place were his natural inheritance.
And so he, too, would slink away when he saw
them approaching, and would hide himself under
the foliage of trees in the suburbs.

He had an end before him, and no hindrance
should discourage him. When the sun poured
down his burning rays at noon he was abroad on
his errand, careless of the stroke that might come
at any moment to lay him prostrate on the ground.
When the rains came—those tropical rains that

fall like a sheet on the earth—he was moving
under them with indifference, buoyed up by a
purpose he had taken in hand. Seeking, ever
seeking, always looking forward and around, but
never finding the object he is in search of:
what does he look for? No one can say—if,
indeed, there be in the big city even one that
would condescend to speculate on the object of his
indefatigable search.

This is the pariah boy, of whom mention was
made in another chapter of this record—the lad
that stood so humbly at O'Dowd's door beseeching
him to visit his sick father; and he is seeking
always for the owner of that robe of fine white
cotton which covered the dying man, and presented
an insoluble puzzle to the Doctor, when he beheld
it stretched out over the wretched couch on which
he lay. He sought Kèsur, longing to get even
a glimpse of her never-to-be-forgotten frail and
graceful form. Not that he would have ob-
truded himself upon her, had she come his way, or
have followed her otherwise than by glances of love
and gratitude. Only if he could see her but once,
he would die happy, and be content to follow his
father to that resting-place for the poor which she
had tried to open for him by instilling into his soul
a belief in a bounteous Providence.

In his wanderings he found himself one day in a
western suburb, near the closed door of a small
chapel, through the chinks of which issued the
odour of fresh incense. Weary and faint he sat on
the marble steps, soothed by the sweet scent.
After awhile he fell into a deep slumber, in which

he seemed to feel a presence of someone bending over him, and telling him to be of good cheer; that the object of his search was near, and would meet him as he passed out of the visible into the unseen world.

He awoke in a perfect calm. Struggling to rise, he fell back on the flags insensible, and lay there without motion until night, when a chilly dew fell upon him, and, soaking through his ragged robe, stilled the gentle motion of his heart, and left him, as he was found in the morning, with a smile on his wan face, and his eyes lifted, in wondering hope, towards the home of the neglected poor.

Within the chapel a dirge was sung that morning, and incense was burnt at a celebration of Sacred Mysteries for the rest of an Indian nun who had just passed away; and a rumour spread from the convent to the city, and from the city up and down the Ganges, that a child of grace had been laid to rest in the convent cemetery, and that she was one who, after a long struggle, had passed from the service of Vishnu the Pure to that of Emmanuel the Beloved; and that she was so fair in the days of her girlhood that she was the theme of a native poet, who had sung of her under the name of India's choicest flower.

THE END.